Dereliction of Duty

By

Daniel McKeown

Inspired Quill Publishing

Published by Inspired Quill: October 2011
First Paperback Edition

Chief Editor: Peter Stewart

Paperback ISBN: 978-1-908600-02-8
eBook ISBN: 978-1-908600-03-5

Typeset in palatino 10/11
By ReallyLoveYourBook, Bridgend, UK.

Printed in the United Kingdom
1 2 3 4 5 6 7 8 9 10

Inspired Quill Publishing, UK
Social Enterprise Reg. No. 7592847
http://www.inspired-quill.com

Dedication:

Dedicated to the memory of my sister, Carole, who passed away in 1998.

For me she will never truly be gone.

Acknowledgments

Writing a novel is seldom a solitary pursuit. I am indebted to several individuals without whom this novel would never have seen light of day. First, I'd like to thank a very close friend, who wishes to remain nameless, for his expertise in military matters and his generosity and willingness to explain, in depth, answers to all my questions. Any mistakes in regards to military procedures, if any, are mine alone.

I'd like to give a special mention to Duane Pescice, who was kind enough to compose the background music and voiceover for the trailer of Dereliction of Duty. The world needs more people like you, Duane. Thank you.

A warm thanks goes out, also, to my beta readers.

Last, but by no means least, I'd like to thank my family for supporting and encouraging my passion and hobby. All those years hunched over a keyboard have finally paid off.

Foreword

With every novel comes an interminable amount of research. At certain points during this one, I've spent more time researching than writing. Despite all of it, however, there have been certain sacrifices of realism in favour of plot advancement.

For instance, there is no such thing as a "Factor X" virus. Nor is there a directory within a computer where a virus can remain undetectable to a virus scanner. Those were invented to further the story.

All places within this novel, with the exception of ATARIC and the FEMA facility at Hunters Point, do exist. However, I may have taken some liberties with certain descriptions.

Enjoy the read.

CHAPTER ONE
THE RUNNING GAME

```
ST. PETERSBURG
RUSSIA
SUNDAY, JANUARY 5TH, 2003
08: 11 MSK
```

The door to the stairwell crashed open, and a heavyset man stumbled through it. A briefcase fell from his hands and hit the concrete steps, sheaves of paper scattering from inside. Behind him, in the hallway, the footfalls of approaching men grew louder.

Ignoring startled cries from the fifth-floor patrons, the man unbuttoned his jacket and cast it aside on the stairs leading up. He discarded the briefcase, closed and locked the door behind him, and began running downwards.

Sweat dripped into his eyes as he hit the fourth-floor landing, though it was not the product of exertion. Above, the door burst open again. The sound echoed through the stairway, accompanied by multiple voices shouting in Russian. They were arguing.

Good. His distraction had worked. Now came the hard part.

Even though his every instinct urged him to run down the last four flights, he knew they would catch him before he made it to the streets. He couldn't afford to let that happen.

He slowed halfway down the third flight, paused for a moment to draw breath, and walked to the bottom. Once there, he stopped and drew the back of his hand across his brow to remove the perspiration forming there. Two different echoes reverberated off the walls above. He didn't have much time.

He found the door to the third floor unlocked and eased it open. Stepping into the corridor, he took in his surroundings with a quick glance. It was empty. The panic hadn't spread to any of the lower floors – yet.

The concrete floor felt cold underneath his bare feet, and he realised for the first time since discarding the jacket that he was naked except for a pair of boxer shorts. He needed to blend in, he needed a phone, but most importantly he needed to survive. It wouldn't be long before they started searching floor by floor, and he knew he would die an agonising death if they found him.

The man continued down the hall and stopped at apartment 314. Pressing his ear against the door, he listened for as long as he dared. The numbers three and fourteen had always been lucky for him.

Confident no one was inside; he stepped back, checked the corridor again, and threw his entire body weight into the door. It gave a loud crack and splintered along the edges, but the deadlock held. He cursed, feeling pain in his left shoulder.

In the apartment next door, he heard the sound of a latch opening. Worse, he could also hear the sharp cries of his pursuers echoing down the hallway.

They were closing in.

He didn't stop to ask himself how they knew which floor he'd taken. Instead, he stepped back and slammed his body against the door in one last, desperate attempt. He tumbled into the room, hitting the floor hard. Wincing, he clambered back to his feet and closed the door against its shattered frame.

The man turned around and studied the room. It was small, maybe twelve feet by ten. Early-morning light streamed in from the open curtains in the far corner. Strewn across the floor and bed were dozens of items of clothing – he borrowed a pair of trousers and a shirt – shoes, and old newspapers. A desk sat adjacent to the right of the bed, a rotary-dial phone atop it. A door opposite the foot of the bed led to a small bathroom. The layout was completely different from the fifth floor, but that didn't matter. He wasn't here to admire the aesthetics, though it looked like the owner had left in a hurry. Frowning, he sat down on the bed and opened all three of the desk's drawers.

They were devoid of clothes.

Closing them, he began wondering if the owner's hasty exit had some connection with the people who were now after him. After all, no one except his handler knew he lived here.

He stood, walked back to the door, and listened for any approaching noises. When he was satisfied that no one was near, he returned to the bed and dialled a number from memory. It belonged to Scott Harden, an old Marine buddy from years earlier who now lived here in Russia – the only person he felt he could trust at this point.

After eight rings a voice croaked, "Hello?"

"Scott? It's Troy Davies." When Harden didn't offer any words of recognition, Davies continued, "You remember that favour you owe me? Well, I'm cashing in on it." He gave Harden an address and asked how quickly he could get there.

"Ten minutes, give or take. What the hell are you doin' in Saint Petersburg?"

"Long story. When you get here, I'm gonna need a distraction."

"Distraction? What've you gotten yourself into now, Troy?"

"Even longer story. I got some goons on my ass right now and I can't walk out of here without help. When you get here, pull the fire alarm. What are you driving?"

"White van. Trust me, you won't miss it."

"Park outside the front of the apartment block. And Scott?"

"Yeah?"

"Thanks. I'll owe you one for this. Now move your ass!"

Davies replaced the receiver, stood up, and walked to the doorway. Now that he had a way out, he wondered if Harden would get here before someone noticed the broken door.

***

The lead pursuer stepped into the third-floor corridor. With practised ease, he withdrew his nine-millimetre Makarov PM from its holster and edged down the corridor as he affixed a suppressor. Behind him, two men shadowed his every move.

They watched with admiration as he glided down the hallway, his booted feet never making a sound on the concrete. They tried to match his gracefulness but only succeeded in looking like rash amateurs.

There were a total of thirty apartments, fifteen on each side. At the beginning and end of the hall, surveillance cameras recorded the comings and goings of the residents. The first one had already been disabled. The leader shielded his face from the second, slipped in under its blind spot, and used his free hand to disconnect the power. Years of tracking people gave him an advantage. He knew his target was on this floor, and he wanted no evidence of the man's death.

He instructed the two men to start checking each door on the left, while he did likewise on the opposite side. When he came to apartment 314 he noticed the door wasn't fully closed against the frame, and daylight could be seen through the aperture. Signalling the others to take position behind, he reached out and gently pushed...

***

As Davies watched the parking lot for Harden's arrival, he noticed movement in his peripheral vision. He whipped his head around just as the door opened fully and the man he knew only as "The Butcher" stepped into the room, gun levelled at his chest. Instinctively, Davies dropped to his knees. Several bullets spat from the pistol, the suppressor reducing the noise to a soft hiss. Behind, lumps of plasterboard exploded in clouds of dust. A white plume descended across much of the room.

Davies couldn't see. His right arm flew up and brushed away filament from his eyes. Where was The Butcher? Left. Right? Goddamnit! He could only hope the dust had blinded the Russian too.

Agonisingly, his vision returned. He saw shapes. Three of them. They were standing one behind the other, rubbing their eyes. He had to move now!

He sprung to his feet. The Butcher was rubbing his eyes frantically, while the other men held position. It was now or never. Lowering his body and charging forward, Davies continued until he hit something solid.

The Butcher toppled over like a bowling pin, falling backwards into the men behind him. Like a set of dominoes, all fell to the ground.

Davies leapt to his feet and thrust his hand blindly towards where he thought The Butcher's pistol had fallen. Hands clawing at the ground, eyes still stinging from the dust, he began to panic when he couldn't find it. Then, just as one of the assailants struggled to his feet, Davies found the Makarov a few inches underneath the bed.

The Butcher began to stand, but Davies swiftly approached and brought the butt of the pistol down hard across the man's skull. The terrorist groaned but stayed conscious. Davies pistol-whipped him again and was grateful to see him slump to the floor. He took care of the other two in a similar manner, and had just stepped outside when a fire alarm began blaring.

It took him a full minute to get to the parking lot and into the van. When he turned to face his old friend, Harden gave him a toothy smile and said, "So what's all this commotion about?"

"Get me to an airport, and I'll tell you everything you need to know."

CHAPTER TWO
FLASH PRIORITY

```
ADI GHAR MOUNTAINS
15 MILES NORTH OF SPIN BOLDAK
AFGHANISTAN/PAKISTAN BORDER
09:07 AFT
```

Sergeant-Major Jack Carlos sprinted across the plateau, hearing the sound of intermittent Kalashnikov and M16 fire resounding through the desert air. He paused at the foot of one of Adi Ghar's many mountains, dropped to one knee, and shouldered his rifle.

Down in the valley, inside a cave as dark as the beard on his face, the flash of automatic-weapons-fire could be seen. Carlos' Force Recon team were laying down suppressive fire from a ridge due west.

Two hours earlier, he and his five-man team fast-roped from a Bell UH-1N Huey into Spin Boldak. Intel suggested the town was being used as a base for supplies and fighters. Upon landing, a dozen Taleban extremists burst from two huts and sprinted north into the desert. Carlos left behind two men to secure the town, while he and the others pursued the runners on foot across fifteen miles of desert to their current position.

Green smoke swirled from the nearby hilltop where he had

just come from. Thankfully, there were no dust-storms today; air support would have a clear line of sight.

"Foxtrot Two," he said into his headset, "flares are hot. Yankee Thunder is five out. Gimme a sit-rep. Over."

Julio Gyle shouted to be heard over the crack of his teammates' gunfire. "Two tangos down, Sergeant-Major. The others are retreating further into the caves. We're preparing to enter now, but once we get inside we'll be out of comms. Over."

Carlos, already moving, replied, "Negative. Hold your position. I'll flank back to the opposite end, come in behind, and flush them back to you. What you don't get, the Super-Cobra will. Over."

"Copy. Over."

"Foxtrot One out."

Carlos had been in Afghanistan for almost a year, and in that time had learned that most mountain caves had two points of entry. He made a beeline for the opposite end of this one, hoping to get there before the terrorists. Heart pounding, legs ablaze, he half-ran, half-stumbled towards the bottom of the plateau, willing himself to continue even as his body screamed for respite.

The voice of the Super-Cobra's pilot came across his earpiece loud and clear. "Foxtrot One, this is Yankee Thunder. Over."

As he neared the foot of the plateau, Carlos dropped to his backside and skidded towards a mound of rock. Momentum carried him forward too quickly, and he clattered rib-first into a small boulder, forcing the air out of his lungs with a grunt. Ignoring the pain, he peeked through a gap between two rocks at the expansive area below. There was no sense in running into an ambush. He could see the rear entrance to the cave, but no sign of any terrorists. Yet.

"Yankee Thunder, this is Foxtrot One," he replied. "I read you Lima Charlie. What's your ETA? Over."

"Three-and-a-half minutes. Be advised, there's an FAC helo bringing up my rear. Over."

Carlos frowned: *Why would a Forward Air Control chopper follow a Super-Cobra into a war zone where no air-strikes were needed?* He put the thought out of his mind and acknowledged the transmission. "Roger that, Yankee Thunder. Two flares are burning on a mountain approximately a quarter-klick south-east of my team's position. From there you'll have a clear view of the tangos when I flush them back out of the cave. Be advised, my team's got recon position on that cave opening, so watch for friendlies. Did you copy that, Yankee Thunder? Over."

"Lima Charlie, Foxtrot One. ETA three minutes. Will watch for friendlies. Over."

"Roger. Foxtrot One out."

Carlos leapt from behind the rock, bringing his gun to eye-level as he sprinted towards the cave entrance forty yards away. In the distance, he could hear the growing whirr of the approaching attack helicopter. Nearing the cave, he hoped the men inside would stay there for another five seconds.

They didn't.

The first appeared as soon as he'd had the thought. A wave of anger washed over Carlos. He drew a deep breath and willed it away. Dropping to one knee, he tucked his M16/A2 rifle hard against his shoulder, flicked the selector switch to three-round burst-fire, took aim at the target's head and squeezed the trigger. Insurgents sometimes wore bulletproof vests, and he didn't want to take any risks. All three bullets struck within an inch of each other, below the terrorist's nose, and exploded out the back of his neck. A spray of red mist erupted and the man crumpled to the ground along with it.

Shouts of defiance and hatred reverberated from inside the cave as the remaining terrorists learned what had happened. Carlos considered shouting some kind of warning in return but doubted any of them spoke English. Besides, bullets were a universal language.

That decision made, he loosed off another burst at the cave wall. Chunks of clay and rock exploded in shrouds of terracotta. An advancing Taleban grabbed his eyes and screamed something in a language Carlos couldn't place. Instead, he fired another burst at the man's head, felling him instantly. Another advancing terrorist hesitated and retreated.

Just as planned.

Crouched now, Carlos flanked around the valley until he had a clear line of sight to the cave entrance. A few men, who he assumed were the rearguard, tried to push past the other terrorists to get outside, only to be held back. Making sure he couldn't be seen, he loosed off three-round-bursts at different areas of the rock formation, giving the impression they were being fired on by more than one soldier. Best-case scenario, it would make them think the entire team had flanked from their overview position on the opposite side.

The sound of the Super-Cobra grew stronger, drowning out Carlos' weapon. Keeping his body low, he dashed from one pile of rocks to another until he came to the entrance. He eased around enough to see inside, ignoring the pain of sharp rocks digging into his back. In the distance, about half a dozen lights were bobbing as their owners moved through the cave. He could see small streams of daylight entering the cave twenty yards farther, appearing like daggers or stalactites.

"Foxtrot Two, this is Foxtrot One. Tangos are coming your way. I repeat, tangos are coming to you. Chopper is imminent. Over."

"Roger that, Sergeant-Major. We'll be ready. Over," came Gyle's reply, this time unaccompanied by sounds of fire.

"I'm going to bring up the rear. If they try to retreat, I'll nail them from this end. Over."

"Ooh-rah! Over."

"Foxtrot One out."

He heard the stifled sounds of breathing from inside, fifteen yards away at most. The Taleban were no fools when it came to organisation – there would be a rearguard left behind, just in case Carlos tried to follow. What came next required no thought.

He removed a pair of night-vision goggles and a gas mask from his satchel and slipped both on. From his rigger belt he extracted a fragmentation grenade, pulled the cotter pin, and flung it into the opening. From inside came sounds of horrified realisation. The same word was repeated three times in five seconds, and Carlos allowed himself the facetious thought that he now knew the Arabic word for "grenade".

He covered his ears and tucked his head to one side as the grenade exploded. Lumps of rock clattered to the ground, spreading a cloud of dust inside the cave. Someone screamed. It was a sound Carlos knew all too well: The excruciating pain of having one's limbs blown off.

He knew he couldn't enter yet. The rest of the front group would be waiting for him. Instead, he grabbed another grenade and flung it farther this time. As it exploded, he spun inside and hurried to a place where he would have a view once the dust settled.

He safed his rifle, took the strap, looped it over his neck, and slung the gun over his head into his back holster. Tight areas like this called for accuracy, so he retrieved his sidearm from its holster.

The thunderous roar of the Super-Cobra rumbled through the cave walls as it circled overhead. For a moment, he feared the combination of it and the damage his grenades had caused might collapse the structure and entomb him. The thought sent splinters of dread through him, but he forced them to the back of his mind.

When the dust cleared, he zeroed in on the two terrorists whose lives were all but over. Carlos had never been the sentimental type, but he spared them the horror of dying from blood-loss by firing a suppressed round into each man's head.

He crept forward, using his goggles to negotiate the cavernous surroundings, careful to avoid looking directly at any sources of light coming from the opposite end. The rest of the group were hurrying towards the daylight, unaware of what awaited them outside.

Carlos hugged the nearside wall, concentrating on keeping his bearing true. Night-vision goggles had a nasty way of reducing peripheral vision, and the last thing he needed was to be blindsided by a retreating terrorist. Another reason why he'd eliminated the rearguard.

The terrorists neared the exit. Carlos slipped his mask and goggles off; and continued forward, one hand on the rock, the other gripping his .45.

Keep moving, he told himself. *Don't give them a chance to turn back.*

***

What the hell is going on?, wondered Master-Sergeant Julio Gyle, his finger poised on the trigger guard, ready to flick it a half-inch backwards to the trigger on the first sight of trouble. He couldn't radio Carlos even if he wanted to – not in those caves.

"Master-Sergeant, we've gotta move in now!"

The adrenaline and excitement had the young lance corporal

pumped up. Gyle could see it on his face. But Gyle couldn't afford the same recklessness – not here and definitely not now. "We have our orders."

"That was a grenade. We gotta get in there and get these guys!"

Gyle wanted to turn and glare at him, but was disciplined enough to know how foolish that would be. The young man did not have the same guile, but he would learn. "I've given you a direct order, Corporal. Continue manning your post until I say otherwise."

The corporal sulked for a moment but turned his attention back to the cave exit. Gyle made a mental note to give him a reprimand later for allowing his attention to waver.

On his other side, Staff-Sergeant Federico Holmes hadn't budged throughout the altercation. His eyes were locked on the exit, waiting – daring – someone to come out. He touched his hand to his face, absently wiping away the perspiration forming on his forehead.

"I don't like this, JG. Something ain't right, man."

Gyle shared that feeling. The caves couldn't have been more than a hundred metres long. It had been three minutes since the first grenade had exploded. Even in the darkest conditions it wouldn't take that long to cover the distance.

"I know, Rico. Give it time. Carlos knows what he's doing."

"I hear you, but these are crafty bastards, and the longer they don't stick their heads outta that cave, the more I'm gonna believe they're planning something."

And the more Gyle thought about that, the more he believed it too.

***

They'd disappeared.

Carlos blinked hard a couple of times, not trusting his eyes in the dim of the cave. No sound anywhere. No movement, either. Ahead, the daylight grew brighter as he manoeuvred closer to the exit. But the group of terrorists were nowhere in sight.

What the...

A crack. The sound of gravel crunching under someone's

boots. Where? Behind? To the side? Carlos didn't know; couldn't know. He snapped his head to the right, squinting to make out the features of the cave. A few rays of light entered through cracks in the cave wall, revealing motes of dust floating in the air. Otherwise, nothing but darkness.

A snap. From behind this time? Had they circled without him knowing? He spun around, free hand reaching for his goggles, gun coming up in tandem with them. The interior became awash in green light. Shapes of two dead terrorists flooded his view, their bodies still motionless.

No, his "six" had not been compromised, the realisation not leaving him any less concerned.

Another snap. Closer this time. To the right? Left? It was hard to judge down here. He turned around to trace it but stopped mid-turn. A powerful light beamed from nearby, filling the green display of his goggles with white searing light.

Carlos hissed, his eyes burning, disorientated. He tore the goggles off and flung them aside. Dozens of white circles coruscated in his vision.

They'd tricked him. *How? Did I let my guard down? Where did they go?*

They'd turned him into the hunted. He had to get out. Which way? Forward, to the daylight? Back the way he'd come? *I can't see!* Somewhere nearby another snap sounded.

He began to see shapes moving. Closing in. He sensed them first, in a way that made the hairs on his neck rise in hackles. They were surrounding him; pinning him in so he couldn't escape. A thousand thoughts flooded his mind, only one constant: He could not stay here. To do so would mean his execution.

His vision returned, bit by bit. Movement again. What was that!? Breathing? He tried to focus his vision to one area, but to no avail. He could see nothing more than shapes. They circled around him, like a group of thugs ready to deliver a beating. Their proximity to him made Carlos' decision easier.

He lowered his body and drove forward towards the first of them, accelerating until the point of contact. He felt his shoulder hit something solid, heard the snap of bone as he angled his body downward, using his legs to force the terrorist to the ground. A sharp cry pierced through the cave, then ceased as they both hit the ground with a tremendous thud, the air exploding from the Taleban's lungs.

Carlos reached down and smashed his forearm into the man's windpipe. The terrorist thrashed wildly, gurgling and wheezing sounds coming from his restricted airway.

He could see daylight again. Ahead. Thirty metres at most. But before he had a chance to return to his feet, strong arms gripped him from behind and did it for him.

Somewhere in the back of his mind, a nagging question persisted: Why haven't they killed me? He didn't know the answer, but as his vision fully returned, he saw how perilous his situation was. No fewer than ten terrorists were standing in a circle around him, the glow of their flashlights glinting off the steel-finish of their five-inch knives.

Yet somehow, that wasn't the scariest thing. There was a crevice to the left of Carlos, light barely emanating from the room behind it. In a moment of chilling clarity, he realised where they'd vanished to and why they hadn't shot him.

On the room's floor sat a wooden box, roughly four foot square. Its lid was positioned against the rear of the cave wall. Carlos didn't need to go any closer to know what it held.

Dynamite.

***

Gyle was officially worried. Perplexed, even. It had been over five minutes since Carlos' last radio contact. In the intervening time, two grenades had exploded within the cave, followed by silence. Gyle began to wonder if Carlos was dead and the Taleban terrorists were waiting to ambush him and his men once they had no other option but to leave their post to check on their commander.

The Super-Cobra was still hovering by the hilltop, the pilot no doubt sharing Gyle's perplexity. He also saw that an FAC chopper had landed on a level area a safe distance away. The rotors were still turning, but a man in full service uniform paced beside it, talking on what looked to be an encrypted tactical radio. Gyle knew the demeanour. An officer. Maybe even a one - or two - star general. His presence only added to the confusion.

Beside him, he felt Holmes tense as though something had

caught his attention. Gyle reproached himself for losing concentration and turned back to the exit, even more astounded to see nothing of interest. What had bothered Holmes?

"What are you thinking, Rico?"

He bit his lip in a thoughtful manner, then said, "If I didn't know better I'd swear I saw lights in that cave."

Gyle frowned but nodded his head. "Okay, but wouldn't that make sense? The Taleban are well-coordinated, but they wouldn't have NVGs. Flashlights would be ideal."

Holmes shook his head. "No, what would be ideal would be nothing at all. You said it yourself, JG – these guys are well-coordinated. They're smart, highly trained, and much more used to this environment than we are. They don't need flashlights to see in the dark."

"So maybe you didn't see light, then?"

"No, I did. About ninety seconds after the grenades exploded. But I haven't seen any since." Holmes shook his head again, his face growing more pensive.

"Which means?" Gyle urged.

"Why here? There are dozens of caves from Spin Boldak to here. Why cover fifteen miles of ground? Why this cave? Unless..." he trailed off, unable to finish his thoughts.

"Unless what? C'mon, I want to hear your thoughts out loud, Rico."

"Unless..." he trailed off again. This time, though, his face twisted in alarm as his mind connected the dots. He turned to Gyle, eyes wide, voice taut with urgency. "Unless it's a trap."

"Move! Get to the far end! I'll come in from this side and push them back to you." He turned to the young corporal and handed him his headset. "Raise the pilot, Smitty. Tell him we need him at the opposite end. We're going to flush the tangos back that way. You stay here and deal with any that get out this end. Don't fuckin' shoot us!" he added, levelling the corporal a hard glare. Then, to Holmes, "Let's move, Rico."

***

Carlos had no hope of making radio contact, even if presented with the opportunity. That put him on his own, and though he'd been in similar situations before, familiarity and comfort were not the same thing. He worried, like any man would, about the case of dynamite three feet away. The terrorists hadn't shot at him because bullets and dynamite did not make a good combination, in the same way explosions and caves didn't either. Yet, the menacing tips of their knives (swords might have been a more accurate description) seemed to suggest they had an alternative death in mind – one which they hadn't attempted yet, for reasons he couldn't begin to fathom.

One of them was toying with Carlos' .45, flicking its light on and off in something akin to awe. Another one had taken ownership of his M-16. He didn't know whether it was the dim of the cave or an act of complacence, but they'd failed to see the rigger belt around his waist. Whatever they were planning, it didn't involve his death...at least not yet. That gave him time.

"Why don't we just go outside and settle – " Carlos began, but was cut off by the butt of his own rifle hitting him square in the jaw, knocking him down again. He landed on the dead body of the terrorist whose trachea he'd crushed. Spitting out a mouthful of blood, and a tooth, he turned away, feeling anger boil inside him. He tried to snatch the dead man's knife but was seized by the hair and yanked to his feet again.

"American pig!" someone said in a barely recognisable tone, then Carlos felt the phlegm.

He dared not move, even though he could not bear the disgusting liquid trickling down his nose. It repulsed him, and he wanted nothing more than to put a bullet in all of their heads. Maybe he would get the chance...

...Carlos wondered why he hadn't seen his sergeant approach. Of course, he'd been a little preoccupied. Nevertheless, he saw him now, moving with stealth in mind. But Carlos knew he had to find a way to extricate himself from the group, otherwise friendly-fire would claim yet another life in this on-going war.

One hand was on Carlos' shoulder, the other at the small of his back. He could feel the knife a couple of inches away from his neck. The proper place would have been closer, to react if a situation required it. He knew he could get out of the hold before the terrorist realised what had happened, clearing the way for Gyle (he assumed it to be him from stature and gait) to dispatch the terrorists.

He waited patiently, allowing Gyle to come to a place where

he could see as much as possible.

Now!

He swung his elbow backwards and caught the Taleban in the solar plexus, forcing the wind out of his lungs. The man let out a muffled cry. Spinning around, Carlos delivered a vicious uppercut which drove the man's nose into his brainstem. Blood gushed from the shattered remains of his nasal cavity. The terrorist crumpled into a heap. Carlos dived to the floor and retrieved his .45 from the terrorist's holster, rolled onto his back, and bathed the closest terrorist to him with its light.

Someone screamed. Carlos would later learn it had been him, screaming at Gyle not to shoot near the illuminated room. He must have gotten the message, because Carlos watched – in the glow of his Surefire light – a well-placed shot to the terrorist's head, instantly felling him.

How many was that? He wondered. *Four? Five?* There couldn't have been many more than a half-dozen left, all of whom would now be aware they were being fired on.

Carlos rose and clicked off his light. Gyle knew his location now, and it made no sense for him to draw attention to himself. It didn't help his vision, but it was better than wearing a sign that said "here I am". Besides, Gyle would be wearing goggles, and Carlos planned to let him do most, if not all, the killing.

***

Gyle had no idea what was in the illuminated room to his right, but it had beset his commander with an anxiety Gyle had never before seen him exhibit. He could only imagine it to be something volatile, else he would not have reacted in such a manner.

Gyle concentrated on dispatching the remaining terrorists. He knew where Carlos had been last, and as long as his commander didn't move again the chance of mistaking him for one of the terrorists was minute. He trusted Carlos to leave the rest of the killing to him and Holmes. Besides, he knew Carlos would be smart enough to know he'd only get in the way.

Gyle was smart enough to avoid looking into the light. In front of him, a couple of terrorists were running around, trying to discern where the latest gunshots had come from. He drew a bead on the nearest one, lined up his tritium-lit sights on the head and gently squeezed the trigger. The suppressor reduced the sound to a small hiss, like sandpaper being scraped across wood, but there wasn't a man in the cave who didn't know what had happened, none more so than the target. His head snapped back with the impact, as the round drove through his jaw, expanded to twice its normal size, and exploded out the back in a cloud of red mist.

This caused a chain reaction of events. The rest of the terrorists now had a general idea from where the gunshot originated. They turned their attention towards Gyle and, for the first time since entering the cave, brandished more than just their knives. They advanced towards him, weapons pointed menacingly, eyes searching the darkness for the figure of a human.

Exactly how Gyle wanted it. On the other side Holmes had sneaked up behind them. The original plan had been to flank them back to the opposite end, where the chopper would deal with them, but there was a chance to get them here and now.

Gyle eased back, careful not to make any unnecessary movements which might attract the attention of their eyes. He didn't know how accustomed to the darkness these terrorists had become, but they had years of experience in environments like this.

Now, Rico!

Gyle didn't believe in psychics, but he'd worked with Federico Holmes for almost fifteen years, and they shared a tight bond which had grown through near-death experiences. There was only one other person on the planet he knew as well as Holmes – Carlos.

Nevertheless, it was as though Holmes read his mind. He hit the first terrorist with a three-round-burst to the back of the head, and had barely released the trigger before lining up his next target. Three more bullets exploded through the air, catching the next nearest terrorist in the back of the neck. Blood aspirated from his mouth as he tried to roar out in pain. He pirouetted and hit the cave floor with an almighty thud.

The remaining three reacted on instinct. They spun around to trace the source of the newest gunfire, not realising they'd signed their own death warrants by doing so. Gyle took aim at the one nearest him, unleashing another three-round-burst that scissored through the air. The bullets impacted just below the base of the neck, a horrible shot in more than one way. Something snapped, and then a piercing scream filled the cave – so loud Gyle reckoned he would have heard it above the noise of the Super-Cobra.

The last two didn't know which way to turn. They snapped their heads back and forth, confused, desperate, and not sure what the hell had happened to their compatriots. Neither Gyle nor Holmes offered anything in the way of sympathy, six more bullets sailing through the air seconds later.

Gyle checked the illuminated room for any stragglers, finding none. The remainder of the cave was then secured thoroughly, each crack and crevice studied for any indication of a room or cubbyhole. When both men were satisfied, they removed their goggles and shouted, "Clear!"

***

Carlos breathed a quiet sigh of relief, but his job wasn't complete yet. He moved towards the illuminated room at a brisk pace, squeezed through the entrance, and located the box of dynamite. He had a mind to leave it here, or let one of his sergeants take it out, but Carlos had never sent a man to do a job he wouldn't do himself, and pride did not allow him to this time either.

Before lifting it off the floor, he checked to see if there were any other boxes in the room. In the first Desert Storm he'd come upon a room in a cave just like this, full of boxes of grenades, AK-47s, and ammunition. Back then it had been the Iraqis who'd used it as a supply station. Ammunition and grenades had been filtered out through a maze of secret tunnels whose exits remained unknown to American soldiers for months. Finding that room had put the kibosh on a lot of the Iraqis' supply to their aboveground troops. This felt like a similar victory, but he'd found just one box...of dynamite, no less. It didn't make sense for the Taleban to have dynamite – not as a weapon, in any case. There were more stable explosives to use.

As he placed both hands around the box to lift it, he had an unnerving thought. It seemed too odd that a single box of dynamite had been left in this room...not without a purpose.

What, though? Why would they leave dynamite? Dynamite's volatile – obsolete in military use; too easily rendered ineffective. You don't leave it lying around for no...

Purpose.

Carlos' eyes widened, the words ringing true, their fear encompassing his entire body. He didn't need to search for it. He knew it was there. Without thinking, he bolted from his crouched position and fired his body through the narrow opening. Once outside, he snapped his head left and right, saw Gyle and Holmes, and screamed, "Move!"

The pale light illuminated the look of fear on their faces, but both knew (or had guessed) what was happening. They made a break first, leading Carlos away from the opposite end where the chopper awaited anybody who might dare exit that way. Even with fifty pounds of equipment strapped to his shoulders, Carlos moved fast for a six-four, two-hundred-pound man. He caught up with Holmes and Gyle just as they neared the exit.

All the time spent wondering where the terrorists had disappeared to, Carlos now reproached himself for not asking *why* they had instead. They hadn't discarded the box. They'd left it there for a reason...a purpose; to maim and kill as many "American pigs" as possible.

Carlos entered the daylight first, hand rising as a shield, eyes squinting as tears flooded his vision. He kept moving forward, stumbling as his desperation grew.

Over five sticks of high-explosive...enough to bring down a small building. What would it do here? How far is the minimum safe distance–

Three rounds exploded at his feet, kicking dust up into his face. Vision gone again, Carlos roared, "What the hell!" On instinct, he collapsed to the ground, both to play possum and to give himself a chance to regain his vision and retrieve his weapon.

Goddamnit! I thought we killed them all! One hand went for his eyes, clearing away dust and tears, while the other blindly grabbed at the holster containing his .45. *Which side? Goddamnit, which side?* He tried to visualise the layout of the ridge, the plateau, and the direction the shots came from; anything to give himself an advantage when his vision did return. But all he could see was the cave and five sticks of dynamite, all in glorious high-definition, taunting him and his inability to think rationally.

"Smitty, cease fuckin' fire! Goddamn it, I'm gonna kick your ass! What'd I tell you! Don't shoot us, you stupid son of a bitch!" Gyle screamed.

Carlos heard Gyle's command, breathed a sigh of relief when

Smitty acknowledged it apologetically, but then flinched as the sticks of dynamite exploded with a deafening boom. A cacophony of collapsing rocks assaulted his ears as the structure caved in, swirls of smoke and dust rising from within. All the time, Carlos just lay on the ground, his mind and body exhausted but nowhere near any danger.

"Jesucristo!" Gyle proclaimed, looking back at the ruined remains. "Mano, you know that was gonna happen?" he asked Carlos, who laughed and nodded his head.

"You think I made you run because I was dying for a leak?" Carlos laughed hoarsely.

"Sergeant-Major Jack Carlos?" a voice interrupted from above.

Carlos opened one eye to look up, saw the medals affixed to the stranger's breast, leapt to his feet and snapped a salute. "Sir, yes, sir!"

"Brigadier-General Edward Triton, Sergeant-Major." Triton returned the salute and then instructed Carlos to be at ease. "I've got flash-priority orders to escort you and Master-Sergeant Gyle to Bagram Airfield, where a C-one-forty-one is waiting to transport both of you back to the States."

Carlos cocked an eyebrow. "Excuse me, General? I never received those orders, sir. We're not due out of here for another four months."

"I appreciate your confusion, but these orders arrived from the Commandant at zero seven hundred this morning. Both of you will accompany me on the FAC chopper, while the Super-Cobra will gather the rest of your team and take them back to base camp."

Carlos shook his head in disbelief. "What's this about, sir?"

"I have no idea. I know you're confused, son, but there will be no more questions. Put Staff-Sergeant Holmes in charge, and both of you come with me to the chopper."

Carlos looked back to Gyle, both trading a look that said 'what the hell?'

CHAPTER THREE
SETTING UP

THE WHITE HOUSE
WASHINGTON, D. C.
MONDAY, JANUARY 6TH
07: 11 EST

Seated behind his desk in the Oval Office, President James
Walsh glanced up from his customary morning briefing report
to see his National Security Adviser, Richard Duke, and his
Chief of Staff, Matthew Clark, entering. Both were Walsh's
oldest friends and accustomed to privileges no other members of
Walsh's administration were. They entered the Oval Office when
they liked, how often they liked, and could call the President by
his first name in private situations like this.

A mess steward entered with breakfast for all three, and
quietly slipped away to let them get down to business.

Duke slotted into a worn leather chair and crossed his legs.
A leftover from his Supreme Court days, it and a briar pipe were
the last remnants of his great image. A former judge, he had first
met the President 35 years earlier at Harvard. Both had
graduated magna cum laude with first-class honours in law.
Walsh went on to be a defence attorney, while Duke became a
prosecutor. Many times in the past they'd had fierce battles in

the courtroom, but their respect for each other never faltered. Some years later, he became a judge, and Walsh ran for the senate and, five years later, the presidency. With the financial backing of Duke, he won the election by a landslide, and Duke became his first appointed adviser.

The President removed his reading glasses and set them and the report on the table. "Good morning, Richard, Matt. Where are we with Operation STRIKE?"

Duke uncrossed his legs and leaned forward. "Morning, James. Most of the two teams are in place. We have a few more recruits arriving as we speak."

The President nodded his approval. "Good. How long before either team will be ready to call on?"

"The best we can expect is three to four weeks," he answered.

"Have either of you decided on commanders yet?"

He shook his head. "Not yet."

"Don't. When it's fully operational, we can do it then."

"As you wish, sir," Clark said. Even though he was allowed to, he didn't call the President by his first name. Not when Richard Duke was present. He liked to think he was the only one afforded that right, and Clark wasn't going to shatter his delusion after all these years. He didn't have the same history with the President as Duke did, but he knew his input was respected just as much, if not more, than the 66-year-old's. A millionaire at the age of 27, Clark had hired Walsh twenty years earlier to defend his son, who had been accused of raping and murdering a white girl. Given the nature of the murder and the colour of his son, it had looked a sure-fire prosecution until Walsh produced two credible witnesses who accounted for the son's whereabouts at the time of the murder. He offered him money as reward but Walsh refused it. When he ran for the Oval Office, Clark wouldn't take "no" for an answer and bankrolled his campaign with almost five million dollars. Though he first refused the job of Chief of Staff, Walsh convinced him to come on-board.

Walsh finished his croissant and asked, "How are things progressing with Jon?"

He was referring to Jonathan Baker, director of the FBI. Baker had organised a sting to uncover an illegal arms-development operation thought to have been masterminded by Pavel Kirov, a Russian freelance terrorist with ties to several Muslim and Islamic freedom fighters. The primary fear was that Kirov was supplying them with weapons to launch another attack on American soil. They knew another attack so soon after 9/11 would cripple the country. STRIKE Force, when fully operational, would be designed to stop such an attack, but they all knew cutting off the Hydra's head didn't kill the beast. They needed to strike at the heart of the operation.

Duke shifted in his chair and glanced back at the door. When he was sure no one was going to enter, he said, "Jon lost contact with his inside man yesterday. He hasn't heard from him in twenty-four hours. We have to assume the worst, gentlemen."

The President grimaced. "Okay. I want Jon's official report on my desk before the day is out. I'd like to know just how much the operation uncovered."

In the corner chair, Clark fidgeted as he mulled over the wording of his next sentence. "Mr President, if I may?" Walsh nodded his head and Clark said, "Sir, I think we should cut our losses and run." Ignoring Duke's disgusted snort, he continued, "This sting operation has been on-going for over a year now and we aren't any closer to uncovering anything untoward about Pavel Kirov's dealings. Let's face it: In all probability our inside man is dead. This is the perfect chance to wash our hands of this."

Duke rolled his eyes. "And do *what*, Matt? Stand back and let this country be attacked again? Spare me your horrified indignation about this whole operation, *please*." He turned his gaze to the President. "James, you know how close we were to uncovering Kirov's operation – "

"Bull!" Clark interjected. "We were no closer yesterday than we were this time last year."

Duke clenched his jaw and folded his arms across his chest. "Now wait just a minute– "

"No! *You* wait a minute. If you recall, we had this conversation fourteen months ago when I told you both this operation was a potential minefield. I stand by those comments. We have nothing! We're no closer to uncovering Kirov's operation. Hell, if anything we're further back than we ever were. They've found our inside man. Do you honestly think we'll ever get another one inside, or even come close to uncovering Kirov's operation now?"

Duke ignored the heated response and turned back to Walsh. "James, we need to deal with this...because if we don't, this country *will* be attacked again."

"Based on what, Richard? The predictions of a bunch of suits in Langley? Or the paranoid delusions of a bunch of analysts at Bolling?" Clark asked, referring to the headquarters of the CIA and DIA.

Duke leapt from his seat and covered the distance to Clark in a surprisingly quick time for a man of his age. "Now you listen to me, you cocky son-of-a-bitch," he began, the veins standing out on both sides of his neck. "Have some respect for the men and women risking their lives so you can sit in that chair like a pompous asshole! Me and James were busting our balls while you were still crawling around in diapers." Clark looked to make a rejoinder but was silenced with a glare. "Your job is to supervise the staff of the White House and organise the President's schedule. You do not get any say in military action!"

The President slammed both fists down on his desk. The beautiful oak table, made from the timbers of the *HMS Resolute*, was a gift from Queen Victoria to President Rutherford B. Hayes in 1880. Both men knew how much the current president thought of the unique piece of art, and knew he was rarely mad enough to slam it like he just had. "I've heard enough! Richard, sit down."

He gave Walsh a questioning look.

"Now, Richard!"

Duke sat back down, crossed his legs and folded his arms like a child whose favourite toy had just been taken from him.

"I have a meeting with the Joint Chiefs at midday. I do *not* have time to babysit you two. Richard, make sure Jon Baker knows I want his report by five this evening. Matt, clear up my schedule for the rest of the day. We will reconvene here after lunch."

Both men nodded, and the President gestured for them to leave.

CHAPTER FOUR
AN UNFORESEEN PROBLEM

ATARIC BUILDING
MANHATTAN
NEW YORK CITY
07:34 EST

Harold Johnson slotted his Mercedes Benz into his reserved space and stepped out into the cool morning breeze. Looking around, he noticed both his bosses, Dave Haskens and James Fielding, were already present. He pulled a Yankees cap over his grey, balding hair and hurried to the entrance.

ATARIC stood on 14 East 38th Street, in a building once owned by another huge computer firm in New York. Many thought the word was an acronym for something, perhaps *Advanced Technological Research Into Computers,* but nowhere on the building or in any literature did it say exactly what, if anything, the name meant. People did know, however, the company had hit a rough patch in recent years and laid off almost half its workers in the last six months. Though its employees created many sellable items, the problem was competing with the likes of Microsoft. ATARIC didn't have the wherewithal to market their products to that degree.

The main working area was a voluminous hall containing

approximately 200 desks and twice as many computers. There were a total of four floors above it, used for staff meetings and the financial end of the business. In the corners of the main hall four suspended offices, with their own stair- and elevator-access, allowed the bosses to watch on-going work with ease.

Johnson, the managing director, climbed the stairs to Fielding's office and found the chairman talking to Haskens, his chief executive officer.

Haskens' secretary, Marie, handed Johnson a cup of freshly brewed coffee and exited. Johnson took a seat and said, "Morning, gentlemen."

"Morning, Harold," Fielding replied. The 71-year-old owned half of ATARIC along with his partner, Haskens. A U.S. Army colonel for fifteen years, Fielding had been forced into early retirement after taking two bullets in the back while fighting in the Ho Chi Minh trail in Vietnam. After years of intense rehabilitation and therapy, he'd recovered almost ninety per cent use of his legs.

"I was just telling David we may have a problem." Fielding sighed and downed the remainder of his coffee. "Jack Reid's new operating system is ready for installation on all our computers. Damned thing is going to save us hundreds of thousands of dollars. Not to mention the money we stand to make when we sell it." He stopped and coughed hard into his hand, shielding blood from their view and wiping it on a towel. "Anyway," he continued, "we've got Charlie Davenport coming on Wednesday to do a financial assessment. I want the new operating system installed by then."

Johnson gave him a look of incredulity. "Are you insane?" He shook his head. "With the staff we have right now, we're talking about a least a week's work – and that's pushing it. You want this done in forty-eight hours? It's just not possible, Jim."

"That's why we need to bring in some people," Haskens said, the corners of his lips turning inward slightly.

"Like who?"

"Peter Hunt, for one." Fielding wasn't surprised by the reaction this elicited.

Johnson clenched his jaw. "Hunt! Are you kidding me? You can't seriously *think* of bringing back Peter Hunt."

"I seem to recall Hunt breaking through our highly

advanced firewall in less than an hour, Harold." Fielding remained calm. He rarely let emotions show.

"Which is exactly why we fired him in the first place!"

Haskens raised his hand and said, "Harry, we didn't fire him." He gave him another false smile.

"Officially, we laid him off – I know that! But need I remind you, Dave, Hunt is more of a liability than any outside contractor you could bring in? You hired me to be managing director because I can read people. So I'll tell you straight up: Peter Hunt is *not* the man for this job."

Haskens' eyes showed a flicker of anger for a second, and then he smiled once more. "I know your history with Hunt, Har –"

"This has *nothing* to do with my history with Hunt! I respect the man – he's got one of the best computer minds I've ever seen, but his people-skills ranks up there with Charles Manson's. Understand this: You bring Hunt back into this building, don't be surprised if you have chaos on your hands within twenty-four hours."

Fielding raised his hand for silence. "Be that as it may, he is the best man for the job. I want you to make it happen. When you do, be clear this is a one-time job. Hunt will not be brought back in any official capacity. He will be paid off the records, and the reason for his presence here will remain between the three of us and Jack Reid."

Johnson almost breathed a sigh of exasperation, but he was secretly glad Hunt wasn't going to get his old job back. "As you wish, Jim. I'll contact him immediately."

Fielding rubbed his hands together and smiled. "Brilliant. Myself and David have some business to attend to downstairs. When Reid arrives, fill him in. Tell him to keep Hunt in line or it's his ass. They used to be friends, didn't they? Well, surely the man can control him. If not, we may have to look for someone who can." He nodded to Johnson, who knew exactly what the old man was getting at.

"I'll see to it he keeps Hunt on a short leash."

CHAPTER FIVE
SECOND CHANCES

PETER HUNT⊖S HOUSE
WASHINGTONVILLE
NEW YORK STATE
07:47 EST

Slumped on his living-room couch, an empty bottle lying in a pool of whiskey beside his outstretched hand, Peter Hunt didn't hear the phone ring the first time. Nor the second, a minute later. It remained unanswered seven times, spanning a period of ten minutes, before Hunt snapped out of his stupor. He stumbled across discarded newspapers, letters, and unwashed clothes and got to it on the thirteenth ring.

"Hello?" His mouth was dry, the greeting barely escaping. He needed a drink. He looked back to the couch and saw the remnants of his last bottle of whiskey. *Dammit! What the hell happened last night?*

"Peter? It's Jack Reid."

Though they'd been friends since the age of five, it still took Hunt a few seconds to place the name. "Jack? Oh, Jack. Haven't heard from you in a while." Hunt couldn't keep the derision out of his voice. *Try since I got fired.* Hunt felt betrayed by both Reid and his own wife, Karen. Both had left him in his time of need. Both had driven him to become his current self, and he hated them for it.

"Yeah, well, things have been a bit hectic at home, you know? Sarah's ridiculing me for working too much."

"Too hectic to pick up the phone – yeah, sure, I understand. So why have you graced me with your time this morning?" Hunt asked, pouring a glass of water from the kitchen sink and downing it in a single gulp.

Reid sighed and said, "Mr Johnson wants to have a word with you, Peter."

"*Mister* Johnson? Was he elected president without my knowledge? Because I damn sure never called him *mister* anything."

"Things have changed around here. Anyway, I'm going to forward the call to his office."

"Nice talking to you too, Jack."

Hunt was tempted to hang up the phone – after all, he had no reason to affiliate with ATARIC anymore – but he couldn't shake the feeling of intrigue.

Harold Johnson had a habit of making people wait for him, so Hunt wasn't surprised it took over five minutes for him to answer the forwarded call.

"How've you been, Peter?"

He almost laughed, though was surprised at the near-sincerity of Johnson's tone. "Come now, Harry. You didn't go to all this trouble just to check up on little ol' me. You tell me what it is you want, and I'll tell you why I can't do it for you."

Johnson's laugh was anything but sincere. "Always like Peter Hunt to deflect with a joke. Okay, Hunt, here's the deal: Your buddy – or should I say *former* buddy – Reid...his new operating system is ready for mass installation at ATARIC. Some issues have arisen and we need it installed on all computers within forty-eight hours. That's where you come in."

Hunt laughed. "You want me to install a new operating system on over five hundred computers within forty-eight hours? For a start, you're talking about at least a week's work. And I'm what – going to help you out because we left on *such* amicable terms?"

"Cut the bullshit, Hunt, and give me a straight answer: Can it be done?"

"With the right team, anything's possible. But you still haven't told me why I would ever want to help ATARIC again."

"Let's get one thing straight: This is a one-time deal, and you'll be well compensated. I'm sure that nest egg of yours is running a little low."

Hunt snorted. "Fuck you, Johnson! I got a severance of five thousand dollars. For eight years of my life? I was making more than that every month. ATARIC screwed me over."

"Screwed *you* over? You've got some nerve, buddy. You tried to break into our secure system. You're lucky you got anything."

"Wasn't much secure, you ask me. What I did, I did for the company. You have any idea how many hackers would make me look computer illiterate? I breached ATARIC's security to prove it could be done. A few weeks before I did, I warned Fielding his computers were unsecure. He didn't listen to reason, so I showed him just how unsecure they were."

"Listen, I don't really care why you did it. Fielding's willing to pay you ten thousand dollars. Think about it – ten grand for two days' work? Where's a rundown, out-of-work bum like you going to come across that kind of money?"

A few years ago, Hunt could have afforded to miss an opportunity like this. His and his wife's salary combined to a total of two hundred and fifty thousand. But it had been nine months since he'd seen a paycheque, and his savings account, though still substantial, had lessened by about fifteen thousand in that time. This was a chance to rectify that. And still, the thought of going back to ATARIC filled him with rage. The company he'd spent a quarter of his life with had stabbed him in the back. Sure, they'd given a suitable reason for his departure, but he knew better. The second he'd breached the system, two security guards straitjacketed him and took him to Jim Fielding's office, where he'd learned Fielding had been watching him for months. A week or so later, they gave him two choices: One, get fired and walk away with nothing. Or, two, leave with his dignity still intact. Hunt had thought the severance package would have been at least twenty thousand, and was too naïve to realise they were going to screw him, so he chose option number two. He received the bare minimum severance pay, and was physically warned not to file for unfair dismissal.

"Hunt? You still there?" Johnson asked, breaking Hunt's reverie.

"I'm thinking."

"Yeah, well, I hate to break it to you but I haven't got time for you to mull this decision over. I need an answer now."

Hunt thought about it for another thirty seconds and made his decision. "First, if I'm going to do this I want fifteen grand. I've got a few debts to pay."

"You're not calling the shots here, Hunt! Ten grand, that's it. Take it or leave it."

He knew how stubborn Johnson was. If he couldn't convince him, he sure as hell couldn't convince Fielding or Haskens either. "Fine, but I want to pick my own team. If not, you can forget this whole deal."

"Okay. I can give you that. So we have a deal?"

"Deal. When do you want me to start?" Hunt ran a hand through his medium-length black hair and rubbed his full-bearded face. He hoped this wasn't as imperative as Johnson's tone indicated. He needed a day to get sober and clean himself up. At the moment he looked like a caveman.

"Right now. How long will it take you to get here?"

With a sigh, he replied, "I need thirty minutes to shave and wash up. It'll take me about ninety to get to ATARIC."

"Two hours? No way. The day will be over. Tell you what: Give me your address, and I'll have the company helicopter there in twenty minutes."

"Are you serious? A helicopter? Fine – whatever." Hunt gave him the address. "I better get paid for this, Johnson, or I swear to God – "

"You'll get paid. Just be ready for that helicopter."

***

After a hot shower and shave, Hunt stopped off in his room and rummaged around for a suit. While he didn't care about appearance or what others thought of him, he also knew there were people at ATARIC who still held him in high esteem, and he didn't want to give them any reason to change their minds.

He found a collection of old suits he had for weddings, funerals, and other such occasions, and picked the one which looked the cleanest.

On the way out the door, he caught a glimpse of himself in Karen's mirror. He stopped and took a long look at his appearance.

Though it was the best he'd looked in almost a year, he was still ashamed of the extra fifteen pounds around his gut. At 32 years old, though, he had a better physique than most men in their twenties. Hunt had always been an avid bodybuilder, but the last time he'd visited his home gym was the day Karen left him. Too much alcohol and fast food had put an end to his once-perfect physique.

Angered with his current physical shape, he stopped off in his gym next. When Karen told him she only wanted one child, he jumped at the opportunity to turn the spare bedroom into a weights-room. He'd stripped out the carpet, put down a wooden floor, and, with Jack's help, moved all his weights from the garage. Now, the twenty-by-twenty room was full of barbells, dumbbells, kettle bells, and even a bike and treadmill.

Hunt had no time for a workout now, but he did want to check something. He picked up a set of electronic scales and set them to pounds. Two hundred and eighty-nine, the readout told him when he stood atop them. Twenty-five pounds heavier than nine months earlier – the last time he'd weighed himself. Disgusted, he threw them back into the corner. As he did, he noticed the framed picture of Steve Young, his American Football idol, hanging above his bench-press machine. It reminded him not to chase after dreams he would never achieve. More importantly, it hid his safe. When Karen had first learned of his predilection for hunting, she'd demanded he buy a safe for his collection of weapons. Hunt had thought wall-mounted safes were a figment of Hollywood's imagination, but the installer had said that belief had the opposite effect on thieves.

He entered the six-digit code, extracted his nine-millimetre Browning automatic, and tucked it inside his workbag.

If they were going to screw him over again, this time he'd be prepared.

As he walked back to the kitchen, he heard the tenuous sound of an approaching helicopter. A few minutes later, at just after half-eight, Jim Fielding's Bell 402 landed on Hunt's front lawn, drawing confused looks from the closest neighbours. Living in the countryside had its benefits, but he had learned country folk were incredibly nosy people.

Wasting no time, he locked the door behind him and climbed aboard the helicopter.

CHAPER SIX
LAST CHANCES

LE ROYAL MERIDIEN NATIONAL
MOKHOVAYA STREET
MOSCOW
RUSSIA
16: 45 MSK

Sergei Ivanovich, otherwise known by his sobriquet "The Butcher", entered the Meridien National hotel just before five p.m., Moscow Standard Time. Still bruised from both the surprise attack and the failure of his last mission, Ivanovich knew the reasons behind his being summoned here were anything but good. When people failed Pavel Kirov they disappeared.

The elegant hotel was, as usual, bustling with activity. One of the finest establishments in Moscow, Ivanovich knew it was also a personal favourite of Kirov's.

Ivanovich stopped at the front desk and signalled the maître d'. In Russian, he said: "Good evening. I'm here to see Mr Kirov."

The middle-aged man eyed him suspiciously for a moment, then said, "Do you have a reservation?"

"Dmitry Fyodorov – he's expecting me," Ivanovich replied,

producing one of his many fake IDs.

The maître d' nodded. "Ah, Mr Fyodorov! Mr Kirov is waiting for you in his usual spot. Please go ahead."

Ivanovich thanked him and continued down the hall towards the Moskovsky Restaurant. He could hear the piano playing from fifty yards away. As he reached the entrance, he couldn't fail to notice the huge sign in Russian above the doors, which read: RESTAURANT OF THE YEAR, 2002.

He found Kirov at his usual table, reserved for the Russian three hundred and sixty-five days of the year. It boasted the best view of the Kremlin through exorbitant panoramic windows. Beside Kirov, his personal bodyguard, Ivor, kept a firm grip on his nine-millimetre Makarov pistol as he eyed Ivanovich with a poker face. The behemoth had a notorious reputation for being over-protective, and even though the restaurant had a strict policy of no weapons, Kirov and his protective detail were the exception to the rule.

Ivanovich knew it had to do with money. Kirov's bank balance far exceeded even the owner's, and he'd been known to make generous donations on a regular basis. It accrued him the best table, the penthouse suite on the third floor, and the right to bear arms. The hotel manager considered the latter dangerous and unjust, but there had never been an incident that required it to be called upon, so the owner continued to allow it.

Ivor stood and gestured for Ivanovich to sit, drawing attention to his gun just in case Ivanovich was tempted to try something. Ivanovich had never been scared of anyone, least of all Kirov's oversized bulletproof vest. As a former KGB and Spetsnaz agent, he'd faced some of the scariest criminals in the world. A fearsome shot with both rifle and pistol, he'd established a reputation for killing, instead of capturing, the people he chased. This had earned him the nickname "The Butcher" – or so he led people to believe.

It had also earned him the attention of Pavel Kirov. Kirov knew, after thorough vetting, Ivanovich would submit to the allure of the dark side. In the end, he'd found the money too hard to resist, especially when people like Kirov paid in excess of one hundred thousand dollars per successful mission, or the equivalent of over three million Russian roubles. It was the kind of money Ivanovich had never seen before. He knew he would never accumulate anything close to it if he stayed in law enforcement, so he joined forces with Kirov, earning enough to retire and live a comfortable life. Now, he could only think of the failed mission, and how much he stood to lose if Kirov decided he no longer needed him.

He had thought about skipping the meeting, retrieving his money, and disappearing before Kirov could inflict a similar outcome on him. But Ivanovich knew Kirov had a list of contacts well beyond anything he had amassed during his time with the KGB and Spetsnaz. If he wanted to find him, there would be no place on earth Ivanovich would feel safe in. Besides, he knew Kirov wouldn't dare kill him in such a public place as this.

He took his seat and downed the glass of wine offered, remarking at how bitter it tasted. Kirov had a penchant for fine wines, but this was obviously not one of Meridien's better ones.

Kirov wasted no time getting down to business. "So, Dmitriev," he began, calling him by his alias. Though he knew his real name, he only used it in private discussions. "What happened in Saint Petersburg?"

Ivanovich cleared his throat. "We underestimated the target. I take responsibility for that. I read his dossier, but I didn't expect him to shoulder-block me like that. Son of a bitch must have been a wrestler in another life." He laughed.

Kirov didn't see the funny side of it. "We needed the target silenced, Dmitriev! He knows of our plans. If he reports back to the *Amerikanos*, we will not be able to conduct our operation as planned."

Ivanovich's smile faded. "So what would you like me to do? I can track him down if necessary." He silently cursed his stupidity. He knew the joke was a stupid idea.

"We have to assume he has reported back to his superiors. Move the operation up. Gather the team and get ready to leave for the States."

"I don't know they're ready for that yet. We had originally planned on another month's training before initiating the mission."

Kirov glared, causing Ivor to shift in his chair as if expecting his boss to lash out. Instead, he calmly said, "Dmitriev, the original plan is finished. The element of surprise was the only thing that gave this mission half a chance of success. Without it, we might as well hand ourselves over to the FBI. So, we move to Plan B. Assemble the team, get them on a plane to America, and wait at the safe-house for instruction. I will call you when the time is right. Go."

Ivanovich knew what was coming next. He'd said similar if not identical lines to dozens of CIs over the years.

"And Dmitriev?"

"Yeah?" Ivanovich replied, wondering in what way Kirov would word it.

"If you screw this up, the next time we meet will be at your funeral."

CHAPTER SEVEN
PRODIGAL

ATARIC
09:04 EST

Peter Hunt had never been in a helicopter before, and as the Bell 402 landed on the helipad of ATARIC, he never wanted to be in one again.

He stepped out onto the rooftop, feeling dizzy, nauseous, and disorientated. The world spun three-sixty constantly, making him want to vomit, but after getting his feet on solid ground and taking a few minutes to recompose himself, the vertigo-like feelings began to dissipate and the butterflies in his stomach lessened enough for him to straighten up and see Harry Johnson standing by the entrance to the stairs.

He smoothed out his suit, brushed back a few loose strands of shoulder-length hair, picked up his workbag, and joined Johnson. No handshakes or words were exchanged, and it remained that way during the elevator trip to the first floor.

Hunt noticed the buttons still had B-1 and B-2 as a selectable option, but he knew to use them required a key which, to his knowledge, only Haskens and Fielding possessed. What those two levels contained was as big a mystery as why he'd been chosen for this job. The top five floors were accessible to anyone.

Even the senior staffroom had been known to be invaded by curious workers, and never once had they been reprimanded, but when he questioned Johnson about the basement levels, he was brought to Fielding's office and told to do his work and mind his own business. Three weeks later, they laid him off.

Hunt didn't mind the silence; it gave him time to think about his first move – something he'd been unable to do over the whirr of rotors.

Installing the new operating system on time would be tough work. Probably ten- to twelve-hour days of staring at a screen, backing up files, wiping the system, installing the new one, restoring the backed-up files, and fixing any ensuing bugs or problems. In an ideal world, everyone ought to have been able to do it themselves, but he knew the majority of ATARIC's workforce knew as much about installing operating systems as he did about weapons-grade plutonium. With a team of ten or twelve competent people, working on twenty-four-hour shift, he felt confident he could make the deadline.

The only problem was finding those people.

The first obvious candidate was Jack Reid. Relationship issues aside, Hunt knew Reid better than anyone else on the planet. He'd first met him at the age of five, struck up an immediate friendship – which continued throughout high school and college – and worked with him for eight years before everything went to hell. In terms of ability, there were few better behind a keyboard than Reid. Without him, Hunt knew meeting the deadline would be impossible.

Other than him, though, no one else came to mind as potential candidates. There were a few people who could install operating systems, but none at the speed which Hunt or Reid could. That left outside contractors, but ATARIC had always been strict on outsourcing work to non-affiliated employees. Hunt decided that had to be the reason why they'd chosen him for this job.

When the elevator reached the first floor, Hunt pressed the emergency stop button. He then turned to Johnson and said, "If you want this job done on time, I need to be able to select my own team."

Johnson shot him a puzzled look. "We already had this conversation, Hunt. I agreed you would be given full control over the team you picked." Johnson reached out to open the doors, but Hunt gripped his wrist like a vice.

"You're not understanding me. I know ATARIC has a strict policy of never bringing in outside contractors to do jobs, but there's gonna have to be an exception made today. The people in this office know how to do their own jobs. They don't know how to install operating systems, and those that do can't do it in the timeframe you've given me. I need to bring in about five or six guys to help out. Along with me and Jack, that should be plenty to get this done on time."

Johnson's features remained poker-faced, even though pain was shooting through his wrist. "I don't know if Haskens or Fielding will go for that. I'll run it by them, though."

Hunt let go of his wrist. "Tell them if they want this job done on time, they'll go for it." He hit the button to open the doors, and stepped out into the main hall of ATARIC.

Nothing much had changed since he'd last been here. In the four corners, all four offices were blinded, just like they had been every day for the past eight years. This was one of many secretive things that had bothered him. He'd begun to feel as though ATARIC was much more than a computer firm, but hadn't had any time to test that theory out. Maybe now would be his chance.

He began walking towards his old desk, thinking Reid still operated from the one next to it.

"Hunt, this way," Johnson announced, gesturing to one of the suspended offices.

"Why? Jack's desk is over here."

"Jack's been promoted to chief of staff. He works from my old office now."

Hunt felt a pang of jealousy but didn't let it show. Instead, he asked, "When did this happen?"

"About six months ago. Come on – let's go see your old pal."

He didn't feel like seeing Reid right now but he followed Johnson up the steel stairs to Reid's new office anyway. Johnson knocked on the door, opened it when beckoned, then left to allow the former friends some quality time.

The mini-fridge in the corner caught Hunt's attention first. Not Reid's new brush-cut hairstyle. Not the two days' growth of beard on his face. Nor even the dismayed look in his eyes when he saw what had become of his former best friend. The fridge was the only thing he could think of, as his stomach craved the sweet taste of another bottle of scotch or whiskey.

"Hello, Peter," Reid finally said to break the silence.

He looked at him for a mere second, then back to the fridge, before saying, "What have you got in there?" He pointed to it, ignoring Reid's shake of the head.

"Nothing you'd want."

"You'd be surprised," Hunt replied, moving towards what he hoped contained alcohol, his raison d'être.

Reid caught him by the arm and spun him around. "Goddamn it, Peter! You're here to do a job, not go on a drinking session. Get your shit together, man!"

Hunt pushed him away but Reid, every bit as strong and powerful, kept his balance and used Hunt's momentum to pull him backwards onto the sofa. He stood, holding his hands up in a gesture that showed he didn't want any kind of altercation.

But Hunt would not be undone. He rose to his feet, pushed past Reid, and pulled open the fridge door. Inside, he found nothing but empty space, and slammed the door shut in frustration.

"I emptied it this morning, before you came. Sorry, Peter, but I'm not going to lose my job because you're too stubborn to kick your habit for two days. And now that that's done, how about we get to work?"

Hunt shook his head and dropped into the sofa. "Looks like somebody's doing all right for themselves." He couldn't keep the bitterness out of his voice, and didn't much care. "You know, I worked here for eight-and-a-half years, Jack. I was the best damned employee this place has ever seen. But what did it get me? Huh? A measly five-thousand-dollar severance pay and a ruined life."

Reid sat down on the sofa and sighed. "I'm sorry about that, but if it bothered you that much you shouldn't have come back. Not even for two days."

Hunt glared at him. "I need the money. And I needed to get out of the goddamn house."

Reid nodded. "Okay. But if you lie here, drinking and feeling sorry for yourself, it's not going to be much different than being at home, is it?"

Hunt wanted to be mad at him, but he couldn't. No matter how much he hated those who had destroyed his life, the truth was that he hated himself more. He could have tried to find a job with another computer firm, but he'd chosen instead to wallow in self-pity and blame everything on his wife and best friend. Maybe if he could get his life back together, he could finally put all this madness behind him, see his wife and son again, and restore some semblance of normality to his otherwise miserable existence.

Resigned to the fact that he had no choice, he rose from the sofa and said, "Okay, Jack. Let's get to work."

Reid sighed in relief. "Great. Where do you want to start?"

"Well, we need more than just us, that's for damned sure. The last time I was here, there were about two other people besides me and you who had enough knowledge to install operating systems – Brad Jones and Tania Anderson. If they're still here, we'll need them."

"Unfortunately they were laid off. But we're going to need more than four anyway."

"That's the problem. I've already spoken with Johnson about it. If Haskens and Fielding agree, I'm going to bring in a few outside contractors."

"Okay. Who've you got in mind?"

He smiled. "Jake Collins, among others."

Reid nodded emphatically and smiled. "I'll go tell Haskens and Fielding I agree with this plan one hundred per cent."

CHAPTER EIGHT
LOOSE ENDS

```
FBI NEW YORK FIELD OFFICE
26 FEDERAL PLAZA
MANHATTAN
NEW YORK CITY
09: 49 EST
```

On the twenty-third floor of the Jacob K. Javits Federal Office building, Deputy Director William Forrester sat in his office drinking his first coffee of the day.

"Red", as he was known to everyone because of his receding mane of red hair, spent little time in Washington D.C. In fact, he'd been to the J. Edgar Hoover Building three times in the last four months. It wasn't that he didn't like the headquarters of the FBI; he had his own office there, with a mini-fridge, plush seats, and other amenities only accorded to a top-level FBI agent. Instead, the problem was that with meetings almost every day, Forrester never found time to keep up with his work.

As a former NYPD officer who'd spent years working his way into the Bureau, Forrester had a reputation of being a doer not a thinker. He rarely, if ever, bothered with office politics or meetings, unlike his oldest friend, the director of the FBI, Jonathan Baker. If it hadn't been for Baker he would have never made it further than special agent in charge (SAC), and would have been content with that. But Baker had recommended him first for the assistant director in charge of this office and then, a year later, for deputy director. In doing so he'd condemned Forrester to a life of meetings, cross-country flights, and complete knowledge of every aspect of the FBI.

After a month of boredom in Washington, Forrester decided to move back to New York, where he now ran the FBI's second-largest office. Once a month (enough, in his mind) he travelled to D.C. to keep himself appraised of goings-on.

Most FBI field offices were run by a SAC. The bigger ones in New York City and Los Angeles were instead run by an assistant director in charge (ADIC). However, there had never been a case where one of the two leading figures in the Bureau had run a field office. For all that, he didn't mind. An old head on even older shoulders, Forrester needed to be a part of the action; to feel like he was making a difference in the world, instead of sitting around a table chatting about how to make that difference.

He didn't get out into the field as much as a fresh recruit, but he still found time to mix it up with the newbies. He knew a lot of people in the office both respected and would take a bullet for him if necessary. To maintain that kind of respect, he felt he needed to do something other than sit behind a desk. Ironically, though, at this very moment he was doing just that.

He was already resigned to the fact that paperwork would be his number-one priority today...until he received a phone call from his oldest friend.

Forrester picked up the secure phone on his desk.

"Morning, Red. Let me guess: You're on your third cup?" Baker laughed.

Forrester returned it. There had always been a friendly competition between the two to determine who could drink the most cups of coffee in a single day. At the moment, Baker held the record with fifteen.

"First, actually, but don't tell me you called me just to brag about breaking the record again?"

Baker's voice became more serious. "Unfortunately not. I've got a bit of a situation here I need dealt with. I could sign it off to a million and one S-A-Cs but I don't trust any of them with this job. I need your help, Red."

Forrester leaned forward in his chair. "What do you need?"

"You remember the sting I had going?"

He nodded, even though Baker couldn't see. "The Kirov one? Yeah, what about it?"

Baker cleared his throat, almost as though people were standing behind him and he couldn't talk. He finally said, "Our inside man was discovered sometime yesterday. We didn't hear from him again until just an hour ago. He's back in the States and has information he claims will bag us Kirov for good. But he's a target now and won't come in on his own. He's landing at LaGuardia in approximately thirty minutes. I'm uploading his dossier to your PDA now.

"Red," he continued, "we need this guy alive. Take a few of your best men, get to LaGuardia, and scout the area for threats. When you have him secured and ready for transport, don't take him back to Federal Plaza. There'll be a Gulfstream waiting for you in hangar fourteen."

Forrester frowned and shook his head. "Gulfstream?"

"It'll take you to Dulles. There'll be a car waiting there to take you to the Hoover building."

"If you wanted me to come in for a meeting, Jon, you didn't have to go to all this trouble," Forrester pointed out with a laugh.

"All kidding aside, Red; this is serious. I need you at LaGuardia on the double. How long will it take you?"

"If I go with sirens, fifteen or twenty minutes. I'll need five or ten to round up a few men, though."

"Take whoever you need, but *don't* tell them what's happening. As far as they're concerned, the man is a potential witness in a high-profile murder case."

"I understand. What's his name?"

"Troy Davies. He'll be coming in on American Airlines flight seven-oh-seven. Any other details you need, I'll upload to your PDA. Call me the second you have him or if anything goes wrong."

"You got it, Jon."

"Thanks, Red. We'll go to the chophouse when you get to Washington – on me."

Forrester knew he was talking about the steak and beer house a couple of blocks from the FBI headquarters. "I'll hold you to that. I'll call you when I have him."

Forrester hung up and smiled. It looked like paperwork *wasn't* going to be the priority after all.

CHAPTER NINE
FAULTS

ATARIC
10: 15 EST

Standing alone in the bathroom of ATARIC, Hunt splashed his face with cold water.

The morning hadn't ended yet and already he craved the taste of alcohol. Having drunk every day for the past nine months, he couldn't do without it, especially considering today's circumstances. Being back in the place that had been the cause of so much pain was hard enough, never mind having to work with people for whom he had an intense dislike.

The obsession with alcohol, though, hadn't started nine months ago. Hunt had always been a drinker.

The only child of Thomas and Katharine Hunt, two of the finest surgeons ever to grace Johns Hopkins, his life was planned almost from birth. He was to be a surgeon, just like his father, mother, and grandfather. From the age of six, medical books such as *Gray's Anatomy* were forced on him.

Having been given a pocket-videogame by his grandfather for his eighth birthday, Hunt grew more and more interested not in the game itself but in the workings of it. Within a few days, he'd disassembled it for study. Soon after, he focused all of his attention on learning everything he could about computers. It wasn't until a few years later, when he discovered his school's library, that he finally found the literature he so desperately wanted to read. Within weeks his parents found dozens of computer books hidden under young Hunt's bed. Because of the shock of seeing him interested in something other than medicine, and because he'd stolen them, they promptly removed him from the school and set about the task of home-schooling.

Due to the time restraints of their jobs, they hired a former medical professor to teach Hunt. That he didn't learn much about other school subjects was of no consequence to them. As long as he learned to read, write, and count past a hundred, they were happy to let the professor spend eight hours a day teaching medicine and just one or two on the rest.

For the first year, Hunt enjoyed the old woman's lessons and began to grow fond of her company. Having been denied a motherly figure for most of his life, it was obvious to everyone but his parents she was becoming a surrogate mother to him. But extremely short-tempered and mercurial, Rosa Reilly began to take her commitments too seriously. When Hunt grew increasingly frustrated with his cooped-up lifestyle, often refusing to listen to her lessons, Reilly became infuriated with his lack of respect. Taking matters into her own hands, she disciplined him. At first she only raised her voice. That worked for a while but Hunt quickly fell back into the old routine.

Her anger grew to violence. It started with light slaps across the hand, but as the months passed her temper became unpredictable and uncontrollable. Reilly beat him. Often with her hands, sometimes a belt, but never anywhere where his negligent parents might see. Hunt – too scared to talk to his parents, let alone tell them something of that magnitude – did everything he could to placate her fiery temper.

It was only through sheer luck that his parents finally found out. On that fateful morning, angered and frustrated by the loss of a patient in surgery, Katharine Hunt came home early for the first time in her career. Entering her room, she found Reilly on top of her semi-naked son, beating his behind with a leather belt. She knew his stifled moans were indicative of someone who'd been through it before and had learned crying often prolonged or worsened the punishment.

Without thinking, Katharine grabbed her son's abuser by the hair, dragged her screaming body out to the landing, and fired her head-first into the banister. The wood, warped with age and disrepair, snapped under the weight of Reilly, and the 72 year-old plummeted three storeys to her death.

Within a few hours Thomas had Katharine and his son on his private jet, heading for the family condo in Spain, while he concocted a plan to get rid of Reilly's body. Using his medical mind and bank balance of over ten million dollars, he made her death look like a suicide. For a quarter of a million, he hired someone to plant an obscene amount of anti-depressants and other drugs in Reilly's home. The same man injected her body with diazepam and moved it there to stage the suicide. Thomas then hired a team of renovators to gut out and rebuild the interior of the mansion. With everything in place, he left for Spain. When the police found Reilly's body, he and his family were in their condo, seemingly because of the on-going renovations to their mansion. The police never questioned it.

Within a few months of returning, though, it was clear that Katharine had problems. Haunted by the death of Reilly, and beginning to lose her ability to function not only in the hospital but in everyday life as well, she became introverted. Rather than risk the shame of being fired, she resigned as head surgeon, citing an inoperable tremor as the reason why.

Hunt, on the other hand, had been allowed to go back to school, where he began to thrive in all his classes. But the pressure from his parents never ceased. As his mother's condition worsened, and as she ironically started taking anti-depressants, her hostility grew evermore. Hunt would often come home and have to study medical literature for entire evenings. Though she never once raised her hand, Katharine adamantly refused to let her son get distracted by insignificant things like television, videogames, or even computers.

Hunt wanted out.

By his fifteenth birthday he'd already attempted to commit suicide. His mother and father were both highly trained surgeons, his attempt to slit his throat had only succeeded in leaving him with a nasty scar.

Pulled from school once more and forced into therapy sessions with a psychiatrist, his depression grew by the day.

Until the shrink one day let slip that a child of or over the age of eighteen could get emancipation from their parents. Hunt pretended he hadn't understood. A few weeks later, the shrink declared his suicidal tendencies were no more. Hunt had seen a way out. All he had to do was bide his time and wait until he turned eighteen.

A few weeks after his eighteenth birthday, he filed a petition for emancipation. After seeing the condition of his mother and the lack of presence of his father, the judge ruled in his favour. He was finally free to live his life however he chose.

It wasn't easy. Thomas had set up a trust fund for when his son turned eighteen – somewhere in the region of three quarters of a million dollars – but the emancipation infuriated him and he cut Hunt off. Desperate to get into college, Hunt first tried to get a loan, but no bank in its right mind would give money to an 18 year-old with no home and very little income. So he turned to Reid, who he'd befriended during elementary school at the age of five. Reid, on a full scholarship to New York University, didn't need the money saved for his college fees but his father didn't feel right not giving it to him. When Hunt found out, he begged him to lend him enough to enrol at NYU.

The enrolment cost less than expected and Hunt, left with over ten thousand dollars of Reid's money, took the advice of his uncle and invested the rest in stock. Within two years he'd quadrupled it and paid Reid back. Thirty of the remaining thirty-two thousand went towards the down-payment for a house in Washingtonville – a four-bedroom dormer bungalow with a price-tag of two hundred thousand. The rest he reinvested in stock, gaining considerable equity over the next few years.

Proud to be fending for himself, and getting top grades in all of his college classes, life appeared to be on the up. In his second year of college, he met Melissa Thompson, a fiery but intelligent blonde studying to become a doctor. They hit it off immediately and were soon inseparable. But the relationship came with a steep price; but having led a sheltered life since the age of four, Hunt's newfound experience of the partying lifestyle drove him to addiction. Late-night weekends became late-night weekdays. He arrived to classes drunk, tired, and tardy. Inevitably, his grades began to slip. A plusses and A's gave way to B's and C's.

The teachers grew tired and suspended him. Sometime later, Thompson broke up with him, claiming he was monopolising her time and was the cause of her academic slump.

Hunt purged his anger and bitterness away in the bottle, falling deeper into depression as a result. Ravaged with guilt over his emancipation, and angered by his father's choice to cut him off, his suicidal tendencies began to resurface. His addiction for partying became simply an addiction to alcohol. He was spiralling out of control but no one could see it.

His stock investments, though, were soaring, adding another one hundred and fifty thousand to his burgeoning bank balance. He had the acuity of a natural marketer. His instincts were sharp, even when dulled by alcohol. In a rare sober moment, he realised he would spend the money foolishly if he wasn't careful, and so, in one of his more proud moments, he'd finished the payment on his home.

But although he'd done himself proud in the absence of his parents, his depression grew evermore. Most nights he'd stare at a picture of Melissa, a bottle of whiskey in his right hand, a knife in his left. The hesitation scars on his wrists were bitter reminders of one more failure in his life.

He medicated with alcohol, antidepressants, hallucinogens; anything else he could think of to dull the pain. He even went to therapy. There, he met Karen Carter. After a few weeks getting to know her, he learned she was studying to become a lawyer. When her father had passed away unexpectedly, the shock hit her hard, culminating in a minor nervous breakdown.

After a few more weeks Hunt found the courage to ask her out. He hadn't expected her to say yes, nor for the relationship to last longer than a couple of dates. It only did because Karen was unlike any woman he had ever met. She inspired him in ways no person ever had or could. Her beauty and intelligence mesmerised him. She challenged (almost browbeat) him to quit drinking, but was smart enough to do so without risking any side-effects. She *did* browbeat him into returning to university and, using all her acquired knowledge of law, coerced the provost of NYU to reinstate Hunt. Not entirely convinced he could make up for lost time, the provost made it a temporary return which could be waived off if his problems resurfaced.

They didn't.

Karen instilled in him a new lease of life. The depression which had ruled him for so long began to dissipate, bit by bit, week by week. Within a month, he had made up all the assignments he'd missed, spurred on by the realisation that someone finally was rooting for him, cared for him, and wanted to do everything in their power to help him. That triggered a confidence boost like no other. With his depression suppressed, and drinking down to manageable levels, his grades soared back into the top percentile of NYU again.

Meanwhile, his stock investments were still generating considerable equity – something that did not escape the attention of James Fielding. ATARIC had only begun to emerge as a high-quality computer firm, but Fielding had already convinced Jack Reid (who'd graduated *magna cum laude* a year earlier) and half a dozen other promising computer programmers, including two he'd appropriated from Microsoft, to join his fledging business. Reid's recommendation had no bearing on Fielding's decision; he had already made up his mind and, on the day of Hunt's graduation, offered him a job and a starting salary of thirty thousand. It hurt Hunt that his parents weren't there to see him graduate or see how far he'd come on his own, but he gladly accepted Fielding's offer and began working for him a week later.

From the start, he showcased exceptional talent. Within a few months he knew every facet of ATARIC's system. Problems were dealt with in a speedy and efficient manner, and Hunt teamed up with Reid to maximum effect. Both were doing a multitude of tasks which would have kept five or six normal computer programmers busy. Viruses were snuffed out before anyone else had even realised they were in the system. Disk drives were defragmented for space, systems cleaned for more speed, programs updated for reliability and ease of use, and programs created both for use and sale.

This work ethic did not go unnoticed. Within six months, they were made co-administrators. Everything computer-related went through them, from problems logging in, to new programs needing installed. They ran the floor, organising work, dealing with problems, and choosing new systems to be installed.

That changed when Fielding decided he needed a chief of staff. Both had good people-skills, handled their responsibilities with ease, and were dedicated to putting ATARIC on the map. Either one of them seemed destined to get the position, but Fielding surprised everyone by bringing in Harold Johnson, former CEO of a small-time computer firm who'd gone bankrupt a few weeks earlier. Apparently, Fielding had been keeping tabs on Johnson, and his reason why Hunt and Reid had been overlooked was that Johnson had more experience and could better handle the rigours of managing ATARIC's growing staff. Reid digested the news better than Hunt who, over the course of the following weeks, began to question Fielding's honesty. To further cement his doubts, he discovered Johnson was not as skilled at management as Fielding seemed to think. In fact, the man was one step shy of an idiot. He knew nothing about computers and even less about tact.

During the following months they had several altercations, the most serious of which led to Johnson publicly firing Hunt – a decision rescinded by Fielding after serious thought. It seemed Fielding had high expectations of Hunt, and being fired was not among them. This intervention did little to quell the fiery relationship, and before long they were back at each other's throat. Any time Johnson made a decision on the floor, Hunt would rescind the order if he thought it inane – the case in most situations. Johnson perceived this as utter insubordination, and since he couldn't fire him, he made it his business to make every minute of his day as miserable as possible. Before long, he'd bogged him down with so much work Hunt hadn't time to leave his office. This freed up Johnson to run the floor any way he liked, and guaranteed Hunt had to work overtime to ensure he kept his job.

But even twelve-hour days were doing little to rid the growing piles of work-orders on his desk, and his patience was reaching non-existence. Stressed out and tired, he contemplated ending his six-month sobriety, but the day he'd quit drinking entirely had also been the day he'd married Karen. He knew breaking that oath would also break his marriage. So, like every other hardship before it, he bottled this one up too. He continued working long hours – sometimes even fourteen- and fifteen-hour-days – even though the strain on both his health and marriage drove him again to the point of bitterness.

He knew that as long as Johnson remained chief of staff, his job would never get easier. He needed some kind of proof to give to Fielding which would demonstrate how little Johnson knew about computers. When he learned Johnson had been vociferously advocating this new firewall as the best ever, he saw the opportunity to return the misery Johnson had reaped on him. He waited until Johnson gave the order to install it on all ATARIC's systems, and then, using an un-networked computer, he hacked into and breached the firewall in less than an hour, showing them just how much their "chief of staff" knew about the world of computers.

For Hunt, this proved to be the beginning of the end. The next day, during an impromptu meeting, Johnson laid his cards on the table: Either Hunt went or he went. After serious deliberation, and a string of other "problematic" questions and actions on Hunt's behalf, Fielding and Haskens made their decision. In respect of his contributions to ATARIC, they refrained from firing him and offered him redundancy instead. Thinking the amount would be a great deal more than it turned out to be, Hunt accepted. A week later, Fielding transferred five thousand dollars to his bank account, along with sending a present to his home. Hunt, strong though he was, could not match the three goons who showed up on his doorstep. Again, he was given two choices: File for unfair dismissal and risk his family's life, or forget about ATARIC and continue his life without the constant fear of looking over his shoulder. He chose the latter. A few weeks after that, he began drinking again. A month later, Karen took her son and moved back in with her mother.

For the past six or seven months he'd lived life one monotonous day after the other, accompanied only by the sweet taste of liquor and the pathetic offerings of daytime television. On those rare occasions that he'd ventured outside, he realised inebriation and daytime activities did not go well together. Certainly hunting did not. A hobby ever since Reid had introduced it to him on the day of Hunt's eighteen birthday, it almost completed the job his suicidal persona had failed to for so long. He would normally never climb a fence with a loaded gun; feeling the pellets whizz inches over his head made him realise he couldn't continue hunting while inebriated. True to character, he decided to continue drinking.

From thereon, he remained indoors for the duration, ordering his food and drink via the Internet. The days became increasingly tedious, and his sleeping pattern began to resemble a vampire's. During the night he would watch re-runs of crappy 90s' action flicks, followed by free-views from the exotic channels. He would then sleep the worst of the day off and wake up around four in the afternoon – just in time for the latest batch of pin-restricted action flicks.

Twice he'd had the shotgun in his mouth, only for the doorbell to ring on both occasions. The first was, ironically, an alcohol delivery. The second was Karen, coming to collect the remainder of her things. She hadn't seen the shotgun, and had been too preoccupied with her own grief to notice how far gone Hunt was. This visit, however, refocused his anger on her and pushed his suicidal tendencies to the back of his mind, if only for a few weeks.

The following weeks leading up to today's phone call weren't much more than a blur. He remembered being drunk throughout, but his only vivid memory was watching a show on *Discovery* about the presence of multiple underground bases throughout the United States.

And now here he stood, in the bathroom of ATARIC, wondering just how long it would be before they screwed him again. As the thought left his mind, he looked down to his feet, where his workbag lay on the floor.

Just try me. I haven't got any family to worry about this time.

CHAPTER TEN
COPS AND SPOOKS

```
CENTRAL TERMINAL BUILDING
LaGUARDIA AIRPORT
QUEENS
NEW YORK CITY
10:25 EST
```

Airports – every law enforcement officer's nightmare. There were too many people, places, and obstacles for any amount of manpower or surveillance equipment to find and track a person. This made them every covert espionage operator's dream.

Forrester knew the person getting off flight 707 would be well-versed in the art of elusion; he'd been picked by Baker for a reason, which meant he'd blend into the crowd without difficulty. He'd be the sort of person you'd look at once and forget. Forrester knew that even though he had Davies' picture, the man would still prove exigent to catch.

Spies and inside-men were by nature paranoid, and not without reason. Forrester knew just how much those people had to lose if their true identities were discovered. Davies would have multiple contingency plans to fall back on if his employers ever decided to deny his existence. At least, that's how Forrester would have done it. He knew Davies would disappear at the first sign of trouble, taking the information with him. So he instructed his four underlings to keep their weapons concealed, and refrain from any hostile actions that would spook their spook.

Flight 707 landed at ten-thirty sharp. The four agents were posted at each entrance, with Davies' picture burned into their brains. In their hands a small phone with built-in PDA provided a backup picture. To appear less conspicuous Forrester had instructed them to dress in casual clothing. The only giveaway was the flesh-coloured earpieces that coiled from their ears, down the inside of their shirts, to the portable receiver/transmitter in their pockets. If Forrester was right, Davies would be looking for someone who stood out, not four men in jeans and tee-shirts talking on their phones like businessmen. That was the plan, at least.

The picture on Forrester's PDA, taken two years earlier, showed a middle-aged man in good physical condition, with a close-cropped head of blonde hair and a pair of rimmed glasses on a fleshy face. But no one matching that description had deplaned.

From his position on a bench inside Concourse A, Forrester glanced up to his four agents, who all shook their heads. "Stay on it," he whispered into the hidden microphone in his breast pocket. A woman a few seats over looked at him with mild amusement before turning her attention back to her trashy magazine. So many people never looked at what was right in front of them, and the woman had passed him off as a weirdo without ever thinking otherwise.

Davies would be different, though. He would surely be able to spot fellow law enforcers a mile away. He'd be careful, methodical, and meticulous. He wouldn't leave the plane last, for fear of drawing unwanted attention. He wouldn't walk alone, and he wouldn't wear anything flashy that might make him stand out from the crowd. Everything about his movement, clothing, and demeanour would scream "mundane". Essentially, he would be a ghost.

The FBI, however, trained its people to both be ghosts and spot them. It was no surprise, then, that Forrester noticed him first, coming off the plane in between two men who were anything but discreet. To his credit, he blended in well, and the extra thirty or so pounds of weight made him look like an ordinary civilian, enough to fool the casual eye, but not Red Forrester.

"Target spotted. Beside the two men in suits. Blue jeans, white top. Five-ten, two-hundred-plus pounds, black carry-on bag. Move in," Forrester ordered as he rose from the seat and converged on the target's location. He could see all four agents moving simultaneously toward Davies.

In an instant he realised his mistake. It wasn't sending four men to Davies' location, which would have spooked even the coolest spy. Nor was it his failure to put in place a contingency plan if things became FUBAR. No, because things were already fucked up beyond all recognition. The mistake, innocuous though it may have been, was also simple.

As the four agents converged on Davies, their casual clothing had the opposite effect on him. Had it been a suit, Davies may have pegged them as law enforcement; but dressed in civvies, he now considered them a threat.

Like any good spy, Davies knew the art of getting a gun on and off planes. As the four agents closed in on him, he dropped to one knee, retrieved his pistol, and levelled it at the nearest agent, whose eyes opened wide in shock as he scrambled for his firearm.

A second later the sound of gunfire echoed through the concourse.

CHAPTER ELEVEN
BACKUPS

```
PAVEL KIROV0S MANSION
CHERNYAVESKY FOREST
PERM
RUSSIA
20: 40 MSK
```

For years the KGB had tried to plant surveillance equipment throughout Kirov's mansion, but he had it swept for bugs three times daily. Further, they'd planted some of their most experienced and trained espionage officers into the mansion's workforce, but Kirov, a meticulous man by nature, countered this by constantly vetting his employees. Those who were suspected of ill deeds were taken to the basement, tortured to find out where their commitments lay, and dealt with accordingly. Any bodies were then incinerated, leaving no proof of any immorality on Kirov's part.

The KGB knew Kirov to be a ruthless terrorist, murderer, and the biggest arms dealer in the Eastern world. His base of operations, however, was not his mansion, and all of his numerous car-manufacturing factories dotted throughout Russia were legitimate – at least at first glance. To get any closer would require more inside men, and the KGB had lost eight agents to such endeavours.

The ironic thing – which the KGB were unaware of – was that the Americans had successfully infiltrated Kirov's organisation and collected significant intelligence during the last sixteen months. Their inside man had also been compromised and Kirov, infuriated by the invasion of privacy, had an hour earlier executed two of his workforce as a demonstration to the remainder of his terrified staff, who were now being vetted again.

Kirov, a man obsessed with the allure of power, had been a Spetsnaz "Vympel" agent for ten of his forty-seven years. Hardened by some of the fiercest training known to any special forces team, he'd seen his share of fierce missions too: Chechnya, North Caucasus, and Afghanistan to name a few. It wasn't until a mission in Dubai, however, that he realised his life had been spent fighting for the wrong side. The "War on Terror" was not as prosperous as the War for Terror, as Kirov came to realise in a mansion in Dubai fourteen year ago.

Shahid Hassan, a sheikh and billionaire, had dedicated the majority of his life to financing terrorist operations. His biggest mistake, though, was supplying the Georgians with high-range weaponry to wage a war on the Armenians, one of Russia's few remaining allies. In doing so, the GRU (Russia's premier intelligence service) decided Hassan had become a liability and orchestrated a black operation to eliminate him. Kirov had been part of the Spetsnaz team tasked with infiltrating Hassan's mansion in Dubai and killing the sheikh, but intelligence had been limited. On arrival, Kirov and his team were caught flatfooted by Hassan's security team. Four Spetsnaz agents were cut down with automatic fire before they'd even set foot inside Hassan's gates. The remainder took cover behind anything they could find, trying in desperation to find a way to counter the enfilade raining down on them.

Trained to perfection in over eighteen different specialities, including infiltration of highly guarded buildings, Vympel's are Russia's finest soldiers. Each agent (like all Russian infantrymen) is given a small spade fifty centimetres long with a blade fifteen inches wide and eighteen inches long. All three edges are as sharp as a knife, and the entire spade is painted dull green so it doesn't reflect sunlight. On this occasion, Kirov used it to dig a trench in Hassan's garden. Within ten minutes he'd excavated enough to hide himself and his gun.

As the day broke and the last of his teammates succumbed to the unremitting hail of gunfire, Kirov finished camouflaging his trench, where he waited patiently until nightfall arrived. When it did, he took stock. All but two of his teammates were dead, although they wished they were. As he watched them die too, he realised he felt no pity for them. The Spetsnaz trains its agents to launch sudden attacks and strike without warning; not to take up defensive positions. But even a fool knows not to fight when outnumbered. Their deaths reflected their own naivety.

Kirov spent two more hours, until midnight, assessing the damage to Hassan's bodyguards, the layout of the house, the most efficient point of entry, and the likelihood of Hassan still being there. Taking everything into consideration, he made a decision to complete his mission.

Spetsnaz agents very seldom use night-vision or any other light-amplification goggles. They rely instead on their own vision, honed to perfection from years of training.

The human eye, properly trained, can see quite well at night. Kirov had learned that using night-vision not only hindered peripheral vision and left the risk of being blinded by a strong light source, it also lent a false sense of security to soldiers who were naïve enough to accept it. He also knew Hassan's bodyguards would not have had proper training since leaving their Special Forces duties behind. Such a high-paying job created a feeling of complacency and, since they had just killed almost half a dozen Spetsnaz agents, that complacency would grip them even more. They would not be expecting another attack, especially from only one man. At just after 0100 the last of the mansion's lights went out, and Kirov rose from his trench. Taking a few minutes to cover the excavation as best he could to avoid premature detection, he finally decided everything was in place. His earlier reconnaissance had revealed Hassan had lost three bodyguards in the fire fight, leaving only five. To a Spetsnaz agent armed with the element of surprise, five men would be child's play. Kirov took them out one by one, disposing of their bodies in his trench-cum-grave.

The inside of the six-thousand-square-metre mansion took his breath away. With three floors, over thirty rooms, a personal swimming pool, library, and entertainment centre, it was by far the biggest house Kirov had ever seen. Now he had to find his target amidst all of those obstacles.

With the bodyguards disposed of, Hassan's workforce posed the only remaining problem. Kirov knew someone of Hassan's incredible wealth would have 'round-the-clock' service to attend to all his needs. And while five-star gourmet chefs weren't likely to win a hand-to-hand battle with a Spetsnaz agent, Kirov also wanted to avoid killing any innocents – murder had not yet become all the rage for him.

He eventually found Hassan in the master bedroom, having just stepped out of a virtually noiseless shower. He was opening his safe as Kirov came into the room. Kirov gave a low whistle to acquire his attention, and then, in one smooth motion, pulled his spade from its keeper and flung it. It hissed through the air, caught Hassan between the eyes, and drove into his frontal lobe. Instant death.

In the open safe he'd found, to his amazement, over a million American dollars and almost four million Russian roubles. Since the mission had been a black op, the team were left to find their own way back to the exfiltration point a couple of klicks south of Hassan's mansion. Kirov knew he could take the money and disappear. By the time someone figured out what had happened, he'd be long gone, and months would be spent trying to find out who'd orchestrated the hit, where the money had gone, and who'd taken it.

That day had changed his life. With his newly acquired cash, he entered the world of terrorism. He started off small, smuggling weapons and fuel throughout his mother country until he'd learned the "rules". He'd discovered making money in the game of terrorism was not as easy as he'd come to expect. Terrorists were by nature dishonest people, and many of them refused to pay him for his services; it required a demonstration to convince other would-be customers he was not a man to be trifled with. Stillian Denisov's skull still hung in Kirov's basement, and Kirov always led his customers downstairs to convey a message to them; that even Denisov, as rich and powerful as he'd been, did not fall outside Kirov's ever-expanding reach.

After a few years, Kirov added another three million US

dollars to the money he'd stolen from Hassan, and used one million of it to purchase a decrepit mansion and the thousand acres of land surrounding it in the Chernyavesky forest. Another half a million was used to demolish the old one and build a new, 7000-square-metre one in its place.

Throughout the construction Kirov had been adamant no unnecessary felling of trees would be tolerated; not because he was a conservationist but because he knew they'd protect his private dealings from the prying eyes of the enemies' satellites and other surveillance equipment. Even though he was not foolish enough to conduct illegal operations out of his home, he also needed a place where he could meet customers and discuss business in private. The mansion provided the idyllic surroundings to put most if not all his customers at ease.

Kirov had gone to great lengths to ensure no one found a way to infiltrate his organisation, which was why he was in a particularly foul mood when his latest customer was brought to the study by Ivor. *That* inside-man had cost him two employees, six months of planning, and almost a million dollars. Kirov's Middle-Eastern associates had taken their business elsewhere when they learned he might not be able to acquire the weapons they desired. So Kirov had to contend with the second-highest bidder's offer, and all because Ivanovich couldn't kill one lousy person!

"Thank you, Ivor," Kirov said as his bodyguard showed his guest to a couch that looked comfortable and expensive enough for a shrink's office. "Have Boris whip up my usual dinner pronto." Kirov turned his gaze to the guest. "What would you like, Vlad?"

"As tempted as I am by that offer, I suspect you didn't call me here to ask my opinion of your chef's food," Vladimir Pushkin replied in his native tongue. Though he could speak fluent English, he chose not to.

"As you wish," Kirov replied, also changing to Russian. "Ivor, have my dinner brought up, and then you may retire for the evening."

"Yes, Mr Kirov," he replied, wondering what his boss was thinking. Kirov never attended a meeting without Ivor present, but he seemed adamant his bodyguard leave now, and Ivor never disobeyed his boss's orders.

"Let's get down to business, shall we?" Kirov asked as Ivor closed the door over. Pushkin nodded and he continued, "I need your services for a very important job, Vlad."

Pushkin's face remained impassive. The Russian had done jobs for Kirov in the past, and had been well-compensated for them. Unlike most of Kirov's other employees, he was not a former member of any Special Forces or law enforcement group. Instead, he offered his services to the highest bidder, which often happened to be Kirov. For that reason, he knew he was the last man Kirov would consider using. Whatever this "very important" job was, Pushkin had a feeling it had been outsourced to someone else first. Were that true, it meant the original person had failed to deliver, which normally meant the end where Kirov was concerned.

"Go ahead," he replied, keeping his voice calm and unenthused. He'd learned years earlier to trust no one, and the scar, stretching from below the lobe of his left ear to his larynx, was a daily reminder of that. That he'd survived was nothing short of a miracle. His partner snuck up from behind, grabbed him around the neck, tilted his head backward, and sliced the knife from ear to ear. The tilting of the head made the blood-loss venous and not arterial, inadvertently saving Pushkin's life. A man out jogging found the Russian a few minutes after the incident, and the paramedics were on-scene four minutes after that.

Today, a thick layer of black beard covered the tell-tale marks, though he could still feel the scar regardless.

"I am not a forgiving man, Vlad," Kirov continued. "I do not tolerate failure, and I have been failed." Kirov took this moment to open a sealed manila envelope which had been sitting on the exorbitant coffee table. The glass top reminded Pushkin of his late mother's finest collection of silverware, used only for special occasions. The table, he thought bitterly, probably cost more than her entire house, bequeathed to Pushkin even though he hadn't wanted it.

"Failed?" Pushkin tried to sound surprised, as though the act of failing someone like Kirov was akin to suicide. "By whom?"

"His name is Sergei Ivanovich," Kirov said, producing Ivanovich's KGB file. The picture showed a young man with long blond hair and a goatee, wearing a pair of sunglasses. He stood in front of a yellow-brick building – the headquarters of the KGB. "There's a more recent photograph here, too."

Pushkin studied the dossier for a minute, then said, "What exactly has this man failed at? From this file, I'd assume him to be highly trained and intelligent. Not the sort to make many mistakes."

Kirov regarded him with a cold stare. "You'd be wrong to assume anything, Vladimir. Your job is not to make assumptions or provide opinion. Your job is to do as I say." Kirov retrieved the file from Pushkin's hand and removed two stapled pages. Holding them up, he said, "This is a copy of an operation I've been planning for months – an operation now moved forward because of Ivanovich's screw-up. He's on his way to America as we speak. Within twenty-four hours I'll instruct him to begin the mission."

Pushkin frowned. "If he's still working for you, what do you need me for?" He was not the sort of man who took kindly to being used.

"I want you to oversee the operation, Vlad...to be ready to step in if Ivanovich fails...and then, regardless of the outcome, to kill him."

Pushkin's face remained a mien of impassivity. The thought of having to kill someone did not bother him. The thought of overseeing this operation, however, did. He pushed his doubts to one side. "What's the pay?"

"Before we come to that, there's one more thing." Kirov removed the last of the pages from the envelope and handed them to Pushkin. This time the picture was of a middle-aged, overweight man with a head of medium-length blond hair.

"His name is Troy Davies and, odd as it may seem, he's an American spy planted inside this very mansion. I sent Ivanovich to deal with him, but he slipped through the nets. According to my sources, he's already left the country. His destination appears to be New York City. He knows everything – the plan, the target, and even the names of the men who will orchestrate it. Without him eliminated, there is no way we can go ahead. That will be your first objective, Vlad. Find Davies and eliminate him before he can report back to his superiors. My private jet is waiting at Bolshoye Savino airport. In it, you'll find five hundred thousand US dollars, along with all the weapons and items you'll need. An additional five hundred thousand will be waiting for you when you complete the mission. Go to New York, Vlad, find Davies, and kill him."

"And if I can't find him?" Pushkin raised an eyebrow.

"Don't worry about that – I'll find him for you. All you have to do is pull the trigger."

Pushkin knew it would be foolish to say no, especially with this kind of money on offer. It took him five minutes to make a decision, though much of this was time-wasting and grandstanding intended to make it look like he wasn't interested. After he accepted, Kirov gave him the file and showed him to a limo which would take him to the airport.

Kirov didn't make the journey, for which Pushkin was grateful. It gave him time to think and study the file. Knowing that he would have to kill both men, he skipped their bios and concentrated on their photographs instead; it was his way of dehumanising his soon-to-be victims. Not knowing their history gave him no reason to be sympathetic, which meant he would have no qualms pulling the trigger. Their faces meant nothing to him, just like the faces of all those countless other people he'd killed over the years.

Vladimir Pushkin was not just a mercenary. He was also a remorseless killing-machine

CHAPTER TWELVE
PROBLEMS

LaGUARDIA
10: 45 EST

Nothing terrifies people more than the sound of gunfire. Even hardened professionals, long since used to the deafening roar, occasionally flinch at unexpected fire. The body's natural reaction is to flee – a stationary target proves much easier to hit.

On one knee, behind the bench he'd been sitting on minutes earlier, Forrester watched with a clenched jaw as thousands of people ran in different directions, screaming, shoving, and trampling those unfortunate enough to get in their way. Security personnel tried to restrain some, reassure others, and restore some kind of normality, but their actions proved futile.

Stupid son of a bitch!

Dressed in casual clothing, his gun tucked inside his blazer pocket, Forrester knew it was best not to draw unwanted attention or retaliatory fire by being foolish enough to run around with a weapon visible. Instead, he used his years of experience to coordinate the movements of his agents based on where he thought Davies would go next.

***

If not for the bulletproof vest hidden under his silk shirt, Special Agent Dan Hollingsworth would have been dead or dying. Instead, he was now spreading outward from the point of contact, trying to trace Davies' steps – not at all easy when thousands of people are running around you. His surging adrenaline kept him from realising how close he'd come to death.

With his gun out of sight, as per Forrester's orders, he moved through the Central Terminal Building, past Port Authority police officers who gave him a thorough once-over before turning their attention to more pertinent matters, and stopped at the escalators leading up to four different concourses. The CTB, six blocks long and four storeys high, comprised thirty-six aircraft gates and two additional three-storey wing annexes.

A born and bred New Yorker, Hollingsworth knew the layout as well as he knew how to fire his Glock. He didn't know, however, that Davies was a trained spook. This current atmosphere suited him a lot more than it did Hollingsworth.

"Hollingsworth, you there?" came Forrester's voice through the tactical earpiece.

Hollingsworth clicked the transmitter in his breast pocket, surprised it had survived two bullets, and said, "I'm here, Red. No visual yet. Heading upstairs now."

"No! Stay on the first floor and cover the exits. He's not stupid enough to remain in the building. In fact, he's probably already gone."

"How can you be sure?" Hollingsworth demanded.

"He knows this place is going to be closed down tighter than the Patriots' defence, and he can't afford to be held up here," Red fired back, unaware of the ramifications of what he'd just said.

Hollingsworth, trying to keep his voice calm but failing, roared, "The guy drew down on me with a Browning, Red! If I hadn't my Type Two on, I'd be dead right now. So whoever or whatever the hell he's involved in, he ain't no damned witness! So you kindly explain to me what the hell is goin' on and why he opened fire on a federal agent in an airport full of people!"

Before Forrester could answer, Hollingsworth noticed the police officer from earlier was now studying him with rapt attention. The young man's hand inched towards a gun on his holster, eyes never straying from Hollingsworth.

C'mon, kid. Let's play it real cool. No need to do anything silly.

"Just listen to me, dammit! Cover the exits, Dan, and I'll explain everything later," Forrester raged.

Hollingsworth never heard any of it. In his peripheral vision he watched the boy – no older than twenty-one – edge closer, hand on the matt-black finish of what looked to be a standard-issue Browning – the kind Hollingsworth had just been shot with. He was only a PAPD officer, but they still knew how to shoot a gun. Point and squeeze, and worry about the consequences afterward. Worse still, 9/11 had given everyone itchy trigger-fingers, nobody more so than the forces marshalling the airports. Any sudden movement and Hollingsworth knew he might once more feel the force of a nine-millimetre round.

"Did you copy, Hollingsworth?" Forrester's voice rose a semitone.

Not now, Red.

The boy moved closer, sidling towards what he perceived a threat, hand still on his weapon.

"Hollingsworth, did you copy that!"

Careful to avoid the movement being seen, he reached to the transmitter and clicked the button three times in rapid succession. The code would let Forrester know Hollingsworth had to observe radio silence. No specific reason, just a quick insurance for situations like this.

***

It took Forrester a moment to place the code. First he thought it meant "agent under duress", but then realised Hollingsworth's lack of response meant he was in a situation which prevented him from maintaining radio contact. He wondered if he'd found Davies, and then countered that by telling himself Hollingsworth would have found a way to inform them if he had.

One thing he did know – he couldn't stay where he was any longer.

***

"Sir, p-please put your hands w-w-where I can s-see them."

Hollingsworth noted the *voice* was shaky, *not* the hand

holding the pistol. He wondered if that meant anything, or if he would have preferred it the other way around. A tremble could lead to an accidental discharge. Lack of one could mean some kind of training – enough, evidently, to allow the kid to remain calm and hold his weapon steady, but not enough to keep the fear out of his voice; and fear made people react in unpredictable ways.

Hollingsworth turned around, the movement slow and deliberate, his hands outstretched. The kid – his nametag read "Jones" – held the Browning loosely in one hand, while the other reached up and wiped away the continuous beads of sweat forming on his brow. An amateur mistake, Hollingsworth decided. He could have easily stepped in and defused the situation before Jones could react, but a glance to the Browning told him the safety was off, which ruled out any sudden movements.

"Interlock your fingers and put t-them behind your head."

Both hands now gripped the pistol firmly. A sign of intent?

"Listen, I'm going to – "

"Just d-do what I said!" The hand wavered, the gun almost slipping from sweat-laden fingers, eyes and facial features imploring an unknown person to obey. "Please...j-just do as I ask."

Hollingsworth nodded, interlaced his fingers, and placed them behind his head. "Listen to me – "

"Please, just be quiet. D-don't move...I'm going to call t-this in. Don't move, understand?"

Hollingsworth nodded, watching Jones remove a walkie-talkie with his free hand, the gun still trained on him. He could see the kid's finger was not where it should have been – away from the trigger. Instead, it was caressing it. Standard-issue Brownings were pre-set to break between seven to eight pounds of pressure. Hollingsworth knew a jerk or spasm could cause the finger to lock around the trigger. He'd already been shot once today, but now there was a real possibility of it happening again.

CHAPTER THIRTEEN
SECRECY

UNDISCLOSED LOCATION
UNKNOWN TIME

The military HMMWV sped along a back road, the rhythmic hum of the tires on the asphalt lulling its passengers into a stupor. On both sides of the road, trees thirty or forty feet high whizzed by. A farmhouse, set against a backdrop of trees and grass as far as the eye could see, sat out on its own, a combine harvester in a nearby field.

In the back seat, sergeants Carlos and Gyle were trying to stay awake, the exertions of the past twelve hours making that close to impossible. Still dressed in the gear they'd been wearing in Adi Ghar, both had not been given a reason for their extraction, nor granted permission to shower and change.

"Soldier, what's your name and rank?" Carlos asked the young driver, whose gaze never left the road ahead. When he made no effort to reply, Carlos continued, "I'm Sergeant-Major Jack Carlos, U-S-M-C Force Recon."

The driver didn't acknowledge the statement, nor make any deference to Carlos' rank. His eyes remained fixed on the road at all times. Carlos, becoming irritated, said, "Listen, son, in the last fourteen hours I've ran fifteen miles; got shot at by a dozen

Taleban; been in a cave wired to explode with dynamite; got pulled out of Afghanistan without any formal reason; sat in a sore-ass C-one-forty-one for twelve hours; was shepherded into a Sikorsky without being allowed to shower or change, and I'm now sitting in a car going to the middle of nowhere. So, I ask you again, name and rank?"

The driver shifted his gaze to the mirror, a smile forming in the corner of his lips. "Captain Jeremy Baxter, United States Marine Corps."

"*Captain?*" Carlos shook his head, his eyes rising to the mirror to study the young man again. He couldn't have been much older than thirty, fresh-faced, with the appearance of someone who hadn't yet seen a tour. Carlos had him pegged for a private; at the very most, a corporal. He could not believe him to be a commissioned officer. He was too young, *and* driving around a man of lower rank than him – something which did not happen in military service.

"I've been 'round the track a coupla times, *Captain*. I'm not dumb enough to think me and Julio here being whipped out of Afghanistan is some kind of prank, but I'm also not dumb enough to believe you're *any* kind of captain. If you are, you outrank both of us. So explain to me why *you're* driving."

"I'm following orders, Sergeant-Major. When the call came, I was every bit as surprised as you are now."

That statement piqued Gyle's interest. He sat forward and said, "What call?"

Baxter's demeanour changed instantly, averting his eyes from the mirror. When he spoke, his voice was guarded, the words chosen with care. "Nothing you need to know about."

Gyle's interest turned to anger. "Where are you taking us?"

"Nowhere."

"Goddamn it, quit being cryptic! We have a right to know where we're being taken."

Gyle threw his hands up in the air and collapsed back into the seat, a mixture of a yawn and an exasperated sigh escaping from his lips.

"You really *are* a captain, then?" asked Carlos.

"Damn proud of it, too. Youngest in over thirty years," Baxter replied, his smile widening.

"Well I'll be damned. Sorry about the...you know." Carlos

tilted his head.

"Insubordination?" Baxter laughed. "Relax. I'm in no position to reprimand you. Besides, happens all the time. Most people think I'm a corporal."

Carlos feigned a smile of incredulity. "For real? Damn. I'd had you as at least a sergeant."

"Sure you did," Baxter replied, returning the smile.

"Not to break up this very touching moment," Gyle remarked, but you still haven't told us where we're going. Even a prisoner gets that right."

Baxter cracked another smile. "I *did* tell you."

"No, you said 'nowhere'."

"*Exactly.*"

Gyle was growing more irritated by the second. "Exactly *what?*"

"The place we're going to does not exist. Much the same way this conversation we're having now does not exist either, right?" Baxter looked up for a nod of confirmation before continuing. "The facility is called Harvey Point, and it's a top-secret CIA base for paramilitary training."

Carlos rose an eyebrow. "*Paramilitary?* You mean some kind of Ranger school? Fort Benning?"

Baxter shook his head. "No. Harvey Point is used to train CIA operatives in explosives, paramilitary combat, and clandestine warfare."

"Aside from the fact we aren't CIA, I thought 'The Farm' was their training ground," Gyle said.

Baxter nodded. "It is, but only for standard training. Pretty much your run-of-the-mill combat and espionage stuff. The Point, though, is hard-core. Advanced EOD, combat, weapons, tactics – pretty much all the training an operative could need. Hell, even the SEALs and the Secret Service participate in the Point's training regime."

"Okay, Cap'n, but that doesn't explain why our sorry asses are being dragged out here," Carlos pointed out. "We're not Navy, Secret Service, or CIA. We're Force Recon. We've already *had* advanced training."

"Exactly!"

Gyle shook his head. "There he goes with the damned 'exactly' crap again! Look, obviously we're not an Enigma machine, so how about you just drop the crypto shit and spell it out for us? What's this about?"

"Like I said, I don't know the specifics. What I can tell you is that you aren't the first soldiers I've driven out here. About a dozen, in fact; all in the last week. And they weren't all Marines, either."

Gyle laughed. "Don't tell me there're swabbies here?"

"That's not all. SAS, GSG-Nine, FFL, USOD-Delta – pretty much a soldier from every major anti-terrorist squadron in existence."

For the second time in twelve hours, Carlos and Gyle traded a look that said "what the hell?"

CHAPTER FOURTEEN
S.N.A.F.U.

LaGUARDIA
10: 55 EST

Forrester moved away from his overwatch position, still worried about Hollingsworth's coded message. As the rest of the hordes of terrified commuters scrambled towards exits or places of safe haven, he walked calmly down the concourse, en route to Hollingsworth's last-known position. Each exit he passed was locked down, three or four PAPD officers manning them. Much as it pained him to admit it, he needed their help. This was their airport.

They looked at him first with suspicion and then with a hint of alarm as he reached into his breast pocket. There was a flurry of activity; hands went for sidearms, some for the walkie-talkies on their belts. Forrester produced his credentials, an anti-climactic moment in comparison.

"FBI?" one asked, his face contorted in what looked to be anger. "What's the FBI doing here?"

Forrester thought about it for a second, then removed his PDA and showed them Davies' picture. "I'm looking for this man. He's a very important witness in a case the Bureau is working. He escaped from our custody a few hours ago," he lied, "and was in your airport as of ten minutes ago. He wounded an agent – the gunshot you heard." Forrester reached into his other pocket, removed a physical picture of Davies, and handed it to the officer. "Show that to all your men manning exits. If he's in the building, I want him detained. *Do not* shoot him under any circumstances."

"Hold on; what if he shoots at – "

A crack of a pistol interrupted the question. Forrester's head snapped up, tracing the origin. It came from the north, where Hollingsworth had last been. Screams filled the airport, as panic once again gripped the commuters. Forrester sidestepped a large man, who then careered into a younger lady and her small child.

"Goddamn it!" Forrester cursed. "Help them up," he instructed the nearest officer. "You two," he said, pointing to the officer to whom he'd first shown his badge and someone who looked like his partner. "Come with me."

As he sped towards the direction of the gunshot, his mind raced with all the possibilities. Had Davies shot Hollingsworth again? Had an officer shot him instead? Or had Hollingsworth shot Davies? He could not bring himself to imagine the fourth scenario.

The two officers followed on his hip, fingering the grips of their service pistols. Forrester noticed the look in their eyes. They would not hesitate to shoot, and in doing so would create a fire fight.

"Let me make something perfectly clear," he said, his voice a little breathless from the run. "If you open fire on the target, your career will be over before the bullet leaves the gun." Forrester didn't bother to turn around to show he was serious. He pushed on faster, brushing aside flocks of confused and terrified people.

At the foot of the escalators, he saw it. It had attracted the attention of four gun-toting police officers, those guns trained on the crouched figure of Dan Hollingsworth. Beneath him lay the body of another officer, his lifeless eyes staring up at the ceiling, blood suffusing the concrete underneath. Forrester closed his eyes and shook his head.

"Jimmy!" The man who'd answered Forrester's questions sprinted to the body, dropping to his knees and ignoring the pain that must have surely coursed through them. He saw the blood, the head wound, and then Hollingsworth. Thrusting his hand into his holster, he yanked out his pistol and pointed it at the FBI agent. "What have you done!?"

"Officer, holster that weapon! Now!" Forrester ordered, arriving at the scene. He then turned to the other officers who were still training their guns on the kneeling Hollingsworth. "You too! Holster those weapons now! This man is a federal agent." He turned his attention to Hollingsworth. "What the hell happened here, Hollingsworth?"

Hollingsworth turned around, his face forlorn. "I tried to show him...my badge, but he wouldn't let me," he began, trying his best to control his grief at the young kid's death. "He said he wanted to call something in. I tried to explain to him the suspect was still in the airport – that it was imperative I get to him – but then Davies came out of nowhere, sir. He came down the escalator, saw me, and opened fire. One shot – that must have been all that was left in the gun. He was...aiming for me, I think. He hit him right in the..."

"Where is Davies now!" Forrester demanded.

"He got away. I had a shot, but..."

Forrester turned to the officer he'd given Davies' picture to. "Get that picture to all the exits! Now! Do *not* open fire on him."

The officer clenched his jaw, the veins on both sides of his neck standing out. "He's just killed this kid and less than ten minutes ago shot your agent. What else does he need to do before you consider him a threat!" he demanded, pushing his nose against Forrester's face.

Forrester shoved him away. "Back off, Officer. This is much bigger than you or me. And make no mistake," he continued, bringing out his gun and pointing it at him. "I will use force to stop you if necessary."

"You're not going to shoot me!"

He lowered the pistol and levelled the officer a hard glare. "Just try me. Get the picture to your men, instruct them to arrest the suspect on sight, and keep your goddamn weapon in your pocket, else you'll be the one going to prison. Are we clear?"

"Like a fuckin' crystal," the officer snorted, stomping off in anger.

"You guys go back to whatever it was you were doing," Forrester instructed the rest of them. "Hollingsworth, come with me." When they were a safe distance away from anyone who might overhear, Forrester turned and grabbed him by the collar. "Now tell me what the hell *really* happened back there, Hollingsworth."

A look of confusion spread over Hollingsworth's face. "What are you talking about?"

"Don't bullshit me, Dan," he replied, releasing his grip and pointing to the escalators. "You said Davies came down the escalator, spotted you at your position, and discharged his pistol."

"Yeah, that's how it happened."

"No, it isn't. If he'd come down the escalator fully, saw you, and opened fire, there's no way he would have missed *you* from point-blank range. And if he'd fired from the escalator, the trajectory of his bullet would have been downward. The entry point of the bullet was just above the nose, the exit roughly the same on the opposite end. Which means that whoever fired at that kid was standing on the same level as him. According to Davies' dossier, he's barely an inch over five-and-a-half foot. The kid's six-foot, give or take a few inches – which is about your height, Dan. So, I ask you again, what really happened here, and why did you shoot that kid?"

CHAPTER FIFTEEN
CONFLICT

```
ATARIC
11:01 EST
```

The arrival of four strangers in suits sparked a frenzy of speculation at ATARIC. Led by two of the firm's security guards, they made their way through the working area, past employees who spoke in hushed tones, and climbed the stairs to Reid's office. Already present were Reid and Hunt. Johnson, who'd earlier convinced Haskens and Fielding to allow the outsourcing of work to non-ATARIC employees, was standing in the corner. He didn't greet any of them, but stood back and observed them like a boss watching a fledging employee handle new responsibilities.

The first one, Jake Collins, had history with Hunt going back to their college years in NYU. They were close friends until one incident: according to Collins – though Peter strongly denied it – Hunt had slept with Collins' girlfriend. The accusation led to a fist fight on campus grounds and another one three weeks later in a bar in Queens. Hunt had won on both occasions, the latter a vicious brawl which had left Collins with a broken jaw. The accusation had not resurfaced after, though the friendship was no more.

Reid was not aware of that part of their history, or else he would have known to refuse Collins' involvement in this job, but Hunt had selected him for a reason. Collins had graduated *summa cum laude* from NYU, and had started his own business a year later. Initially a small firm catering to a wide range of clients with computer problems, the company flourished and within a few years had amassed over ten million dollars, as well as employing over a hundred workers. Collins also had one of the brightest computer minds in New York, if not the country.

"Hello, Jack. Been a while. What have you been – " Collins hadn't recognised Hunt because of the long hair, but he did a double-take now, realising who he was, and suddenly his mouth gaped. "What the hell is *he* doing here? I thought he was fired!"

Hunt allowed a conceited smile to play on his lips. "Sure I was. But, see, the only person here with half a brain is Reid...and, well, they just *had* to call me back in to sort out this mess. You were their second choice."

Collins' face turned red. Levelling an admonishing finger at Reid, he said, "I'm not working with, for, or anywhere near that son-of-a-bitch, you understand!"

"Why the hell not, Jake? I thought you guys were friends?"

"We were. Until he slept with my girlfriend. I swore I'd never have anything to do with him again."

Hunt laughed dismissively. "You're still bandying that crap around, Collins?" He turned to the other men in the room. "He thinks I slept with his girlfriend, yet he went ahead and married her."

Collins' eyes filled with rage, and he charged towards Hunt like a maniac. "You shut your mouth, you miserable piece of shit!" He swung a wild punch that Hunt blocked with ease. With a firm grip of Collins' wrist, Hunt pivoted on one foot, arched Collins' arm up, and spun it behind his back. He gave it a small jerk, causing Collins to yelp.

"You hadn't the beating of me in college, Collins, and you damn sure don't have it now."

Through gritted teeth: "Fuck you, Hunt."

Hunt twisted further and Collins grimaced, trying to avoid another showing of pain. Hunt whispered in his ear, "And for the last time, I never touched Katharine. So get over your pathetic paranoia."

Reid moved beside Hunt, intent on using force, if necessary, to break the quarrel up. "Let him go, Peter."

Hunt gave him another conceited smile in response.

"He may not be able to take you," Reid continued, "but you *know* I am. Let him go *now*."

Hunt released his grip and pushed Collins away from him. "Whatever you say, Jack."

Johnson, though amused by the whole altercation, decided it would be wise to intervene. "As much as I would love to see Hunt get his ass kicked by Reid, I'm afraid that would be rather counter-productive. So, whatever issues you guys have, whatever bad blood there is between you all, sort it out on your own time."

Collins, rubbing his arm, shook his head and said, "No, I'm not staying here. You can get someone else to do the job. Me and my men are leaving."

Johnson stepped in front of them, cutting off their path to the door. "I'm afraid that's impossible. Half the money was already wired to your account – "

"You'll have it back before the hour is out," he replied, sidestepping Johnson.

Johnson moved in front of him again. "Like I said, I'm afraid that's impossible. This company does not accept refunds."

Collins glared at him. "I don't care what your company 'accepts'. Now, if you'll kindly excuse me..." He gestured for him to move but he stood his ground.

Johnson crossed his arms. "Let me explain how this works: When you accepted this job and the transfer of money, you essentially signed a binding contract. If you really want to nit-pick about this, I'll have our lawyers explain to you the minutiae of the situation. Suffice it to say, it won't be very favourable for you. So, let's avoid all of that unpleasantness. You sit your ass down in that chair, Mr Collins, and start instructing your men to do the job they were hired to...or you might just find yourself in a *very* unpleasant situation. Are we on the same page now?"

"Let me get this straight: I'm being forced to do a job I don't want to? I don't care about unpleasant situations. Have your lawyers contact mine, and I'll be in touch. Now get out of my way."

Before Johnson could launch a retort, Reid said, "Jake, just give me five minutes, okay? Alone. If you don't like what I have to say, you can walk, regardless of what Mr Johnson tells you."

Collins' eyes oscillated around the three men, finally landing on Reid. "Five minutes, then."

"Great! Thank you. Just give me one minute first." He turned his attention to Hunt. "Peter, can I have a word with you outside?"

Hunt frowned but followed Reid outside, who closed the door and paused at the top of the steps.

"As one of very few friends you have left, Peter, let me give you some advice: Quit being an asshole. It doesn't suit you. I know you feel you were screwed; I know Karen left you and took your son; but I'd've thought you'd've learned your lesson from the last time. You're getting a *third* chance here and you're blowing it. You've only been here a few hours and already you're looking like a liability. I'll reiterate what I said earlier: Get your shit together, man!"

"I never touched his girlfriend – "

"I don't care. If the two of you can't put your differences aside – however true or untrue they may be – and work together, one of you will have to leave. And I can tell you right now, it's looking like you. You notice the way Johnson didn't care much about you but seemed obsessed with Jake leaving? He doesn't give a rat's ass about you. He's waiting for a reason – any reason – to send you home."

"It's not like I'm going to have a job at the end of this, is it?"

"Definitely not the way you're going at the minute." Reid sighed, then said, "Listen, you need the money, but you don't need the hassle. And I gotta tell you, I don't think you'll last another hour here," he finished, looking at the beads of sweat dotting Hunt's forehead. "When's the last time you had a drink?"

Hunt glared at him. "You think I'm drinking on the job? I haven't touched a bottle since last night," he spat.

"My point exactly. Have you forgotten those years of medical training you had? You're sweating, which is one of the first symptoms of DT."

"I don't have delirium tremens. It's only been eight or nine hours since I've had alcohol. Rapid-onset DT takes at least twelve to twenty-four hours to appear."

"You've been what – drinking at least five or six bottles every day for the past eight or nine months? You can't just expect to go cold turkey for the next couple of days and not experience any side effects."

"Yeah, I *have* been drinking at least that, but the key words here are "eight or nine months". DT is a condition prevalent in chronic alcoholics, which I'm *not*."

"All I'm saying is you don't look so good," Reid replied.

"That wouldn't have anything to do with the fact I haven't been in this environment for almost a year? I don't want to be here anymore than you want me here, but I need the money. So go have your chat with Collins, convince him to stay, and let's get this done, 'cause I don't need to be here any longer than absolutely necessary."

"And you'll quit being an asshole?"

"Jack, just go. I'll do what needs to be done for the job," Hunt said and then, as an afterthought, added: "Besides, I'm not the one you should be worrying about."

Reid dismissed Hunt's concerns with an unworried wave of his hand. "Jake will be fine. I'll placate him."

"Not Jake. Johnson. There's no way *any* of us are gonna feel comfortable with him standing over our shoulders. We'll get this done a lot quicker if he's out of the picture."

"I agree with you, Peter, but I'm in no position to tell him to leave."

"I don't think he'd leave even if you were. But I got a better idea."

Reid cocked an eyebrow. "Go on."

"The way I figure it, we have to install the OS on one computer first – an un-networked terminal. That way we can check if it's going to cause problems. That's going to take a couple of hours, what with configurations and other bits and pieces. If that installation is successful, we're good to go on all the systems. Okay so far?"

"Get to the point."

Hunt nodded. "Okay, if we can get Johnson out of our hair for a few hours, we should be okay. And I think I have a way to do it."

"Go on," Reid urged.

"We upload a virus to ATARIC's network. A low-key one

that won't cause a lot of damage but will take some time to find and destroy."

Reid looked at him as if Hunt had gone mad. "You want to upload a *virus* to ATARIC? Are you crazy! If we're found out we'll be fired or, worse still, arrested. You can't be serious!"

"We won't be found out. I'll do it from my laptop. Once Johnson finds out, he'll be on it like flies on manure. He won't trust the folks downstairs to handle it. I'll hide the virus in a place where their scanner won't find it. They'll have to run manual checks, and by the time they've done that, we'll know if our OS is compatible."

Reid looked like he was considering it. "And you're sure you can do it without anyone ever finding out?"

"Am I a wizard or not, Jack? I can do it with my eyes closed and one hand tied behind my back."

Reid deliberated for a second. Then, with a sigh, he said, "I can't believe I'm saying this, but okay...get back in there and do it. And please, for both our sakes, don't get caught."

CHAPTER SIXTEEN
DECISIONS

CENTRAL TERMINAL DRIVE
11:05 EST

Troy Davies hadn't been in New York City for a few years. Outside LaGuardia was a maze of roads, one-way traffic systems, and more vehicles than on the freeway. He didn't know the layout, and was in no particular mood to walk, so he put two fingers in his mouth and whistled for a cab. A yellow one with an NYC registration pulled up to the footpath of the CTB before he'd removed his fingers. He glanced back over his shoulder, saw that no one of interest was watching, and hopped inside.

"Where to, pal?" the cabbie asked without bothering to look at his passenger.

Davies thought about it for a moment. He had no idea who those men were, but they'd converged on him in a manner which suggested a degree of professionalism. He'd considered the possibility Kirov had him followed from Russia, but it didn't seem likely. He had made sure no one had tailed him from his apartment. He'd left all three men unconscious, though now he wished he'd put bullets in their heads. Whoever these men were, Davies knew he couldn't take any chances. He needed to regroup and figure out his next move.

The cabbie looked up to the mirror. "Hey, buddy, I haven't got all day. Where to?"

"Sorry...first, I need to go to the Washington Mutual bank on West Seventeenth Street in Brooklyn. Then, I need to go to Seagate."

"Sure thing, but it's gonna take about an hour in this traffic."

"If you get me to the bank before midday, there's a hundred-dollar note in it for you."

"It's your wallet, buddy."

The quaint town of Seagate was a gated community at the western end of Coney Island. Although it had been over two years since Davies had last been there, he was still a registered member. His photo-ID card – in a safe deposit box in Washington Mutual – would allow him access.

And then what? In his mind were the secrets of a Russian terrorist, a man whose plan was both ingenious and potentially suicidal. The Powers-That-Be needed to know what he had planned. They needed to know how much they stood to lose if Pavel Kirov succeeded. How had he found out? How had Kirov discovered Station Blue? And how long would it be before he initiated his plan?

" – a New Yorker?" the cabbie asked, breaking Davies' reverie.

"Sorry?"

"I said, are you from around here? I don't meet many New Yorkers willing to part with a hundred dollars for a twenty-mile cab journey."

Davies shook his head. "Not a New Yorker, no."

"So what brings you here?"

Where do I start? "Business."

The cabbie took Davies' laconic response at face value. He got rude customers all the time, and usually charged them extra or lengthened the journey. Those customers didn't offer him a hundred dollars for a twenty-mile journey, however. This one, though...there was something about him. He decided not to ask what the business entailed, afraid of knowing. For the rest of the journey, he stayed silent.

How did Kirov find out I was a spy? Did I get sloppy? Did my handler turn me in? How, damnit!?

Three years spent getting inside Kirov's crew; months on

cover and background stories; the constant vetting of all personnel; the things he'd done to earn the trust of the fiercest terrorist in the Occident; hours spent in the company of Kirov and his lackeys, drinking booze and eating some of the finest gourmet meals in the world; and all of it now pointless.

Kirov had learned about Davies before he could find any incriminating evidence to bring Kirov to justice. Except for this one plan – what was it The Butcher had called it in Kirov's living-room the night before he'd tried to murder Davies? A "master-plan". *The* master-plan. And now someone was trying to kill him because he knew about it. Someone had blown his cover, and now Kirov would stop at nothing to ensure Davies did not get word back to the FBI.

For the first time in his life, he wondered who he could trust. Jonathan Baker had masterminded the sting; he was the only one who knew the entire details of it. Which also made him the number-one suspect in Davies' mind. He'd called the Bureau from the flight, told Baker he had something massive which couldn't be shared over a phone, and then...what? If those men had been agents, why weren't they dressed as such? Why had they approached him in a hostile manner? And what if they had intended to do something else?

What if they wanted to take me to the middle of nowhere, put a bullet in my head, and bury me? If that were true, where could he go? Who could he trust? And, most importantly, who could he tell about Kirov's plan for Station Blue?

CHAPTER SEVENTEEN
ACCUSATIONS

CENTRAL TERMINAL BUILDING
11:10 EST

Hollingsworth glared at Forrester. "For the second time; what the hell is that supposed to mean? Are you insinuating *I* had some part in that kid's death?" he demanded, trying to control the redness seeping into his face.

"Convince me you didn't," Forrester replied, his face deadpan.

"You're serious! Jesus Christ, sir, why would I kill a fellow law enforcement officer? That's insane!"

"You tell me. Maybe things got a little heated. Maybe an accidental discharge. Or maybe he came at you and you had no choice. Whatever the case, that officer is dead and I'm not buying into it that Davies came down the escalator and shot him."

Hollingsworth shook his head and levelled a finger at Forrester. "I can't believe I'm hearing this! You're going to stand there and accuse a fellow agent of murder? I don't care if you're the deputy director of the FBI. You're not going to accuse me of something I haven't done! I didn't kill no kid, y'hear me!?" Hollingsworth said, too loudly, drawing startled looks from those civilians who were brave enough to stand in one place for longer than a few seconds.

"I've been an agent longer than you, Hollingsworth, and a cop a hell of a lot longer than that; reading people is my speciality. You're not telling me something about that kid's death, and whether or not that 'something' incriminates you, I don't know. What I do know is I don't have time to deal with this right now. Every minute we spend arguing is another minute Davies has to get away. Go seal off the perimeter and all the exits. Make sure every officer knows what Davies looks like. Go!"

As Hollingsworth sped off for the exits, Forrester took one more look at the scene. One of the officers had been smart enough to cover the body and take it out of sight, but the blood still lingered on the ground, its presence a tell-tale mark of what had occurred minutes earlier. *What* had *occurred?* Forrester mused, his mind wandering to all the possibilities. From his knowledge of spooks, he knew they weren't usually well-trained in marksmanship. The accuracy of the shot suggested the shooter was someone with a background of weapons-training. One perfect dot, just above the bridge of the nose. Instant death. The heart would have been more reliable, but officers wore vests. And vests, though normally useless at close range, were capable of stopping anything up to a .45.

Forty-five? Why's that ringing a bell...What are you thinking, Red? Why's a forty-five calibre relevant? C'mon, think!

But he couldn't. Not in any coherent manner. Rapid thoughts flitted through his head. The shock of the last half-hour had done something alien to him. What had originally been a simple pickup had now escalated into a bloodbath, and he had not been prepared for that. He'd been involved in a shootout once in the last ten years – the price of becoming a "suit". He now wondered where his love of the chase had gone. Why had the thrill of an adrenaline-pumping mission like this lost its appeal? Was he getting *that* old?

You've been behind a desk for too long, Bill. For Christ sakes, you just accused a man of murder without a shred of evidence to back it up! You're losing it.

He claimed to be a good reader of people, yet he hadn't read Davies, nor had he believed the man to be capable of murder.

You approached this all wrong, Red! He's been undercover for God knows how long; what else is he going to do but suspect everyone? And we came in and approached him from all sides like a goddamned bunch of terrorist lackeys! No wonder he opened fire! He was probably scared out of his freakin' mind.

Enough to kill an officer, though? That part still didn't make sense. It would have made *more* sense to get out without any altercations. But good planning had to allow for all contingencies, and in high-stress situations like this even the holiest men were capable of taking a life. Besides, who knew what Davies' mindset would be after so many years undercover, of looking over his shoulder, afraid his next move might also be his last. People like that were one step shy of insanity.

Okay, so what would I do if I were in his position? Where would I go? I have information about the most illusive terrorist since Ilich Ramirez Sanchez, but I've been out in the cold too long. I don't know who to trust, where to turn, or what to do. I'd go to someplace I feel safe; someplace I know no one else knows about. From there, I'd figure out my next steps. Okay, so where –

The sound of his phone jarred him away from his thoughts. He removed it from his pocket and flipped the cover open, not thinking to check the caller ID. "Hello?" The answer was laced with anger.

"Red? Just what the hell's going on down there!?" a furious Jonathan Baker demanded. "I'm getting intel that there's been *two* separate cases of shots fired at LaGuardia. Jesus Christ, I asked you to secure an undercover agent, not shoot up a goddamn airport!"

"Your *undercover agent* shot at us first. We were moving in to identify ourselves, and he fired at one of my agents. So the next time you want to jump down my throat about something, have the full story first, Jon!" Forrester was perhaps the only man, save for the President, who could speak to Baker like that without worrying about his job.

On the other end, Baker gave a quiet sigh. "Sorry, Red. I guess I'm a bit tightly coiled today. I'm headed for Station Blue this afternoon. The President wants a status report on some of the new weapons. I'm not particularly looking forward to being there."

"Oh? You haven't been to Blue in ages. I didn't know you

were still the President's primary liaison with them."

"Unfortunately. Anyway, give me a sitrep. How long before you and Davies are sitting beside me in the Hoover building?"

Forrester hesitated long enough for Baker to ask, with a sigh, what was wrong.

"When he shot my agent, he somehow managed to evade us and get away." Forrester grimaced, expecting a backlash.

"Please tell me he's still in the airport and you've locked it down," Baker replied, his voice calm and level.

"All exits are closed, and all men manning them have Davies' picture – don't worry, they think he's a federal witness, like you wanted. If he's still in the building, we'll find him, Jon."

Baker seemed preoccupied with something, and when he finally spoke, he didn't reply to Forrester's reassurance. "Why did he open fire? I mean, I can understand running, maybe brawling, but *shooting?* And how'd he get a gun on a plane? Did he? Or did someone give it to him when he deplaned?"

Forrester knew Baker was thinking out loud. He liked to bounce ideas off other agents, both to bring new perspective and to get his thoughts out where he could make sense of them. Some, Forrester had already thought of. Others were piquing his interest.

"We don't admit this readily, Jon, but spooks are trained to get weapons into otherwise impossible places. It wouldn't surprise me if Davies had a way of smuggling one on-board."

"Maybe before Nine-Eleven, but not now. There's no luggage that isn't checked, no carry-on bags that aren't fully searched, and no gun that doesn't show up on a metal detector, contrary to what Hollywood would have us believe."

"You think he has someone on the ground? No, no – I don't," Forrester disagreed, shaking his head. "We watched him deplane. He was..." he trailed off, the words he'd said less than an hour ago coming back to him.

Target spotted. Beside the two men in suits.

CHAPTER EIGHTEEN
SUBTERFUGE

```
HARVEY POINT
CIA TRAINING FACILITY
HERTFORD
NORTH CAROLINA
11: 16 EST
```

The captain brought the HMMWV to an abrupt stop, throwing his passengers forward, who did well to avoid hitting their heads off the seats. He pulled the brake and turned to face them; both were throwing him askance looks, which made him smile. These abrupt halts had been the only fun he'd had all week.

"Hey, what the hell gives, Cap'n! You trying to knock us out, *mano*?" demanded Gyle.

He reached into the back, past Gyle, and opened the passenger door. "Afraid this is as far as I can take you, Master-Sergeant," he said, gesturing for both to leave his vehicle.

Carlos opened his window and peered outside. Ahead, a single gate stretched the width of the road. The top of it was lined with barbed-wire, the gate itself littered with "no entry" signs. To the right of it, a large wooden sign proclaimed *HARVEY POINT DEFENCE TESTING*. To the left, off the tarred road, a black SUV was parked in the shade of numerous trees.

Behind the gate stood something that looked like a guard post, but Carlos couldn't see anyone manning it.

"Where do we go from here?" he asked, coming back inside.

Baxter gave a sly smile. "Now begins the fun part. The EOD and paramilitary training buildings are about a quarter-klick east of this gate. You'll have to walk there..."

Gyle looked up, a frown etching his face. "Why do I get the feeling it won't be as simple as that?"

Baxter smiled again. "That perception of yours is good, Master-Sergeant. You're going to need it. As you can probably see, there's no guard posted at the gate. Everyone here is aware of your arrival. It's your job to get to the EOD building without being spotted. There are maybe a dozen soldiers out here in this forest, and you're going to be judged on how well you can evade them and reach your target."

Carlos punched the back of the seat, his face growing redder by the second. "We're out here playin' games in the middle of nowhere, while my team are back in Afghanistan getting shot at by the Taleban! I was dragged out of a war zone for *this* bullshit? I don't know what this is all about, Cap'n, but God help me if I ever see that baby-G again. What the hell was his name, Julio?"

Gyle scratched his forehead. "Triton, I think."

"Yeah, that's it. Personally – and you can quote me on this if you like – I think this is a bunch of crap; taking us to the middle of nowhere to see who the best anti-terrorist squadron is." Baxter turned away at that remark. "Yeah, that's what I thought," continued Carlos. "A game orchestrated by men in suits who've nothing better to do with their time than jerk soldiers around. I'll get out now, but I won't be walking no quarter-klick *anywhere*; you understand me?"

Baxter shook his head and blew out a pent-up sigh. "You're not the first soldier who's reacted that way, Sergeant-Major, and I suspect you won't be the last either. I'll tell you what I told them: If you leave here without permission, you'll be court-martialled and most likely dishonourably discharged from your unit."

"On what grounds?" a defiant Carlos demanded.

"Insubordination. Failure to comply with orders. Any number of things, really. Like I said, I don't know the minutiae of what's happening here, but I can follow orders. Mine were to make sure you got here and were made aware of what you had to do. Yours are to make your way from here to the EOD building as best you can." Baxter reached into the glove compartment and pulled out a couple of items. Handing them to Carlos, he said, "A map, compass, and MREs. Here's hoping you won't need the latter."

Carlos tossed them to Gyle, shaking his head in frustration. "That's it? No paintball guns, no last words of encouragement, or maybe a key for the gate?"

Baxter cracked another smile. "Afraid not. I'm assuming you know how to read a map, so there's no need for me to point out the EOD building. I will say one thing: Beware of wild animals. This area is notorious for alligators."

"You're kidding me, right?" Gyle asked with a wide-eyed stare. "We have no weapons!"

"You'll get your standard-issue equipment when you reach the EOD. Until then, I hope you're fast runners."

"*Wonderful.*" Gyle threw his hands up into the air. "I can't believe I'm saying this, but right now I hate my own country. Give me Afghanistan any day of the week. Fuckin' alligators."

"Gentlemen, time's a wasting. I guess I should have told you this earlier, but if you don't make the EOD building before midday, you'll have failed."

For the first time in ages, Carlos cracked a grin of his own. He took an over-exaggerated stare at his watch, then said, "A quarter-klick in forty minutes? I could do that crawling."

"It's interesting you say that, because you just might have to," Baxter finished, giving him a look that showed he was serious. "Now kindly get out of my Humvee."

***

A hundred feet back from the main entrance, two soldiers, dressed in woodland camouflage and crouched behind a row of trees, watched the newest arrivals exit the HMMVW. The driver then sped off, and both exchanged a glance, the first nodding to the gate.

"Twenty quid says one of those tossers tries to jump it," remarked Sergeant Larry Lansdale.

"*Quid?*" replied Oberfeldwebel Kürt Fromm, in a highly

pronounced German accent. *"Tossers?"*

Lansdale gave him a look of incredulity, then smiled. "Never mind." The German understood and spoke English fluently, but British terms were lost on him.

Lansdale wondered if he should throw in a few Cockney slang words for the hell of it, but knew Fromm was not a man to play games with. They'd only been at the Point for a week now, but stories had already been told, ranks exchanged, and camaraderie established between over a dozen multinational soldiers, all of whom spoke fluent English. In typical masculine fashion, the toughest member of the "team" had been determined. There was still some dispute, but the now widely held belief was that Kürt Fromm, of Germany's Special Forces team KSK, had to be a robot. In training, he never missed. Not with a rifle, handgun, or even the large sword he liked to call a "knife". During mealtime, he told stories of training at the German Mountain and Winter Combat school in Mittenwald – stories that made some soldiers cringe; a unique occurrence given that they too were no pushovers when it came to toughness.

Part of KSK's 5th platoon sniper unit, Fromm's appearance belied his reputation as a tough man. An inch over six foot, the German did not possess the biggest body of all the soldiers here, most of whom were hard-core bodybuilders. But appearances were deceiving, and Fromm had the preternatural strength of an ox. Wiry and harder than the wooden stock of his Walther WA-2000 sniper rifle, his biggest strength was his unerring accuracy behind a scope. Rumour had it he held the record for the longest sniper kill in German Army history: 2105 yards, *if* rumours were to be indulged. If true, it put him in the company of only a handful of snipers to have achieved a kill at over two thousand yards. That alone commanded respect.

As a member of the British SAS, it took a lot for Lansdale to consider someone else tougher or stronger than he. At two hundred and forty-five pounds, he outweighed Fromm by seventy-odd, though stood only an inch taller. His arms betrayed years of weight-training. Where Fromm had his sniper record, Lansdale held an equally proud record back at Hereford for the heaviest bench-press in Regiment history: two hundred kilograms.

For both men, the novelty of their current situation had worn away after the first week's training. They had not been told why they were training or on whose authority, either. After all, who had jurisdiction over a group of multinational soldiers? And who had the power to second them to the United States, even if only temporarily? There were a lot of questions, but no answers had been given yet, and new soldiers were arriving by the day.

"Our friends are at the gate," announced Fromm. He then interlaced his fingers and cracked all his knuckles.

There was very little that scared an SAS operative, but Lansdale admitted to himself – begrudgingly – that the black German, who kept a razor in his pocket because his beard grew almost as fast as he could run, scared the hell out of him. He found himself wondering who would win if Fromm encountered one of those alligators all the soldiers had been warned about. The scary part was Lansdale couldn't decide, even though logic told him an unarmed human didn't stand a chance against an alligator. Fromm was not entirely human, though. Or at least it seemed that way.

"I see 'em." *Now, one of you try to jump it,* he thought, chuckling inwardly.

***

"Like hell I'm jumping that. Those *pendejos* can afford to pay for a new fence," Gyle said, producing, with a cheeky grin, a Swiss Army knife from inside his Kevlar vest. He'd constructed a secret hiding place in the lining of the fabric so if captured nothing less than a thorough search would reveal the knife.

Carlos laughed, slapping his sergeant and close friend on the back. "I like your style, Master-Sergeant." Spreading the map out of in front of him, he added, "Now, let's see if I remember how to read one of these damned things."

"You've been chasing that desk job at the Pentagon for so long that you've forgotten everything you learned in the field, Sergeant-Major," Gyle replied in an inflected tone, referring to the position of top-level enlisted planner that Carlos had been offered on two separate occasions but had respectfully declined. He wasn't ready to leave the field yet, despite the protestations of his CO and the Marine Corps Commandant.

Carlos gave a wry laugh. "You looking rid of me, Julio? I'm not ready to sit behind a desk yet. I'll leave that stuff to the COs."

"Who in their right mind would have thought Baxter was a *captain*, Sergeant-Major? Guy barely looked thirty."

Gyle found the most suitable tool for cutting through the fence and began working, while Carlos got a bearing for the Explosives Ordnance Disposal building.

"Tell me about it. He was too refined for my liking. Tours are supposed to take that pompous edge off, but I'm guessing he went to officer school a lot sooner than most."

Gyle snipped another bit of high-tensile steel, the gap now widened nearly enough to allow a man through. It would need to be widened farther in this case, however. "Did you really mean what you said about walking away?"

"Hell no," Carlos replied. "I just wanted to screw with him. I was serious about this being bullshit, though. I don't like leaving Rico and the others back in Afghanistan."

"I hear ya. Rico's a good kid, though. He's got enough guile" — the pun made Carlos smile — "to command the team."

Carlos knew he had, but avoided the topic. Folding the map up, he said in a disapproving tone, "What the hell are you doing – sawing through the damned thing? You slacking on me, Master-Sergeant?"

The great thing about Carlos, Gyle thought, was that he could be serious when necessary, but knew when to break up a tough situation or conversation with humour, and that couldn't be said about most of the commanders of the other platoons in Force Recon. He even allowed his sergeants to address him as "Jack", though out of respect for his seniority and experience, most didn't.

"*No, sir!* I will have an entry made in approximately one half-minute, Sergeant-Major!" Gyle replied with standard military inflection.

This time Carlos' response was serious. "Dammit, Julio, keep your voice down."

Gyle grimaced, angry at himself for allowing complacency to creep in. There were still obstacles to negotiate, highly trained soldiers to avoid, and alligators – *fuckin' alligators* – to run away from like scalded cats. And here he was, bellowing to the sky like a hyena, and probably telling every godforsaken thing within a hundred yards his precise location.

He lowered his voice, the reply sheepish. "Sorry. Don't know what the hell I was thinking."

Had it been another soldier Carlos might have reprimanded him further, but because it was Gyle he allowed it to pass. He wouldn't have anyone else as his second-in-command. NCOs didn't come any better than Julio Gyle, a Puerto Rican with a fiery temper second only to his ability to "read" a war-zone. Gyle never made the same mistake twice, and very rarely *once.* He understood things quickly, delegated with the best of them, and was as tough as his two-hundred-and-fifty-pound, six-foot-four frame could demonstrate.

"There." Gyle stood up to reveal an opening about five foot square, the edges of which were bent backwards to preclude either man being cut to pieces. "You got a bearing?"

Carlos nodded and retrieved the compass. "Yeah, quarter-klick my ass; It's more a half-klick. Follow me."

Both men squeezed through the opening without any problems. Inside, the road stretched as far as the eye could see, but the buildings indicated on the map were hidden behind hordes of trees. Carlos wondered how many other things were also hidden. The thought caused an inexplicable shudder of something he could only assume to be fear...or possibly dread. Yet both of those were alien to him, much like the flora and fauna of North Carolina.

This area is notorious for alligators.

Carlos found himself thinking what else it was notorious for. How many snakes, spiders, and other creatures inhabited this locale? And how many of them would take your life as quickly as you could swat them away? He was familiar with forest environments, just not North Carolinian ones, and too many soldiers died from having no knowledge of their environment.

"I don't know what's more disquieting, *mano.* That we're wearing desert fatigues in the middle of a forest, or that there's a bunch of soldiers stalking us," Gyle said.

"I'm more worried about what else might be stalking us, Julio. You know anything about North Carolina?"

Gyle smiled. "Apart from it having really crap sports teams?" He shook his head. "No. Why do you ask?"

"You think Baxter was screwing around on the whole alligator thing?"

"I don't think he'd be the sort to, Sergeant-Major. But if there are alligators out here, we best find a weapon of some kind," Gyle replied, looking around.

"Eh, Julio? Your knife!" Carlos gave him a friendly clip around the ear.

"I meant a weapon for you. You're off the wagon if you think you're getting my Swiss Army knife."

Carlos ignored Gyle's rejoinder. If there *were* alligators out here, nothing short of a firearm would prove valuable anyway.

"Okay, Master-Sergeant. It's eleven-hundred-and-thirty hours. We make it to the EOD building before eleven-hundred-and-fifty-five, or we don't make it at all. They may be able to spin some story about us being one or two minutes late according to their watches, but five is a bit much.

"The entire area between here and the EOD is lined with trees – makes for low visibility but lots of places to hide. Eyes and ears open, Julio. I'll take point, you bring up my six. Check behind you at all times. I don't want any surprises. We move in cover formation. Tripwires, bear pits, deadfalls, foothold traps – check for it all. We don't know the environment and we aren't taking any chances. Understood?"

Gyle nodded.

"All right. Complete silence from here on. Let's be safe, Julio," Carlos finished, offering a fist which Gyle bumped with his own.

The road continued north-east, cutting a trail through the forest and gradually winding back around to the south about another five hundred yards farther on. If Carlos wanted, he could stay on it all the way to the EOD building, but that put him out in the open. Ironically, it was no safer to trek through the forest. While this area was closed off to civilians, animals didn't possess the same docility. And where there were animals, there were animal *traps*.

He signalled Gyle to follow him into the shrubbery on the right. Brushing past leaves of trees and bushes, he noticed the grass was flattened, lying halfway to the ground. Not enough to have been done in the last hour, but within the last two or three, someone – *or something* – had been out here.

Carlos spread out a hand and moved it in a zigzagging motion. Gyle nodded, knowing Carlos wanted him to follow behind in a veering course. If anyone tried to follow their trail, it would be a lot more confusing. Of course, it meant Gyle had to more careful; veering off the beaten path meant a greater chance of encountering traps. As quietly as possible, he broke a three-foot-long branch off a tree and used it to gently prod the grass in front. It was tedious work, which a lot of soldiers wouldn't have the patience to do, but it was necessary. The EOD building was only a half-kilometre away, and both men could run that in two or three minutes. Getting there on time was no problem. Getting there in one piece, however...

Most soldiers know when someone is in close proximity to them; more so in jungle environments where every step could alert an enemy. Carlos could feel it – somewhere, in the midst of all these trees, someone was stalking him, watching his every move with military precision. Perhaps even the same person who'd disturbed the grass. The feeling caused his skin to crawl. He'd been stalked, tracked, and followed countless times in his military career, just never in a way that made him feel trapped. Even in that cave in Afghanistan, surrounded by a dozen Taleban, he hadn't felt trapped.

Carlos came to a sudden stop, his right hand rising in a fist, signalling Gyle to stop too. Though it wasn't necessary, he turned around and placed one finger on his lips. When Gyle nodded, he turned back and looked to his left, staring at one spot for more than half a minute. Every breath was rationed, every unnecessary noise filtered out until all that remained was the chirping of birds and the rustling of foliage. His hearing became hyper-acute. He closed his eyes to avoid a sensory overload, and concentrated solely on the noises of the forest.

There!

A snap. Barely audible but there. About fifty yards to his left; the sound of a twig snapping under weight. *The weight of what, though?*

His eyes snapped open, zooming in to where he thought the sound originated from. He searched for anything incongruous, anything that didn't belong in a milieu of trees; an outline, a shadow, or part of the jungle that appeared to move on its own. The problem with jungle camouflage, he thought, was that it lent soldiers an illusory belief of being invisible.

Carlos had been concentrating so hard he failed to notice Gyle until he came in behind and laid a hand on his back. Only superhuman conditioning, the kind exclusive to Special Forces soldiers, kept Carlos from jumping out of his skin.

"Christ, Julio," he hissed. "Don't do that!"

"Sorry, Sergeant-Major. Everything okay?" replied Gyle, whispering.

"I don't know. It might be nothing, but..."

Gyle nodded. "Yeah, I feel it too. We're being watched. Not sure from where, but someone's out here."

Or some thing...

Carlos tried to push his fears to one side, knowing they were inappropriate for a soldier of his stature; but fear was indiscriminate. He knew some of it came from the realisation they weren't dealing with ordinary soldiers.

"...pretty much a soldier from every anti-terrorist squadron in existence".

Baxter's words, if true, were chilling. A conglomerate of Special Forces soldiers in an environment rife with hiding places and prime for all kinds of traps? This forest – nay, *jungle* – was made for such a unit. And who could be trusted to leave behind all differences if an opportunity to kill a hated enemy arose? Whose brilliant idea was it to bring together a group of multinational soldiers to a place like this, where they could disappear, kill, or turn on their commanders with the stealth of a chameleon? The bigwigs hadn't thought this through, because in Carlos' mind the cons far outweighed the pros.

There! Again. The noise came from a different place this time, about ten or fifteen yards east of the original one, but closer to Carlos. *Has to be a human!* If it were an animal, the sounds would be indiscriminate. But these sounds...they were something else. The sounds of someone trying but failing to stay silent as they negotiated the jungle. Carlos knew moving around out here without making a sound was virtually impossible, even for the most elite soldiers.

Garnering Gyle's attention, he touched two fingers to his eyes and then pointed to where the last sound had come from. Gyle nodded, moving out of the undergrowth and staying low all the way back to the road. There, he stopped, concealing himself behind a cypress tree. On the other side of the road were dozens more of them, interspersed among Spanish moss and other deciduous plants. Gyle focused his vision and watched for any movement.

Another snap. Even more eastern than the last, but closer still. Gyle nodded, knowing what was happening; they were flanking from the opposite side, staying off the road and using the jungle to make a complete circle. Smart. Gyle figured they'd been watching from the beginning, waiting for him and Carlos to pass so they could flank around and sneak in behind. They hadn't counted on the forest giving away their position.

Gyle slipped back in beside Carlos and gave his commander a sitrep. "At least two," he began, whispering. "No way you send one man alone in this environment. Reckon they've been watching us from we got here; probably think we're halfway to the EOD by now. They're using the jungle to flank in behind us and stay off the road."

"You saw them?"

Gyle shook his head. "They're good enough to be invisible, not *inaudible,* so no visual. But it's what I'd do."

Carlos thought about it for a few seconds, looked at his watch, then said, "I've got an idea."

***

Lansdale didn't like it. This was supposed to be easy. Track the two new soldiers, box in and capture them, and bring both to the EOD building. He and Fromm had watched them from the main gate until they'd disappeared into the undergrowth. They weren't supposed to go that way. The most optimum route, as indicated on the map, was to the left, where capturing them would have been simply a matter of waiting. They'd deviated from the norm, requiring Lansdale and Fromm to regroup and follow behind.

Even then it should have been easy enough. Just a simple matter of following their trail. Except that it was random at best. From what Lansdale could discern, it veered left and right without any explanation. In a way it seemed almost careless – or perhaps even care*free*. Certainly it didn't look like the trail of a trained soldier every bit as afraid of possible traps as he would be of the animals they were designed to snare. Which made Lansdale think the trail couldn't belong to either soldier.

Worse still, since losing sight of them in the undergrowth, he hadn't heard a sound nor seen a glimmer of movement. Had they been wearing jungle camouflage he could have accepted that. But knowing they were in desert...nobody was *that* good.

"They are good, my friend," Fromm announced from behind, as though he'd read Lansdale's mind.

"I know." Moving through a jungle without making a sound required time, patience, and skill. These guys could maybe tick one of those boxes, but all three?

There we are! Lansdale smiled. The snap of a twig, about fifty yards farther down the trail.

He signalled Fromm to take point, even though Fromm, a master-sergeant, outranked him. There were no ranks in this unit, though. At least not yet. And Lansdale, who hated being point-man just as much as he hated being in a jungle in North Carolina, knew Fromm was a sniper, and snipers made very good point-men.

Lansdale stayed close, confident from his two weeks here that no traps were in this vicinity, but careful nonetheless. It enraged him that weapons hadn't been issued to any of the soldiers other than during morning and afternoon training. Yes, they'd been reassured numerous times that the odds of encountering dangerous wildlife were infinitesimal. And yet Lansdale couldn't trust anyone who used words like "infinitesimal" to describe odds. Maybe the chances of being struck by lightning could be described that way, but what the hell else would one expect to encounter in the wild *but* wildlife! And the majority of those suckers were dangerous. Lansdale wondered if there were spiders out here, sure as his head was bald that there were. They had those in England, some big ones in recent years, too, but nothing compared to the humongous ones in this country. Not to mention snakes, alligators, and crocodiles...he shivered at the thought.

And these "welcoming parties" for the newest soldiers were at best pointless. He could understand testing soldiers to determine their capabilities, but you did that in training, not here. And since none of the men had made it to the EOD building without being captured, Lansdale began to wonder if the bigwigs wanted it that way.

Fromm shared his partner's concerns. He covered the last few metres, to the point where he believed the sound had originated, and raised his hand. Eyes oscillating in a 180-degree arc, he searched the forest ahead for signs of human presence, finding none. The trail which had earlier veered inexplicably left and right now vanished. Not in a gradual way, as might be expected. Within five yards, the grass went from being bent to standing erect. From there, no further signs of disturbance could be seen. Even more confusing, the trail did not end near the road, which might have explained the grass. No, it ended in the middle of the jungle, right beside a...

Verfluchte scheiße!

Fromm looked up, fearing the worst.

***

Carlos waited until the point-man saw him, then launched himself from the tree. The soldier tried to sidestep, but it was already too late. Carlos collided with his chest, locked his arms and legs around the black man's body, and used his weight and momentum to bring him crashing to the ground. The soldier threw up one arm in a feeble attempt at resistance, but Carlos grabbed it and pinned it to the ground. He didn't need to look over to know that Gyle had the other one in a similar predicament.

Below him, the soldier nodded his head. "*Ja*, you guys *are* good."

"German?" Carlos asked, almost as though he didn't expect a German to be black.

"Kürt Fromm, master-sergeant, KSK."

He figured Fromm would have offered a hand had both not been pinned to the floor. Carlos didn't know much about KSK, other than it was one of Germany's elite Special Forces units. The man beneath him had an athletic build more suited to track and field, which made Carlos think he was a sniper. Those guys trained for endurance, not strength. Not to mention Germany's hard-core mountain schools...

"Jack Carlos, Sergeant-Major, United States Marine Corps."

"Marines!" the other one snorted from five yards away, trapped under the huge frame of Gyle. "Can't believe we got outsmarted by a bunch o' jarheads."

"Watch your mouth, *muchacho*," Gyle warned with a smile. "What's your name?"

"Larry Lansdale, sergeant, SAS. Now get the hell off me, you Spanish prick!"

"*Pensando en pajaritos preñao, cabrón.*"

Lansdale gave him an incredulous look, then glanced to Carlos as if to ask what had just been said, since Gyle's face was a picture of amusement and it didn't look like he intended to translate.

Carlos smiled, shaking his head not in amusement but in an equally incredulous way. "I'm American, mate. Haven't a clue what he just said."

"You look Spanish too," Lansdale observed, giving Carlos a thorough stare.

"Mexican father, American mother. And I think we've humoured you long enough." Carlos turned his attention to Gyle. "Tie him to the tree, Julio. Time's a wasting."

Gyle yanked Lansdale to his feet as though he weighed nothing, shoved him against the tree, and removed a coil of rope. He triple-lapped it around him, securing it as tight as he dared without cutting off circulation. When he finished, he helped Carlos do the same with Fromm.

"So, *Julio*," Lansdale said, deliberately mispronouncing it 'who-lee-o', "what the bloody hell did you just say to me?"

"Name's 'Jew-lee-o', *hombre*. And I said that you were thinking of the pregnant birdies." Gyle cracked a goofy grin.

"Pregnant...? What the 'ell are you on about?"

Carlos laughed, having a fair idea what Gyle was getting at. "He means you have your head in the clouds, soldier. Of course, not literally, 'cause then you would have seen us in the trees." It was hard not to smile.

"You daydreaming," Gyle said, coming nose-to-nose with the Englishman. "Get your head out your ass. If this was real, you're now captured or dead." Gyle turned away, heading for the trail, but stopped and turned back, adding, "And I'm Puerto Rican, *pendejo*."

"Fuck you!" Lansdale shouted as Gyle and Carlos disappeared into the forest. "There's dozens more soldiers out here!"

"If they're anything like you," Gyle called back, "we shouldn't have a problem."

Carlos continued along the trail, checking his watch: Eleven-forty-two. They still had the best part of half a mile to negotiate in thirteen minutes. He wondered if Lansdale's statement was meant to scare them, or if there *were* more soldiers out here. Barely had the thought entered his head when he felt the presence of someone nearby. He tried to move, to react, but something cold came to rest against his jaw before he could; a rifle. In his peripheral vision he could see someone else had a gun to Gyle's head too, but before he could turn that direction a figure, clad in black and wearing a ski mask, stepped in front of him. A third man. A leader, judging from his gait and demeanour. Carlos realised his clothing differed from Lansdale and Fromm's. The black Nomex suit was familiar to him. Force Recon Marines used a similar one for black operations – during clandestine warfare, night time incursions, and top-secret missions where stealth and anonymity were paramount.

It can't be what you're thinking, Jack!

The leader's eyes moved up and down, back and forth, studying Carlos, their anger visible even in the confines of the mask. "Name and rank!" he barked. The eyes were scary; a steely, almost maniacal, warning that disobedience would not be tolerated. Carlos didn't. Name and rank told no one anything.

"Carlos, Jack. Sergeant-major."

"What is your unit, Carlos?"

"United States Marine Corps."

"Sergeant-Major Carlos of the United States Marine Corps, you are in a CIA facility. Are you aware of that?"

Carlos didn't reply.

"Once more, Sergeant-Major: You are trespassing on CIA ground. Are you fully aware of the consequences of this?"

Carlos remained stock-still, refusing to blink or acknowledge the question. "My name is Carlos, Jack. I am a sergeant-major in the United States Marine Corps. I have nothing else to declare."

The leader came within an inch of Carlos' face, then spoke in a menacing tone: "I will ask this one time only, and if you do not respond, I will put a bullet in both your heads. This is a top-secret facility. What are you doing here!"

As if to prompt a reply, the other two cocked their rifles.

CHAPTER NINETEEN
CRAFTMANSHIP

ATARIC
11:43 EST

Jack Reid had spent the last half hour pacing the main floor, deep in thought. When asked by various employees what he was doing, the answers were laconic and not at all informative.

He'd never known Peter Hunt to be reckless. Not in school, nor college, and certainly not on the regular hunting trips they'd gone on before Hunt's dismissal; the man was the antithesis of recklessness. So why had he seemed so eager to suggest an idea that was, for him, completely out of character? The plan would work, of that Reid had no doubt, but it was not a plan Hunt would ever consider. Unless...

Reid bolted up the stairs. He burst through the door to his office, startling all the men in the room, and yanked the laptop off Hunt's knees. When he looked at it, he saw a new screen open in Visual Basic. Nothing else. No lines of code, no virus to be uploaded to ATARIC's mainframe, just a screen awaiting commands. He noticed also that Hunt had not connected to the network. The power cable was the only lead extending from the laptop.

"You okay, Jack?" Johnson asked with a bemused smile.

His head jerked up, his eyes darting from Johnson to the wall behind. "Yeah – yeah." He nodded. "I'm fine," he said, his mind desperately scrambling for an excuse for his behaviour. "I thought Peter was going to install the new OS on his laptop...and I guess I wanted to make sure he'd wiped it first." He gave a sheepish grin. "Everything appears to fine, though." His gaze locked on Peter. "I have to clear up a small issue downstairs. I'll be two minutes."

The subtle signal and code in Reid's message told Hunt everything. He waited until two minutes had passed and then excused himself from the room. Reid was at the foot of the stairs, his fingers impatiently drumming on the steel banister. Hunt joined him at the bottom and flashed him an angry glare.

"What the hell was that?"

"You tell me, Peter."

"Oh, I see...you *wanna* get caught? If Johnson had half a brain he'd be all over us right now!"

"This 'plan' of yours – where'd you come up with it?"

Hunt frowned, his nostrils flaring. "What's *that* supposed to mean?"

"I've known you my entire life, Peter. You don't have a reckless bone in your body. All of a sudden you're suggesting a plan to upload a virus to ATARIC? You just happened to have a virus on your laptop?"

"No, I'm hacking it together right now. Why do you think I was in Visual Basic?"

"It's not you. You don't suggest wild ideas like that. I should have noticed it sooner, but I guess I was too naïve. You're not interested in money or doing this job for ATARIC. You're only interested in revenge." Reid shook his head, the disappointment etched on his face.

"Is that what you think?" Hunt sighed. "If that's so, Jack, why would I upload a measly virus instead of one that would cripple the company? I've been sitting at home for close to a year. You *know* how good a hacker I am. If I wanted revenge, ATARIC would have viruses in their system every day." He lowered his voice to a whisper and continued, "Truth is, I want my old job back. I want my old *life* back. I miss my wife, my kid, and I miss doing this stuff with you every day."

Reid felt a tinge of sadness and pity. No matter what had

happened in the last year, Hunt was still a close friend. He deserved the benefit of the doubt, but he would keep a close eye on him. "I just have one question: Can we do this?"

"The virus is easy – "

"No. I mean, can we install all these operating systems in time?"

Reid had the look of a man who feared for his job. Hunt could empathise, but he wasn't going to leave himself open to become a scapegoat if they weren't able to complete the job.

"If we get the OS installed on an un-networked terminal first and without any problems, I don't see any reason why not."

Okay." Reid nodded, acknowledging the deflection. "Get that virus uploaded and let's get started on this thing."

Uploading the virus was child's play. Picking the proper drive to put it in – somewhere a virus scanner would search last or wouldn't search at all – that was the problem. ATARIC's virus scanners were high-tech. Ironically, it was Hunt who'd suggested their installation, but that worked in his favour this time.

He'd lied to Reid. He wasn't hacking the virus together now. He'd done so months ago, in the hope he'd get a chance to upload it to ATARIC's system. Not a "measly" one. This one he'd worked on for months, when his mind had been sober enough for him to write it. The computer nerds called it a "Factor X" virus. It would destroy the hard drive of every computer on the network and render them useless. No anti-virus software could detect all the strands. If someone tried to install a new hard drive, the virus would lay dormant until the computer was reformatted and the hard drive installed, and then it would flare up again. This meant new computers would need to be bought – over forty thousand dollars' worth.

But now Hunt was having second thoughts. It wasn't just his livelihood on the line anymore. If he uploaded the Factor X virus, a lot of people would lose their jobs. As much as he still hated ATARIC for what they'd done to him, he couldn't do that to his former co-workers. There had to be another way to get even...

A few weeks before his dismissal, he had discovered a strange anomaly within ATARIC's main file-storage system. The stored data was copied to a backup system somewhere else in the building. Along with keeping a record of users' personal data, it also kept hourly logs of workers' login and logout times, programs installed, websites accessed, and a whole host of other routine checks. This, however, wasn't strange at all. Hunt knew backup storage systems were essential for large companies like ATARIC, and the majority of those checked their workers' computers to see what they did on their breaks. No, the destination of the data afterward was the strange part. After some major hacking, Hunt discovered it was sent through a secure filter to an offsite generic email address: *jamiesignfeld@youmail.com*. When he'd probed a little farther, he'd found the email address to be non-existent and the amount of data being sent five times what ATARIC's computers accumulated daily.

A quick visit to the mail provider told him their daily limit – nothing close to what was actually being sent. That had sounded alarm bells. After some phishing, he procured an administrator's login details for the mail provider and discovered there was no email address under that name, nor were there any registered Jamie Signfelds at *all*. The email address was bogus, but data was being sent *somewhere* by the hour. And along with it another five times as much...*what?* he'd wondered at the time. What files could possibly be that size, and why would they be sent *away* from ATARIC? The secrecy part hadn't surprised him.

During his first week of unemployment, when Karen had still been living with him and he hadn't progressed to alcoholism again, Hunt decided to do a little sleuthing on ATARIC's clandestine operations. As most computer programmers do, he'd left a backdoor into the system, but to his horror he'd discovered that, barely twenty-four hours after being fired, his account had been erased. Not only that, but Reid had changed his own password also. So, he spent a few hours on ATARIC's website studying the names of all its current employees. Then, he Googled those names to find out if any of them had Web pages of their own, and found most had accounts on Facebook or other social networking sites. There, he discovered that many of them had posted personal details, including names of spouses and children. With this information, gaining access had taken only a matter of hours.

There, he'd encountered his first setback. As an

administrator, Hunt had access to the majority of ATARIC's systems, but his hacked account had no privileges. He couldn't access the data storage system, and didn't want to hack it because he had no idea of the security involved.

For the following week, he played the scenario out in his head repeatedly, trying to find some explanation for it. His epiphany came when his electricity bill arrived. After more studying, he learned a company with five hundred computers would use around four thousand kilowatts of power in a ten-hour day. He knew the computers were all shut down at night (Fielding had been adamant about that) so it would make sense that scant power would be consumed thereafter. A difficult hack of the local electricity company revealed that the daily power consumption exceeded eight thousand kilowatts – enough to power a computer company twice the size of ATARIC.

Whatever that backup system did, it used the same amount of power as five hundred ordinary computers. That kind of power consumption was something Peter Hunt had never encountered in his computing life.

CHAPTER TWENTY
OFFICE OF PROFESSIONAL
RESPONSIBILITY

GRAND CENTRAL PARKWAY WEST
QUEENS
NEW YORK CITY
11:45 EST

"Listen, I don't give a good goddamn what you have to do! I want his records unsealed *now* and on my desk before lunch. If you need any more clarification, I'll have Director Baker on the horn before you can say 'what the hell'. All right?" Forrester demanded. He was in the backseat of an FBI jeep heading northwest towards the New York field office. Beside him, Hollingsworth cut a forlorn figure as he stared at the passing trees along the parkway. Forrester paid him no attention, listening to the response from the other end instead. Satisfied with it, he thanked the man and hung up.

"What was that about?" Hollingsworth asked, continuing to stare out the window.

"Nothing *you* need to worry about, Hollingsworth. You've got more important things at hand. When we get back to the office, there'll be an OPR representative waiting for you. He'll have a few questions to ask you."

Hollingsworth finally turned away from the window. There came a look of concern first, followed by anger. "What are you saying? I'm being investigated? Hold on! Were those *my* records you were talking about?"

"I already told you that was nothing you needed to worry about. What did you think was going to happen? You were present when an officer was shot! The Port Authority PD are going to be all over this like stink on shit! They'll wanna question you too. So don't give me the whole 'I'm a victim' look, Dan." Forrester turned and looked out the window. "Unless, of course, you want to tell me what really happened back there," he finished, turning to face Hollingsworth, whose face suddenly turned redder than what remained of Forrester's hair.

Hollingsworth's answer was said with just enough of a menacing tone to make his point but not enough to merit disciplinary action. "I already told you what happened, and frankly I'm getting pissed off with the implication."

"Fine, but you need to be prepared for the possibility of an investigative inquiry. This won't just go away. Until we find Davies and corroborate your story, you'll be the main focus of the PAPD's rage."

Hollingsworth punched the passenger seat in frustration. "Goddamn it, sir! I was shot less than an hour ago, and now what are you telling me – that I'm going to be subject of an investigation for something I didn't do? Respectfully, sir, this is bullshit!"

"And because you were involved in *two* separate shooting incidents, there will need to be a formal investigation. You know that's the SOP in this situation. I'm also putting you down for counselling – "

"Sir – "

"Don't argue! We both know this isn't the first time you were involved in a shooting– "

"Baltimore was different!"

"Stop interrupting me, Dan!" Forrester levelled him an angry glare. "First, you'll be taken to a holding room where the OPR rep will ask you to recount in your own words what happened in both shootings today. He may bring up the Baltimore incident. You need to be prepared for that." Forrester paused on seeing the look of disgust on Hollingsworth's face. He continued, "You will give your full co-operation during this hearing, Hollingsworth. If I find out you've been in any way insubordinate, I will place you under house arrest and detain you at Twenty-Six Federal Plaza until the investigation is complete."

"You can't do that!"

"Oh, I can and will. I don't like seeing fellow agents being investigated, but we also have a credo in the FBI – a code that agents live and die by. 'Fidelity, bravery, integrity'. I'm assuming they taught you that at Quantico. So, if I believe an agent has done something that goes against that code, it's my duty to report it."

"I haven't done anything that goes against the code! You're making unfounded accusations with zero proof to back them up! You're going to crucify me because of something that happened five years ago! Baltimore was a righteous shoot, dammit!" Hollingsworth gestured with a finger and continued, "I'll tell you something right now – I am *not* going down for something I didn't do. I will fight tooth-and-claw with you on this, and I don't care if it costs me my job. You're not going to sully my reputation with this *bull*shit."

"Your reputation was already sullied, Dan. And Baltimore was *anything* but a righteous shoot. I don't know what strings you pulled to keep your job after that fiasco, but if you're found out to have *any* involvement in what happened at LaGuardia today, I'll make it my business to see you really *are* crucified."

CHAPTER TWENTY-ONE
KNOWNS AND UNKNOWNS

HARVEY POINT
11:46 EST

Carlos wanted to spit it out on his polished boots, or maybe in the eyehole of his mask, but that would only incur more wrath. Damned if those M-16s didn't have one hell of a sturdy stock, he thought, spitting the blood as far away from the leader's body as he could. He ran his tongue around the inside of his mouth a couple of times to check for any loose teeth that might choke him. Then, he turned his gaze back to his captor, giving him a look that said "is that all you've got?"

The leader nodded to the nearest man, who drew back the M-16 for another onslaught. This one, though, was mercifully lower. The diminutive lackey smashed the stock into his solar plexus with all the might he could muster. Only superhuman conditioning prevented Carlos from erupting in laughter when it hit his rock-solid abdominal muscles and stopped with a muffled thump. Behind the mask, the eyes darted left and right, horrified Carlos hadn't doubled over in agony.

"Goddamnit!" The leader stormed over and grabbed the rifle. "Gimme that!"

Carlos prepared himself for another attack on his stomach, but the leader stepped behind him and jabbed the M-16 into his kidney instead. Pain erupted up the left-hand side of his body. Searing, burning agony that caused him to buckle over. The leader raised his foot and shoved it into Carlos' behind. He collapsed, and with his hands secured behind his back with rope, fell face-first into a puddle of muddy water.

Big mistake, you son of a bitch. You'll pay for that.

"Get him back on his feet!"

Both men seized Carlos around the stomach and yanked him to a standing position. Across the way, he saw Gyle tense as though he wanted to do something to protect his commander. Using only his eyes, Carlos warned him to cool it. The time would come for that. Whoever these people were, they had no intention of killing either him or Gyle. If they had, Carlos would already be dead for not answering the leader's earlier question. No, this was something else. Scare tactics, probably. Maybe even a test to see what the newbies were made of. For all Carlos knew, this might even be an initiation – a hazing, of sorts.

On that idea, he had an unnerving thought: *What if this isn't what we were told it was? Oh, shit! What if this is SERE!*

A Survival, Evasion, Resistance, and Escape drill would explain the secrecy, the location, the men with masks, but not the removal from Afghanistan during the middle of a war. *Could it be possible? Would they actually pull us out of a war for a goddamned test? Why would Baxter lie? To set us at ease? To make us think we were going to a CIA facility?*

Whatever this was, one thing Carlos knew for certain was that, one way or another, they were being tested. And if they failed or broke under duress, their military career would be over.

"Take them to the holding cells." The leader turned his gaze to Carlos, and with a grin, added, "We have people there who'll be a little more forbearing."

Even though Carlos didn't show any signs of fear, the leader laughed.

***

They threw Gyle in first, ten minutes later, having stripped him of everything except his underwear. Next, the lackey tried to throw Carlos in, but only succeeded in making him stumble across the threshold. Angered with the looks of amusement in the eyes of his comrades, he smashed his stock into Carlos' other kidney, felling him. This time, though, his hands were free to protect his face.

Gyle had seen enough. But before he'd moved two yards, Carlos' aggressor re-gripped his weapon and spun it to face him.

"Don't even think about it. Back against the wall!"

He knew it was futile to resist. He needed to know what they were up against first, before he could formulate any kind of plan. It didn't make seeing his commander treated like that any easier, though.

"Whatever you say," Gyle replied, retreating. "But just so you know, I'll be getting my clothes back, *pendejo*."

The lackey laughed and closed the door of the cell. "Sure you will."

He bent down to examine his commander. "You okay, *Papi*?"

Carlos gave a grunt in reply. "Help me up."

When he had him back on his feet, Gyle said, "Damn, *mano*. You're one hell of an *oso*. You didn't even grunt when he hit you."

"I'm too strong for my own good, Julio." Carlos laughed weakly.

"I think I'll call you 'Bear' from now on." Gyle gave him a smile and a light slap on the back.

"I've been called worse things."

Gyle laughed. "In all seriousness, though, just what the hell have we got ourselves into here?"

Carlos wished he had the answer. As he moved gingerly around the room, he studied the walls, the bars of the cell, and the single bed against the back wall. Above the cell door, he noticed a small-framed camera recessed into the stone. He nodded to Gyle and arced his eyes that direction. He gave the slightest nod in return and moved along the side wall, slithering his way to the cell door until he could manoeuvre under the camera's blind spot. There, he studied the device for a few seconds, then moved back to his earlier position.

"Stationary camera. It's covering the bed and the exit. No swivel. No mic either...Bear." Gyle gave him a grin. "Just a video feed. They can't hear us."

Carlos shook his head and whispered, "I'm betting they can, Julio. They want us to think they can't. Okay, huddle in," Carlos ordered. He gestured to a corner outside the camera's scope, and both huddled together on their hunkers. Carlos began, whispering, "It's some kind of test. Don't know what. Could be an initiation hazing or something. Might even be SERE." He looked to Gyle to see how he digested that, but he didn't even flinch.

"It's too elaborate for it to be a SERE drill, Sergeant-Major. No way they'd pull us out of Afghanistan for that."

"Maybe, maybe not. But it's a test. If it's for a new anti-terror team, or if it's a SERE drill, doesn't matter. We fail, we're out. And I ain't getting kicked out of Fore-con for this crap."

"*Semper Fi!*"

"*Semper Fi!*" Carlos gave a nod of approval. "We stay tough, we stay strong, we stick together. They're gonna try and break us. Name, rank, unit – no more. We clear?"

"I ain't even telling them that much. *Pendejos.*"

"That's what I like to hear, Master-Sergeant. If it's SERE, it's three days. Keep your mind strong. God knows what they plan to do to us."

"What about part four?"

Carlos nodded. "We find a way, do it. Day or night – doesn't matter. Plenty of places to hide out here. We get out, head for the EOD. I want answers."

"Damn straight. You okay to go another round?"

"I'm good. They'll maim me before I break."

Gyle smiled. "Yeah, I'm *definitely* calling you 'Bear' from now on!"

"Whatever happens, don't let them fool you. I'm not breaking, you're not breaking. They'll try to make us believe the other has turned." Carlos turned his eye to the camera, making doubly sure he was out of its range. He then ran a finger along his upper lip, whispering, "This is the signal for 'A-Okay'. He moved the finger to his forehead and swiped it across in the same manner. "That's 'danger'. Got it?"

"*Alto y claro,*" replied Gyle, meaning "loud and clear".

"It won't happen, but if they do manage to break one of us, remember the signals."

"They ain't breaking me, *Papi*." Gyle's steely look of determination demonstrated how serious that statement was.

"Okay, I dunno where the listening devices are, but if you need to say anything you don't want them to know, say it in Spanish. Less chance there's someone here who understands it." Carlos hadn't lied about his heritage; he *was* an American citizen... but he *could* speak fluent Spanish.

"What about the Swiss?" Gyle asked with a wink. "If I can get past the fatigue."

"I'm afraid your foreign cousin's gonna have to wait, Julio. Too early for sex on the first date."

Gyle nodded. The code was simple, though ingenious. He'd reminded Carlos about the Swiss Army knife inside his military fatigues. Carlos had replied by saying it was too early to think of responding with violence. Along with using Spanish, they could communicate this way without giving anything away.

There was a rustle of keys at the cell door. Carlos looked up to see the leader open it, a bemused smile on his face. From what he could see, tattoos lined his entire body. His hair was shaved tight to the scalp, revealing a scar barely half an inch wide by about four inches long. It looked like someone had taken an axe to his skull but hadn't succeeded in finishing the job.

"I think your friend is more interested in the opposite sex." The leader laughed, nodding to Julio. "The Swiss cousin a six-foot man, soldier?" he asked with another laugh. "You boys getting all hot and bothered in here, eh?"

"You must have misheard, *pendejo*. I didn't say 'Swiss'. I said 'your momma'."

"Take him away," he ordered his two lackeys.

The first one secured Gyle's hands behind his back, while the other snuck in behind Carlos and dealt another savage blow to his kidneys. Carlos doubled over, unable to prevent the groan escaping from his lips.

"So, you are human after all. Don't worry; you're next," the diminutive one said with a cruel, mocking grin.

"I look forward to it," Carlos replied, locking eyes with his aggressor.

The door closed again, and Carlos moved to the bed. It

would be a long couple of days, and he needed all the rest he could get. He had barely placed his head on the mattress when Gyle's first roar of pain pierced the humid North Carolinian air.

It wasn't a drill. Nor a test. Not anymore.

No, now it was personal.

PART II

Divide and Conquer

12:00 – 16:00

CHAPTER TWENTY-TWO
ARRIVAL

```
PRIVATE AIRFIELD
VALLEY STREAM
QUEENS
NEW YORK CITY
12:03 EST
```

Vladimir Pushkin would think twice before accepting another mission from Pavel Kirov. To his great relief, the Tupolev Tu-144 had slowed to a merciful speed and not the cruising one of 1,430 miles per hour at which it had careered across the Atlantic Ocean. A journey which would have lasted anywhere up to eight hours on a commercial flight, took little over three in Kirov's behemoth jet. The fact that he'd given it to Pushkin to fly halfway across the world was suggestive of the importance of this mission.

Kirov had a long-standing relationship with many of the airports in Russia – under falsified names and identifications, of course – but the same was not true in America. His contacts there, though, had arranged a significant bribe for the owner of Rogers Airfield, who happily took the fee and turned a blind eye to the landing. As an additional precaution, the Tu-144's transponder had been turned off.

The Tupolev taxied to a stop along the only runway, and

Pushkin made his way to the cockpit to inform the pilot he'd find his own way back to Russia. The pilot informed *him* that he'd been instructed to refuel and fly back to Russia immediately, in any case.

The landing stairs were extended and he stepped out onto the taxiway, greeted by a man dressed in a three-piece suit. A pair of sunglasses hid his eyes, though Pushkin could tell from the slight quiver of his lower lip that the young man was afraid. A goatee and ridiculous Elvis-style sideburns made him look like TV's stereotypical Texan, but Pushkin knew the facial hair had an altogether different purpose; to give him the appearance of being older and more experienced than his otherwise youthful face conveyed. Behind him was a ubiquitous SUV, entirely black except for its windows. Tinted windows only drew unwanted attention.

"Who are you?" Pushkin spoke in English for the first time in months, unsure of whether or not Elvis Junior spoke Russian. He certainly didn't look Russian.

"I'm Gray...um, Kenneth Gray. Kirov sent me to...well, I'm your driver."

Gray looked like he would have preferred to be anywhere else but here. He didn't know whether to offer his hand, take Pushkin's luggage, or say something else. In the end, he took the middle choice, stored Pushkin's belongings in the trunk, and opened the door to the backseat.

"Something wrong with me sitting in the front?" inquired Pushkin with a raised eyebrow.

Gray slammed it shut as quickly as he'd opened it, and said, "No, sorry. It's just...I usually...I mean, my usual passengers sit in the back."

"There's nothing 'usual' about me, Gray," Pushkin replied, grabbing the handle of the passenger door before Gray could. "And I can open my own fucking doors, okay?"

Gray nodded. "Yes, sir."

"Let's get one thing straight: I don't like being treated as some kind of invalid. I don't need drivers, lackeys to open doors for me, or any other pampering from Kirov. I work alone. Now, I'm going back to the jet to get the remainder of my things. When I come back, the only thing I want to see on that runway is your SUV. Not you. Got that?"

"But Kirov – " Gray didn't know why he was protesting, but the words found their way out of his mouth. He was relieved when

Pushkin stopped him mid-sentence.

"You let me worry about Kirov. I will not make the offer twice. Get out of here."

Gray nodded, and was gone before Pushkin had turned his back.

Pushkin shook his head, walked to the back of the SUV and shut the trunk, then slipped into the driver's seat. The two cases in the back were the only items he'd brought with him. One of them was filled with weapons; the other, money.

Kirov had provided him with a safe house in Brooklyn, and the first port of call was to stash the money there. Pushkin trusted Kirov would not try to reclaim it or do anything foolish like that. He had a special bullet reserved just in case he did.

The ironic part was Ivanovich's involvement. Right this moment, the notorious former KGB agent was on a commercial flight to New York City, having left a couple of hours before Pushkin. He would not be here for at least another three. Soon thereafter, he would likely be instructed to begin a mission that, regardless of the outcome, would result in his death.

For the most part, Pushkin believed Kirov wanted it that way. He had no compunction when it came to killing people who'd failed him – another reason why Pushkin had in waiting a bullet with Kirov's name on it. He'd learned that to get by in this business you needed to prepare for every contingency.

He started the car, shifted into drive, and found his way off the airfield to the nearest road. There, he stopped and punched in the address Kirov had given him. The GPS pinpointed the locale and gave him the most optimal route as well as a timeframe and alternative routes if traffic proved to be a problem.

First, he'd stash the money and most of the weapons. Kirov had eccentric habits when it came to supplying his workers with arms. The second case had a Dragunov SVD sniper rifle, a couple of nine-millimetre Makarovs, hand grenades, an Uzi nine-millimetre, and a H&K MP5-SD. Either he thought Pushkin was a horrible shot, or he had a thing for overkill. Either way, Pushkin didn't need the hassle or danger of carrying around that amount of weapons. A single Makarov would be enough.

He needed to find Davies before he could use it, though.

If only he'd known that the man he sought was less than twenty miles away.

CHAPTER TWENTY-THREE
SAFETY DEPOSIT

WASHINGTON MUTUAL BANK
BROOKLYN
NEW YORK CITY
12:05 EST

Troy Davies exited the cab and handed the driver the necessary fare plus the hundred-dollar note he'd promised him. The man took it and sped off in case Davies changed his mind. He'd done excellent work to negotiate the traffic, and Davies wasn't going to argue with him over five minutes in any case. Besides, along with his photo-ID card, the safe deposit box also held an additional forty thousand dollars of emergency money. Funds were one thing he didn't lack.

The passport in his pocket identified him as "Karl Williams", an altogether ubiquitous name in a city like New York. It listed his occupation as a freelance information-technology consultant, and he could give a thirty-minute discourse on the ins and outs of computers with complete ease. Two other passports hidden inside the fabric of his bag identified him as two completely different men whose occupations and mannerisms he could assume in the blink of an eye.

For all his exorbitant habits over the last eighteen months, for all the weight he'd put on, Davies was much the same man he'd been two years earlier when Jonathan Baker had made an unannounced visit to his house and asked him to make the biggest decision of his life.

The FBI's bailiwick was not espionage, and as such they didn't have agents trained in the art of deep-cover infiltration. Davies was the closest thing they had – a veteran law-enforcer (with no immediate family to inquire as to his whereabouts) who'd been undercover in various sting operations on American soil, but never anything as elaborate or dangerous as what Baker had suggested. It seemed more akin to something the CIA would have undertaken, and Davies had gone as far as to ask why *they* hadn't attempted to infiltrate Kirov's administration. For all the CIA's awareness of foreign terrorists, though, they had no knowledge of Pavel Kirov or the arms trafficking he was believed to engage in.

After some reluctance and a few months to mull the offer over, he agreed to Baker's proposal. The next morning a car arrived at his home. He was taken to an undisclosed location in the middle of a forest, where he'd spent the next year being taught the art of deep-cover infiltration from an ex-officer of the CIA's Special Activities Division, a highly secretive covert organisation who specialised in the art of collecting intelligence from foreign and hostile countries. Along with Director Baker, Deputy Director Forrester, and President Walsh, this man was the only other person who knew the full details of the sting operation.

And at this moment, he was the only one Davies could trust.

In his house Davies had a safe containing the small amount of paperwork he'd been given in the lead-up to the sting operation. He'd been trusted to burn it, but those surveillance notes, subject profiles, and detailed blueprints of Kirov's mansion were his insurance against an attempt on his life. Among them were the contact details for the ex-officer. First, he needed to get his photo-ID card.

He felt like screaming. All this running through hoops and he was no closer to the finish line. He wanted to tell someone what he knew, but it seemed there were people on both sides who wanted him dead. As much as he wanted to, he couldn't break cover now. Not until he knew who he could trust. His information in the wrong hands could do more damage than Kirov's plan. He would have to remain disciplined until the opportunity to end all this presented itself. He'd done it for the last three years. What was a few more days?

The Washington Mutual bank on West Seventeenth Street, Brooklyn – a dull, brown-brick building on the corner of an intersection – was not the kind of bank you would expect someone of Davies' stature to use, but that was the point. Positioned around a half-dozen other banks within two miles, this one was the last place anyone would think of checking.

Davies walked through the white-marble portico, keeping his head down, and headed for the middle desk. Behind it, he found a middle-aged woman typing furiously with one hand and holding a phone with the other. She gave him a signal to wait one minute and he nodded in a subserviently. He'd been taught that loud or obnoxious people stood out. The ones that were the least memorable were those who were polite, reserved, and somewhat reticent.

While he waited he scanned the interior. There were three security guards; two on the exits and one roaming around the floor. The bank continued around a small corner, behind which was a row of private desks and, further on, the entrance to the safety deposit boxes. It had been almost two years since Davies had last been here. He couldn't remember if there was a third exit in the private section. He didn't think so. If the need arose, he would exit through the second door, out onto West Sixteenth Street, shake his pursuers, and double back to the door he'd first entered.

There were also two stationary cameras; one above each door. From his current position, neither had the range to pick him up in an identifiable way. He remembered there was another one in the safety deposit room, which might cause more trouble than he'd anticipated. Though he was almost convinced no one would ever think to check this bank, he hadn't survived for so long by taking chances.

In the far corner, on a bench beside the second exit, he saw someone had forgotten their New York Yankees baseball cap. The bench was currently unoccupied, but it was too close to the camera for Davies to think of trying to pilfer the cap. It would raise too much suspicion if he tried to do so while avoiding the camera's line of sight.

"--take you now, sir."

Davies turned around, wondering how long the woman had been talking. He flashed her an embarrassed smile and said, "I beg your pardon? I'm afraid I missed that." He was angry at himself for allowing his mind to wander. Strange people were memorable, and he could not afford to be memorable at this point.

"I'm able to take you now. Sorry about the delay."

Davies shook his head. "Not at all. I was just admiring the aesthetics," he said with an embarrassed laugh.

"They get less admirable when you have to look at them every day." She returned the laugh. "What can I do for you, Mr...?"

"Williams. Karl Williams," Davies replied, producing his passport. "I've come in to withdraw the contents of my safe deposit box."

The woman nodded. "I see. Do you have your account number, Mr Williams?"

"I have it...now where did I write it down?" Davies made a show of trying to remember, even though he'd burned the number into his brain years before. People who recited their account numbers from memory raised more suspicion than a disorganised but charming man from out of town. After thirty seconds of fumbling, he withdrew a slip of paper, saying, "Ah! Here it is." He read the number off the slip, squinting at every other digit; it was all a part of the act. He wanted his mannerisms, vocal tones, and behaviour to be completely different to Troy Davies'. That way, no one could make a connection between his real identity and the bumbling computer consultant Karl Williams.

The woman finished typing on the keyboard and said, "Mr Williams, if you'll just sign this," she said, producing a slip of paper, "you'll be ready to go."

Davies hesitated for a moment, trying to remember how he'd signed his name as "Karl Williams". He quickly grabbed the piece of paper to avoid raising suspicion, and wrote the letter "K" down as slowly as he dared until the signature pattern came back to him. When he'd finished, the woman took it with a smile and checked it against the signature on file.

After an agonising minute, she said, "Okay, Mr Williams.

Everything appears to be in order. Here's your key." She handed over a golden key with the insignia of the bank engraved on both sides. "Box number twenty-eight." She raised her hand and clicked her fingers. The security guard who'd been roaming the floor started to approach. "This man will accompany you and see that everything is to your satisfaction."

He turned around to view the approaching guard, keeping his face as impassive as possible. "Is that entirely necessary?" This was not an act.

"I'm afraid it's standard procedure, Mr Williams. The security guard must check that no one else is in the safe deposit room. For your safety, you see. It is not meant to be an inconvenience."

Davies nodded and then shook his head. "No, no – it's okay. It's been a while since I was here and I'd forgotten about the procedure."

"That's quite okay, sir. When you've finished your business, leave the key back with me. Have a good day, Mr Williams."

He nodded again and thanked her. The security guard led him around the corner, past the rows of desks where more sounds of furious typing mixed with conversation could be heard, and stopped outside the safe deposit room. Here, he raised his hand and told Davies to wait while he checked the interior. Davies got the feeling this was the part of the job the young man loved. It wasn't every day you got to boss around people who earned considerably more than you.

After two or three minutes, the guard returned and gave the A-okay. He held open the door for Davies, waited until he went inside, and closed it without accompanying him. Davies immediately scanned for the camera. He spotted it above the middle of the chamber, swivelling to take in the entire room. Tilting his head downward again, he moved at a brisk pace, passing the boxes in numerical order until he arrived at the third row and number fourteen. There, he inserted the key, opened the door, and slid out a black lockbox. Davies had always been a cautious man. He'd stored the belongings in his own lockbox (as many clients did) and carried the key, along with the fake passports, in the fabric of his bag. Stuck to the top of the box was a seal that remained undisturbed. There was no way to open the box without breaking it, so he knew nothing had been tampered with.

He stored the lockbox in his bag, closed and locked the door, and kept his head down on the way back. After one knock the guard pulled the door open.

"Everything to your liking, sir?" he inquired.

"Everything is fine, thank you."

"Do you require an escort to your vehicle?"

Davies shook his head. "That won't be necessary. Thank you for your hospitality."

"My pleasure, sir. Make sure you return your key, and have a nice day."

Davies made his way back around the corner, careful not to look directly at the camera on the rear exit. He stopped at the desk, and with a friendly smile handed the key back to the woman, thanking her, too, for her hospitality.

On his way towards the exit, he noticed the baseball cap had been lifted from the bench. He praised himself for not attempting to lift it earlier, as it would have probably caused a scene when the person returned to find it missing. But as he turned back to the door his eyes caught the familiar insignia, and for the briefest of seconds he allowed his gaze to settle on the wearer of the cap. The man was watching him, and when Davies caught his eye, he quickly looked the other way. He tried to calm down by reassuring himself people generally acted that way when they were caught staring, but alarm bells were ringing.

Davies changed course to the left, angling from the exit and keeping his head tilted away from the camera. He reached a rack with different pamphlets on it and picked up one on loans. As he began "reading", he turned and walked directly towards the camera, keeping the pamphlet above the bridge of his nose. At the entrance, below the camera's blind spot, he stopped and took inventory. The man was standing in the same place, his feet absently tapping the ground as if to suggest impatience. He didn't look in the direction of Davies, instead keeping his eyes on the desks and occasionally glancing to his wristwatch.

There was something about his demeanour, though, that Davies didn't like. His mannerisms appeared too contrived, almost as though he knew someone was watching. If that were true, it meant he had had experience in adopting false personas. The way he held himself, too, screamed "agent". Not "detective" or "police officer". There was something distinct about how a government agent held themselves; a conceited swagger barely visible in some, ever-present in others, but there in every single one. That was something even the highest ranking officer or detective never displayed.

Or maybe Davies was being paranoid. One could only spend so much time looking over one's shoulder before everyone became a potential threat. The milkman could be a spy. The weirdly dressed man in the mall could be a hired gun. The mind began playing tricks. The bulge in a pair of trousers – in reality a bunch of keys – became the shape of a firearm. The man staring at you in a bank became an agent, when in reality he might just fancy you. When paranoia gripped to its full extent, nothing on earth could compare to the fear. It petrified you, rendered you unable to move, and turned you into a walking time-bomb. Davies had already walked that path, and he did not want to again.

Slowly, he set the pamphlet down on a windowsill and eased through the exit, back on to Seventeenth Street, eyeing the Yankee as he did. The man made no effort to move, nor did he look in Davies' direction. Davies turned left, walked along the side of the bank to a crossing, and jogged to the other side. Going on to Sixteenth Street now would be stupid. Instead, he slipped into a food store on the corner of Mermaid Avenue and stopped just inside the door. From there he could see the bank exit clearly. He waited five minutes but not a single person exited.

Aware that people in the store were beginning to stare, he stepped out onto the street and flagged down a taxi. Like he had at LaGuardia, he checked to see if anyone was watching, and when satisfied, slipped into the back seat and told the driver to take him to Seagate.

CHAPTER TWENTY-FOUR
FRONTIERS

WHITE HOUSE SITUATION ROOM
WASHINGTON, D. C.
12: 10 EST

President Walsh's eyes locked onto General Peterson and, through gritted teeth, he said, "What are you telling me, Chad?"

Charles "Chad" Peterson looked around the room for some kind of backup and, when none was offered, said, "I'm telling you it won't succeed, sir. That is my professional opinion."

The President glared at him. "You already said that. Now I want to know why. You can't tell me this won't succeed without showing me some kind of proof to back that up. So where is your proof, General?"

Peterson sighed, folded his arms. "The territory is unknown. We have no men in any of our Special Forces groups who have been to this location, Mr President. *None.* With all due respect, sir, what you are suggesting is doomed to failure."

Peterson had been vocally supportive of the President's decision to send more forces into Iraq and Afghanistan, but this was different. Walsh was considering sending troops to the Northwest Frontier Province of Pakistan, and the 61-year-old Chairman of the Joint Chiefs did not approve. Not only was the terrain treacherous, even for the locals, the province also sat between Jalalabad and Islamabad, home to numerous Islamic, Afghani, and Pakistani freedom fighters. It was a suicide mission; but sketchy intelligence reports had indicated that Sayid bin Laden, Osama's half-brother, had been seen in the province days earlier. Rumour had it he was overseeing the training of Islamic jihadists, having been sent there by Osama. The President had called for an immediate meeting today and had, minutes earlier, announced his plan to send half a dozen Spec Ops units into the territory to scout for Sayid. But the President would not bow to Peterson's recommendation to confirm the intelligence first. He wanted teams in the region yesterday, and Peterson knew how stubborn Walsh was; he would not change his mind unless confronted with solid proof the mission had no chance of succeeding.

"With all due respect to you, General, I think that's a bunch of crap." Walsh turned his gaze to the rest of the table. "Does anyone else think our men don't know the territory well enough to succeed out there?" When no one answered, the President looked at General Rogers and sharply said, "Vince, weren't your Force Recon guys close to that region a few months ago?"

The Commandant of the Marine Corps glanced to Peterson – who warned him with a hard stare not to say anything to refute his claim – and then back to the President. "I believe they were in the territory, sir. Maybe not specifically *that* territory, but close enough." Rogers ignored the look of rage on the Chairman's face and continued, "I also believe this is too good an opportunity to pass up. If we get Sayid we stand a good chance of finding where Osama is hiding."

Peterson stabbed an index finger at Rogers and shouted, "You're willing to risk the lives of dozens of soldiers on a goddamn hunch! Do you know how many doppelgängers bin Laden and his kind have? We have *no* solid proof this is even the *real* Sayid." Peterson turned his gaze on the President. "Sir, the probability of us finding Sayid bin Laden there is about a million to one. You send men in, the only thing we'll be unearthing is a dozen more graves at Arlington."

"Jesus Christ, Chad! You're talking like our men aren't the best soldiers in the world," spat Admiral John Beckett. The whey-faced 76-year-old was the Chief of Naval Operations and had served his country for fifty years. While adamant the Navy SEALs were the proper team for this mission, he didn't like anyone downplaying the abilities of any section of the United States military.

Peterson's face flushed. "I'm not saying anything of the sort, John! I'm saying we stand a better chance of finding a homosexual in a brothel! With all due respect to the President, this mission is pointless."

There was a moment of shocked silence while everyone digested what Peterson had said. It was one thing to disagree with a plan of Walsh's. It was quite another to call it "pointless".

The President took a moment to compose himself. He shifted in his seat at the top of the desk, took a deep breath and cleared his throat before saying, "You've made your position on this abundantly clear, Charles, but I'm the Commander-in-Chief of this country and I make the decisions." With that sentence the President froze Peterson out of the conversation. "Admiral," he continued, turning his gaze to the naval commander. "How soon can you have a SEAL team ready for deployment?"

Without hesitation, Beckett replied, "SEAL team five is on standby as we speak. They can be wheels-up and boots on the ground in ten hours, sir."

The President nodded his approval. "Very good. Vince." He turned to the Marine Corps Commandant. "You have a Force Recon team not far from there, I believe."

Rogers hesitated for a moment. "Eh...I believe so, sir." He looked away from the President. "Spin Boldak, I think."

The President ignored the hesitation. "How long would it take to move them into position?"

"A matter of hours, sir." This time he didn't hesitate.

The President nodded. "Give the order, General. Tell them to hold position until the SEALs arrive."

"Yes, sir."

The President eyed the Chief of Staff of the Army, General William Ramsey. "Will, have Delta on standby. I probably won't use them, but it doesn't hurt to have them ready."

The 44-year-old was the youngest man in the room, but the rest respected his opinion nonetheless. "Yes, sir. I'll alert the Colonel right away."

As Admiral Beckett began to establish points of entry and

landing zones, General Peterson's phone bleeped. He apologised with a rise of his hand, turned away from the group, and answered the call. After a few seconds, he hung up. "Pardon me, Mr President, but something has come up that requires my immediate attention. May I be excused?"

"Anything you'd like to share?" The President looked sceptical.

"Nothing that has any relevance here, I'm afraid."

Walsh gave a curt nod. "Okay, Chad. I expect to see you back here tomorrow, and I want you fully behind this mission."

"As you wish, Mr President."

***

Outside, Peterson was joined by his Secret Service detail, who followed the Chairman out of the basement of the West Wing to the main foyer of the White House. There, Peterson told them to wait five minutes, and stepped into his limousine.

He dialled a number from memory and a familiar voice answered after just two rings. "Are you okay to talk?"

Peterson ignored the question. "Why on earth would you call me during a meeting with the President? I'm trying to keep a low-profile about this whole thing, dammit! Do you know what would happen if someone found out about this?"

"I'm sorry, sir, but it's vital we meet immediately."

"I'm on my way back to the Pentagon now. You can meet me in my office in fifteen minutes."

"No way! What I've got to say can't be said there. Can we meet anywhere else?"

"What is this about?"

"I can't say over the phone, but it's definitely something you want to hear, and definitely worth interrupting your meeting over."

"I'll be in the Ritz-Carlton in fifteen minutes."

"I'll be there."

Peterson hung up and instructed his security detail that he was ready to leave. As the car rolled out through the main gates, he began wondering what his man had discovered. It had to be something huge for him to risk calling Peterson during a meeting with the President. He held the position of Sergeant-

Major of the Marine Corps, the highest non-commissioned officer in the field, and served as Peterson's Senior Enlisted Advisor. He was also the Commandant's right-hand man, and privy to almost all information pertaining to the Marines, though Rogers had no idea he also worked for Peterson. It didn't bother Peterson; Rogers was a conniving son of a bitch who hung out others to dry as often as his maid hung out his clothes.

Something fishy was going on though. Peterson had been a general for ten years, never had he been to a meeting in the Situation Room without at least one member of the National Security Council present. But Walsh's main advisors were nowhere to be seen, and that struck the wily old fox as incongruous. The decision to move troops into a foreign country needed to be made with the backing of SecDef. Rainey wasn't there, which meant he'd already acceded to the President's demands to deploy troops, which also meant Rainey had something more important to do.

Peterson wanted to know what.

CHAPTER TWENTY-FIVE
HONOUR

```
ATARIC
12: 16 EST
```

The sound of Harold Johnson's two-hundred-pound body bounding down the stairs from Reid's office was both music to Peter Hunt's ears, and hilarious. After a stop-start last half-hour, Hunt had finally found the most suitable place for the virus and uploaded it to the network. He'd decided not to use the Factor X one. Instead, he'd hacked together a "measly" one which would keep ATARIC's employees guessing for a few hours. Unsurprisingly, it had taken ten minutes before anyone downstairs had noticed its presence.

"What do you mean, 'it's not working'? What's wrong with it?" Johnson's voice could be heard as though he were still standing in the room. "What is it, a *virus*?"

"I... answer... sir... until... know... more," answered what sounded like a terrified worker.

"Start running some goddamn tests. I'll be back in a minute."

The stairs rumbled again, and a few seconds later, Johnson re-entered the office, strode towards Hunt, and levelled a finger at him. "What the hell's going on down there?"

In the corner, a flicker of fear passed across Reid's face, but he composed himself and found something to do.

"What are you talking about, Johnson?" Hunt's face remained nonchalant. Johnson wanted to point the finger at someone, and the most suitable person at this minute was Hunt.

"Something's just happened the entire ATARIC network, and I want to know what the hell it was!" Johnson replied. Blood seeped into his face as he struggled to control his temper.

"Let me guess: You think I had something to do with whatever's happening down there?" Hunt replied with a grunt. In the corner, Reid jerked slightly but caught himself before anyone noticed. They did notice, however – everyone but Johnson and Hunt – the arrival of Dave Haskens, who'd ghosted up the stairs and was standing outside the door listening to the entire conversation.

"It's not a huge leap, Hunt! Within hours of you coming back to ATARIC, the system has a virus in it! And don't feed me some bull about it being a huge coincidence. Pack your stuff. You're outta here."

Before Hunt could make a riposte, Haskens announced his arrival. "Harry, may I have a word with you outside?" For all his tough-man act, Johnson was first and foremost a coward. When Haskens spoke, he jumped like someone had just shot a gun. Swallowing, he turned to Haskens.

"Dave, I was just – "

"*Now*, Harry." Haskens stepped back outside the door and Johnson reluctantly joined him.

Hunt was beginning to think this hadn't been his smartest idea ever. Johnson would tell Haskens about the virus, blaming it on Hunt and, if he was in any way convincing, the chances were he'd be out the door before lunch. He couldn't afford to let that happen. In the next ten minutes, he would find a way to convince Reid to give him administrator privileges – the first step in finding out what was going on at ATARIC. For now, he had to convince Johnson he had nothing to do with the virus.

In the corner, Jake Collins studied Hunt and Reid. Aside from being a millionaire, he also had the astuteness of a man twice his age. He knew something was out of kilter. They were plotting something, and the latest occurrence had done little to convince him otherwise.

"If I'm going to stick around, I want keyed in on whatever it is you two are planning," he announced. His two employees looked up with genuine intrigue, until Collins instructed them, with a hard glare, to get back to work.

Reid's answer was a little too quick and much too defensive. "What are you talking about, Jake? We're not planning anything."

"I've known both of you for years. Before Hunt got fired, you were like peas in a pod. I don't know if you had anything to do with the commotion downstairs, but I know you've been doing something you ought not to have been."

Hunt looked to Collins' employees. "Leave." The two men looked to their boss, who said nothing. "Now!" he said forcefully. "Get out."

Collins nodded his head. "Go get some fresh air."

When they'd left, Hunt exchanged a glance with Reid, who bobbed his head. "We needed Johnson preoccupied with something – anything." He lowered his voice and continued, "We had to get him out of the picture. None of us were going to be able to work with him staring at us. I know how this must sound, but believe me, we would never jeopardise this company." He paused, wondering how true that statement was. "Harry Johnson is a sycophant, Jake. He'll do anything to prove to Jim Fielding and Dave Haskens that he knows what he's doing. I knew if there was a problem with the system he'd be all over it."

Collins nodded slowly, allowing Hunt's confession time to sink in. After thirty seconds, he said, "What would happen if either Haskens or Johnson learned of this?"

"We'd probably be fired," Hunt replied.

"No 'probably' about it. We'd be out of here faster than Johnson sprinted down those stairs," Reid replied with a laugh.

Collins nodded again, a tiny smile forming in the corners of his lips. "I guess me and Harold Johnson have a little talking to do, then."

Both men's eyes opened wide.

CHAPTER TWENTY-SIX
COURAGE

HARVEY POINT
12:20 EST

Carlos' attempt at sleep had lasted a mere five minutes. The toughest soldiers were trained to sleep in the roughest locales, but when the screams of brothers-in-arms pierced the air, sleep was unattainable. Not to mention the daylight that skewered into the room through the bars of the cell. So he had paced around, studying the bars, walls, and any other areas that might be vulnerable. He'd avoided the camera as best he could.

Then the screaming stopped. Five minutes passed. Ten. No sign of Gyle, no more screaming.

It had now been fifteen minutes. Were they finished with him? Had he broken? Or were they letting him rest before starting up again?

These questions sounded off in his head and, as the time passed, his pace quickened. Julio was his friend, and Julio was being tortured. All throughout his career Carlos had made an oath not to leave a fallen man behind. He wasn't going to break it now. Whoever these people were, they'd just savaged a Marine, and Marines were brothers. What you did to one, you did to all.

Semper Fidelis – Always Faithful.

It was written all over Carlos' face. These men fought together and would die for each other. No amount of orders, drills, or tests would ever change that. By torturing Gyle, regardless of the reasoning, they'd just made the biggest mistake of their lives. And if that son of a bitch Triton was here, Carlos would maim him.

He knew the biggest part of withstanding torture was the mentality of the person being tortured. Gyle had said he would never break, but every man had a breaking point. If you prodded hard enough, there were ways to make a person talk. The human threshold for pain, even in those soldiers who'd been readied for the possibility of capture during SERE school, lowered the longer torture lasted. Some people lasted days, others months, rare ones sometimes years, but break enough bones, crack enough ribs, and everyone got to the same place: "*Enough, please!*". Torture was inhumane, but prolonged bouts of it yielded results. And for the all the military's codes and rules and drills, they were primarily in the business of getting results.

Carlos grunted at the thought. For twenty years he'd served his country admirably and dutifully. He'd *gotten* results. He'd survived missions where dozens of his comrades had died. He'd gone from a scrawny private to leader of a fearsome group of Force Recon Marines. And now what? They'd pulled him from Afghanistan to test his loyalty? To see if he had what it took to lead a new fearsome group of soldiers? *Then test* me! *Leave Julio alone and try and break* me!

He hid his fear well on the outside, but on the inside he was breaking up. Gyle meant more to him than a terrific soldier and second-in-command. He was a brother. Neither man had a girlfriend or wife, but when off-duty both shared an apartment in El Paso, Texas. They liked to pull pranks, sabotage each other's meals, and generally make asses of themselves. When work called, though, they returned to commander and second-in-command. But when alone on missions, they still riled and cracked jokes. Carlos was certain their kind of bond occurred in only three places: Between mother and child, husband and wife, and men who had faced death together. The latter was what made the bond between soldiers so great, and why many considered their teammates more than just teammates. When you stared Death in the eye with someone and survived, it changed your outlook; changed your perception. And with every scream of Gyle's, Carlos felt his muscles clench, his body ache, and his temper surge to the surface.

The sound of a baton clanging across each bar of the cell broke his reverie. He looked up and noticed the diminutive scumbag from earlier. *You're the first one. Yeah, smile all you want, you little bastard. I'm going to take pleasure in wiping that smile away.*

"Your mate isn't doing too well." He paused and then, with a smile, added, "We had to stop for a while. But he's in bad shape. One of the guys got a little too eager...cut him real bad." He paused again to let that sink in.

For a split second, Carlos' eyes showed a flicker of fear, but he curbed it quickly. "You're lying."

He shook his head. "'Fraid not. Looks like you got a bit of a dilemma, but I'll lay it out for you. If you tell us what it is you're doing here, we'll let you go and you can take your friend to the nearest hospital. Hell, we'll even give you transport."

Carlos looked down to the ground, torn between recognising a lie and trying to protect his best friend – his *brother*. What was a career compared to a man's life? *No, this is what you warned Julio about! You said they'd try to play us against each other – use our relationship to make us talk. Don't do it! But Julio's life – Julio is fine! They're not going to risk killing him, no matter who the hell they are! There are rules! These people aren't terrorists. They play by the rules just like everyone else.*

But what kind of rules allowed for this fiasco?

"My name is Carlos, Jack. I am a sergeant-major in the United States Marine Corps. Do what you will."

"Oh, we will, but we won't do it to you." The man laughed. "We'll do it to him. How long will you be able to sit there knowing your friend is getting closer and closer to death? How long before you'll put his life over the rules of your unit? Will you let him die before you tell us what you're doing here?"

"Carlos, Jack, sergeant-major, United States Marine Corps," he replied defiantly.

The man laughed again. "As you wish, 'Carlos, Jack, sergeant-major, United States Marine Corps'," he mocked. "I'll be back in thirty minutes. I just hope your mate can hold out that long."

As the man walked away from the cell, Carlos jumped off the bed and sprinted to the bars to look out. He watched him walk back into the forest to the east, where he disappeared into the foliage after fifty yards. Carlos glanced around the rest of the immediate area, checking for any lingering guards. There didn't look to be any, and the grass had not been significantly disturbed to suggest anyone other than the diminutive captor had been out here recently. At least now he had an idea which way to go if he did manage to break out. He'd thought it would be an on-off session. Gyle for thirty minutes, then Carlos. But it was now apparent these punks were playing by different rules.

Breaking out had now become priority number one.

CHAPTER TWENTY-SEVEN
REVELATIONS

RITZ-CARLTON HOTEL
SOUTH HAYES STREET
ARLINGTON
VIRGINIA
12: 27 EST

The General arrived at the hotel wearing attire devoid of any markings which would classify him "military". The Ritz-Carlton, five minutes from the Pentagon, was a hotel Peterson frequented. The concierge at the front desk recognised him immediately and instructed a chaperone to take him to his usual table. The man led him into a dining hall which was unusually bustling for such an early hour.

As he waited for his guest, he looked around to see if anyone was watching. Pentagon officials were known to dine here, and Peterson didn't want to risk the chance of someone overhearing the conversation or seeing the two together. Satisfied that no one was, he ordered a brandy and tried to relax.

When his guest entered five minutes later, Peterson didn't make eye-contact, trusting the man to find him on his own. The Sergeant-Major – also wearing no distinguishable military attire – knew Peterson's usual spot and found the General without bother.

He ordered a sherry and waited until the bartender returned with his change before starting.

With a casual glance, he checked to see if anyone was watching *him*, and then said, "You're sure it's safe to talk here?"

"It's a hotel, Wesley. You see? I can call you by your first name. Nobody bugs hotels. Now, start by telling me what's so important you had to interrupt me during a meeting with the President."

"You said you thought Commandant Rogers was up to something, right?" Peterson nodded and Wesley continued. "You were right."

He looked over his shoulder again, Peterson observed. It seemed to be a nervous habit. Peterson felt guilty for putting him in this position, but he needed answers, and he hoped the man from Kentucky had them. Wesley Anderson, son of a black father and white mother, had joined the Marines to get away from his drunken, deadbeat parents. Service had turned him from a scrawny kid to a barrel-chested powerhouse who'd been awarded the Medal of Honour for his contributions in the first Desert Storm. For him to be scared like this, it meant he had something huge.

"Go on," Peterson urged.

"In the last two weeks, three Marines have been pulled from various parts of the Middle East and shipped home. At first I thought maybe there was some kind of family emergency and they were granted leave. But not all three. I asked a few buddies of mine in the Army and they told me a few guys had been shipped home from their unit too."

Peterson was becoming more intrigued. "Okay, what do you think is going on?"

"The three Marines were from Force Recon, and the Army guys from Delta Force. You don't pull your best men from a war-zone like this. Not unless you've got something more important for them to be doing."

"What could be more important than the war we're in right now?"

"I don't know, General. Did you notice anything different about the Commandant this morning? More evasive about things – something like that?"

Peterson furrowed his brow. "Come to think of it, there was a moment during the meeting where he hesitated. I didn't think much of it at the time but..." He paused as he tried to remember what Rogers had been talking about when he'd stumbled. "...he hesitated when the President asked him if he had a Force Recon team close to Pakistan."

Anderson nodded. "Sure, he had a team out there. He also pulled two Marines from it twenty-four hours ago. I was supposed to be the one who flew over to bring 'em back, but he decided to send a brigadier-general instead."

"It's obviously not something everyone is supposed to know about, then. I got the feeling he didn't appreciate the President putting him on the spot like that. Okay, so if the President – and I'll assume he's aware of this – is pulling troops from the best anti-terrorist teams in the country, why?"

Anderson took a sip of sherry and said, "Some kind of top-secret mission? Something he doesn't want Congress or the Joint Chiefs to know about?"

"How many people in the Marine Corps know about the men being pulled?"

"Very few. I'm not even supposed to know. I'd venture to say no one lower than colonel knows about it."

Peterson frowned. "How could something like that be kept secret?"

"Lots of things are possible with a presidential order. Plus, the threat of being demoted from a four-star to a one-star general is scary enough – just imagine going from colonel to second lieutenant! There are ways to keep soldiers in line."

"But if you found out about this, that means others have too. I don't buy into this secrecy thing."

"There are things in the United States military that neither the Joint Chiefs nor Congress know anything about. Which brings me to my next point. Have you ever heard of Harvey Point, General?"

"No. Should I have?"

"I wouldn't think it would be your domain. Harvey Point is a top-secret CIA training facility in Hertford, North Carolina. It's where they send CIA operatives to learn about explosives, paramilitary training, and other things pertaining to espionage."

The general frowned. "How do you know all this?"

"I have a friend in the CIA – we go way back. We served together in the first Desert Storm. Don't ask me his name – just trust this information has been verified."

"Fair enough, but what's this 'Harvey Point' got to do with

anything?"

"About the time these soldiers started disappearing from the Middle East, the CIA were issued a writ ordering them to vacate Harvey Point. It didn't go down too well, but they complied. Within twenty-four hours, all nonessential CIA personnel had left the premises. By the next day, the remainder had followed suit."

Peterson raised an eyebrow. "That's not the kind of thing you see every day."

Anderson took another sip and shook his head. "It's not the kind of thing you see *ever*. The CIA is a civilian outfit. It doesn't fall under DoD jurisdiction. The only way they would leave is if the writ was issued by the President."

"You think this has something to do with the soldiers being pulled?"

Anderson leaned forward. "Well, for a base vacated almost a month ago there sure is a lot of activity at it right now."

"Wait a minute – you think the soldiers are *there*?"

"*Somebody* is there. Whether it's the soldiers, I don't know. Whatever's happening, though, it's beyond 'top-secret'. We're talking black ops, General."

Peterson thought about that for a moment, his face set in a pensive stare. "This 'Harvey Point' place, can you get me there?"

"I suppose. Why do you ask?"

"Completely off the record?"

"Sir, if General Rogers knew we were having this conversation we'd be court-martialled. I'm not going to open my mouth."

"The President is going to move troops into Pakistan in the next ten hours. I want to know why. He asked for Force Recon, the SEALs, and Delta Force to be ready to deploy to Pakistan, so why the hell is he removing men from their units? If Harvey Point holds the answers to those questions, I need to get in there."

"I'll see what I can do." Anderson's expression became more serious. "Sir, the second we set foot on Harvey Point there's no turning back. You have to accept the possibility our careers will be over. Are you sure you want to go through with this?"

Peterson returned an equally serious expression. "The President is making irrational decisions, Wes. If it costs me my career to bring them to light, so be it."

"I'll start looking for a way into Harvey Point, then."

CHAPTER TWENTY-EIGHT
RECRUDESCENCE

```
SEAGATE
BROOKLYN
NEW YORK CITY
12:31 EST
```

The photo-ID granted Davies access, even though the guard at the gate had never seen him before. He ushered Davies through and closed the gate behind him, tucking back into a sandwich and his mystery book thereafter.

The taxi drove along the main road, past houses whose garages were worth more than most people's homes, through streets crowded with children playing all kinds of ball games, and past a police station and medical centre both of which had "Seagate" preceding their official titles. Davies knew this community was tight-knit. Everyone knew everyone else, they all got along, and Seagate had all the amenities needed to ensure no one ever had to leave. In addition to the police and medical facilities, it also had a small fire brigade on standby. The community was self-sufficient, and the residents enjoyed the freedom of not having to traipse into the city for every little thing.

For Davies, it was the perfect place for a safe house. Without a photo-ID card, no one could enter. For added protection, the cards were made with an imbedded hologram which was virtually impossible to recreate. Seagate wasn't a fortress, but he had seen military communities with less security.

As the driver drove towards his house, he looked out the window at the seagulls flying overhead, and it brought back vivid memories of the last time he'd been here, two years earlier.

He'd bought the house for two hundred and fifty thousand dollars – money bequeathed to him by his father. The old man had expected his son to go to college, become a city engineer, and continue the family tradition; but when he'd been murdered a day before Davies' eighteenth birthday, Davies' entire persona changed. College became inconsequential, and vengeance filled his mind and clouded his vision.

He moved out of his parents' house and used ninety of the three hundred thousand dollars left to him to buy a ramshackle one-bedroom estate in Clinton, New Jersey. Another twenty thousand renovated it to a liveable condition. A few months later, after several unsuccessful attempts to track down his father's murderer, Davies joined the NYPD. He figured he'd use their resources to find the killer and then ditch the job. But within a few weeks he had discovered the lure of the chase did something for him. Something he'd rarely experienced before – it thrilled him. His father's killer suddenly didn't seem worth losing his life over. But he couldn't let him live, and when he found out his identity, he confronted him. The man hadn't denied it – in fact, he'd almost basked in the glory of it...until Davies pumped two bullets into his head.

He had taken the body to a new construction site in Brooklyn. At the time, Seagate was a small community with about twenty houses, but new funds had become available and the people wished to expand it by an extra forty. It had worked out quite well...the foundation of his new house becoming the gravesite of his father's murderer. When the concrete had cured, so too had his lust for revenge. He closed that chapter of his life and began anew, with a fresh purpose, a goal to help rid the streets of people like his father's killer. The 22-year-old had one dark moment in which he desired to kill and bury those who had wronged others, but vigilante justice like that had only one possible outcome, and he refrained from letting his anger rule him.

Three months after his twenty-fifth birthday, and having subsequently passed the detective exam two years earlier, Davies was promoted to sergeant. This came as a surprise not only to him but to the rest of the officers, who hadn't envisioned him as chevron material. By the time he was thirty, he was the lead lieutenant of the precinct and pushing for captain. His arrest/conviction record was second to none, and he'd closed more cases in five years than most officers had in their entire careers.

During a high-profile federal case against the Mendoza brothers – two scumbag mobsters who thought they owned Chinatown – he had first met Jonathan Baker, then an SAC. Baker had been impressed by the way Davies had handled both the case and the Bureau's intervention. He had helped Baker by giving him all his accumulated intel on the Mendozas – ten pages' worth which, when combined with Baker's, helped incarcerate the Mendozas for a twenty-year stretch. In return, Baker had convinced the then-director of the Bureau, Jules Cochrane, to give Davies a trial run. Davies had been content to remain NYPD and hold out for promotion to captain, but he'd learned a lot of key players in the precinct weren't impressed with his cooperation with the FBI (which had allowed them to take the credit for the Mendoza bust) and some had even suggested he be demoted to sergeant...or, worse, detective. Concerned with the matter, he spoke with the deputy chief, who pulled no punches. He told him he would not be demoted, but neither would he be promoted. He would remain lieutenant for possibly the rest of his career. A few days later, Davies took up Baker's offer and tried out for the Bureau. When he received word he'd passed, he walked into the deputy chief's office and handed in his shield, gun, and uniform.

For the first eighteen months, it seemed like he'd made the biggest mistake of his life. New FBI agents – facetiously referred to as "Fuckin' New Guys", euphemistically as "FNGs" – were the lowest of the low, and treated as such. Shackled with the most mundane assignments, tedious paperwork, and put through enough training to guard a small country, their jobs were nothing more than robotic monotony designed to distinguish the wheat from the chaff. Several men, who'd joined up when Davies had, dropped out within the first few months. Every other month someone else did, too.

He had serious thoughts of joining them. After all, he was a 34-year-old who'd made it as far as lieutenant in the NYPD, and yet was taking orders from a clean-cut kid from Arkansas who looked young enough to be in high school. The NYPD officers casting aspersions on Davies' ability to function as an officer was bad enough, but he'd cooperated with the FBI and gave up his career to join their ranks. He'd expected to be treated more fairly by them.

As the months passed and the treatment continued – even worsened – he cursed his naïveté. He'd been stubborn up until that point, but the lack of respect infuriated him, and on the way home that Friday evening he made up his mind he would hand in his resignation on the Monday.

He didn't need the job at the Bureau, but his pride had kept him there for as long as he could stand. He had proven everything he needed to prove, and would be content to live out the rest of his days in the blissful confines of Seagate. He'd even envisioned fishing in Lower New York Bay, or surfing, or even taking up golfing – Seagate had it all. He would live. To hell with the Bureau.

He didn't get the chance.

That weekend, Jonathan Baker arrived at his house and told him about the sting. As an added incentive, he also told him the job of assistant director in charge of the Buffalo field office awaited his return. Davies had taken some time, but ultimately had made the decision he felt best suited him. He wasn't the sort to play golf, anyway.

The day before he'd been taken away for training, he removed from his Seagate house everything that identified him as "Troy Davies" and stored it in the basement of his house in Clinton. He then removed forty thousand dollars from his inheritance and stored it and the photo-ID card in Washington Mutual. The FBI would deny his existence if something went wrong, and he needed an insurance policy in case they ever considered him expendable.

As he left Seagate behind to begin a new journey, Davies had the disquieting thought that, if the FBI screwed him over, his father's killer would be joined by more corpses. More horrid still, that did not frighten him – only the realisation he might be capable of doing it.

"That'll be five-fifty, mate," the driver announced, breaking Davies' reverie. He handed him a ten-dollar note and told him to keep the change. As he stepped out onto the footpath, the driver muttered genuine words of gratitude and pulled away.

Before leaving, he had given his dog to a little girl four doors down, whose parents were mightily upset at the gesture. In all of his planning, though, he'd forgotten about the lawn at the back of his house, which had grown so wild it would require a combine harvester to cut it. He laughed at the thought whilst also wondering how the neighbourhood watchdogs had failed to notice it. Seagate had strict codes, one of which was that lawns needed to be "presentable".

Like a portent of the horrid things that might happen in the near future, the heavens opened as he stepped into his front yard, and rain sluiced from above. Before he could fish out his keys, the deluge drenched him. He threw open the door and sped inside.

He removed his sodden top and jeans, and threw them on the table in the utility room. The house was devoid of the majority of paraphernalia associated with most homes. Davies had moved only the bare necessities from his house in Clinton. He'd never understood why, but he wanted nothing that would remind him of his past life.

He towelled off and found in his room a change of clothes loose enough to cover his considerably larger-than-before girth. While there, he opened his wall-safe and extracted the second of his lockboxes. This one held all the documentation on the sting operation, including the contact details for his training officer. He took the proper slip of paper and returned the rest to the safe, keying in the code afterward. Paranoia had made him buy the safe; common sense made him choose a digital one.

The rataplan of rain on the roof became louder as the storm grew more intense, with flashes of lightning flickering through the darkened sky in intermittent bursts. Davies was used to it now, having spent almost two years in Russia, as mercurial a country as you could get when it came to weather. As he looked at the address on the slip of paper, he cursed his choice to let the cabbie go, and wondered how long it would take another one to get here.

He pulled on a sweater and zipped up his jeans, moving out of the bedroom towards the living room. On the way, he passed his bathroom and thought about taking a quick shower, but decided against it. Al Kingston's house was in West Chester, Philadelphia, at best a two-hour drive. Kingston would have to excuse the lack of hygiene.

As he continued forward, something caught his eye and he stopped suddenly, turning to face his front door. It lay open, fluttering back and forth in the wind, the rain pounding off its frame. He'd closed it. Of that he was deadly sure.

Locked it, though?

Goosebumps formed on his arms and neck, chilling him to his soul.

The gun! Where had he left it? His mind raced as he tried to remember what he'd done with it after using it in the airport. He moved forward to the door, eyes sweeping across the mahogany floor for some kind of weapon. The utility room swam into his vision. Something went *click*. The gun! *In the pocket of my trousers!*

Davies angled right, cursing as his bare feet squeaked on the slippery floor. The jeans were still sitting on the table top, the bulge in the right pocket giving Davies cause to breathe a sigh of relief. Before he could reach them, a loud thump sounded from down the hall. Then another. Another. Until finally the sound of broken glass replaced the hollow thumping, replaced once more by glass crunching under the soles of booted feet.

Davies dashed for the gun.

CHAPTER TWENTY-NINE
MAGNA OPERA

ATARIC
12: 34 EST

When Jake Collins came back through the door alone, Hunt seized him by the arm and slammed him against the mullion of Reid's office window. Through a gap in the closed blinds, Collins could see the floor below, twenty feet down. This time, though, Reid made no effort to stop or restrain Hunt.

"Hold on! It's not what you think!" screamed Collins. Fear washed over his face.

Hunt snarled. "Really? And what is it I think, Collins?" He pushed him harder against the glass.

"I didn't give you guys up! I told that SOB it was me."

Hunt released him. "What do you mean?"

"It seemed the perfect way for him to throw me the hell out of here. So I told him I planted the virus on ATARIC's systems."

"What did he say?" Reid interjected.

"He told me to get back up here and do the job I've been paid to do. If I didn't make any more trouble, he said ATARIC would consider not suing me for everything I've got."

"Why would you risk your entire career to pull a stupid stunt like that, Jake?" Hunt demanded. "We had this under control. You didn't need to do anything."

"I figured if I could convince Johnson I was a liability, he'd let me go."

"And you didn't think there'd be a backlash?" Hunt looked at him with incredulity. "He could bankrupt you, for Gods' sake!"

"Well, he could try. But since there were no witnesses to hear what I said, it's his word against mine. Even the most unscrupulous lawyer in the world wouldn't take on that kind of case."

"Well...thanks...I guess." Hunt found the words hard to say, as though doing so might actually make Collins think he was grateful. Either way, more important things were at hand. He quickly changed the subject. "And now that that's over, let's get started on this damned OS." He turned his attention to Reid. "Jack, I'm going to need admin privileges for a few hours." He cast the hook, hoping the bait would entice the minnow.

"What for?" Reid asked, frowning. "We're installing the OS on your laptop first. You don't need admin privileges for that."

"No, *you two* are installing the OS on my laptop. I want to run a systems diagnostic test on the main ATARIC network."

Reid shook his head. "What the hell for?"

"I want to make sure everything is compatible and that we're not going to create more problems by installing your OS, Jack. It may be the best part of a year since I've been here, but I still know my way around the system. I installed it, for crying out loud!"

"Be that as it may, you still don't need to do *any* checks. I've made sure everything is compatible. I've run every check known to man on this. Trust me – it's my ass on the line if I'm wrong."

"All the more reason why it would make sense to get a consult on it. A second opinion won't hurt, Jack. I'm not going to screw around here. I want paid, and that isn't going to happen if this OS doesn't meet Fielding's requirements."

"I don't have the authority to do what you're asking, Peter," Reid said pointedly. "Even if I wanted to, I can't give you admin privileges."

"No, but you can enter your password and look the other way," Hunt replied, extending the bait fully.

Reid levelled him a cold stare. "What you're suggesting

violates every ATARIC rule in the book. I could get fired, and you could be arrested. Think long and hard about your next words, Peter: they may be last ones you say as a free man."

Hunt scoffed. "Don't be ridiculous. Strictly speaking, I'm on the ATARIC payroll. You'd merely be giving an employee administrative access for company reasons. Certainly not a crime, and probably nothing more serious than a slap on the wrist if discovered."

"Well, gosh, when you put it like that..." Reid rolled his eyes and then shook his head. "No, I'm not doing it. Any administrative work that needs to be done, I'll do. You concentrate on installing the OS on your laptop and making sure there's nothing untoward about it."

Collins, who'd been standing to one side, interjected, "What about me? What'll I do?"

"As soon as Peter makes sure everything is okay with the OS, you and your team start installing it on all the computers downstairs."

"What about the virus?"

"If they haven't snuffed it out by then, me or Peter will kill it."

"That's great, Jack," Hunt broke in, "but you still haven't told us what you'll be doing."

"As soon as you give me the A-okay, and when the virus is out of the picture, I'll start backing up and wiping the systems. Jake and his guys can follow behind me and install the OS on the wiped systems. You should be finished on the laptop at that point, Peter, so you can restore the backed-up files to the new systems."

"There might be a problem with that."

Reid gave him a look. "Which is?"

Hunt wheeled around in his chair. He grabbed his bottle of water and took a swig. The taste was bitter, but he decided it was because his mouth had become too used to the taste of alcohol. If he wanted to stay sober, he was going to have to get used to other beverages again. With a smug look, he said, "Well, last I remember, a task like that requires admin privileges. So it looks like you have a choice to make, Jack. Give me admin privileges and risk losing your job, or don't give me them and definitely lose your job."

CHAPTER THIRTY
TORRENT

SEAGATE
12: 37 EST

Davies advanced down the corridor, gun extended, feet shoulder-width apart in the traditional Weaver stance. The ground beneath him creaked. He moved faster, towards the room – *his* room – where the sounds of glass crackling would, he hoped, mask his approach.

Ahead, the door was slightly ajar. Davies moved, tightly hugging the left-hand wall, crouched down on his knees, moving along on his haunches.

Heart thumping, ears pounding, he paused at the end of the corridor, then brushed open the door with his free hand, and rose into the room. Reflexively, his arms swung left and right in tandem with his eyes. Bed, clothes, dressing table, pair of shoes, glass on the floor. Wind howled through the broken window like a banshee, and rain pelted the rug floor, but there was no one in the room.

Davies was about to leave and check the rest of the house when he remembered his room had an adjoining en-suite...the door of which was closed. He switched the gun to his left hand and moved towards the bathroom, holding onto the bed with his right and following its contour to avoid stepping on glass. The door was closed tight against the jamb, and for a brief moment Davies thought it might be locked. From inside, he could hear the sounds of heavy breathing and grunts. He switched his gun-hand again, gripped the knob easily, tested it to see if it would open, and positioned himself to the left of the door when he found that it would. He put his shoulder tight to the door, ready to barge it when he turned the knob.

Three, two, o –

Out of the corner of his eye, he saw something move. Most people's instinctive reaction would have been to turn around, but Davies had already figured what was coming. With impressive agility for a man of his size, he dropped to the floor seconds before the baseball bat smacked off the door with a sickening thud that made him grimace. Knowing another barrage would be forthcoming, he rolled to the left. The bat smacked off the carpet with a muffled thud, right where Davies' head had been seconds earlier.

Davies tried to scramble to his feet. He slipped on the rain-slicked rug and fell arm-first into shards of glass. *Move!* his mind commanded but his body had already reacted on instinct. He rolled again to the left. Glass sliced through his new tee-shirt and blood suffused the damp rug beneath him, but the alternative was worse. Somewhere above, he saw blurred shapes moving, but tears clouded his vision. He squinted desperately. Quick-fire bursts of pain stabbed through his back and stomach, but he willed them away. Rain pelted against the leg of his trousers, adding more sensation to his aching body. He had to keep moving! But he couldn't see. Could only hear. What were they doing?

The bat fizzed through the air again. Davies tried to roll, but hit something solid – the bedpost. He desperately tried to turn the other way, but it was too late. The bat caught him on the shin, searing pain exploding up his legs. His scream lingered for a second, soon drowned out by the howl of the wind which seemed to cry in tandem. He turned onto his stomach to protect himself, and felt something hard dig into his ribs – the gun

Davies hand fumbled for his Glock, his fingers clawing at the carpet.

Scratching, tearing, ripping.

Where was it? *Find it or you're dead!*

Motion. Above. The bat rising again! *Find it! Where the hell!*

Davies rolled left, and felt it dig into his ribs again. *Shit! The other side!* Rolling back, he clawed with his other hand until he felt the solid stock of the Glock. The bat arced down again; he thrust the gun upward and pulled the trigger.

There came a moment of stunned silence, followed by something clattering to the floor. Davies squinted his eyes rapidly, trying to clear them. From above, he could hear no screams of pain, no gasps of horror, nor anything which might indicate someone had been shot or killed. Just silence. Eerie silence accompanied by howling winds.

Move! Get up! his mind commanded, though his body refused.

"Take another step and I'll blow your head off!" he screamed, waving the gun for emphasis. The threat was an empty one, but the intruder didn't know that.

"All right, man, all right! Just calm down!"

Davies struggled to his feet, keeping the gun trained on their frames. With his free hand, he rubbed his eyes until they were clear. Standing in front of him were two petrified kids wearing letterman jackets and jeans. The baseball bat was lying on the floor, and a hole the size of a fist visible in the plasterboard wall behind them.

"Who the hell are you and what are you doing in my house!" Davies said through gritted teeth.

"We didn't know anyone lived here!

"So you thought you'd break in!" Davies replied, scooping up the bat and flinging it through the broken window. "Why the hell did you attack me?

"We thought you were a cop. We came here to smoke weed."

"Shut up, Ray!" the other one snarled.

"He's got a gun, Billy!

"Shut up, both of you!" Davies ordered.

"Hey, mister, we're really sorry. Shit, it started to rain and we just – I donno – we just broke the window to get inside," said Ray.

"You're lucky I didn't kill either one of you! Now get the hell out of my house before I *call* the cops.

Both looked like they couldn't believe they were been giving a chance to walk away without the involvement of the police, but they didn't hesitate to dash out the window and make off into the downpour.

When they'd left, Davies fell back onto his bed and let out a sigh of both frustration and relief. Frustrated at letting two high school kids get the jump on him. Relieved he hadn't killed either. Of all the days to pick to smoke weed! He wondered how often other people had used his house in his absence, and was glad he'd chosen to leave most of his valuable possessions in Clinton.

He reached down and gingerly rubbed his shin. It didn't feel broken, but it would hurt like hell for a while. He pulled his trouser-leg up and surveyed the damage. A nasty, elongated gash extended from his foot up three inches to the base of his leg. Blood was matted to the hair, and more dripped from the wound. On his chest were dozens of tiny abrasions and one large gash. He didn't know in what condition his back was, but he knew he couldn't show up on Kingston's doorstep looking like this.

Five minutes later, he was standing under his shower, protecting his gun from the sluicing water.

CHAPTER THIRTY-ONE
INTERROGATION

26 FEDERAL PLAZA
12: 45 EST

"Would you like to begin, Mr Hollingsworth?" the OPR representative – Hatchett – asked, with a gesture of his hand to indicate the stage was Hollingsworth's.

"Begin? Okay, I'll begin by saying I'm hungry."

The man looked around at the two-way mirror in the interrogation room as if to order someone behind it to bring in some food. He turned back and said, "That can be rectified. Now, let's start from the beginning."

Hollingsworth nodded. "Okay, in the beginning was the word, and the word was God." Hollingsworth started to smile, but stopped when he saw anger flare behind the man's blue eyes.

"Your CO assured me you would be co-operative, agent. The more you stonewall me, the greater the repercussions will be. So, again, start from the beginning."

Hollingsworth decided he didn't like the baldy old coot. No more than he liked being imprisoned in an interrogation room for this crap. But he realised refusing to co-operate only made the rep's job easier. He wanted any excuse to suspend Hollingsworth, and insubordination was the quickest way to do so.

"I'm not trying to stonewall you. I just think this is bullshit. Why do I have to be here? Okay – I know *why*, but why *now?* The guy who shot that cop is still out there. This bureaucratic nonsense can be left 'til later," Hollingsworth said with a sigh.

"You're here because you were involved in *two* shootings this morning. The standard operating – "

"I know what the SOP is. Doesn't make this any less pointless. Look, you wanna know what happened? Okay, here it is: We were instructed to go to LaGuardia and pick up a witness in a high-profile murder case." Hollingsworth paused, wondering about the validity of that statement.

Before he could continue, Hatchett said, "Instructed by whom?"

"Deputy Director Forrester. He said it was a simple pickup. In and out. No real problems."

Hatchett picked up on the doubt and anger in Hollingsworth's voice. "You didn't think it would be?"

Hollingsworth shook his head. "No, nothing like that. It just seemed...I don't know, strange, I guess."

"What seemed strange?"

"He said it was an easy pickup, but he came with us. I know he likes to get out in the field, but he didn't need to be with us on this one."

"Why was he?"

Hollingsworth hiked his shoulders. "I don't know. I guess – "

The door to the interrogation room opened and a short, stocky man wearing horn-rimmed glasses entered and set a tray containing sandwiches and two cups of coffee on the table. He left without a word.

"Go on. You were saying?" Hatchett pressed; took his cup and plate and began eating. Hollingsworth looked unsure, but eventually downed a slug of coffee.

"I guess he had some kind of personal stake in the operation. To be honest, I don't know," Hollingsworth replied.

"Okay. What happened when you got to the airport?"

"We had to recon the area – make sure it was safe for the pickup."

"And the witness – when did he enter the equation?"

"Probably 'bout ten minutes after we got there. It was Forrester who saw him first."

Hatchett nodded. "Then what happened?"

"He told us to move in and secure him. I was the closest, so I got there first. I was about to remove my ID, but he pulled a gun before I could – "

"The *witness* pulled a gun?" he asked for clarification.

"Yeah. He pulled it 'fore I got a chance to tell him who I was."

"He shot you – how many times?"

"Twice, in the chest."

"Then what?"

"Everything went crazy. People started running, screaming. I was stunned for about a minute, then I got up and saw the witness running. I followed him but he slipped away. So I kept searching – trying to figure out where he might be going. That's when the cop spotted me."

"The PAPD officer who was shot and killed?" Hatchett queried.

"Yeah, he started looking at me suspiciously. A cop is a cop, you know? Whether they're Bureau or Port Authority, they're still a cop. He knew I was carrying."

"What makes you so sure?"

"Like I said, he's a cop. He may only have been PAPD, but they're still given basic training. I can't explain it better than that. You just know. It's an intuitive thing."

"Fair enough. What happened next?"

"He drew down on me. I tried to calm him down and explain the situation, but he wouldn't listen. He got hysterical – starting talking about calling it in and having to arrest me. I didn't want to make any sudden moves. The kid was nervous enough. But I knew I was wasting time. So I told him who I was and I was about to reach for my badge when the witness came down the stairs."

"Wait – he was upstairs?"

"Yeah. I saw him and I knew he was going to try to kill me, so I went for my gun. The kid – he reacted to the sudden movement. I thought for sure he would have pulled the trigger, but he went to move in beside me. That's when the witness opened fire. The shot was meant for me, but the kid got in the way."

Hatchett leaned forward in his seat and steepled his fingers together. "The witness shot the PAPD officer?"

"Like I said, it was meant for me. But yeah."

"Did you retaliate?"

"No."

"Why not?" Hatchett probed. "The witness shot a fellow law enforcement officer. That gave you every right to open fire. What happened?"

"I wanted to help the kid, and the witness was out of bullets. Besides, our order was to bring him in alive. No exceptions."

"But you let him get away?"

"No. I ordered him to stop, but he kept going. I had a shot I couldn't take. I figured we could catch the witness later – the kid was dying."

"You put the wellbeing of a fellow officer before the arrest or capture of a man who'd tried to kill you on two separate occasions. Why?"

Hollingsworth could feel his temper begin to boil. "Like I said, he was *dying*."

"No, he was dead. Shot in the head. You couldn't have done anything for him."

"Listen, I was a Ranger before joining the Bureau. I was taught to never leave a man behind."

"However admirable that may be, the PAPD officer was already dead. It doesn't make sense you stayed with him and let your mark go."

"What do you want? Me to say I screwed up by letting the witness go? I know that! I don't need some suit telling me it, too. I stayed behind and tried to help the kid. If I'd chased after the mark, you guys would be sprouting some similar bullshit about me leaving behind a dying kid. Damned if I do, damned if I don't."

Hatchett realised the session was spiralling out of control. He'd pushed too hard too early, and the risk of alienating Hollingsworth had increased twofold in the last few minutes. To pacify the agent, he said, "Why don't we grab some proper lunch and reconvene here in an hour?"

"Hoo-fuckin'-ray for that."

Hatchett smiled. The break would also give him the chance to review the inconsistencies in Hollingsworth's statement. He suspected something was amiss from the start, and this interview-cum-interrogation had convinced him of that.

CHAPTER THIRTY-TWO
FIRST MOVES

CLASON POINT
THE BRONX
NEW YORK CITY
12:55 EST

Vladimir Pushkin pulled into the driveway of Kirov's safe-house and parked the SUV in the shade of an English Box hedge which formed the property line. Exiting the vehicle, he closed and locked the white gates, then headed up the stairs into the two-storey town house.

The quality of the interior surprised him. Although Kirov had riches beyond Pushkin's wildest dreams, he wasn't the sort of man to whittle it away in exorbitant real estate which he had no intention of residing in. Yet the town house must have cost at least a quarter of a million dollars, not to mention what Pushkin found inside.

In the back bedroom were two computers, what looked like a high-tech communications system, and a row of eight monitors which were turned off. He figured them to be a CCTV feed, and he flicked the power-switch to find out. The screens made a sound, flickered for an instant, then buzzed to life. For a moment, the picture was black-and-white, but colour gradually seeped into the monitors. He wondered if that was an indication of the length of time since they'd last been used. Either way, he saw the monitors depicted the entire exterior of the house, including views from up and down the street.

In the kitchen, he found neither food nor any indication anyone had occupied the residence in the last six months. The table was empty, the floors spotless, and the blinds drawn. The cupboards were devoid of even cutlery or china.

In the forward bedroom, he found the blinds drawn, too. A map of New York stretched the width of the wall. On East 38th Street a building was encircled in red. Two others three blocks to the west of it were too. On closer examination, Pushkin discovered these were law enforcement buildings. In the corner, beside the shuttered window, a black-light board sat.

He backed out of the room and closed the door. The stairs leading up were pine, finished with a veneer that squeaked under Pushkin's booted feet. There were only two rooms up here, and neither contained anything more than carpets and blinds.

This couldn't have been a safe-house, he decided, scratching his scar pensively as he returned downstairs. It had to be an operations centre. Both rooms containing the equipment and intelligence were close to the door to facilitate a quick getaway. The CCTV cameras were hidden from plain sight and ensured no one could come within a hundred yards without being seen. And there was nothing in the house which wasn't entirely necessary. If Pushkin didn't know better, he'd have said the place was being used for a stakeout.

He walked outside to the SUV, removed his bags, and hurried back inside before anyone might see. He took the bag containing the weapons to the back bedroom and stored it behind the two computers, but not before removing the Makarov and ammunition. From his personal luggage, he removed a satellite phone and dialled Kirov's number.

Unsure of the time in Russia, and after eleven subsequent rings, he began to wonder if Kirov was sleeping. As he went to hang the phone up, a hoarse voice croaked a "hello".

"It's me," Pushkin replied in Russian. "I'm at the house.

From the other end came the sound of gurgling, spitting, and finally, in a more coherent voice, "What time is it there?

Pushkin looked at his watch, which he'd set to New-York-time at Valley Stream. "One in the afternoon.

"Good. Our 'friend' shouldn't be landing for another few hours.

"What about our other 'friend'?

"He's in New York right now. He was spotted in LaGuardia this morning, and then in a bank in Brooklyn a few hours later.

"Which bank?

"Washington Mutual on West Seventeenth Street. Unfortunately, the area was too crowded for my men to do anything.

"Did they follow him?

"They lost him."

Pushkin could hear the anger in Kirov's voice. He thought about asking what kind of bumbling idiots Kirov had as employees, but it wasn't his place to meddle. "What do you want me to do?"

Kirov laughed. "I've never known anyone as persuasive as you. Go to the bank. My contact in New York will be waiting for you there. He'll explain everything you need to know. One more thing..."

"Which is?"

"After he does, put a bullet in his skull."

Pushkin, not missing a beat, replied, "That wasn't part of our arrangement."

"There's an extra hundred thousand waiting for you if you do."

"Consider it done."

"Excellent. If anything new breaks on our *friend's* location before you start persuading, I'll let you know."

Pushkin hung up without exchanging goodbyes. He emptied the bag of his personal belongings, leaving only the satellite phone, a map, a wad of hundred-dollar notes, and the Makarov. The latter he stored in an easy-access pouch on the front, ensuring first it was loaded with a full clip and a round chambered.

Outside, he tossed the bag into the back seat of the SUV. After he'd backed out onto the main street, he pulled the brake and closed the gates again. Just as he was about to slip into the driver's seat, a voice called from twenty yards away.

"You new in the neighbourhood?"

Pushkin turned around and appraised the man approaching. He was middle-aged but in good shape, completely bald, and had, across his cheek, a scar similar to Pushkin's.

Pushkin eyed his bag surreptitiously, then said in his best American accent, "No, just making a few alterations for the owner." A foreigner in this neighbourhood would raise too much suspicion, and he needed the safe-house to remain free of suspicion.

"You know him personally?"

"You could say that."

"Yeah, well, we aren't too happy about the riff-raff he rents his house out to. Could you tell him that?"

"That really isn't my department. I'm paid to look after the house; not its occupants."

"I understand. Sorry to bother you."

"Not a problem. Have a good day."

As Pushkin drove north on Beach Avenue, he began to wonder what caused the man to have such a low opinion of the occupants of Kirov's town house. It didn't seem likely any of Kirov's employees would be dumb enough to draw that kind of unwanted attention. From his initial reading, he got the feeling the neighbour was ex-military. Probably only for a few years, he decided. He didn't have the hardened persona of a veteran soldier, but that scar was indicative of a shrapnel wound. The injury could have been severe enough to allow him to play the disability card and get out the war – probably Desert Storm, judging by his age. And ex-military-types knew how to spot trouble. If this guy realised something was amiss, he could prove to be more trouble than Pushkin needed.

And if he'd been inside Kirov's house...well, that produced even more complications.

The question now was: did it produce enough to merit his death?

CHAPTER THIRTY-THREE
QUAGMIRE

```
LEO & WALKEN LAW FIRM
MANHATTAN
NEW YORK CITY
13: 01 EST
```

Karen Hunt ducked into the ladies' room and closed the door tightly behind her. With a surreptitious glance, she checked all of the stalls for the presence of any other employees. When satisfied she was alone, she moved over to the washbasins, trying her best to mute the clack of her three-inch stilettos. She set her purse on the table and removed a Kleenex from inside, dabbing it against her eyes and cheeks where her tears had ruined the makeup.

What she saw in the mirror disgusted her. Karen had always prided herself on being a strong, independent woman. She'd learned early on that men were only interested in beautiful women for one reason. Most of her boyfriends, before Peter, had flaunted her like arm candy. He was the first man who had loved her for her, and for that reason he would always have a special place in her heart. But somewhere along the way they'd both lost track of who they really were, and the repercussions of that had been too severe for her to bear. She'd fought hard to make Peter a better person – to bring him from the doldrums of a life that no person, male or female, should have had to live. It was a battle she'd thought she'd won. To see him throw it away had broken her heart.

Ironically, her tears were not shed for Peter or herself. They were, instead, shed for what would happen next. Peter would find out, of that Karen had no doubts. And when he did, he would kill him. Karen had said no, had pleaded with him to leave her office and go home to his wife, but he hadn't listened.

She flung the Kleenex to the ground, fighting back tears, and turned on the faucet. The cold water cleansed her and made her feel better, but the soap stung her. Trying hard not to break down again, she dried off and removed her makeup kit. Then, she carefully dabbed concealer over the purple bruise under her right eye. A layer of foundation hid the most noticeable parts, and a slight spray of fake tan did the rest. When she'd finished, she loosened the band around her ponytail and let her long black hair fall into place around her shoulders.

Her mind filled with questions, most of them laced with accusing tones, making her the villain and not the victim. Why did you stay on late? Why did you wear that skirt? Why did you wear that perfume? Did you really need so much makeup? But she omitted the most important one of all: why did you wait so long to stop him? He'd kissed her for a good half-minute before she pulled away. And then he'd grabbed her by her hair, and despite her screams of protest, tried to force his lips on hers. Tried to pull her blouse off. Until she'd slapped him. Hard, but not as hard as he'd hit her in return, his eyes burning with fiery rage. For a moment, Karen had thought he would kill her. But when he realised what he'd done, he backed away, stumbling, and put his hand across his mouth as his eyes morphed from anger to utter terror. He knew what he'd done had not only cost him his career, it had probably cost him his life too.

Almost as though to make a weak attempt at amends, he'd hurried over and helped Karen off the floor. She'd told him forcefully to leave. He gave her apology after incessant apology and pleaded with her not to tell anyone what happened – that it was all just a horrible mistake and he would do anything to rectify it; give her money, recommend her for promotion, anything she wanted. She'd stormed out of her office without a word, and drove home to her mother's house in tears.

The next morning, she called in and used her sick-day. She'd spent it curled up on the sofa in a ball, watching reruns of her favourite television shows. Her mother knew something was wrong, but she assumed it had something to do with Hunt. And try as she might to pry, she could not get an answer out of her stubborn daughter.

Karen had decided she wasn't going to lounge around her house feeling sorry for herself like a certain husband of hers. She had a son to provide for and a retired mother whose pension wouldn't put food on a plate. So, against all of her better judgement, she went to work this morning, a mere thirty-six hours after the worst day of her life.

For the past four-and-a-half hours, she'd avoided her office. Karen Hunt, née Carter, had been a lawyer with Walt Leo and Johnson Walken's law firm for the past seven years. She hoped to become a partner in the next three, and a scandal like this could jeopardise her entire career. She'd considered pretending it hadn't happened, but sexual harassment was taken seriously by this firm, and hiding it could be potentially worse than reporting it. Until she figured out what to do, she wanted to avoid running into him, and the first place he would look was her office.

With a depressed sigh she shoved her makeup case back into her purse, looked at herself in the mirror one more time, smoothed her blouse and skirt, and walked to the door.

He must have had someone watching the toilets. Or he'd been watching them himself, waiting for her to use them. Either way, he was standing outside the door when she opened it. Karen screamed, but quickly put her hand across her mouth to stifle it.

"We need to talk," he said candidly. "We can do it in my office or yours, but we're doing it...right now."

"I haven't got anything to say to you!"

"Then I'll do the talking. Let's go."

Karen looked around the lavishly furnished main hall of the law firm, to the lawyers' desks, and to Walt Leo and Johnson Walken's office which sat above them all, the blinds drawn. No one was paying any attention to her, despite the scream she'd stifled. If they were going to do this, it would be here, and not in an office where she couldn't be heard.

"I'm not going anywhere. Say what you have to say here."

He looked puzzled but nodded his head and acquiesced. "Okay, here's fine."

He was attractive in a far-out sort of way. Nothing close to Peter's natural handsomeness, but he had his appeals – except for a hideous beard that did nothing for his high jaw-line. His hair was curly, medium-length, and blond. His body language exuded confidence, and he had the swagger of a sexually active man. His physique denoted an active man. Despite all of those things, he was not a six-four, two-hundred-and-fifty-pound slab of muscle like Peter. Fit though he may have been, Karen knew her husband would destroy him in a brawl.

"Who've you told about it?" he asked, glancing over his shoulder.

"*It?* You mean your assault?"

"Keep your voice down!"

"Don't see why I should. Everyone will know about it before the day's out. I've made my decision."

A flicker of horror washed over his face. "You don't want to do that."

Karen placed her hands on her hips and gave him an indignant stare. "And why not? Because you'll assault me again?"

"Listen – what happened was a mistake. I didn't mean to hurt you, Karen. You have to believe me."

"You know, in all of this there's one thing that's been bothering me. How many *other* women have you silenced with lavish gifts and promises of promotions? How many haven't got off as easily as I did? You hide behind a façade of friendliness. You advocate a policy of zero-tolerance towards sexual harassment. But beneath it all, you're a hypocrite. You're more twisted and bitter than the majority of the people this law firm represents. I despise people like you, and you're not going to get away with it. It may cost me my job, but I won't let it cost me my dignity."

"You don't want to go down this road...I promise you that. Because if you do, I will promulgate so many rumours about you that everyone in this office will think you are promiscuous. If it even goes to court, your credibility will be zero. And let's face it – who's a jury going to believe? A woman divorced from her husband, with a history of sexual relations with the workmates in her office? Or the respected lawyer of male persuasion who was innocently caught up in the tempestuous desires of that woman? You also have to ask yourself who your husband will believe, seeing how you divorced him and took his only child."

"You son of a bitch! You wouldn't dare."

"You're lying to yourself if you think I won't. Drop it and you'll be a partner before the end of the year."

Karen gave him a cold stare. "I don't want to be a partner in this company. And when I'm done, you won't be a senior one, Mr Walken."

CHAPTER THIRTY-FOUR
SOD'S LAW

ON-BOARD CASPIAN AIR FLIGHT 434
SOMEWHERE OVER THE IRISH SEA
18: 05 GMT

Dozing fitfully in his seat, Sergei Ivanovich didn't notice the movement until the last of them walked past. When he sat up and cleared his eyes, he couldn't believe the sight in front of him. Three men approached the cockpit door. The barrels of weapons protruded slightly from underneath the fabric of their Bishts. They walked in single-file, calmly, their heads bowed as though in prayer.

Ivanovich tapped his second-in-command, Amos York, on the shoulder and gestured towards them. York stiffened in the chair, but his face remained impassive. The same could not be said for the woman two seats in front of Ivanovich, however. She screamed when she saw the gun, but quickly stifled it with a hand.

This reaction caused the hijackers to break out of their trance. The rear one pivoted quickly, his arms coming out from underneath the Bisht. The word "AK-47" instantly flashed through Ivanovich's mind as the rest of the first-class occupants screamed.

The other two reached the cockpit door, uncovered their weapons, and unleashed a flurry of bullets into the locking mechanism. The screams grew in number, most of them coming from the rear cabins. The front-man drove his boot into the door and charged into the cockpit.

"Everybody remain calm!" the rear one said in a highly pronounced Middle-Eastern accent. "Nobody try to be a hero, and nobody will die. If you move out of your seat, we will shoot you dead."

Son of a bitch! thought Ivanovich. *Of all the flights in the world, you stupid morons picked this one.*

The screams reduced to whimpering now, though many still shed tears – just silently. Up front, the leader – Ivanovich assumed the one who'd kicked in the cockpit door was in charge – would likely be telling the pilot to change course, radio some authority and cite a list of demands, or some other nonsensical thing. Either way, they were now in control of the plane. Which did not bode well for him and his deadline.

"Well fuck a duck," York whispered. "Looks like we got more than we bargained for on this flight, Sergei. Two sets of terrorists on one goddamn plane! What are the chances of that?"

#3 heard the end of the sentence, stormed over, and shoved the barrel of his rifle into York's cheek. "What are you whispering about!" His eyes burned with hatred.

"I was telling him I should have taken my gun with me too. Then we could have hijacked this thing together. Know what I'm saying? You feeling me?"

#3 looked confused but not angry. "Silence! You feeling *me*?" he asked, stressing the word "feeling" as though it were alien to him.

York nodded. "Sure, sure. I'm 'feeling' ya, Towel Head. I mean, 'Muslim'. No, 'Islamic'. What is it they call you people these days?"

#3 roared in anger. He spun the AK-47 and smashed the stock of it against York's jaw. "Say another word and I will *kill* you."

York, holding his jaw, raised his free hand and said, "It's cool, man, it's cool. Please don't kill me!"

The Muslim turned away, disgusted with the American pig. When he'd left, York massaged his jaw and cracked a smile at

Ivanovich.

Ivanovich glared in return. "What the hell was that?" he said in an even lower whisper.

"A little test."

"Test? To find out how hard the stock of an AK-47 is?"

"No, to see if he had the stones to kill me. He failed."

"Meaning?"

"Meaning these guys are a bunch of pussies. They aren't going to kill anyone. If they were, he'd've killed me when I called him a towel head."

Ivanovich gave him a hard stare. "And what if he *had* killed you?"

"Then you'd know to take the sum'bitch seriously," York replied, stifling a laugh.

"Okay, O' Fearless Leader. What do we do now?"

"Now we wait."

"For what?"

"To see how many there are, what their plans are, and how quickly we can kill the fuckers."

CHAPTER THIRTY-FIVE
SQUAWK

```
AIR TRAFFIC CONTROL CENTRE
SHANNON INTERNATIONAL AIRPORT
COUNTY CLARE
REPUBLIC OF IRELAND
18:10 GMT
```

John Riordan checked the radar screen twice to make sure he'd read the number correctly, then bolted from his seat and charged up the stairs to the shift supervisor's office. He knocked on the door twice, then entered without being beckoned.

Sally McGuiness looked up from the paperwork on her desk, glared at the door, and then did a double-take on seeing Riordan's serious expression.

"What's wrong, John?"

"I've just got a seventy-five-hundred squawk from a Boeing plane in our airspace."

McGuiness rolled her seat back and rose quickly. *"What!* Is it scheduled to land here?" she demanded, looking out her window to the runways below.

"No, ma'am. It's a Caspian Air flight. They don't use this airport."

"And you're sure it's been hijacked?"

"The pilot squawked twice. It's not a mistake."

"My God!" She looked to the ground for a second, as though trying to figure out what to do next. Hijackings weren't uncommon, but they were for the smallest international airport in Ireland. When she looked up, Riordan was studying her expression, a bewildered smile on his face. She ignored it and said, "Okay, find out where the flight originated and where its destination is. Then, if the hijackers haven't disabled the transponder, find out if it's still on course."

"Yes, ma'am." Riordan turned to leave.

"And John?"

He turned back. "Yeah?"

"Let's keep this quiet until we know more. We don't need any distractions down there. When we find out where the plane is landing, we can radio the airport and let them contact the proper authorities," she finished, dropping back into her seat with a heavy thud.

"Sounds like a plan."

Riordan exited the office and calmly sauntered back down the staircase to his desk. As the senior air-traffic controller, he was in charge of the floor when McGuiness wasn't stomping around it in her four-inch pumps. The rest of the crew respected him, but they were plenipotentiary. Their actions were learned by rote, and they made decisions of their own volition. The last thing any air traffic control centre needed was someone to let two planes smash into each other at forty thousand feet because they were too scared to make a decision without permission. No, everyone knew their job and did it with a minimum of fuss. They were a team, of course, but each individual could – and did – function on his/her own. Which was why, when Riordan slotted back into his seat, no one thought to ask why he'd bounded up the stairs to McGuiness' office.

Settling back into his chair, he spread and cracked his fingers, and began working them across his keyboard at a frenetic pace. In a few minutes, he'd found the contact details for *Caspian Air* and dialled the number. A female voice answered with a friendly greeting.

"Hello – yes? Is that *Caspian Air*?"

"Indeed it is, sir. How may I help you?"

"How are you doing? I'm calling from Shannon

International Airport. Could I by any chance speak with the president of the company?"

"I'm afraid he's not currently reachable. He's on vacation. Can I ask what this is pertaining to?"

What gobshite goes on vacation in feckin' January? "Could I speak with the vice-president of operations, then?" replied Riordan, deliberately ignoring her question.

"I can put you through, but without an idea of what this concerns, I can't promise he'll take your call, sir."

"Put me through, please."

"Yes, sir."

A warbling dial-tone replaced the sweet voice. Riordan cringed involuntarily. In ordinary circumstances, he would have been far more courteous, but these weren't ordinary circumstances, and lives hung in the balance.

After eleven rings, a voice finally spoke: "Ed Kennedy, V-P of *Caspian Air*. To whom am I speaking?"

"Ah, yes, Mr Kennedy? I'm John Riordan, senior air-traffic controller for Shannon International Airport, Republic of Ireland." Riordan paused, not to allow the information to sink in but to word the next sentence in his head. "You have a flight in-air today; flight four-three-four, registration number EP-ATR. Can you verify that, sir?"

The sound of keys clacking followed for the next minute, and then: "That's correct. Why do you need to know that?"

Riordan, again, ignored a question. "Sir, can you tell me the specific route for that aircraft?"

"Moscow to New York City. Now, tell me what this is about, Mr Riordan."

"Sir, your aircraft just squawked seventy-five-hundred twice in the last five minutes. We have reason to believe it has been hijacked."

CHAPTER THIRTY-SIX
CRY "HAVOC"

HARVEY POINT
13: 15 EST

Carlos couldn't wait to get his hands on someone...anyone. Right now, he didn't care who. When – or perhaps *if* – they came to take him away, he'd grab the first one around the neck and strangle the SOB, and if there were any more, use the strangled one as a human shield and fight his way out. It wasn't much of a plan, but with a camera watching his every move, finding another way to break out was virtually impossible. The element of surprise was the only advantage he had.

Except that no one had come for him yet. It had been almost an hour since the diminutive guard had informed him of Gyle's ostensible injury. SERE training usually involved alternating torture. Hour on, hour off. In this case, they should have already begun on Carlos. That they hadn't suggested something different was happening. Something he had never encountered before.

Gyle's screaming hadn't started again either. Maybe that was just a ploy to make him think his friend was severely injured. *But if that's the case, why haven't they started on me! What are they playing at?* Maybe they'd decided Carlos' threshold for pain would aid him in withstanding torture better than Gyle, so they'd concentrated their efforts on breaking Gyle. So why wasn't he screaming? Why, why, why!? It didn't make sense. If they weren't torturing Gyle, they should have been torturing *him*.

Sighing, Carlos backed away from the cell door and plopped down on the bed. In the last twenty-four hours he'd slept a total of five minutes. Both his mind and body were exhausted. But he fought on, summoning courage and strength from the inner reservoir of energy all soldiers possessed. Now was not the time for sleep.

He studied the camera again, wondering how robust it was. Being recessed into the wall made it harder to break, but the lens would still be susceptible to attack, surely? The problem he faced was that it was eight feet above the floor of the cell, and his only weapons were his fists. The bed was shackled to the wall, and there were no other items in the room. Breaking the camera would be nigh-on impossible. But if he tried to, someone might see. And if they saw, they would want to stop him...

Carlos sprung off the bed and moved towards the camera. With a powerful leap, he jumped into the air and smashed his fist against the lens. The glass remained intact, but that was immaterial. He repeated the manoeuvre until he was confident enough time had elapsed for someone watching to have seen his actions. Though his hand was red and bleeding, the lens refused to break. Nevertheless, his actions warranted the intervention of one of the guards, surely, and if he continued, they would have no option to open the cell and restrain him.

Carlos continued to pound it until he grew exhausted from the effort. With laboured breaths, he fell back onto the bed and listened attentively. The only sounds he could hear were birds and crickets chirping, the rustle of foliage in the wind, and the eerie silence of a place which now seemed deserted.

He threw his hands up in disgust. "Where the fuck are you! I'm right here. What are *you* waiting for! Huh? *What are you waiting for!"*

Silence.

Not even the birds and crickets wanted to answer him.

***

Almost...there!

The tether securing Larry Lansdale to the tree finally snapped and he fell forward on his face. He turned around, half-expecting to see Kürt Fromm having a laugh at his expense, but the German's expression was emotionless. With a sigh, Lansdale returned to his feet and cut Fromm free. Fromm didn't fall forward though, displaying impressive balance to stay on his feet.

"Well this wasn't part of the bloody plan," Lansdale pointed out, shaking his head. "For all we know they could be at the EOD right now."

"I doubt it."

Lansdale gave him a look. "Any particular reason why?"

Fromm stroked his rapidly growing beard and said, "They've been captured."

"*Captured?* By who, and how the hell could you possibly know that?"

"You didn't feel it? There was someone else out here."

"*Someone else?* Like who? Some of the other soldiers?"

"Don't know, but there was definitely someone here, and they took our friends with them."

Lansdale gave an incredulous sigh. "You can't possibly know that."

"I was trained to track people. I have the hearing of a dog. After we were tied up, our friends got about fifty yards before they were ambushed."

Lansdale shook his head and wondered what else about this German freak of nature could scare him. The man was nothing short of a beast, and even though Lansdale considerably outweighed him, he had the disquieting thought that Fromm would tear him apart if the need arose. And then eat him.

"So what do we do now?"

"What else can we do? We head back to the EOD and get a sitrep."

CHAPTER THIRTY-SEVEN
THE DOGS OF WAR

```
CAMP LIBERTY
1st FORCE RECON HEADQUARTERS
ONE MILE FROM SPIN BOLDAK
AFGHANISTAN
22:50 AFT
```

Staff-Sergeant Federico Holmes acknowledged the radio transmission and replaced the handset in its cradle, his face a pensive mien. With quick strides, he marched out of his tent and covered the short distance to the command hut, where the executive officer of 1st Force Recon, Captain Tom McCoy, sat behind his desk typing on a laptop. Though Jack Carlos was Holmes' commanding officer, McCoy was the resident commander in charge of all 1st Force Recon's platoons in Afghanistan.

Holmes snapped a sharp salute, which McCoy returned.

"At ease, Sergeant. What have you got for me?" McCoy closed the lid of the laptop and leaned back in his chair. The 42-year-old should have been somewhere in Washington, wearing a suit and tie and on the payroll as one of the many Marine Corps' commissioned officers who'd gone on to be senior military advisors. But this tour would hopefully be his last, and if he played his cards right he would be in line for promotion to major.

Holmes let his hands fall to his side, but kept his posture rigid. "Cap'n, we've just received a flash-priority call from SOCOM." Special Operations Command was responsible for the deployment of Marines throughout Afghanistan.

McCoy leaned forward and gestured for Holmes to continue.

"Sir, under orders from the Commandant, we're being redeployed to the Northwest Frontier Province of Pakistan. Our mission is to locate and apprehend Sayid bin Laden, who was spotted in the area a few days ago."

"Did you authenticate this message, Sergeant?"

"Yes, sir. The codes matched. The message is legitimate."

"Okay, Holmes. Get some rest. You move out first thing in the morning."

"Cap'n, our orders are to deploy immediately. They want us in Pakistan by sunup."

A look of confusion spread over McCoy's face. "Wait a minute...why are *you* coming to me with this? Where's your commanding officer, Sergeant? Where's Jack Carlos?"

"Sir?" Holmes looked at him as though he'd grown a set of horns.

"Where is your CO, Sergeant?" he replied in a sharper tone.

"Cap'n, Sergeant-Major Carlos and Master-Sergeant Gyle were shipped home yesterday."

McCoy bolted out his chair and hurried around the desk with the speed of a man ten years his junior. "*What!* On whose authority?"

"The order came from the Commandant. You didn't know?"

"No, I damn well didn't know!" McCoy slammed the door and turned back to Holmes. Gone was the laid-back demeanour, replaced by an incensed expression. "Okay, Sergeant, you better start telling me everything that happened in Adi Ghar yesterday."

For the next five minutes, Holmes went over everything in explicit detail, omitting nothing. For the most part, McCoy allowed him to continue without interruption...until something peculiar caught his attention.

"You said this guy was a brigadier-general. What was his

name?"

"Edward Triton."

"Never heard of him." McCoy knew all the generals in the Marine Corps. Triton was an uncommon name, and not one McCoy would forget. "If this guy's a brigadier-general, he must have made oh-seven in the last few months, because that name is unfamiliar. What did he look like?"

"Didn't see a lot of him, Cap'n. He had the usual attire. Couldn't see his hair, though his beard *was* thicker than regulation-length."

"Let me ask you a question, Sergeant. You got back here from Adi Ghar when?"

"Just before midday yesterday, sir."

"I didn't debrief you, so who in the hell did?"

"Major Miller, sir."

Without warning, McCoy grabbed him by the shoulders, his eyes wide with shock. When he spoke, his voice was taut and urgent. "What do you mean Major Miller debriefed you!" Miller was the company commander for 1st Force Recon – McCoy's commanding officer.

"I was supposed to report to you for debriefing, Cap'n, but one of the sergeants told me Major Miller wanted to speak with me. He asked for a status report on what happened in the mountains. When I told him about Carlos and Gyle, he said they were needed stateside for something he could not divulge. He also told me to tell no one but you, Cap'n."

McCoy's eyes grew wider still. "Major Miller is here?"

"What do you mean 'here', sir?" He frowned. "I'm sure he's in his tent sleeping, or he's in the command centre."

"Sergeant...Major Miller hasn't been in Afghanistan for six months!"

Now it was Holmes' turn to be wide-eyed. *"What?"*

"Which begs the question, Marine: If you didn't give Major Miller that sitrep...just who in the hell *did* you give it to?"

CHAPTER THIRTY-EIGHT
FIRST MANOEUVRES

CASPIAN AIR FLIGHT 434
18: 20 GMT

In seat 34-C, Richard Denton leaned back in his chair, stretched his arms out, and yawned for a couple of seconds before stifling it with a hand. He looked around to see if anyone had noticed, but only the pretty blonde-haired teenager in the seat next to him passed any remarks. She rolled her eyes and shook her head. Typical teenage angst, Denton decided, wondering where her parents were and why they'd allowed their precious daughter to board a plane on her own. She hadn't said a word the entire flight thus far, but Denton had noticed her derisive facial expressions and a holier-than-thou attitude that Paris Hilton herself would have squirmed at.

Denton returned the PDA to his pocket, satisfied it had sent the message. At the Transportation Security Administration building in Arlington, Virginia, an alarm would be blaring across the computers of the deputy and acting administrators of the TSA. A simple three-letter code would inform them of a hijacking in progress. Attached to the code was a short synopsis detailing the flight number, passenger total, number of hijackers, and the scheduled destination of the aircraft. This information would be forwarded to the secretary of the Department of Homeland Security, who would in turn inform the President that a flight scheduled to land in New York had been hijacked.

With the touch of a button, Denton had set in motion events even he could scarcely have imagined.

***

"Looks like there's only five, Sergei," York whispered, unable to contain the grin.

"We're not armed, Amos."

"So what? We take them one by one, shouldn't be a problem. We isolate them and kill 'em without any of their buddies growing a brain."

"Why are we even considering this? We just wait it out and see what happens."

York leaned in beside him so close Ivanovich could smell the stink of garlic. "You don't complete this mission today, you're dead. We don't take these guys out of the equation, we ain't landing. We ain't landing, you ain't completing the mission. You don't complete the mission, you're dead. You leave them in charge of the plane, they'll likely crash it into some goddamned building and we're all dead. So, whatever way you look at it, the odds are pretty much shit. Way I figure it, you got one option...take them down and let the plane land where it's supposed to land. Then we slip away in all the carnage. Oh, did I mention that if you don't complete the mission today you're dead?"

"You might've said it once or twice or a million times. But we screw this up and we're dead too."

"Yeah, but at least this way we have a chance of *not* ending up dead. And let's face it...our other odds basically say we're screwed. Which leaves us with only this."

"Do we get the rest of the guys involved?"

York shook his head. "No. The more people who know what we're doing, the more chance they'll screw it up. We do it on our own."

Ivanovich didn't like how fast this was spiralling out of control, but desperate times and all that clichéd crap. "Okay.

Whatever way I look at it, I'm screwed. We do it your way."

"You were Spetsnaz. If your team was on the plane right now, what would be your first move?"

"Exactly what you said: Isolate and neutralise. Terrorists aren't the sharpest knives in the drawer, so chances are they aren't using low-velocity ammo. We can't risk a single shot being fired. Unless in dire straits, we take them down with CQC. I know it's been a while since you had to use your fists for anything, Amos, but you'll have to adapt," Ivanovich finished with a smile.

"Okay, so we're clear. Isolate and neutralise?"

Ivanovich nodded. "The latter part's easy. Getting them separated...not so much."

***

The girl was going to be a problem. Like a typical spoilt teenager, she had her feet on her seat and her knees resting against the back of the one in front. A white snarled lead extended from the pocket of her jeans to her ears, where a pair of earphones blared an incessant tune he was glad he couldn't fully understand. She was oblivious to everything going on around her, unbelievable though that seemed to Denton. She hadn't looked up, but it would only be a matter of time.

He needed to get her attention without startling her, and ask her to switch to his window seat. If she made a scene, chances were they'd kill her. But there was no way she wasn't going to make a scene. The second he asked her to do anything, she'd whine like a petulant child. The only way to do this was to be rude.

He rose fast and pushed her legs out of the way like a man in need of serious relief. In the midst of her cries of protest, he yanked clear one of her earphones and silenced her with a sharp glare and a finger across his lip.

"Move to the window seat. *Now!*" he ordered in a low but menacing tone. When she tried to make a retort, he added, "Don't argue!" She muttered something about him being a psycho, but relented and slipped over to the window seat without another word. To emphasise her distaste she jammed the earphone back into her ear, with an icy glare that would have made a drama queen proud. It baffled him how she could remain oblivious to the goings-on around her, but it made his job easier; moody silence trumped screaming hysterics.

At least now he had the aisle seat. Better still, none of the terrorists had noticed the altercation. With the element of surprise, he could take them down.

CHAPTER THIRTY-NINE
THE PERSUASION OF POWER

WASHINGTON MUTUAL BANK
13:30 GMT

According to the GPS in the SUV, four police precincts bordered Coney Island. This gave Pushkin cause for concern, but he was a reasonably fluent speaker of English and could pass for an American when required. This came from his ex-partner, who he had been fond of before the backstabbing SOB tried to decapitate him. Still, it had taught him a valuable lesson, one he was about to pass on to Kirov's New York contact: Never trust anyone.

He parked on a footpath beside the intersection of West Seventeenth Street and stepped out into the drizzling rain. Closing the door, he zapped the automatic lock and thrust his hands, keys and all, into the pockets of his jeans. With his head tilted downwards, he crossed the street to the bank and hurried inside.

Luckily for Pushkin, lunchtime was the bank's quietest period, so it was deserted except for a few employees and a man wearing a New York Yankees baseball cap. Without needing to ask, he knew this was Kirov's contact. He nodded to him and arched his head toward the door. Outside, they crossed the street to a salad bar and stood by the door, in the shelter.

"You Pushkin?" the man asked in impeccable English.

Pushkin nodded, checked around him for anybody watching, and said in an American accent, "What was Davies doing in the bank?"

"Withdrawing cash, from what I could make out."

He wanted to ask him how he'd let Davies give him the slip, but he figured there wasn't much point. Instead, he asked, "Which teller did he deal with?"

"The middle desk. Her name's Kate Shaw."

Pushkin cocked an eyebrow. "You know her?"

The man shook his head. "I pulled a few favours and got her jacket. She's twenty-nine years old, has lived in New York all her life, and has a husband and eight-year-old daughter. What are you gonna do?" he finished with a slight tone of concern.

Pushkin could understand why Kirov wanted the man dead. He let emotions rule him. He would not make the hard decisions for the good of the mission, and people like that were useless. Pushkin would take pleasure in putting a nine-millimetre round above the bridge of his nose, but for now he needed the man alive.

"I'm going to have a chat with Mrs Shaw. Is she back from her lunch break yet?"

"A few minutes ago. So what are you going to do?"

Pushkin smiled. "What I said I was. I'm going to have a chat with her. You stay here and watch for any cops. You think you can handle that?"

The man's eyes flickered with anger for a brief moment, but he nodded like the subservient lackey he was. "Sure."

"Tell me everything else you found out about this woman," Pushkin ordered and listened to him ream off details about Shaw's life for a few minutes. When he'd finished, Pushkin crossed the street and re-entered the bank.

Kate Shaw was a strikingly beautiful woman. Her shoulder-length auburn hair glistened under the bank's fluorescent lighting, and her radiant smile was infectious. She was a very sophisticated woman, the kind banks cherished. It wouldn't surprise Pushkin to learn she'd charmed many a man out of his money.

She sat behind the middle desk, talking in a professional tone to the person on the other end of the telephone. Pushkin decided it wasn't her husband or daughter. With the right persuasion, he could convince her to come with him. Making sure no one was watching, he moved quickly to her desk, waited until she made eye-contact, and then said in a low but audible tone, "If you ever want to see your daughter alive again, follow me."

Kate went wide-eyed in surprise, dropped the phone like a thousand volts of current had suddenly pulsated through it, and bolted from the seat. "What did you just say!"

"Your daughter, Mrs Shaw. Think very carefully about your next move. Make the wrong one, I'll hit the speed-dial on my phone and the man on the other end will put a bullet in Katie's pretty head."

Kate tried to control herself but tears began streaming down her face. "Who are you? How do you know my name? Where is my daughter?"

Pushkin looked around to make sure no one had noticed the commotion, before saying, "Katie's dead if you don't get off that seat right now and follow me outside."

Kate hesitated for a moment, but maternal instinct trumped survival instinct and she followed Pushkin out of the bank, her heels clacking across the tiles. He didn't take her to the salad bar, but crossed the intersection to Mermaid Avenue and slipped into a Chinese restaurant. He walked past the gathering flocks of lunchtime customers and took Kate into the male restroom. There, he performed a thorough sweep for any other occupants. When satisfied there weren't any, he extracted two items from his breast pocket. The first was a picture of Troy Davies, and the other, his Makarov.

"Yes, this is a real gun, Mrs Shaw. I would love for you to give me a reason to use it," Pushkin said and levelled her with a glare. With his free hand, he gripped her right hand and placed the photograph in it. "This man came into your bank earlier today. Do you remember him?"

Kate nodded.

"I don't like liars, Kate." Pushkin leaned in and sniffed her perfume erotically. "If you lie to me, I'll lock that door and you won't like what I'll do next. Okay?"

She shuddered at the thought, tears streaming down her face, but she nodded and barely mouthed, "Yes."

Pushkin sniffed her perfume again, his mind filling with

images of Kate's voluptuous body...of it naked in this very stall and of him straddling her, ignoring her screams and whimpers of protest. How he would love to – *No! Not now! You have a job to do.* Yes, that was true. But when it was over, maybe he would pay Mrs Shaw another visit – a more intimate one.

He continued, "Or, I could ring my friend and he'll take little Katie to a private place and teach her some grown-up games."

"No, please! I won't lie to you! Please don't do anything to my daughter!"

"This man"—Pushkin pointed to the picture—"what did he want in your bank?"

Through tears, she answered, "He came in...to withdraw the contents of his safe deposit box."

"What was in it?"

"I don't know – "

"Kate..." Pushkin warned.

"I swear to God! Bank officials don't know the contents of our customers' safe deposit boxes. We can't!"

"That's okay, Kate. I believe you. What was this man's name?"

Kate hesitated for a moment. Not because she was afraid of giving away privileged information, but because she couldn't remember it. "Something "Williams". I'm sorry! I can't remember the rest of it. But I can get it for you! I have his file on my computer."

"Does it list his current address?"

"I think so."

"Okay, we're going to walk calmly out of here and go back into the bank. You're going to print me a copy of Mr Williams' details. If you do that, my friend will let your daughter go, unharmed."

"Yes. I'll do whatever you want. Just leave my daughter alone!"

"But," Pushkin continued in a sterner tone, "if the police receive a call in the next few hours and a description of me is released to the general public, I will kill her. I know where you live, Kate, and I know where your mother and father live, also. I'll kill your entire family and I'll make you wish I'd killed you too."

"I never want to see you again! I'm not going to tell anyone!"

"Good. Let's go."

CHAPTER FORTY
PLATITUDES

ATARIC
13: 35 EST

As Hunt came back into the office after a short toilet-break, he noticed Reid and Collins had skipped their lunch to concentrate on ensuring all ATARIC's computers were backed-up and ready to receive the new operating system. Collins was finishing the installation on Hunt's laptop, and Reid was doing something in the corner station.

At a quarter to one, Reid announced all of ATARIC's systems were backed-up and it was now only a matter of individually wiping the current OS and installing the new one onto each computer.

"So we're good to go?" Collins asked as he munched down a sandwich Reid had offered.

"Everything looks good here, guys. The diagnostics check revealed no problems. Thanks for the admin privileges, Jack."

"Thanks for going over it for me one more time. Okay, so we get a quick snack and then we push on. That sound good?" Reid inquired.

"Sounds like a plan. Jake, how many men can you get here in the next thirty minutes?" Hunt asked and glanced up to

Collins.

"As many as you want. Why?"

"Get about nine or ten – " Hunt's phone suddenly came to life with the tone of AC/DC's *Gone Shootin'*. With an apologetic rise of his hand, he grabbed his workbag and unzipped it. As he went to retrieve his phone, the bag slipped from his hand, hit the table, and tumbled to the ground beneath. He looked on in horror as his gun spilled from inside and landed on the ground with a hard thud. Both Reid and Collins jumped back in shock, expecting the deadly weapon to discharge, but after a few seconds of spinning, it settled on the ground.

"What the hell is that doing in there?" Reid turned his gaze to Hunt. His eyes were burning with rage and his fists clenched in anticipation of violence.

"Jesus!" Hunt replied quickly. "I thought I took them all out!"

"What does that mean?" Reid demanded sharply.

"I mean, this is my hunting bag, guys. I couldn't find anything else this morning – Hold on while I get this...Hello?" Hunt said, turning away from their glares to answer the call.

"Peter? Are you at home?"

"Karen? Hold on a second..." He squatted down and lifted the gun, put it inside the workbag, and zipped it up. He then turned to Reid and Collins and said, "Get your lunch. I gotta take this. I'll be back in a few minutes." He hurried down the stairs and into ATARIC's restroom, which he found empty. "Karen, you still there?"

"Everything okay, Peter? You sound like you have company."

Maybe it was just his imagination, but Hunt thought he detected a tone of accusation in Karen's words. "I'm at ATARIC, Karen," he replied without any emotion.

"ATARIC? What are you doing there?"

"Jack needed my help with a few things, and he convinced them to bring me back...for a while, anyway."

"That's great, Peter! But, are you...?"

"What, drunk?" This time his emotions were clear.

"I didn't mean it like that, but are you okay?"

"I'm fine, but you didn't call to check up on me. What's wrong?"

Karen hesitated. "It doesn't matter. I can tell you're busy."

"Karen," he said sternly. "What is it?"

"I can't tell you over the phone. Can you come over to my office?"

"Karen, I really can't leave here. We're on a deadline, and Jack needs me. Is it something serious? I mean, something that can't wait until tonight? We can – " Hunt was about to say they could talk about it at home tonight.

"Listen, how about I come over there?" Karen suggested. It's only thirty minutes away."

"Well...okay, I suppose I could pry myself away for ten or fifteen minutes. When you get here, give me a call and I'll come down to meet you."

"Okay. Thank you, Peter."

"See you in a bit."

Reid and Collins were waiting for his return, standing, strangely, in the same position they'd been when he left. He wondered if his story had curbed their curiosity and outrage, and wasn't surprised to find it hadn't.

"Why have you a gun in your workbag, Peter?" This time it was Collins.

Hunt blew out a sigh. "I told you already. That's my hunting bag. I take my guns in it when I'm hunting. I couldn't find another bag for my stuff this morning, so I cleared it out instead. I mustn't have seen that gun."

"You leave your guns in your bag?" Reid demanded.

"Yes, I do, Jack. Ever since Karen left, I haven't bothered putting them back in the safe," he spat matter-of-factly.

"What *did* Karen want?"

"She told me Sarah was up for it, and she wanted to know if I was interested in another threesome tonight."

Reid's face flushed, and though he wanted to lash out at Hunt, he controlled himself. "As facetious as that comment is – especially with your *history* with Jake – I'm going to ignore the lecherous remarks aimed at my wife."

Hunt shook his head. "I'm sorry, that was uncalled for. Karen wanted me to come over to her office, but I told her I didn't have time. So, she's coming here in about half an hour. And since we haven't got time for dawdling, how about we accept my reason for the gun being in my bag and get on with the job at hand?"

"Fine," Reid replied. "But just so you know, I've taken the gun for safekeeping. You'll get it back when we're finished tonight."

"Fine, *Mother*," Hunt replied evenly. "Now can we get back to work?"

CHAPTER FORTY-ONE
UNCOVERINGS

QUANTICO MARINE CORPS BASE
QUANTICO
VIRGINIA
13: 50 EST

Wesley Anderson had spent the last hour working on a pretext for General Peterson's visit to Harvey Point. The best – and *only* – one he'd come up with so far was for them to masquerade as an inspection team sent by the President to make sure all CIA personnel had vacated the premises. Anderson had forged a presidential letter – a crime in itself – and was confident that, without major scrutiny, it would get them into the base.

When his phone rang, he expected it to be Peterson calling to inquire how much longer he'd be. The voice on the other end, though, was of an old friend whom he hadn't seen in years.

"Well I'll be damned! If it isn't my old gunnery-sergeant Thomas McCoy! How the hell you been, Gunny?"

"It's Captain Tom McCoy now, Sergeant-Major."

"Well I'll be double-damned! You gonna pull rank on me now, Marine?"

McCoy laughed. "I ain't that full of myself yet, Sergeant-Major. Besides, I know you're the right-hand man for the

Chairman of the Joint Chiefs."

He returned the laugh. "So what can I do for *Captain* Tom McCoy today?" He could feel the mood change with that question.

"I gotta ask you a few questions that are gonna sound strange, sir. And I gotta know we're on a secure line and that this is between me and you."

Anderson leaned forward on his rocker chair and closed the door to his office. "We're secure, Captain. And we've been friends long enough that I don't need to answer the second one. What's up?"

"Well, one of my sergeants just told me he gave a sitrep to a major yesterday."

"What's so strange about that?"

"Well, the major in question hasn't been in Afghanistan for months."

That comment piqued Anderson's attention and he began to listen more attentively to McCoy's words.

"Thing is, sir, there's a lotta strange things going on around here. First, the sergeant tells me he gave a sitrep to Major Robert Miller. I know for a fact Rob hasn't been behind enemy lines for months now. I was talking to him just the other week to give him a sitrep myself, and he's lamenting the fact he's in D.C."

"Could it have been a case of mistaken identity?"

"I don't see how. The major – or whoever it was – identified himself as Major Miller and specifically asked to speak to the sergeant. I'm not blaming the kid – Holmes – at all. I mean, if you get wind of a major wanting to speak with you, you show up. Thing is, Holmes shouldn't have been debriefed by anyone at all. He's not the leader of his platoon – that's Jack Carlos. But Holmes told me Carlos and his second-in-command, Julio Gyle, were shipped home yesterday. Now, the order didn't go through me. They bypassed me, sir, and took two of my best men without so much as a by-your-leave. Plus, the guy who took 'em – Brigadier-General Edward Triton – I've never heard tell of him. So I don't know what the hell's going on back there, but I would appreciate a little heads-up. Can you find out?"

Anderson already knew what was going on, but he couldn't tell McCoy that. His voice became guarded: "Tom, how many people besides me have you told about this?"

"None. Holmes and the rest of his team are the only ones who know. Why?"

"I need you to drop it."

"Sir?"

"I'm already looking into it. This goes way deeper than anything I've seen in twenty years. Heads are going to roll on this, Tom. Forget we had this conversation and continue your work over there like nothing happened."

But McCoy would not be undone. "What the hell is going on, Sergeant-Major?"

"Dammit, Tom! I'm trying to save your ass! You remember those 'missions' in Desert Storm? The LGD lacings outside Baghdad?"

"Yeah, I remember. What about it?"

"No one knew what we were doing. Hell, no one even knew Fore-Con were involved. That was black ops. This stuff I'm dealing with now – it's beyond black. There's going to be fallout. And the less you know, the better your career will be for it. Now, I'm going to terminate this conversation, and I hope for your sake and mine you forget everything we've just said to each other."

When Anderson hung up the phone, it had barely settled back into the cradle when it rang again. This time it was Peterson, and he wanted to know why the hell the line had been busy for five minutes.

"Sir, I'm ready to go on this end, but I've just heard something you might be interested in..."

CHAPTER FORTY-TWO
TAKEDOWN

CASPIAN AIR FLIGHT 434
18:55 GMT

Enough time had elapsed, Ivanovich decided, eyeing the terrorist nearest him. He was about thirty feet away, walking down the aisle towards him. The leader was still inside the cockpit, with his second-in-command guarding the entry. The final two – Ivanovich hoped there weren't any more than five – had gone into the rear cabins.

With a flick of his wrist, Ivanovich alerted York that it was time to go. The terrorist closed the distance to twenty yards, and Ivanovich watched both his eyes and those of his second-in-command. The latter were staring off into the distance, perhaps in silent prayer, and Ivanovich knew he wouldn't get a better chance than this.

***

It was now or never, Denton decided, watching the advancing terrorist. The pretty girl beside him had still yet to notice the commotion, but that was immaterial.

Come on, you son-of-a-bitch. Just come another few yards. That's it, keep coming. Now!

With the swiftness of an eagle, Denton lunged out of his seat. Caught unaware, the terrorist jerked in reaction to the movement, but luckily his finger hadn't been on the trigger of his rifle. The first priority was to rid him of his weapon. Denton smashed his forearm down on the stock with all the force he could muster. The rifle tumbled out of the terrorist's hands and crashed to the floor.

Instinctively, the Arab followed it down. Denton, now on his feet, brought his knee up into the crouching frame, catching him square on the jaw. The terrorist toppled over and hit the ground with a hard grunt.

Denton ducked down and grabbed the man's AK-47, ignoring the look of horrified confusion from the blonde in the seat next to him. He then grabbed the terrorist around the waist and hefted him into his seat. The blonde's expression changed from horror to disgust, and for a moment Denton thought she might start crying, but he again silenced her with a finger to his lips.

Pulling his hoody over his head, he advanced deeper into the rear cabins, searching for the other terrorist patrolling this route. Along the way, he saw people tense in their seats, others rise to offer help, and his reaction was the same in both cases: a spread hand to tell them to relax and not get in his way.

***

Ivanovich didn't know what the hell was going on in the rear cabins, but it had attracted the attention of his terrorist. As the man walked by Ivanovich's seat, Ivanovich took one last look at the second-in-command, gave York a jerk in the ribs, and rose out of his seat with the grace and light-footedness of a ballerina. Without a sound, he closed the distance to the unsuspecting terrorist. He thrust his arms forward and grabbed the Arab around the neck, and with a savage jerk, spun his head until he heard the satisfying snap of bone. The terrorist dropped to the ground with a lifeless thud. Ivanovich grabbed the rifle and pirouetted to face the cockpit door.

York was already halfway there. At the last second the terrorist looked up and tried to shoulder his rifle, but York had the advantage. With a shoulder-block a linebacker would've been proud of, he drove into the man at chest height. Both collapsed through the cockpit door and fell inside, the AK tumbling from the grip of the terrorist.

York lashed out with a punch that sent blood cascading into the air and rendered the terrorist useless. In his peripheral view he saw the AK-47 lying another five feet forward, behind the chair of the third officer. With a desperate lunge, he clambered over the motionless body and thrust out a hand to grasp the butt of the rifle.

The leader, though, had already anticipated it. A heavy booted foot dropped onto both the rifle and York's hand. With a groan of pain, York yanked his hand from underneath, tearing skin as it abraded the rubber. When he glanced up, he saw a bearded man whose face bore a striking resemblance to Osama bin Laden, and whose smile suggested how much pleasure he would take in sending York into whatever afterlife awaited an infidel.

"*Allahu Akbar,*" the leader screamed, aimed his AK at York, and gently squeezed the trigger, savouring the moment for its every worth.

"No, Sergei Ivanovich, actually, but I'll tell Allah you rang," Ivanovich called as he stepped into the room and levelled his AK at the leader's head. The Osama wannabe roared something incomprehensible, and then made the biggest mistake possible. He turned to get a bead on Ivanovich, not realising the extra two seconds of time required to do so had given Ivanovich an advantage the Russian could not have otherwise gained.

What if I puncture the damn –

But there was no time for that. Ivanovich steadied his aim, sucked in a deep breath, and pulled the trigger once. The bullet covered the distance before Ivanovich's arm had even recoiled. It smashed into the forehead of the terrorist, and the 5.56 mm NATO round fragmented on impact, hit the skull and shredded the brain into minute pieces. Without a sound, the leader collapsed to the cockpit floor amidst a pool of blood.

***

Denton heard the shot but he was already otherwise committed. The terrorist, who'd been facing away from him, now spun around. Denton, caught out in the open, moved to dive for cover but realised doing so was futile. The terrorist looked at him in confusion, and then asked something incomprehensible. Denton understood – the hoody had hidden his face and the terrorist was confused. That confusion bought him all the time needed.

He'd never fired a gun on a plane before, and certainly not an AK-47. The rifle came up at a weird angle, almost something akin to the way a gangster held a pistol in Hollywood, and he cursed silently. The movement, though, had alerted the Arab. Rage washed over his face, followed by a scream of "infidel", and then his rifle came up in exactly the right place.

Denton knew he would only get one chance. Tucking the stock hard against his shoulder, he lined his sights below the terrorist's nose and squeezed the trigger.

He felt something hard jolt him in the chest, and for a split second he thought – or perhaps hoped – it was the recoil. First, he looked up and saw the terrorist collapse to the ground, a red dot on his forehead indicating how woeful Denton's aim had been. But when he looked down, he saw blood gathering on his own chest. In an oddly serene way, he nodded and collapsed to the floor below.

All he could think of now was how much he wanted to sleep.

***

"Who the hell are you guys?" the first officer demanded of Ivanovich and York.

"Just concerned citizens," replied Ivanovich.

"'Concerned citizens', my ass! I know a thing or two about guns, and there's no way a 'concerned citizen' would be able to take down a team of trained terrorists like you guys just did. So, who the hell are you?"

"Let's just say there was a time in our past where we served our respective countries. And now, Captain, we need to go check the rest of the flight for any stragglers. By the way, did the terrorists change our flight course?"

"No, sir. They wanted us to fly to New York. The bastards were probably going to try another nine-eleven."

"What's the standard procedure now? Do you fly on?"

"I can't radio-in because they shot the radio. I have no choice but to continue on my original course."

There was another question that nagged at him as he walked down the aisle to check for stragglers. Why had they hijacked the plane so quickly? It would have made more sense to wait until it neared New York City, which would have lowered the margin for error. But they'd hijacked it four hours from its destination, allowing ample time for anyone on-board to assess the situation and come up with a plan.

When Ivanovich walked by the pretty blonde, with a rifle in his hand, she screamed and pushed the unconscious form of the terrorist out of the seat and jumped back into her own, in a foetal position. Ivanovich couldn't help but smile as he gestured for York to secure the limp body.

Farther down the aisle, he came on a confusing scene. Two men were lying on the floor. One of them was undoubtedly dead, but the other had a faraway look in his eye, and as his chest heaved up and down, it made a sucking noise. Pink froth gathered at the corners of his mouth. Ivanovich had seen such a thing before. A punctured lung, no doubt. The man would be dead before a doctor would have time to even remove his shirt.

Who are you? Ivanovich silently asked the dying man. Stepping around the downed frame, he checked to make sure the other terrorist was dead, before securing his rifle. When he turned back, he found York rummaging around in the dying man's pockets.

"Flight marshal," he announced, producing a bloody ID from the man's breast pocket. "Richard Denton."

You picked the wrong day to play hero, Mr Denton.

"Keep an eye on him. He's not going anywhere, but he might be armed, and he might think we're the bad guys."

York laughed. "We *are* the bad guys, Sergei."

That irony was not lost on Ivanovich. "Yeah, I know. Just keep an eye on him. I'm gonna go check the rest of the flight."

"You think there're more?"

"Maybe..."

"What else you thinking?" York asked.

"Something about this isn't right. I'm going to go check on a few things. If Mr Denton there dies while I'm gone, go ask the captain where we can get something to tie the unconscious one up...and somewhere we can store the dead ones."

"And if he doesn't die?" York pressed.

"Then help him along," Ivanovich replied nonchalantly.

CHAPTER FORTY-THREE
FOOL ME TWICE

OUTSIDE SEAGATE
14: 00 EST

With a smile on his face and one less bullet in his Makarov, Vladimir Pushkin pulled up to the entrance of Seagate and alighted from his SUV. According to Davies' – AKA "Karl Williams" – file, he had a residence both here and in Clinton, New Jersey. Since this was the closest, Pushkin had decided to check it out first. To his chagrin, he'd discovered the community was more secure than the bank he'd just left.

With a sigh, he hit the zapper and lifted the trunk. Lifeless eyes stared back at him. The sight caused him to smile again. As he had predicted, the murder had brought him a great deal of satisfaction.

He closed it again and walked to the security hut, where a stocky man in his late fifties sat reading a novel appropriately entitled *Endgame*. Pushkin coughed to acquire his attention, and the man grunted as though someone had disturbed him sleeping.

"Yeah?" he asked

"I need to get inside," Pushkin replied in perfect English.

"Photo-ID card, please."

"I don't have it."

"Then you ain't getting in. Good day."

Useless son-of-a-bitch.

Pushkin walked back to the SUV and slipped inside. He flicked the key once, twice, a third time without letting the engine start, and then, with a thump of the steering wheel, feigned complete disgust. Continuing the act, he stepped outside, slammed the door shut, and marched to the security hut.

"You wouldn't have any idea 'bout this piece of crap SUV, would you?"

The guard set the book on the table again and rose out of his seat. "What seems to be the problem?"

"She won't start for me." Pushkin had to mentally remind himself to say "she" instead of "he".

"I'm no mechanic, but in the interests of getting your car the hell out th' road, I'll take a look."

Pushkin allowed the guard to get as far as the door and then withdrew his Makarov. With an even greater smile, he shoved the pistol into the back of the man's neck and pulled the trigger once. The head snapped forward as blood exploded from an inch-and-a-half exit hole, and the man collapsed into Pushkin's waiting arms. The Russian dragged him to the back of the car and heaved him into the trunk. With a satisfied clap of his hands, he closed it again, walked to the security hut once more, and opened the gate.

After five minutes, he finally found Davies' house – not because he'd located the number, but because the broken window outside it seemed incongruous for a place like Seagate. He eased the car to a stop about fifty yards downwind and idled it. For the following five minutes, he watched for any activity, coming or going, from the residence, while doing recon on the rest of the area.

For a small community, it sure did get its share of traffic. From the time Pushkin stopped his car until the time he exited it, no fewer than six cars came and went. Soon, they'd discover the main gate was open to the world, without a security guard in sight. He had to move fast before someone sounded the alarm.

He jogged to the opposite side of the road and ducked into Davies' front yard. Darting past the front door, he stooped down below the level of the windowsills and moved towards the broken window. Every now and again, he stopped to check his six and make sure no one had snuck up behind him. When he reached the window, he found the curtains pulled to ward off the rain which was still drizzling. He opened one of them enough to allow him to see in. When he saw no one inside, he hopped through and landed lightly on the carpet inside, avoiding the glass he was sure was there.

The room was in shambles. Rain and blood slicked the rug carpet, bedclothes lay strewn across the floor, and a large chunk of plasterboard was missing from one of the walls. Pushkin crouched down and fingered the blood on the rug. It hadn't fully coagulated. There had been a serious tussle here no less than an hour ago, he decided.

Continuing forward, he checked the en-suite bathroom and found, in the sink, a half-empty bag of white crystalline powder. From what he'd read of Davies' file, the man had no disciplinary problems that stemmed from narcotics abuse. This was not his bag of cocaine or heroin. Whoever had broken the window had also not realised Davies had been home. The question now was: Were both still going at it somewhere in the house, or had the druggie done Pushkin's job for him and killed Davies?

Out in the corridor, he extracted his Makarov and eased down the hallway, checking each door along the way. All of them were wide open...except for the last on the left. He positioned himself along the right-hand side of it and gently lay against it.

Silence.

He tried the knob. Slowly, he spun it until the door popped open, and then he grabbed his Makarov in his right hand and, taking a step back, shouldered the door with his left side. It burst open into the room and clacked a tiled wall behind. Pushkin rolled into the room and landed in a crouch, hands extending forward, eyes and gun sweeping across the room in tandem.

Bath, wash-handbasin, shower, and a bidet.

He rose and edged toward the closed shower door. In his mind a thousand warning bells fired off simultaneously. Keeping his gun tight in his right hand, he reached out with the left and slowly drew the door back until he could see inside.

Empty.

But water dripped down the tiled wall inside...

Pushkin hurried back out to the corridor and checked the last room downstairs. He found the kitchen empty, as he had expected to, but those warning bells now escalated to full-blown alarms. Something bugged him. The broken window, the blood on the rug, the bag of drugs, and the used shower. What connected them? If Davies had fought off an intruder who had broken his window to get in, how did the intruder have time to stash his drugs in Davies' bathroom? *Why* would he stash them there? Why did Davies take a shower after? Why wasn't he still here? Pushkin was aware that Kirov had called Davies a spy. Paranoia ran wild in spies. If this was Davies' safe-house, it lacked the security which would bring comfort to a man of his standing. Sure, the community was tight-knit and had impressive security, but that wouldn't be enough for someone like Davies. No, this residence had all the hallmarks of a backup safe-house. But why –

"...before he finds us," a voice murmured from nearby.

Pushkin spun quickly. He moved out of the kitchen with slow, deliberate steps, the gun continuously oscillating from side to side just in case someone was lying in wait. Down the hall, in the lower bedroom, he could hear the sounds of rustling. He moved faster, covering the distance in a few seconds, and burst into the room much the same way he'd entered the bathroom.

"What the hell was that? Go check it out, Ray," a voice called from inside the bathroom.

"Like hell! C'mon, man, just grab the stuff and let's get outta here," replied Ray.

The two of them exited the bathroom together, one holding the bag of drugs. They looked at Pushkin, saw the gun, saw he wasn't Davies, and dashed for the broken window.

Pushkin weighed up his options. They'd seen his face. They probably wouldn't remember it, given the situation, the darkness of the room, and the fact the gun was more memorable. But they'd seen him.

Even in the dim of the room, he could see the sights of his Makarov perfectly. The gun came up like an extension of his arm.

The closest one to the window first, Vlad, he told himself. The bullets barely made a noise as they exited through the suppressor. They hit the first one in the side of the jaw and exploded the head like a ripe melon. The second one stopped in his tracks, almost tripping over the downed body of his mate. He turned to face Pushkin but never completed the move. Pushkin double-tapped him in the temple and he dropped.

He dragged the bodies to the adjacent bedroom and closed the door. He checked upstairs, finding nothing but empty space, before going back outside and reversing his car as close to the front door as possible.

CHAPTER FORTY-FOUR
LEADS

26 FEDERAL PLAZA
14: 10 EST

While Hollingsworth's interview continued in the interrogation room, William Forrester perused Troy Davies' jacket which had arrived in his office minutes earlier. The manila envelope was as thick as a small novel, and the information inside just as shocking as the contents of those espionage thrillers Forrester read religiously.

Apparently, Davies had spent twelve years in the NYPD before joining the Bureau. While this wasn't uncommon, Forrester had never heard of the other man before Davies had started working with the FBI, which was surprising given the reputation he'd carved for himself. According to the file, he had convicted almost a hundred criminals. Along with a staggering ninety-per cent arrest/conviction record, he'd also liquidated several small-level narcotics rings in New York City. These feats earned him promotion after promotion, and he'd looked a certainty to become captain before a federal case against the Mendoza brothers unhinged all of his hard work. The official report stated Davies had been solely responsible for their arrest, but Forrester remembered the case well. He'd just joined the Bureau a year earlier and it was his first taste of action. He'd been partnered with Jonathan Baker, but Baker had done most of the work while Forrester had to contend with getting coffee and other menial tasks. The one thing which stood out, even all these years later, was that the Bureau had taken credit for the entire bust.

An official note, hidden towards the back of the jacket, read:

To: Commissioner Alan Partridge
From: Deputy Chief Richard Flynn
Re: Lieutenant Troy Davies

Dear Commissioner Partridge,

It is the opinion of the department heads of the NYPD (precinct thirteen) that Lieutenant Troy Davies, shield number 5273, is unfit for duty as captain at this time and for the foreseeable future. Furthermore, we believe Davies' current state of mind negates his ability to function as an officer of the NYPD. We recommend that he be suspended for an indefinite period of time, pending a full investigation pertaining to his actions during the Mendoza case.

As with all NYPD officers, we expect a degree of loyalty and a measure of common sense when liaising with sister law enforcement agencies. It is with great sadness that I report Davies as failing in both of those requirements. While we do not wish to see any NYPD officer suspended, we must also consider the hostile environment he could create if he remains in our precinct.

Deputy Chief Richard Flynn.

Further towards the back, Forrester found Baker's recommendation to Jules Cochrane, which vitiated Flynn's claim that Davies was unfit to be captain. The panegyric went on to say that Davies' co-operation with the FBI had been invaluable in helping the Bureau incarcerate the Mendoza brothers. The recommendation and request for a try-out had been granted by Cochrane. Further to that, Davies' certificate of graduation from the FBI academy followed, but then all documentation, to the surprise of Forrester, ceased. No reports, no recommendations from superiors, and no performance reviews for Davies' first twelve months in the Bureau. Forrester knew the sting didn't commence until about six months after Davies' graduation; even the least active agent had some form of paperwork to fill out. The more he studied the file, the more he began to believe someone had removed certain documentation from it. He could understand the secrecy involved and the choice to seal Davies' jacket, but if you were going to seal something, why remove anything from it? Getting the records department to unseal it had taken numerous threats and promises of repercussions, but anyone with clearance lower than Forrester's wouldn't have had a chance. It didn't make sense.

For all intents and purposes, since joining the Bureau Troy Davies had become an unperson. No files, no paper-trail, no records. And while Forrester could understand why, it still didn't explain what had happened during those first six months and the previous twelve in the academy. FBI personnel files were stored in some of the most secure databases known to man. It was unlikely Kirov, even with his ever-expanding reach, could hack the system. Was there something in Davies' past which had been expurgated from official documentation? And if so, what could have been so serious to deem that kind of action?

Forrester was so immersed in the file that he didn't notice Special Agent in Charge Mike Delaney come into his office. The 42-year-old had a florid complexion which had earned him the nickname "sizzle" or just "siz". But being reticent and unable to speak to females were the only faults Delaney possessed. With a gun, he could hit an egg at sixty metres. With a rifle, almost six hundred. Delaney had been present with Forrester earlier in the day at LaGuardia.

"Sorry to bother you, sir, but that 'favour' you requested earlier?"

Forrester set the file down and closed the cover. "Yeah, what about it?"

"We got a hit. One of the taxi drivers we canvassed recognised the picture. He said he left the guy in Seagate about an hour ago."

Forrester snapped his fingers and said, "Get O'Leary and Bastich, and bring the car around. We're leaving."

CHAPTER FORTY-FIVE
PERPLEXITY

CASPIAN AIR FLIGHT 434
19: 15 LOCAL TIME

The co-pilot, under advisement from Ivanovich, made an announcement over the intercom that the attempted recovery of the plane had failed, costing the lives of a flight marshal and two other law enforcement officers, and that the terrorists were remaining in the cockpit henceforth. If anyone tried any more heroics, the pilots would be killed. Ivanovich didn't know why he'd coerced them to lie, but something didn't feel right to him. Until he knew what he was dealing with, it was best to keep everyone in the dark.

Back in his seat, after spending the last fifteen minutes carefully scouting the plane to see if any terrorists were left or any of the passengers reacted to his presence, Ivanovich was happy to learn the standard procedure for this was to continue on course, but something still bothered him about the whole scenario. Turning to York, he shook him awake and said, "Let's say we were going to hijack this plane..."

York groaned, shifted in his seat, and rubbed his eyes. "We're hijacking what now?"

"No, let's *say* we're going to hijack a flight – this flight. Let's also say we want to take control of the plane...crash it into a building, à la nine-eleven." Ivanovich said the last part in a whisper on the off-chance someone might hear and cause a panic. "Okay?"

"Yeah, I guess. Where are you going with this?"

"What way would you do it?"

York frowned. "I'd do it the way these guys just did. Attack the cockpit, get control, and dissuade the passengers from being heroes.

"Exactly. But if you were going to crash the plane into an American building," Ivanovich whispered again, "why wouldn't you wait until it had crossed international waters? Why hijack it four hours from its destination?"

"Come to think of it, that was a pretty amateur move on their part. I'd wait until damn near final approach before I'd storm the cockpit. Less chance of a reaction that way. But these guys...yeah, you're right. It doesn't make sense they hijacked it so early."

"Either they're extremely stupid or..."

"Come on, Sergei. You've been musing for the past thirty minutes. Spill your guts. What are you thinking?"

"Nine-eleven changed everything, right?"

"In what way?" York asked, becoming more confused by the minute.

"In every way, but especially in regards to flying. New preventatives, new law enforcement agencies, the presence of more flight marshals on planes. It was hard enough to get a weapon on-board pre-nine-eleven, but now we're supposed to accept that a bunch of Islamic terrorists got no fewer than a half-dozen AKs on-board today? How? It sure would have been handy for us to know how to smuggle weapons on and off this flight."

"The best security is only as strong as its weakest link, Sergei. Our guys found a way around it...or they kidnapped a flight attendant's family and forced the guy to help. Terrorists will always find a way; you oughta know that."

"Okay, I'll give you that, but we've worked with Islamic terrorists before. They're damned formidable, wouldn't you say? They're not the sort of people to screw up something like this. These guys, though...it's like they're either incredibly stupid or incredibly confident."

"But why would they be incredibly confident?"

"Exactly! Why would *anyone* be that confident after all the security measures in airports and on flights over the past eighteen months?"

"Maybe these guys just didn't do their homework?"

"Hell no. We're talking about the most organised terrorist group since the IRA. This thing would have been planned for months, right down to how many times per flight the captain left the cockpit."

"So why'd their planning get shot to shit on this one?" York asked with a frown.

"What if it didn't?"

York fidgeted in his seat. "Dammit, I hate when you go all cryptic on me, Sergei. What the hell you thinking, man?"

"You and me both, Amos – we know how terrorists think. If we were going to do this, we'd damned sure have a backup in case everything went to hell."

"So what's these guys' backup plan?"

Ivanovich turned to him, his face deadpan. "Somewhere on this flight...there's a sleeper agent."

CHAPTER FORTY-SIX
STUPEFIED

ATARIC
14: 25 LOCAL TIME

Standing outside ATARIC, Peter Hunt looked at his watch for the umpteenth time and wondered where Karen could be. Even in the heaviest New York traffic, she should have already been here ten minutes ago. And, judging from the quiet streets outside the building, traffic was at a lull. He could only wait ten more minutes and then he would have no choice but to go back inside. Reid needed him, and if Johnson found out where he was, all kinds of hell would break loose.

Something odd caught his attention on Madison Avenue, a block away from East 38th Street. Three black SUVs turned left towards ATARIC, boxed in between by a small stretch-limousine with tinted windows and what he assumed were federal plates. All four vehicles drove past ATARIC's parking garage and front entrance, continued down 38th Street, and turned right onto 5th Avenue. Sixty seconds later, two police cruisers made the same manoeuvre, lights on but sirens muted.

Hunt noticed no one either side of 38th Street passed any remarks at the incongruity of seeing a small motorcade drive through the area. They continued their daily routines, oblivious to everything and everyone around them – a normal day in the life of a New Yorker. Something about that bothered him, but he couldn't figure out what.

For the next five minutes he watched the traffic come and go down the rain-slicked street. Thankfully, the deluge had eased but the conditions still made for careful commuting. Perhaps that explained why Karen was running late, but as the time moved towards twenty-five-to-three, he decided he couldn't wait any longer.

After trying Karen's cellphone and getting no answer, he dialled the operator and got the number for her law firm.

"Hello, this is the Leo and Walken law firm, New York office. How may I help you?"

"Hello. Could you put me through to Karen Hunt's office, please?"

"Indeed, sir. May I ask who's calling?"

"I'd rather not say."

"As you wish, sir. Transferring the call now."

The sounds of Journey's *Don't Stop Believing* filtered down through the handset, bringing back memories of the eighties, both good and bad. Hunt had always been a hardcore fan of rock n' roll, especially AC/DC. No matter how depressed he got, or how bad his life seemed, listening to an Angus Young solo always perked him up.

He was about to give up, after eight rings, when a voice answered, "Hello?"

Hunt frowned, wondering why Karen was still in her office. Had she got tied up with a client, or had she blown him off? There was something about her voice too: an edgy tone to it.

"Karen? You're still in the office? Is everything okay?"

"Peter? What are you talking about?"

"Did you forget?"

"Forget what?"

"What – are you playing games, Karen?" demanded Hunt, feeling his temper boiling up into his throat.

"Peter, what are you talking about? Why are you calling me?"

"Me calling *you!* You called me almost an hour ago and told me you had something to tell me. I told you I couldn't get away and you said you'd come to me. I really don't have time for games, Karen. Are you coming or not?"

There came an exasperated sigh from Karen, and then, "Peter, I haven't talked to you in almost six months. I sure as hell didn't call you today. I don't know how drunk you are, but I'm hanging up now."

Suddenly everything became quiet. So quiet Hunt could hear his heartbeat, which thumped with every passing second. The world began to spin, like it had when he'd exited the chopper on the roof of ATARIC this morning. He tried to stifle it, but couldn't, bending over and heaving into a storm drain as a wave of nausea crashed over him. Stumbling, he fell towards the front doors and held himself upright with one hand, squinting in a desperate attempt to quell the vertigo-like feelings. His brain pounded against his skull, almost like something inside wanted to extricate itself. On the other end of the phone, he could hear Karen demanding to know where he'd gone to, but no matter how hard he tried, he couldn't steady himself to answer her.

What the hell had happened? Did she call and have second thoughts, and was now trying to cover up her mistake? Or had she called at all? If she hadn't, it left only one other explanation.

"Peter – fine, I'm hanging up. God – "

Steadying himself to hold the phone, Hunt mumbled, "Karen..."

"Listen, Peter, I have work to do. If this is some kind of game – "

"Karen, listen carefully, please. Call Jack. Tell him I'm at the front door of ATARIC– "

"ATARIC? What are you doing there?"

"Then...call an ambulance."

"An ambulance? Peter! What's wrong – "

But another wave of nausea hit Hunt. His knees buckled and he collapsed at the foot of ATARIC's front entrance, to a cacophony of screaming from the handset which tumbled to the ground with him and smashed to pieces.

Then the world went black.

***

White light disorientated him.

Hunt shut his eyes quickly, as stars coruscated in front of his vision. When he opened them again, it took a moment for his pupils to contract. He blinked a few times to clear them, and studied his surroundings. Around him, numerous machines performed tasks he couldn't begin to imagine, their bleeping alarms much scarier than their backlit displays which he didn't understand.

Looking down, he discovered he was tethered to a gurney. Above him, two men in security guard uniforms alternated their attention from him to the machines. Their demeanours were coldly professional.

At the back sat two more men. Both had their heads in their hands for differing reasons. One looked to be in shock, but the other was talking on a phone and shielding his ear from the constant cacophony of bleeping.

Hunt tried to move, but the straps securing him held tight. With sudden acuity, he realised he was in an ambulance, and the men weren't security guards but paramedics. The two men behind were Jack Reid and Jake Collins. Karen had called the ambulance. Hunt felt himself breathe a sigh of relief. She still cared. Unless, of course, this was someone's facetious idea of Heaven.

"Easy there, big fella," one of the paramedics said. "You had yourself a nasty fall. Don't go moving until we're sure you haven't done any damage."

Reid and Collins looked up, the former breathing a sigh of relief almost as huge as Hunt's. They moved to get up, but the other medic warned them to keep their distance. Hunt didn't understand why, but he had a feeling it had something to do with his head, which throbbed.

"What happened?" asked Reid as he took his seat and assured the person – Hunt hoped it was Karen – on the other end of the phone that everything was okay.

"You tell me," Hunt dissimulated. "I can't remember."

"Do you remember calling Karen?"

"No," Hunt lied.

"She said you called her about you two meeting up," pressed Reid.

"I really don't know, Jack."

"Do you *know* that you disappeared on us?"

"What do you mean?" he replied.

"About half-one, you said you needed to go for a toilet break. We haven't seen you from then until now. Where did you go?"

"What are you talking about? I came back..." Hunt stopped, his eyes widening. "My bag! Where's my workbag!"

"Your *workbag*? It's probably where you left it. *That's* what you're worried about?"

He didn't take it! My God, what the hell is going on? I didn't go back to the office. Karen never called me. Jack never found and took my gun. I hallucinated the whole thing! Jesus, I've lost an entire hour. Where did I go? What did I do?

"I'm sorry, I'm not thinking straight. Must be the shock. How are we on the OS?"

"Don't worry about the OS. The medics want to take you to Lenox Hill," Reid announced.

Hunt shook the only part of his body he could move. "I'm not going to *any* hospital."

"Sir," began one of the medics, "you've had a – "

"Yeah, yeah, a 'nasty fall'. I don't care. I'm not going to the hospital; so you do whatever you have to do here and then let me go."

"I must strongly advise against – "

"Listen: Either you remove these restraints, or I remove them for you. We on the same page?" demanded Hunt, gesturing with his eyes to his obscenely large arms.

"As you wish, sir. We'll run our tests, give you some medication, and you're free to leave."

"Thank you."

Hallucinations aren't a symptom of rapid-onset delirium tremens, nor any other condition stemming from alcohol abuse. I didn't collapse because of DTs.

I collapsed because someone wanted me out of the way.

CHAPTER FORTY-SEVEN
COURAGE UNDER FIRE

HARVEY POINT
14: 35 EST

Carlos had no more time to debate the incongruity of his current situation. The fact that no one had responded to his cries or attempts to break the camera was reason enough for him to decide something wasn't right; you didn't break people by leaving them alone in their cell. If you were smart, you knew men like Carlos were more dangerous held captive than they were out in the open. Gyle had been gone for too long, and his lack of screaming only added to Carlos' worries.

With a sigh, he eased off the bed and moved to the cell door again. Outside, foliage stretched as far as the eye could see, meandering off where the buildings began some hundred yards farther on. But he couldn't see enough of them to determine if people were coming and going, and Gyle's earlier screams seemed to have come from farther west than those crop of structures. If he remembered the map correctly, three subsequent buildings surrounded the EOD complex. From his viewpoint, Carlos could see two alongside an edifice which he assumed to be the EOD. If it was, to the northeast a two-foot-wide pipe served as a storm drain for all three buildings. If he could get to it, he could access them unseen.

There was still the problem of getting out of his cell. But he had a small inkling of an idea. Throwing himself prone on the floor, he wiggled his way underneath the bed so the camera couldn't see him. There, he spun onto his back and worked his fingers into the screws securing the springs.

After five minutes of arduous labour to remove two bolts, he finally had what he needed. The coil snapped when enough pressure was applied, and the piece of spring came loose from the base.

He spent another five minutes straightening the material, before coming back from underneath the bed. Concealing the spring, he dashed to the cell door again to see if anyone was coming.

Silence.

Carlos decided it was now or never. He worked the length of spring into the locking mechanism and began tinkering with the tumblers. From his position, the camera couldn't make out what he was doing. Someone would have to come to find out, and either way, that was a win-win situation.

Carlos allowed his mind to wander to the possibility of escape. If he could get out, the storm drain seemed the most advantageous position to take up. From there, he'd work his way to each building individually and find out where they were holding Gyle. After that...well, he hadn't thought that far ahead, but if Gyle was truly injured, someone would pay, and he didn't care who.

***

Sitting alone in the soldiers' quarters, Sergeant Larry Lansdale went over Brigadier-General Triton's words again and again in his head: *Those two soldiers failed the mission, son. They've been shipped back home. Don't worry about them. Your mission continues this afternoon, Sergeant. Get some chow and be ready for action at fifteen hundred hours. Sharp!*

Sir, yes, sir!

Failed the mission? How? Why? They'd done what no other soldier before them had – capture the two men sent to capture *them*. They were the best soldiers Lansdale had met so far. They weren't just Marine Corps. No, they – what were their names? – were Force Recon, not a doubt about it. If they'd failed the mission, it was because someone wanted them to. Or, as Fromm had alluded to earlier, because someone had ambushed them.

The arrival of Chief Petty Officer John Mason, formerly of Navy Seal Team Six and, until recently, part of the Navy's top-secret tier-one counter-terrorism unit DEVGRU, broke Lansdale's reverie but darkened the mood somewhat. Though both shared many similarities – bald, an inch apart in height, and had the exact same weight: 245 – their former squadrons, whilst having mutual respect for each other, had for years been the subject of debate over who was the finest counter-terrorist team ever devised. This had led to some bad blood between certain members, and Lansdale had kept his distance from all the swabbies until now.

Though Mason had an intimidating build at six-three, his arms weren't as defined as Lansdale's, and Lansdale knew he would have the upper hand if the bald Yank wanted to throw down. But the arrival of Mason's designated partner, Gunnery-Sergeant Nathan Murphy, changed the mood even more.

If Fromm was the toughest and scariest at the Point, Murphy had to be a close second. At seven foot tall and weighing three hundred pounds, he towered over every single soldier by almost half a foot and outweighed them by forty-plus pounds. Where most of the other soldiers' strength came from power-lifting, Murphy's was natural. He'd never lifted a weight in his life, but he'd military-pressed Mason for six reps during the first week.

As a member of the Marine Corps, Murphy's full-bearded face wouldn't have been tolerated for any other soldier, but because of extenuating circumstances he was allowed to grow it. It gave him an aura of uniqueness.

Murphy didn't have to say much to intimidate, but his impressive physique, coupled with a coarse voice, accentuated his fearsome persona. When he spoke, everyone listened. Everyone, that was, except for Kurt Fromm. The German had no tolerance for bravado. While he didn't mind the bonhomie between soldiers, he felt the treatment of new ones sometimes went above and beyond accepted standards.

"So, Larry, get tied to any trees lately?" Mason asked with a laugh.

Since the debriefing between Triton, Lansdale, and Fromm had been private, Lansdale wondered how Mason could have found out about it. He came to the conclusion he couldn't have, which meant Mason (or someone else) had been in the jungle and saw them get tied to the tree.

"Go screw yourself, swabbie," replied Lansdale.

Mason's friendly demeanour vanished in an instant, replaced by palpable rage. "What did you call me?"

"You heard me, unless you're deaf as well as stupid."

"You know," began Mason, "I hear we only got so many spaces on this team, Nate. I'm thinking this pussy here doesn't deserve a spot. Let's make sure he's not in a position to get one." Mason advanced on Lansdale, who sprung out of his seat and readied himself for an assault.

Murphy moved to close the door, but only got five feet. Kurt Fromm stepped into the room. Before Murphy could react, he delivered a vicious left hook to the American's midsection, dropping him to one knee. His right came up immediately thereafter, catching the Marine square under the chin and depositing his blood halfway across the room. The huge soldier's body arced backwards and collapsed in a heap on the cold, concrete floor.

Fromm advanced forward, his eyes set in rage. "We got some kind of problem here, *ja*?" he asked Mason.

Though Mason stood six-four to Fromm's six foot, and outweighed the German by a considerable amount, he shook his head and raised his hands in capitulation. He helped his mate off the floor and scurried out of the quarters like someone had told him a deadly neurotoxin was present inside.

"Are you okay?" Fromm asked when he'd left.

"Fine, but we're on their radar now. They're gonna have it in for us."

"*Have it in?*"

Lansdale shook his head and laughed. "Never mind. So, did you find out anything about where our friends got to?"

"I can tell you where they're *not*. There are three buildings around the EOD complex. I checked them all, along with the EOD. No sign of our two friends."

"So maybe they *were* sent home?"

Fromm shook his head. "I doubt it very much. All the

trouble to bring them here to send them home again because they 'failed' one thing? That doesn't make sense. I don't know where they are, but they're still on this base. I'll bet every Deutsche Mark I own on that."

"Aren't you guys with the euro now?"

Fromm glared at him. "Let's go. We still have a schedule to keep, and we don't want to give anyone reason to 'kick' us out."

CHAPTER FORTY-EIGHT
VENEER

CASPIAN AIR FLIGHT 434
18: 45 GMT

With fleeting glances, Sergei Ivanovich checked the entire row of economy-class seats for anyone who appeared out of place in a milieu of ordinary citizens. Most passengers cast him a mixture of confused, annoyed, and concerned glances, but he continued forward until he reached the curtained entrance to the first-class compartments. Here, a pert young woman raised her hand to signify he could go no farther.

Ivanovich removed the badge he'd stolen from the dying – now dead - flight marshal stored in the avionics compartment with the other dead terrorists and, covering the photo, showed it to the attendant.

"Ma'am," he began in his best American accent, "I'm a TSA-registered flight marshal. I'm not even supposed to be on this plane, but someone screwed up the itinerary this morning and I got the short straw. Listen," Ivanovich continued, taking the confused woman by the arm and leading her through the curtain. "I'm just after getting off the satellite phone with the deputy secretary of the TSA. They're raising holy hell on the ground." Ivanovich paused and cast a feigned nervous glance at all the first-class passengers. Continuing in a whisper, he said, "They think there's a chance somewhere among these passengers is another terrorist; one who has a remote detonator for a bomb."

The attendant's eyes widened and she motioned to scream before Ivanovich clamped his hand over her mouth and led her back into the economy section.

"Please! We don't need a panic here, Mrs...?"

"*Ms* Ford. Holly," she replied, trying to keep her nerves in check. Jerking her thumb toward the cockpit, she said, "What's the situation with the pilot?"

Ivanovich led her by the hand to a quiet place and said, "Holly, I need you to listen very carefully. I'm about to tell you something you cannot tell anyone else. We subdued the terrorists from earlier. The pilots are alone in the cockpit. But if this sleeper agent finds out they're dead, he might blow up the plane right now. We can't let that happen. So, what I need you to do is to remain calm and act as though nothing's changed."

Holly shook her head vigorously. "I don't think I can do that!"

Ivanovich grasped her shoulders. "You can. And I need you to keep this quiet. The less people who know about this, the better chance we'll have of making it to the ground in one piece."

Holly's eyes grew even wider this time. "God! How can this be happening? I mean, I was only sixteen when nine-eleven happened. I wondered how awful it would have been to be on those planes, and now – "

"Holly, I need you to stay calm. Please. Just go back into the first-class cabin and serve the people. If you see anyone or anything suspicious, come and tell me immediately. Can you do that for me?"

"Okay." She nodded. "I guess."

"Okay. Good girl. Just one more thing: I've requisitioned the help of a police officer on-board. So, if you see a large black man walking around the aisles, he's with me."

"Right. Just please find and arrest these bastards!"

Ivanovich stifled a laugh at the irony of that statement and followed the attractive attendant into the first-class cabin. To her credit, she continued her duties devoid of anything resembling fear or concern, and he used her as a distraction to gain more time to study the occupants of the cabin.

Many were businessmen, apparelled in expansive Armani suits and working on exorbitant laptops. Others were affluent vacationers who Ivanovich assumed to be idiotic for choosing Russia as a holiday destination. And some wore suits but carried nothing which would identify them as businessmen. It was these who Ivanovich studied carefully, committing their individual mannerisms and appearances to memory. They were the ones who stood out amongst the crowd. Their lack of business equipment sounded alarm bells immediately; companies who reserved first-class seating for their employees did so to provide a quiet, harmonious surrounding for them to work in. Somehow it didn't seem right for a "suit" to be without *any* kind of office-work.

What Ivanovich didn't see, much to his chagrin, was the presence of a final Islamic terrorist. While there were numerous foreign citizens on-board, none had the distinctive characteristics of a Muslim, and none possessed the hardened and chiselled facial features of one who despised the "infidel".

"Got a possible in the rear economy cabins, Sergei." York's voice came through as though he were standing next to Ivanovich. The transmitters and earpieces were for the mission – if they ever got that far – but York had rooted them out of his bag for now. It would allow them to keep in contact while doing recon of all the cabins. The only downside was that they would look insane to the people around them.

"Any devices in his hand?" Ivanovich asked, ignoring the look of bewilderment – which he knew was coming – from a woman sitting with her husband and two children.

"Like what? A big one with a sign saying: 'Hey, this is the device for remote-detonating the huge' "—he whispered the next word—" '*bomb* we have on the plane?' "

"Yeah, something like that. Christ sake, York, has he got any kind of PDA device in his hands?"

"That would be a no. I think I would have mentioned it earlier. Don't you?"

"So why is he a 'possible'?"

"That might have something to do with the beard and the striking resemblance to his Islamic brethren."

"Okay, noted. Keep looking. It may be our guy, it may not, but he isn't going to *detonate* until we reach New York. We keep searching until we're sure there's no one else."

"Whoop-de-do."

Ivanovich thought about reprimanding York for his cheerful pessimism, but the American made him laugh – a rare occurrence these days. Instead, he finished his sweep of the first-class cabin, checking everywhere, including the toilets.

Ivanovich didn't notice him until he returned down the aisle for a second time. In a corner seat in the middle of the first-class cabin, seated beside a large man who'd hidden him the first time, Ivanovich saw a face from the past.

Jesus Christ, it's Levsky!

Ivanovich would never forget the face of Aleksandr Levsky for the rest of his life. He had no doubts – this was him. Those same hard, blue eyes. The same ragged hairstyle, albeit now greying with age. And, at his feet, an expensive cane which had been retrofitted to hold eight highly poisonous darts.

Ivanovich shielded his face from view and hurried back to the economy section. He stepped into one of the toilets so his conversation couldn't be heard.

"Amos, we've got a serious problem."

"No shit, Sherlock! Where've you been all day?"

"Not that! We've got *another* problem. Levsky's on the plane."

"Levsky! *Aleksandr* Levsky?"

"Yeah."

"*The* Aleksandr Levsky, former director of the KGB?"

"One and the same."

"Fuck me! Do you think he'll recognise you?"

"Oh, I think he'll remember me. After all, I did kill his family."

CHAPTER FORTY-NINE
MASSACRE

SEAGATE
14: 50 EST

The first indication of something being amiss came when Bastich drove the Bureau's SUV through the open gates of Seagate without anyone stopping him or asking for identification. The security hut lay open to the world. Inside, a damp novel fluttered in the wind, the text indecipherable.

Forrester took a moment to study the surrounding area. The gates were lined at the top with barbed wire and controlled from a power box located inside the hut. The rest of the gated community was horded off by an eight-foot perimeter block wall atop which was a row of razor-sharp spikes. A large sign on the wall beside them read: TRESPASSERS WILL BE SHOT. Forrester didn't believe the security guards were even armed, let alone allocated the authority to shoot trespassers; but the sign, along with the intimidating structure, would be enough to dissuade all but the craziest people from attempting to enter.

Forrester slipped back into the jeep and told Bastich to drive. According to the canvassed taxi driver, number fifteen was Davies' house. They passed by several mammoth dwellings, all with lawns, separate garages, and expensive cars. If anyone had discovered the gates were open, they had yet to do anything about it.

The smell of freshly cut grass wafted in from outside, but Forrester couldn't hear a lawnmower. He couldn't see anyone outside their house either, but he suspected that was because of the mercurial weather.

When they reached number fifteen, he took a deep breath as he surveyed the scene. The front door lay open, swaying in the wind like the book. Though the rain had ceased, the wind still whistled through the neighbourhood. Across from the door, beside the garage, the bedroom window had been smashed. Forrester wondered about the incongruity of that: Why would someone smash the window *as well* as break in the front door?

"Bastich, go around the back and make sure no one's hiding in that field back there. O'Leary, go through the broken window and clear the house from there. Delaney, you're with me. We'll go through the front. Weapons visible, safeties *on*. If you see the mark this time, fire a warning shot and tell him you're authorised to put his damned ass in the ground if he doesn't freeze. Got it?"

"Got it," all three replied in unison.

"Let's move!"

Forrester kept his gun holstered until he crossed the street and disappeared from view behind the latticed fence. O'Leary branched to the left, Bastich the right, while Forrester and Delaney bore down the middle.

Forrester took the lead, pushing the door open fast and stepping into the house, oscillating the gun from side to side. In his peripheral vision, he took in the different rooms on each side. He acknowledged but ignored them, instructing Delaney to secure them. The right-hand side of the house was his concern now.

Off to the left, he could hear Delaney making his entrance. He blanked it out, focusing instead on the kitchen in front of him. He paused beside the closed double doors, slipped into place alongside the wall, and turned his head far enough into the room to allow him to see inside.

The room was devoid of anything resembling kitchenware. It was oddly sparse, with just a dining table and a few chairs inside. A sliding door led outside into the backyard, where

Forrester could barely make out the shape of Dave Bastich as he probed through the lengthy grass for any signs of their mark.

Forrester spun into the room. His gun remained extended, not trusting that the kitchen was as empty as it appeared. But there was nowhere for anyone to hide. Frustrated, he turned back to discover Delaney had cleared the rooms on either side of the front door. No one had been in those, either.

Forrester was about to go upstairs when the voice of O'Leary boomed through the house, "Jesus Christ!"

Forrester's face turned red, and for a moment he wanted to dash to O'Leary's position and punch the naive whippersnapper in the face for doing something so stupid, but he realised upstairs remained unchecked. He could deal with O'Leary in a minute.

"Sir, I think you better come look at this," Delaney announced, returning from O'Leary's position, his face as white as the kitchen walls.

"What is it?"

"Sir, I really think you should come take a look."

Forrester shook his head in disbelief. "Fine. Clear upstairs, Delaney."

As Delaney recommenced his search, Forrester moved to the rear of the house, fully intent on giving O'Leary the biggest reprimand he'd ever given an agent. He stormed through the door into the bedroom, glared at Tim O'Leary's blanched face, and dropped his eyes in tandem with the horrified agent's.

What he saw shocked him. Across the width of a double bed, four bodies lay juxtaposed. Each of them had the same distinctive markings: two bullet holes two inches above the bridge of the nose. On the floor were tear-shaped droppings of blood, along with one large and seemingly coagulated pool.

The victims were all men, Caucasian, between the ages of eighteen and forty. Two of them, Forrester observed, weren't much older than schoolchildren.

"That's not everything," O'Leary muttered softly.

Nor was it. If the sight in the bedroom shocked him, the one in the en-suite repulsed and enraged him. On the tiled floor, a once strikingly beautiful woman lay spread-eagle, her pretty dress torn asunder. Her breasts and vagina were exposed, her hair laid neatly away from her face. Her death, however, had come about through different means, though she may have preferred to have been shown the mercy granted the other victims. Instead, hers had been a more gruesome ending. Both her carotid artery and jugular vein had been sliced open, from ear to ear, and a large aperture in her neck allowed Forrester to see into her throat.

Either side of her recumbent body was a pool of blood, about two pints' worth, but the strange and disturbing thing was that none of it so much as touched her or the fabric of her clothing. She had been killed here, of that Forrester had no doubt, but her murderer had taken great time and expense – not to mention *care* – to position her body in exactly the right manner. It had the feeling of being done by someone who had taken great pleasure in every moment.

In contrast, the other deaths appeared rushed and impetuous. Forrester could not get an image out of his head; of Davies coming home to find his wife had been sleeping around, and then killing each of her lovers, raping her, and then taking great pleasure in her final moments.

He rose from the body and said, "For Godsakes, O'Leary, quit standing there! Find something to cover her up."

"Yes, sir. Sorry."

Forrester stepped out of the room and drew in a deep breath. What had started off as a simple pickup had now escalated to multiple homicides, not to mention the attempted murder of an FBI agent. Had Davies snapped? Forrester knew undercover agents subjected to intense and prolonged bouts of deep-cover work had a tendency to forget who they really were. Their behaviours began to resemble the person they were masquerading as.

Everything pointed to that scenario. Davies had apparently lost his identity, lost his sense of right and wrong, and reached breaking point. Forrester didn't know the man's history, what he had seen or done in Russia, or any of his background other than what he had read in his file. But only a talented hand could have grouped the bullets in that manner, and only a sick mind could have done that to the woman.

And those two things, at this moment in time, were synonymous with Troy Davies.

CHAPTER FIFTY
THE HUNT BEGINS

OUTSIDE SEAGATE
14:58 EST

In his own SUV, a hundred yards away from Davies' house, Vladimir Pushkin watched the FBI agents scurry around like headless chickens, and took amusement in the fact they didn't have a clue what had happened or was happening. With the discovery of five bodies inside the house, most of the Bureau's manpower would now be concentrated on this one scene and any leads stemming from it.

The two kids and the gateman were unfortunate bystanders, but Pushkin hadn't stayed alive and out of prison this long by taking chances. Still, there had been some upside. Kate Shaw had proven to be a pleasurable experience, to say the least. Despite her whimpers of protest, she had, to Pushkin's infinite surprise, aroused him. Her perky breasts and voluptuous figure had made him feel something he hadn't felt in years. He would take that moment with him to his grave.

The one downside, though, was that the FBI had almost caught him. Barely had Pushkin egressed the house when the SUV rolled to a stop outside. Another five minutes and he would have been in the back of it, bound hand-and-foot in cuffs.

That would have been a disaster. He hadn't expected the Fee-bees (as the North American gangsters liked to call them) to be so prompt, or to have been there at all. He knew they, too, were searching for Davies. He also knew that, if they were as good as their reputation seemed to suggest, they would be with him every step of the way. And while he hadn't intended the bodies to be discovered for another few hours, they now provided him with the leverage needed to keep the Bureau at arm's length.

He wasn't worried about a connection to him. He'd made sure to wear gloves, and his semen wasn't on the Bureau's extensive database. There was the possibility they would catch him and take a sample, but Pushkin didn't think that likely. No, Kate Shaw had been a worthwhile risk...

The sudden bleeping of a phone confused him. No one had the number for his satellite phone. Tracing the sound, he discovered, on the floor of the passenger side, a disposable cellphone. He slipped on his gloves again and keyed the answer button.

"Hello?"

"Vladimir? Where is Kenneth Gray?" a confused Pavel Kirov demanded.

"Kenneth who?"

"Your driver! That is his phone you are using."

"I sent Gray home. I don't want or need a lackey."

"He was no lackey! He was the only one who knew which flight Ivanovich was coming in on!"

"Don't worry about Ivanovich," replied Pushkin. "When the time is right, I'll find him."

"You better pray that turns out to be true. Where are you now?"

"Trying to find and put Davies in the ground, like you asked. Why are you ringing Gray? Are you looking for a status report? Is he your eyes and ears on the ground?"

"Never mind that. I have Davies' location," Kirov announced triumphantly.

"Where, and how did you find it?"

"Let's just say I have more contacts in America than I originally thought. Apparently he chartered a taxi to take him to Philadelphia."

"Philadelphia! What the hell's there?"

"I haven't the slightest idea. But whatever it is, it's in a place called West Chester. I have my men working to find out his connections there but it might take some time. You should get going. The GPS in the SUV should take you there, and I've added a little surprise."

Pushkin keyed a few numbers in on the GPS until a large map came up. On it, his location in Seagate was marked by a green dot, but about twenty miles west, a red dot pulsated as well.

"What is this?"

"My technicians found a way to hack the taxi's LoJack transmitter and display it on your GPS. Impressive, right?"

"What kind of challenge is this? Where's the fun in the hunt if you already know where the prey is?" a disappointed Pushkin demanded.

"Dammit, Vlad, just get him and kill him. We haven't time to be screwing around. It's a two-hour drive to West Chester, and Ivanovich is landing in two hours. You have to intercept Davies before he gets to where he's going. Understood?"

"With this thing, I'll pick him up in thirty minutes. Relax, Kirov. He'll be dead before Ivanovich touches the ground."

"He better be. Quit wasting time talking to me and get a move on."

CHAPTER FIFTY-ONE
THE LESSER OF TWO EVILS

PEOC BUNKER
THE WHITE HOUSE
WASHINGTON, D. C.
15: 00 EST

As the Joint Chiefs returned to their various offices around the country to co-ordinate, in the event of action needing to be taken against the hijacked plane, the President and three members of his Cabinet were ushered to the Presidential Emergency Operations Centre under the East Wing of the White House. The tube-like bunker, hardened to withstand a ten-megaton nuclear blast, had last seen use during 9/11.

"What do we know?" the President asked, in a weak voice, as he watched CNN on one of many televisions in the room. No news station had discovered the hijacking yet, but it was only a matter of time.

National Security Adviser Richard Duke made a show of lighting his briar pipe before switching on a computer beside him. On the wall above the large, adorned table they were seated at, a wooden panel slid back to reveal a fifty-inch television. A picture of an airplane filled the enormous screen.

"*Caspian Air* flight four-three-four, inbound from Moscow

International Airport. This picture comes courtesy of a British predator drone," Duke announced, taking a long puff. "Apparently, the plane was hijacked about two hours ago."

"What do you mean 'apparently'?" asked Matthew Clark, the President's Chief of Staff.

"At precisely ten minutes past one this afternoon, our time, the pilot squawked seventy-five-hundred to indicate a hijacking was in progress. Thirty minutes later, he squawked seventy-six-hundred to indicate, supposedly, the plane was back under his control."

"Civilian intervention?" the President queried.

"I'm not sure. In the intervening time between the first and last squawks, the pilot ceased radio contact with air traffic control. Shortly thereafter, the transponder went off-air. There's a possibility the pilot was under duress and forced to squawk, but I don't know if terrorists are as knowledgeable as that when it comes to pilot codes. Most pilots are trained to squawk seventy-five-hundred an additional time if a hijacking has been resolved. Not seventy-six-hundred. It may be the pilot changed codes to let us know it isn't a legitimate resolution."

"Where's the plane now?" the President demanded.

"Somewhere over the Atlantic Ocean. It's about two-and-a-half hours from American soil," Duke replied.

"And there's no way to contact it?"

"With the transponder down, it's coming, sir...blind, deaf, and fast. We have no way of knowing where it is."

"My God! Are you telling me there's a plane on a collision course with our country again?"

"I believe so, Mr President."

The President's weakened and tired demeanour changed instantly. In a flash, he stood from his seat, paced to the television screen, and pointed at the airplane. "I want our fighter planes in the sky right this minute. I want two stationed at all easternmost airports along the Atlantic Ocean. And I want every – and I mean *every* – airplane to make radio contact with air traffic control before they are granted permission to land."

"Sir," Duke began, "we've already launched fighter planes, but we need to look at the possibility this plane isn't going to land."

"I'm well aware of that, Rick, but we need to find it first.

Whatever it takes! I will not have another nine-eleven during my term."

"We're all overlooking one major issue here." Attorney General Walter Norman spoke for the first time during the briefing.

"What's that, Walt?" the President asked.

"We seem to be candy-assing our way around one thing: the possibility we'll have to shoot this plane out of the sky."

"We can't – " Clark began but was abruptly cut off.

"The hell we can't! We've been training for this moment for over eighteen months. If there's a direct threat to our country or the people in it, we have the right to take affirmative action."

" 'Affirmative action'? Jesus Christ, Walt! You're talking like a madman," the President fumed. "Do you realise the mass uproar we risk if we shoot down a plane later discovered to be safe? My God, we'd be committing state-sponsored murder. Not to mention career suicide."

"Would you rather let the plane crash into a building and kill thousands of people? What would *that* do for your *career*, Mr President? Let's face facts here, gentlemen: We have a hijacked four-hundred-ton plane on course for American soil within three hours. We have no way of communicating with it, finding it, or even knowing where it's going to strike, for Godsake! Do you want to make an announcement on the five o'clock news that this Cabinet knew about the plane but didn't do anything about it because of bureaucratic red tape?" Norman demanded.

The President slumped back into his chair and looked at Duke and Clark for reprieve. When they didn't offer any, he began in a strong tone, "We're talking about five hundred people here! There's no way I can justify killing that many people, even if we could prove the plane was intended to be used as a weapon. We'd be finished."

"Sir, we'll be finished if another nine-eleven happens. It's the lesser of two evils. Would you rather walk out of this office as the man who had the guts to prevent another nine-eleven, or as the man who let another catastrophe happen because of fear of the consequences?" inquired Norman.

The President shook his head. He rose from his chair again and walked to the door, where a joint service military officer opened the bulletproof entry. "I can't make this decision right now. I need time to think. Have our fighter jets on constant alert. I want four-three-four found and made land – whatever it takes."

"Sir, I really don't think you should leave the PEOC right now," Clark said.

"I need to clear my thoughts, Matt. I'll be back shortly."

The President left the PEOC, entered the elevator, rode it to the first floor of the East Wing, and walked briskly towards the Executive Residence. His Secret Service detail struggled to match his pace, but they were excused when he reached his room. With a knock, he entered and found his wife, Michaela, present along with a makeup artist and scriptwriter. The First Lady had a scheduled interview with a talk-show host at four. Walsh couldn't remember what for, but he politely asked the entourage to leave the room for a moment.

Michaela immediately knew something wasn't right. She rarely saw her husband during the day, and right now his bedraggled features caused her more worry than going live in front of millions of Americans.

"What's wrong, James?" she asked, coming over and giving her husband a hug and a kiss.

Michaela Walsh had aged gracefully. Her forty-something face looked as fresh and youthful as it had in her college days, and her shoulder-length auburn hair seldom needed to be attended to by her aides. Walsh couldn't figure how he'd managed to win the heart of such a beautiful and smart woman but, being part-Irish, he wondered if he'd ever kissed the Blarney stone – his luck had to have come from somewhere. Their relationship was as good now as it had been when they'd first met, and Walsh confided in Michaela about most presidential decisions.

"We have a situation downstairs."

"Come on; come over here." Michaela took him by the hand and led him to their bed. They sat on the edge of it and she asked, "What's going on?"

With a sigh, the President began. "A couple of hours ago a plane en route from Russia was hijacked. We think it's coming here, Mi."

Michaela eyes widened. "My God! You don't think...?"

"We don't know yet," Walsh replied, caressing her hand.

"And we don't want to start a panic. We know where it is," Walsh lied, "and we won't let it get anywhere near our cities."

"You're worried you're gonna have to shoot it down, aren't you?" The First Lady had always been quick on the uptake.

"There's a possibility it might come to that."

"James, if you have to make a decision between the lives of thousands of Americans and the lives of a plane-full of people, which do you think the American public will be more forgiving of?"

"Walt said something similar," Walsh replied with a sigh.

"Walt's a smart man." Michaela smiled to break the tension and give her husband some reason to be optimistic. "Neither I nor Walt can make this decision for you, though," she continued in a serious tone. "You have to do what you feel is right. Whatever that decision is, this country will support you. Your cabinet, too. But most importantly, so will I."

Walsh leaned in and kissed his wife as fervently as he had the first time they'd made love. "Thanks, Mi. I needed to hear that from you."

"Don't let them browbeat you into doing something you don't want to. You're the President of the United States. The repercussions fall at your feet, not theirs, so you make sure the decision is yours and yours alone."

"Sometimes I think you're the President." Walsh laughed for what felt like the first time today.

"Well, I do look *awfully* good in a suit, but then you don't look that good in a dress," Michaela teased. "Go on," she said, shooing him with a perfectly manicured hand. "Go make an executive decision. I have a date with Oprah."

"You wish," laughed Walsh as he scurried away from her swinging arm.

"You gotta start small, my love. One day, I'll *be* Oprah."

"You planning on changing skin colour and adding fifty pounds?" Walsh laughed as he ducked one of his wife's high heels. The dagger-like shoe hit the wall and the stiletto pierced through the plasterboard sheeting. Walsh fell to his knees as Michaela looked at the wall with a horrified expression.

"Quit laughing! It's not funny," she protested but couldn't help laughing as well. Gulping for air, she said, "How are we going to explain that?" she asked, pointing to the stiletto.

"Rough sex?" Walsh queried with a raised eyebrow, and rushed out the door as Michaela grabbed the other shoe.

The banter with his wife had allowed Walsh to clear his thoughts and analyse the situation from an unbiased point of view. Both she and Ed were correct; doing nothing was worse than shooting a plane-full of innocent people. It was gross negligence, and if it got out – more likely *when* – the American public would never support him for standing idly by and allowing another catastrophe to happen.

Sometimes the hardest decisions were the ones that sacrificed one thing for another. While many of his potential voters believed the ends never justified the means, they would quickly turn the other cheek if Walsh did nothing, and criticise him for it. Regardless of what way he looked at it, it was a no-win situation. Over three thousand Americans had died during 9/11. He could not and would not allow something like that to happen again. If it meant killing five hundred people, it was a decision he could live with.

CHAPTER FIFTY-TWO
SURVIVE. EVADE. RESIST. ESCAPE

HARVEY POINT
15:05 EST

Somewhere off in the distance, Carlos could hear the muffled thumps of human feet as they moved through the jungle. Not the men who'd captured him; their footfalls would be more direct and less cautious. These were some of the other soldiers, probably engaging in some new exercise, perhaps even to bring new soldiers for Carlos to meet and greet.

Except that they would be meeting an empty cell.

Carlos worked the last tumbler until he heard the satisfying click, and the cell door opened with a noisy creak. He pushed it open full and after closing it again behind him, darted into the jungle. His eyes quickly adjusted to the sunlight and he saw, about twenty yards due east, a large clump of brush he could hide in. Sprinting, he covered the distance in ten seconds, and slid to his belly in the knee-length grass.

The prison sat out on its own. Its walls were covered with what looked like ivy, and the surrounding area, save for the entrance, was dwarfed by grass as tall as five feet. The place looked to have last been inhabited years earlier, but Carlos hoped the map he'd memorised was still accurate.

He found the storm drain, to the northeast, covered by years of grass and brush, and it took five minutes of labour to remove the thorned foliage from around the four-foot-wide metal enclosure. An additional three minutes were spent moving the seized hinges enough to gain access inside without risking the lid falling and chopping him in half.

As he dropped inside, he hit water first and then the concrete pipe. His knees buckled with the unexpectedness and for a moment he thought he'd hyper-extended his right one. But after wriggling it, he was confident he'd only lightly sprained it.

The water covered him as high as his thighs, and Carlos wondered if his plan was such a great idea after all. The interior of the four-foot-wide pipe was darker than expected, though light emanated from another entry-point about two hundred yards farther downstream. Without the aid of a flashlight, the journey from here to the EOD building could take an hour.

Feeling pain in his right knee, Carlos pushed forward through the murky water. It felt like walking through treacle with led-encased boots on, but he soldiered on as thoughts of missions in places like East Timor and Kazakhstan flooded his subconscious. The water there had been stagnant and in many cases riddled with diseases like Legionnaires', not to mention loaded with poisonous creatures which killed you slowly and agonisingly. The thoughts brought, for the second time in twenty-four hours, a shudder of incomprehensible fear, for fear was something Force Recon Marines were not allowed to possess. Carlos shrugged it off again and covered the distance to the next opening. There, he paused to catch his breath and recall the map he and Gyle had been given when they first arrived. The storm drains continued for about a quarter-mile, at which point they branched off to feed the four different buildings. He didn't know exactly which building was which, but trial and error would determine that.

The most frustrating thing was not knowing where they were holding Gyle. If it had been a normal mission, Carlos would have broken out and made a beeline through the jungle to the buildings. But there was nothing normal about this mission. The secrecy involved made him decide to indulge in his own surreptitious approach.

These people wanted to play a game; they wanted to test the best soldiers in the world. How unfortunate for them the soldiers they were testing had minds and codes of their own. The motto for the Marine Corps was *Semper Fidelis,* the Latin meaning "always faithful". But the motto for Force Recon was *Celer, Silens, Mortalis:* "Swift, silent, deadly". Like a snake, Carlos would slither in from below, play possum until the moment arrived, and then strike with venom.

***

How ironic that the latest "exercise" was a SERE scenario.

Crouched behind a clump of some godforsaken plant, Larry Lansdale checked his six for the third time in the last half-minute. About fifty yards to his west, Kurt Fromm lay in underbrush and wriggled his way toward "Checkpoint Charlie". Lansdale hadn't thought to ask who'd come up with the lame name, but it seemed irrelevant right now.

Even more ironic, the exercise involved getting from the EOD building *back* to the main gates of the facility without being spotted by the ten-man team of Special Forces soldiers led by – Lansdale groaned at the thought – John Mason and Nathan Murphy. Well, at least it was more fun than being tied to a tree for two hours.

Neither did Lansdale think to ask why they were skipping the first three letters of SERE. Escaping was the easy part. The other three, not so much.

He had slipped away from Fromm and moved into an overwatch position to scout the area ahead. "Checkpoint Charlie" – nothing more than a barren four-foot-square strip of jungle – appeared empty, but Lansdale didn't trust that observation. Special Forces soldiers moved with ease through environs as concealed as these jungles. For them, hiding out here would be as easy as breathing.

Garnering Fromm's attention, he touched two fingers to his eyes, then pointed them to the checkpoint. He followed that by making a clockwise circle with his finger to indicate his intentions. Fromm nodded, understanding what Lansdale meant.

The SAS man dropped and veered off to the west, slithering through the damp grass as quietly as the situation allowed. Fromm moved at precisely the same moment with a north-by-northeast bearing.

Lansdale knew somewhere else in these clumps of grass were eight more soldiers, all trying to prove they could sneak past a conglomerate of the best soldiers in the world. Everyone here had nothing to prove but everything to lose, and for that reason he was determined not to be shown up by the "enemy".

Though he had only been a toddler when Vietnam was in its prime, he had some experience of jungles. To say he hated them was an understatement, and yet he found comfort in the knowledge they were a hell of a lot better than running around a bleak desert where hiding places came along about as often as wells did. At least here you had somewhere to hide if the shit hit the fan.

To make things even more difficult, both teams were given identical standard-issue jungle camouflage. No dog tags, arm bands, nor anything to distinguish one team from another. Any soldier Lansdale encountered could be the "enemy", and because no one knew any different, it was basically every man for himself. Except for Lansdale and Fromm. The two had formed a bond in the past week and had decided teamwork favoured them; because they knew each other's gait, posture, and appearance better than any of the others did. Not to mention that jungles were Kurt Fromm's fiefdom. The German Mountain and Winter Combat school in Mittenwald contained some of the most gruelling terrains in the world, most of which had jungles like this one.

As Lansdale continued forward slowly, he felt something land on his nose and, despite the sudden desire to swat it away, his quick thinking allowed him to wriggle and scare the unsightly beast off. Barely had he done that when he felt something else. Not on his nose. Nor his legs. Nor any other part of his anatomy.

Lansdale "felt" the presence of a soldier as he came within ten yards of his position.

***

Though the water got cooler the further Carlos advanced down the storm drain, it seemed to become shallower. The pain in his knee, which had gradually dulled in the cold water, now returned as it lowered to shin-level. Carlos didn't mind. It focused his thoughts and kept him alert. Being without sleep for almost thirty hours had left him groggy and in need of rest. Twice, he'd thought of falling asleep in his prison cell, and had Gyle been present he might have afforded himself that luxury. But to sleep alone was to relinquish control, and he couldn't accept that. Control was the only thing he had.

He had served as a sergeant-major for almost five years now, yet he still found himself needing the advice of his former squadron leader, Sergeant-Major Wayne Roland, who'd been like a father to him during his time with the Marines. Whatever situation they were in, however bad, Roland always found a way to make his team laugh. Carlos had done his best to imitate the SOB's sunny disposition but even he, as funny as he was, couldn't live up to Roland's Irish charm. He had no doubt, however, that Wayne, if here right now, would be going about this the exact same way.

The element of surprise served as his best advantage. By now, someone would have discovered he'd escaped. They'd be co-ordinating search patterns and trying to figure out where he'd gone. That would take at least fifteen minutes. Then, they'd start searching the periphery of the jungle, fanning out from the prison cell. It would be hours before someone had a brainstorm and decided to check the storm drain. This way, he could come and go like a ghost, leap up and ensnare his prey, and disappear into the darkness before anyone knew what had happened.

This way, Carlos became what so many soldiers feared.

An invisible hunter.

***

Lansdale dared not move.

Less than ten feet from his head, a Special Forces soldier moved in a zigzagging formation. With the barrel of his rifle, he prodded each blade of grass, each clump of brush, and anything else he thought might hide the form of a combatant soldier.

Lansdale kept his breathing shallow and controlled. As carefully as possible, he moved his right and left feet backwards simultaneously, edging farther away from the soldier's current search pattern. Each movement was painstakingly done with as little noise as possible. Had the soldier been a little farther back, Lansdale might have tried to turn. As it was, turning now would only give his position away.

Thorns ripped through the fabric of his jungle camouflage. Grimacing, he ignored the shooting pain and continued backwards...right into a damned nest of them. He veered sharply to the right; felt them rip through the rest of his fatigues; felt the blood drip from the wound. About a dozen embedded into flesh, tearing through his skin as he tried to wrench free. It seemed no matter how far he edged away from them, he couldn't get out of their ensnarement.

The soldier heard the snap of a branch, and jerked his head in Lansdale's direction. He froze, and waited to see what the soldier would do, quietly moving away from the spot when he saw him advance.

The remaining thorns clung for dear life, as though they wanted to rid him of his leg. He gritted his teeth and yanked from their grip, tearing more skin as he did. The pain shot through him like daggers, but used his high threshold for pain to keep from screaming in agony.

The soldier closed in. Lansdale watched as the barrel swished aside grass barely five feet from his head. Throwing stealth out the window, he pivoted on his knees and spun one-eighty. Legs and arms pumping, he bore left, heading for the taller grass.

Behind, the soldier heard the rustling but couldn't see what had made it. He followed the sound, thrashing at the ground with his rifle. Fear gripped Lansdale as he imagined the bayonet of a rifle piercing through his heart like a bullet through sheet-wood. He shrugged it off and pushed on faster.

Twenty yards later, he bumped into something.

Lansdale's veins turned to ice as a soldier spun around and aimed a rifle at him.

CHAPTER FIFTY-THREE
DISCOVERY

ATARIC
15: 10 EST

Back at his desk – after ignoring Reid and Collins' recommendation to go to a hospital – Hunt tried to put his suspicions to the back of his mind and concentrate on the job at hand. But despite his best attempts, he could think of nothing except the last two hours of his life.

The scene in this office and the men's toilet had been so vivid, so coherent, that he could scarcely believe it hadn't happened. According to Reid, Hunt had left around one o'clock to go to the toilet. The next time Reid saw him was in the back of the ambulance over an hour later. Even stranger yet, his gun was still intact in his workbag, and the conversation about it and Reid's wife appeared to have never happened.

Vivid hallucinations were uncommon in cases of *delirium tremens*. There had been, to Hunt's knowledge, several incidents of hallucinations involving rats, snakes, and even elephants, but in the majority of those cases the animals attacked the person. He could not recall a case where someone's hallucination had not been their worst nightmare. His worst nightmare was that Karen would never take him back, but in his hallucination she rang him. Not to mention DTs typically involved confusion, diarrhoea, agitation, fever, tachycardia, and severe tremors, none of which he had. Aside from being a little weak, he felt better than he had in months.

For those reasons, Hunt aired on the side of suspicion. If it wasn't DTs, the hallucination could only be explained by one other thing: drugs. There were many people in the office he knew, but only a few who had serious issues with him to do something like that. Harry Johnson sprung to mind first. From the beginning, he'd held a serious grudge against Hunt, culminating into an eventual war which had cost him his job. Hunt being called back today would have hurt Johnson. And for someone whose reputation and pride came before all other things, Johnson wouldn't have been impressed by Fielding and Haskens practically demanding he be brought back, if only for a day. Johnson would have been upset, but capable of drugging him?

What if someone just wanted you out of the way? A little cocktail to knock you out for the rest of the day so they could...what?

Suddenly, it made sense. He'd been asking too many questions, asking for administrative permissions, and creating a hostile work environment.

By getting me out of the way, they take all the credit and it looks like I've fallen asleep or got drunk. I get sacked again, and they end up smelling like roses! The person who has most to gain by your failure is Johnson. He warned them not to bring you in, didn't he? If he's proven right, his credibility rises like a balloon, while your reputation sinks like a stone.

The reality was most of the people he was now working with had issues with him: Collins over their past, Reid over Hunt's current behaviour, and Johnson over their history. All three had reason, motive, and means to drug him. And they all had something to gain by his departure.

But right now, he didn't have the time or resources to investigate it further. Much as it pained him, he needed to get his mind back on the job he was being paid to do. *Wait a minute; if the events in the office and toilet never took place, did Jack give me admin privileges yet?*

Hunt wheeled over to his station and logged in using his temporary username and password. The old operating system took ages to do everything – one of the reasons why Reid's new one was being installed. After a few minutes, he discovered Reid *had* given him administrative control. Frowning, he began wondering if he'd mentioned it before the office hallucination, or if some part of the hallucination conversation had actually happened. The more he tried to remember, the more confused he became. Cursing silently, he put it to the back of his mind and began doing what he'd come here to do.

After ten minutes of searching, he found the mail-storage system and discovered arbitrary pieces of data were still being sent to the address *jamiesignfeld@youmail.com*.

Browsing through the sub-directories and various other subnets in the ATARIC system, he discovered the pieces of data were not only being sent to that address, they were being sent to two additional ones also. The first was something called DESTINY, though its listed website sold "kitchenware at affordable prices". The other one...Hunt frowned. It led to a website with a message stating the owner hadn't paid his hosting fees and the site was in abeyance until he did. Its name was STATION BLUE. Hunt Googled it and found various sites, including transportation services, wildlife committees, and even exotic material. But all of them were still operational, and none held the domain name "www.stationblue.com".

He tried another search, this time using the hyphenated version of the title. The returning hits were mostly the same as before, but buried towards the bottom of the seventh page, he found an article on a conspiracy website entitled "'Station-Blue': The Top-Secret Military Base The Government Don't Want You to Know About". Hunt glanced over his shoulder to make sure no one was coming, and clicked the article:

Friends and conspiracy theorists alike: For too long we have been duped by the United States government into believing places like Area 51 and other aboveground bases are the most secretive complexes in the country. They are not! They are a façade created to draw attention away from the REAL secret bases. What you are about to read will blow your minds, my fellow theorists.

In the aftermath of 9/11, several large and small businesses were liquidated following the stock market collapse. One of these buildings was bought out by a shell corporation owned by Uncle Sam, himself. As work began on Ground Zero and workers poured into the area to begin the reconstruction of the Twin Towers, several other machines and workers began "gas-main repairs" on the street outside the military-owned building. These ostensible repairs went on for eighteen months, during which time the entire block was closed off to all but pedestrians. Though several complaints were filed everywhere from 26 Federal Plaza to City Hall, none ever found their way to the desk of anyone important, and the pleas fell on deaf ears.

The site itself was kept more secure than Ground Zero was during the subsequent twenty-four hours after 9/11. Several people reported being turned away by military personnel, while others had their cameras and recording equipment confiscated. These acts alone suggest more was going on than "gas-main repairs", my friends. A LOT more.

Several fellow theorists managed to take photographs from a distance, risking their freedom and lives to do so. These photographs show concrete trucks numbering in the hundreds; trucks with steel girders and beams; trucks with coils upon coils of electrical cable. Further to this, large excavations were happening at an abandoned waste-disposal facility three miles from this building. Both of these went largely unnoticed, what with the entire country up in arms about 9/11.

While we were all worried about the greatest threat of all coming from without, the US government were working from within to build, right under our noses, the single greatest secretive facility in the history of this "free" land. They used chicanery on us, my friends. While we mourned the deaths of our compatriots and swore revenge on those who had wronged us, they used that distraction to build a secret underground base right here in New York City. Yes, you read that right. An underground base. Here, in the Big Apple.

It would be remiss of me, since Big Brother knows who am I and where I live, to give out the exact location of this base. However, take a drive up to Hunters Point on the north-western tip of Long Island City and you'll discover a FEMA building resides in the old waste-disposal facility. Numerous suits patrol this location day and night. Beside this building is a tunnel which leads to the Queens Midtown Tunnel. The reason for its existence is supposedly to allow FEMA, in the event of an emergency, to egress from their facility as quickly as possible. I must warn you, fellow theorists, Hunters Point is guarded by overbearing bodyguards in suits who won't hesitate to bring you, if caught on their property, to an undisclosed location and interrogate you for days on end. Be careful snooping around.

I have yet to discover what is going on at this 'Station-Blue', but I'm sure, with recent developments in the War on Terror, it involves our military in one way or another. We must bring this and other bases to the attention and knowledge of our fellow citizens, else we may end up in a totalitarian world the likes of which Hitler and Stalin could scarcely have imagined!

Copyright © 2002, Daedalus.

Farther down the page, Hunt found the photographs. Daedalus' article was corroborated by several black-and-white shots of numerous haulage trucks offloading everything from concrete to reinforcing steel. In many of them, men in suits watched proceedings from nearby entrances. In others, the pictures revealed the same men standing on rooftops and watching with binoculars. All of them wore sunglasses and had earpieces which coiled from their ears and disappeared down the back of their necks. In one picture, Hunt saw the outline of a holster. Still, even that wasn't the shocking part.

In the last two pictures, he saw a short-haired man walking out of a building whilst talking on a phone. In one shot, the man had his head down, away from the photographer. In the other, his face, though dappled, could be seen clearly enough to identify.

The man was Jack Reid and the building was ATARIC.

CHAPTER FIFTY-FOUR
SLEEPER

CASPIAN AIR FLIGHT 434
17: 15 GMT-2

Though the plane had already passed through seven different time-zones, Sergei Ivanovich couldn't relax enough to lie down in his seat and fall asleep, as much as he wanted to do just that. Aside from one extremely pissed-off terrorist tied up in the captain's bathroom, plus the strong likelihood of a sleeper agent on-board, there was also the slight matter of Aleksandr Levsky.

Ivanovich paid a visit to Levsky's house fifteen years earlier, five days after his dishonourable discharge from the KGB. The director wasn't home, but his wife and three kids were sleeping in the master bedroom. Ivanovich took care of the wife first, slitting her throat with a Russian military knife and laying her down on Levsky's bed. Though he wasn't fond of killing children, Ivanovich wanted to avoid possible revenge missions in years to come. He killed them humanely – a syringe of Phenobarbitone each, and they passed away without any pain or suffering.

When Levsky discovered their bodies ten hours later, he went berserk. Within hours he had every known murderer both in prison and on parole lined up for interrogation. Several were shot dead when they refused to answer his questions, others tortured until they did. Several months and hundreds of bodies later, Levsky discovered Ivanovich had murdered his family.

For the next eighteen months, he had every KGB agent worth his badge searching for Ivanovich. Every airport, train station, and bus depot in the country had pictures of him. Every motel within a hundred miles had them also. Ivanovich had to leave the country in Pavel Kirov's jet.

He spent the next two years in the States. After facial reconstruction, he did several small jobs for Kirov until the Russian felt he could trust him. After he'd earned Kirov's money and respect, Ivanovich became his second-in-command, gaining charge of more and more high-level missions in various countries as a result.

But Levsky continued chasing him, despite the facial alterations, hairstyle changes, and multiple identities. Like some kind of insatiable maverick on a trail of justice, he followed his every footstep. If Ivanovich did a job in Kiev, he would discover, hours later, Levsky's troops had filed into the area right behind him. Levsky afforded him no respite. He hounded him like a dog...until he finally caught him.

During a hit in St Petersburg, Ivanovich took a round in the shoulder from a sniper guarding his mark. After calling off the mission and struggling back to his safe-house, Ivanovich discovered four men waiting for him. Three of them were Spetsnaz agents, and the last one, Aleksandr Levsky. The agents softened Ivanovich up, and Levsky finished him off with three bullets to the chest.

Or so he thought.

The Spetsnaz agents had been bought by Kirov, and they'd replaced Levsky's gun with a fake. All they had to do then was signal Ivanovich to drop like a stone, which he duly did. Thus, Sergei Ivanovich "died" and Aleksandr Levsky called off his dogs.

But despite the facial changes and the subsequent twelve-and-a-half-year period of separation, Ivanovich had no doubt Levsky would recognise him. You never forget the eyes; not of someone who butchered your family. And if Levsky saw him, the rage and hurt he'd cemented over with the passing years and the "death" of Ivanovich would erupt out of him again like a volcano. He would become a man without conscience; without remorse. And in that intoxicated state, he would be capable of anything.

How strange and ironic it was that now the most dangerous man on the plane was not the sleeper agent, nor the remaining terrorist hog-tied to the captain's toilet, but Aleksandr Levsky, the former director of Russia's infamous KGB.

"Ivanovich, you there?" came the voice of York, breaking through Ivanovich's reverie.

"Found anything?"

"You mean, apart from the bunch of passengers who think I'm insane?"

"York, you *are* insane." Ivanovich laughed.

"Yeah, but they don't know that, do they?"

"You wouldn't happen to have any useful information, would you?" Ivanovich asked flatly.

"Look, there's like five hundred people on this damn plane. You want me to eyeball every single one of them for a device you tell me looks exactly like a PDA? How long we got? 'Cause I could go through this fuckin' plane with a microscope for the next three days and not find anything," replied York.

"I'll take that as a 'no', then."

"So we don't get this guy – what's the worst that could happen?"

"Aside from us getting blown to pieces? Nothing much."

"What if I said I had a plan?" York threw that out as a feeler to see if Ivanovich would wave it off or accept it.

"I'd say that would be a first." Ivanovich laughed first but curbed it when he heard York's disapproval. "Okay, what?"

"What if we make the sleeper come to us?"

"How would we do that?"

"We get our 'friend' in the toilet to help us out. Make him confirm some story about him hiding when the shit hit the fan. If we can convince the sleeper the last terrorist isn't being coerced, maybe we can draw him out into the open. Take him down that way."

Ivanovich nodded, even though York couldn't see the gesture. It was a good plan. Not foolproof, but a hell of a lot more likely to succeed than what they were doing right now.

The only problem was convincing the last terrorist to go

along with it.

"How do we convince our 'friend' to draw out the sleeper? He's not going to do it because we threaten him. These are suicide bombers, after all," Ivanovich pointed out.

"He'll do it – after I cut off all his fingers and threaten to do the same to his balls."

"You really *are* insane, aren't you," Ivanovich asked rhetorically, then added, "Okay, let's do it."

CHAPTER FIFTY-FIVE
INTRUDERS

HARVEY POINT
15: 17 EST

"What the hell are – " Fromm's voice dropped from a whisper to dead silence as Lansdale's eyes widened and his head shook vigorously. The German dropped the rifle and watched Lansdale jerk his head upwards seconds before a shadow fell across both of their prone frames.

They were dead men, Fromm knew. Whatever chance one of them had of avoiding an enemy in this situation, with both in close proximity to each other, it was only a matter of time before they were spotted. They had no choice. The soldier would have to be neutralised – quietly – or they were goners.

He signalled his intentions to Lansdale. He nodded and turned slightly to get the soldier's bearing, who had now closed the distance to within five yards, concentrating solely on blades of grass about five feet east of Lansdale's current position. His viewpoint took in their location. Neither could rise without alerting him.

The problem with moving in grass as tall as this was it bent, revealing to anyone with sharp eyesight your exact location. To counter this, Fromm brushed it aside with both hands as he moved. This allowed it to return to its original position once he passed.

Without knowing exactly what the plan was, he moved away from Lansdale, towards the soldier who continued to stab at the grass with his rifle. The morning dew had evaporated, but the foliage still felt damp in his hands. The sensation brought back memories of Mountain School, where he'd traversed jungles warmer and more deadly than this one, and where he'd learned survival was as much about mental strength as it was physical. Those days had been some of the worst of his life, but they'd prepared him for what had come after. Nothing on the battlefield had compared to that training. In that respect the German Army, certainly KSK, could lay claim to being the most prepared military unit in the world. In Kürt Fromm, they'd produced probably the finest sniper in German history, for whom a rifle was merely an extension of his arm, and for whom taking down targets at a ridiculous range was as easy as breathing. And yet the irony was Mittenwald had not prepared him for a jungle in North Carolina replete with twenty-odd Special Forces soldiers whose weapons were also an extension of *their* arms.

For a moment he felt like a fly trapped in a web. But then he realised that he was not the fly but the spider. For the spider waited patiently until the fly bumbled into his trap, and then, like a predator, it seized the initiative.

Fromm waited until the soldier thrashed at the grass beside him. The weapon came within inches of his face, and the German lashed out with both hands and grabbed it around the stock. The soldier yelped in surprise, but Fromm quickly yanked the rifle towards him. Caught off balance, the man staggered forward, tripped on Fromm, and plummeted to the ground beside him. Wasting no time, he seized him around the neck, shoved his forearm into the man's throat, and held him down until lack of oxygen-flow to his brain caused him to pass out.

"Bloody hell!" exclaimed Lansdale, coming up beside him and shaking his head. "I'm glad I'm not on their side."

***

At just after twenty past three, Eastern Standard Time, an S-76

Sikorsky thundered over the top of Harvey Point. The military helicopter kicked up dust as it settled into a clearing, landing fifty yards inside the main gates. Two men exited in a crouch, the first a huge, barrel-chested African-American attired in military fatigues.

As the second man straightened fully, the sunlight gleamed off the extensive array of medals affixed to his pinstriped suit. With his free hand, he donned his hat and walked briskly towards the nearby buildings.

In his other hand, a five-page dossier rustled in the wind. On its cover was a picture of Harvey Point.

***

What Carlos would have given for a flashlight or, better still, a pair of night-vision goggles. As it was, he had to rely on his own keen vision to keep from slipping into the wrong storm drain and ending up in Hicksville. For all that, though, it wasn't too difficult. Each branch also served as an exit, which allowed light to filter inside. With the aid of his photographic memory, Carlos kept on the right path until he came to an exit where he heard, to his surprise, voices.

"...know...am...sonny?" barked someone in an authoritative voice.

"Sir...this is...and we have the authority...United States."

"I don't care...you have. Get me...superior...before I...patience."

Though Carlos could only hear snippets of each man's words, he got the feeling the mood had just changed. Whoever the deep-voiced man was, he didn't belong here, but his presence had disturbed the soldier replying to him. The apprehensive tone in his replies told Carlos the new arrival was a high-ranking officer. He knew only one kind of person who made soldiers react like that – a general.

Carlos asked himself what, if anything, this changed. The presence of a general on-site could mean the entire operation would be discovered, terminated, and everyone would be free to go back to their previous posts. But these guys had usurped a CIA training facility for their own use, and had kept the entire country and its leaders, save the President, in the dark about it.

Until now. And while this surprise visit would have caught them off-guard, they would have factored it into their original planning. They would have contingencies in place for this. Of that, Carlos had no doubt. They would find a way to explain everything.

Unless...

***

"Are you the commanding officer of this facility?" demanded Charles Peterson, Chairman of the Joint Chiefs. He was standing in the foyer of a large building. To his left and right, partitioned rooms contained various items, most notably communications equipment, and high-tech surveillance equipment. Straight ahead, a set of stairs led up to another floor.

The man being questioned – a brutish Latino with a bald head and numerous tattoos inked all over his anatomy – nodded his head. "Mr Chairman, I am the interim commander of Harvey Point. To what do we owe this pleasure?"

"What is your name and rank, son?" Peterson replied, ignoring the question – he would be the only one asking anything today.

"Major Eddie Dominguez, U-S-M-C, sir," Dominguez replied automatically, then grimaced.

"You are aware, Major, this is a top-secret CIA facility, yes? What business does the Marine Corps have here?"

"Sir, you'd best take that question up with the President. We're here under his orders."

Peterson glared at him, causing the young major to break eye contact. "As the Chairman of the Joint Chiefs, I am privy to all military action. If you so prefer, I will have Commandant Rogers issue you your dishonourable discharge papers. One last time, Major: What is the United States Marine Corps doing here?"

Dominguez blew out an exasperated sigh. "Sir, all I can tell you is this is a training exercise, authorised by the President of the United States. We have full authority to be here. I am also under obligation to tell no one any more than what I've just told you."

"Very well, Major. If that's the way you want to play it."

Peterson turned around and signalled Anderson to come forth.

"What are you doing, sir?" Dominguez demanded.

"Consider this a military inspection team, Major Dominguez. Notify your troops accordingly. Myself and Sergeant-Major Anderson are going to perform a complete check of every Marine, soldier, and person on this base, commencing right the hell now."

"You'll do no such thing, Chad," called a new voice as it made its way down the stairs from above. Peterson immediately knew who it was. In fact, he'd been expecting him. It confirmed his suspicions that something beyond top-secret was going on here.

The man was Secretary of Defence Edward Rainey.

CHAPTER FIFTY-SIX
BLACK SITE

```
HUNTERS POINT
QUEENS
NEW YORK CITY
15: 30 EST
```

As one military vehicle landed in North Carolina, another, less noticeable, turned into a recycling plant on the north-western tip of Long Island City. This time, though, the entry gates were patrolled by a rifle-toting guard who stopped the car immediately. After two or three minutes of scrutiny, and then another to verify the registration and driver, the guard opened the gates and waved the car through.

At first glance the plant seemed to be like any other of its kind. Numerous men and women in hard hats and high-visibility vests perambulated from building to building. Others in blue and orange coveralls worked at various machines dotted around the plant. What looked like rubbish constantly revolved on huge conveyor belts, disappearing into a building marked REC 1. Other machines crushed various metals and solid materials, transferring them to another conveyor belt whose destination was marked REC 2.

At the back of the facility, where East River glimmered in the afternoon sunlight, a ramp leading downwards gave way to a huge door, not unlike the blast door of a fallout shelter. The limo headed directly for it.

Above the thirteen-ton behemoth of an entrance, a camera – fitted with night, heat, and infrared-vision – scanned the hologram embedded in the number plate of the Cadillac and then the number itself. Comparing the two, it then scanned through the tinted windows and analysed the retina of the driver. When these three checks were complete, a huge groan emitted from the pit, and the blast doors opened surprisingly quickly, considering their weight.

The limo drove through, descended for about ten seconds, then continued driving level for a quarter-mile, whereupon the road veered steeply downhill before levelling off again. On either side, walls of concrete arched around and joined above, creating a cylindrical enclosure. Every ten yards, large halogen lights, powered from the plant, illuminated the 2.7-mile tunnel which had cost over a hundred million dollars to construct.

In less than five minutes, the limo approached the end, where another camera scanned the limo once more. It opened to reveal an underground parking garage containing approximately a dozen-and-a-half cars, vans, and jeeps. In the southeast corner, a red light flickered above the doors of an elevator. On the wall beside it, two boxes, one atop the other, glowed in the darkened surrounds of the lot.

The driver slowed to a stop beside the elevator, opened his door, and got out to open his passengers'. Out of the vehicle stepped Director Jonathan Baker, FBI, and Director Roger Clemence, NSA. The latter pulled a cap over his bald head and followed Baker to the elevator where, one retinal and fingerprint scan later, it opened with a groan almost as loud as the blast door's.

"Don't you think it's time someone fixed that damn thing?" Clemence complained as Baker selected option B-3 and took a seat on the specially constructed bench. The four-minute journey from here to topside had a tendency to get bumpy, especially since the elevator's speed exceeded forty miles per hour.

"Why don't you go take it up with the city engineers?" Baker joked.

Both men knew that would never happen. The President

had used the distraction of 9/11 to construct this tunnel and underground facility. Here, it was at its lowest – six thousand feet under New York. The engineers who'd worked on it were sworn to secrecy, and it was their recommendation to have the submerged part under East River only five hundred feet below the water. Once back on land – on the Manhattan side – they claimed the soil at that depth was too weak to risk building, so they bored down an extra four thousand feet until they found a solid foundation. From there, it had been a matter of continuing the tunnel to "Station Blue" and boring up to meet its pre-existing basement.

Of course, work then had to be done to stabilise the structure and construct the elevator shaft. Thousands of cubic metres of concrete were poured in from outside using a concrete pump. This helped with stabilisation as well as providing an entirely new basement section that could only be accessed from this elevator and a special "hatch" in the level two basement of "Station Blue". This airtight hatch could not be opened without a key-card, fingerprint scan, and a retinal comparison. Made from DuPont Kevlar, it was impervious to every cutting material and explosive known to man. For this reason, access to "Station Blue's" basement level-three complex could not be achieved through devious means. In that regard, it was the safest facility in America. And it needed to be.

Level-three "Station Blue" was a black site. For that matter, so were levels one and two. About fifty people in total knew of its existence, and only ten of those were privy to the entire details. Such was its secrecy and security that not even the President himself could access the entire facility on his own. He needed the presence of at least one other cleared member to bypass each security measure.

The facility was built with one thing in mind: Weapons development. A team of a dozen technological geniuses worked around the clock to build the kind of weapons limited to science fiction and fantasy novels. In addition, they constructed new, high-tech gadgets, worked on creating new vests and armour to withstand the highest velocity bullets, and found other time to tinker with pre-existing items in order to improve their effectiveness and efficiency. Once these weapons passed a batch of rigorous tests, they were shipped off to a top-secret testing facility in Los Alamos, New Mexico, where they underwent more scrutiny until they were deemed safe, reliable, and effective for use in their designated environment.

The workers, most of them MIT and Cal Tech whiz-kids, were provided with houses, cars, and anything else they so desired. The one stipulation, aside from the secrecy, was they all live in a gated community just outside Forest Hills in Queens. The estate, guarded day and night by ex-Marines masquerading as security guards, had every amenity known to man. Tennis and basketball courts, swimming pools, its own lake, a forest with animals to hunt, various helicopters and pilots, a golf course, and a rally track cut through the forest, for those who liked that sort of thing. Coupled with a salary a senior lawyer would be proud of, their jobs and lives were blissful in the extreme. With one phone call they could have, within reason, anything they desired.

Every three months, though, the President requested a progress report. An external verifier, always Baker but sometimes accompanied by Clemence, made the arduous journey from Washington to "Station Blue". Here, they met with the two leading men in the operation, as well as a handful of workers, and had a symposium about the status quo and plans for the future. This meeting, recorded for efficiency, was hand-delivered by Baker to the President within hours of leaving "Station Blue". And while Baker thought of it as nothing more than a waste of time and resources, he and Clemence were the only two people in law enforcement agencies who knew anything about the facility, and therefore had drawn the short straw.

With nothing on his schedule for the next three hours, Clemence had decided to tag along this time; partly because he was bored, but mostly because it had been over a year since his last visit. Curiosity had got the better of him, and he was anxious to see how one particular item had progressed: The microwave gun.

Originally masterminded by DARPA in the early eighties, but cancelled after lack of funding and technology, the weapon was still in its prototype stage the last time Clemence had seen it. Back then, it had been attached to the turret of a tank, but modifications from "Station Blue's" geniuses – and a new wave of seemingly limitless technological advances – had downsized it considerably and now it was intended to be used as a handheld rifle.

Using a mixture of particle beam and microwave technology, the weapon fired red-hot bolts of energy at speeds exceeding fifty miles per hour. The problem, though, arose from the heat generated by each shot. After a half-dozen were fired, the firing mechanism, and several other moving parts, became so hot they virtually melted. To counter this, all internal parts had been coated with fire-resistant material which could withstand over five hundred degrees centigrade. However, prolonged use eventually destroyed it, leaving the weapon with a shelf-life of only six months to a year depending on use. If the "Station Blue" geniuses could figure a way to extend it, it would give America an inexorable advantage in the War on Terror.

"Seems to me an awful waste of money, seeing how you can access this facility through the level-two complex," Clemence said.

Baker threw him an incredulous look. "Because a dozen whiz-kids from MIT coming into the building every morning, going down the elevator, and disappearing until that evening – yeah, that's not going to raise any suspicion."

"Hey, listen" — Clemence rose his arms in capitulation — "all I'm saying is it seems pointless. I mean, what's the point of having this tunnel here if you can access the facility from up top?"

Baker laughed. Clemence had always been a pessimistic son of a bitch, even during his twenty-year spell with the LAPD. Regardless of how good a bust he or the precinct made, he'd always wanted more, or found something to complain about. That fact notwithstanding, Clemence was one of the most tenacious cops Baker had ever worked with. Now into his sixties, he'd forged a career out of this sheer tenacity, and had earned his place in the elite pantheon of agency directors.

"Yeah, make 'em drive thirty minutes out of their way to get from level two to three. See how well that goes down," Baker said with a shake of his head.

"We have to do it. What – them MIT whiz-kids too good to do a little driving, eh?"

"I'm gonna start ignoring you now, Roger," Baker said with

another shake of his head.

"Hmph. Nothing new there."

The doors finally opened, revealing level-three "Station Blue" in all its splendour. The giant laboratory bustled with activity. In each and every corner, men and women in white lab coats hurried from one place to another, seemingly unaware of anything other than their work. Upstairs, in the main offices, staccato sounds of weapons being fired and other items being tested could be heard.

Both men stepped out of the elevator and were greeted by two familiar faces. The first was a young, sprightly man with a full head of black hair. He smiled, and handed both a pair of earmuffs.

"Welcome to Station Blue, gentlemen," he said, cracking another smile.

Baker knew him well, and knew the smiles were fake. He returned them, though, and offered his hand.

The second, a much older and less able-bodied man, refused to shake either's hand, but greeted them instead with a nod and a polite "welcome".

"Good to see you again, Jim," Baker said, wondering how long the old man had left. Stage-two liver cancer had turned the once youthful and exuberant James Fielding into a frail old man. He had, from the looks of it, another six months left – if even that.

"Why don't we go somewhere quiet where we can conduct our business in private?" Dave Haskens queried, another fake smile spreading over his face.

CHAPTER FIFTY-SEVEN
INCOGNITO

HARVEY POINT
15:35 EST

"What are you doing here, Ed?" Charles Peterson demanded of Rainey.

Wearing a white suit, white loafers, and with his brown hair also starting to whiten, Rainey looked like some kind of angel. But despite his appearance, there was nothing heavenly about the Secretary of Defence. Possessed of one of the sharpest and quickest minds in the game, he was both a highly successful entrepreneur – with two companies and fifty million dollars to his name – and a Machiavellian. When it came to politics, few could catch him out on any subject. And he took great pleasure in making other people sweat. For all that, Peterson didn't fear him. Rainey was a cocky and arrogant son of a bitch, but he only thrived on others' fear. Peterson's poker face never showed anything.

"I could ask you the same question, Chad," Rainey replied, signalling to the brutish Latino to leave. Rainey's walk, much like everything else, was a swagger. To him, appearance meant everything.

"Now what possible reason could there be for the Secretary of

Defence being at a top-secret CIA facility?" Peterson asked with a raised eyebrow.

Rainey smiled. "It's interesting, isn't it?"

"What?"

"I figured someone outside the Cabinet would stumble onto this. There's no such thing as secrets in today's world, Chad."

"Not with – "

"What...surveillance? If only the CIA or NSA were half as good as they purport themselves to be...then we'd have an intelligence community to fear!" Rainey waved his hand. "But enough about that! Like I said...I figured someone would find out. Never thought it would be *you*, though."

"What is this about, Ed? What's going on here?"

Rainey encompassed the entire building with a sweep of his hand. "This...this is all about the future, Chad. The future of not only the United States but the entire world."

Peterson realised Rainey sounded like a teacher behind a lectern preaching about the future of education. There was no doubting his passion, but the Chairman of the Joint Chiefs wondered if it were *only* passion and not the lunatic ramblings of someone insane.

"How would that be, Ed?" he replied, raising his voice a semitone to feign interest.

"The problem with this country's armed forces is that even though we have some of the best soldiers in the world we still haven't got the most formidable anti-terrorist team as a result." He gestured to a chair in one of the cubicles, and both men sat down. Rainey crossed his legs. With another smile, he began, "We have soldiers...great soldiers...but the problem is they're divided between different factions of our military forces. Just imagine what we stand to gain if we combine the greatest soldiers in all our military!"

Even though Peterson knew most of it already, he acted surprised. "That's what this about? So why all the secrecy? This seems like something the American people would support without blinking."

Rainey nodded. "Sure they would. If they knew about it right now, I'm pretty sure three-quarters of them would agree wholeheartedly with what we're doing." Rainey flashed another smile – this one dissimulative. He wanted Peterson to push on.

That way, he had the opportunity to say he'd been coerced – more or less – into talking.

"So what's the problem? Why are we sitting in a CIA facility, talking in hushed tones about something that isn't even worthy of such clandestine actions?"

"It's one thing to second soldiers from different American military groups. It's quite another to take them from all over. There's no precedent for that sort of thing."

A look of shock flickered over Peterson's eyes but he quickly curbed it. *That* was a surprise. He'd known about soldiers being seconded from various US military forces, but nothing could have prepared him to learn foreign soldiers were also a part of the plan. Rainey was correct – there were no precedents for this kind of thing. The only well-known anti-terrorist team with any resemblance to this was NATO. Something similar would need to be put in place here to determine who had control over soldiers of various nationalities. *That* was why it had to be secretive. Something like this would not go down well with the American public.

"So, let me get this straight," Peterson began, keeping his voice level. "You guys are pulling soldiers from all over the world – I don't even know what kind of paperwork would be involved with that, but I'm sure it's not something you do over the phone. But you're taking them from their units, bringing them all the way over here, and training them to be some elite conglomerate of anti-terrorists designed to...what? Where are their loyalties? Who do they work for? Which country do they serve?"

Rainey laughed. "You think we haven't hashed all this out already, Chad? We've picked the right soldiers, with the right history, and who have the qualities we're looking for." A devious smile.

Peterson watched Rainey's right hand twitch. He subconsciously craved a glass of wine. Obsessive over image, he had also the need for either alcohol or a cigarette when putting on his little show. Maybe it was part of the image, but Peterson suspected it was because it calmed him down.

"What kind of 'qualities'?"

Waving his arm, Rainey said, "I'm not going to discuss the minutiae of it with you, Chad. We have everything under control. Now, if you still want to be Chairman of the Joint Chiefs come tomorrow morning, I suggest you leave now."

Peterson knew Rainey resided over all of the Joint Chiefs. He didn't have to power to terminate any of them, but he did have a very good relationship with the President. And since Peterson and the President weren't on the best of terms at the moment, he had little choice but to accede to Rainey's demands.

"If I've figured this out, Ed, you know it won't be long until someone else does too. You can't keep something like this a secret forever."

"On the contrary, far greater secrets than this have been kept over the years. This one's child's play in comparison."

Peterson shook his head. This had all the hallmarks of being a brilliant idea, but it also had the stigma of the last fifty years of military brusqueness. America had alienated themselves from a lot of their allies, and the last true one they had was Britain. Constructing a team like this – a team comprising various nationalities – was like playing Russian roulette. Soldiers were soldiers, yes, but loyalty to one's profession was not the same as loyalty to one's country. Many of them would be considered traitors for joining such a unit. The team would be a powder-keg of emotion and bravado, and the slightest thing might be enough to set them against each other.

"This has the potential to be either a brilliant coup...or a train-wreck. My money's on the latter." Peterson turned to Anderson, who'd been leaning against the partition listening to the entire conversation unbeknownst of Rainey. "Sergeant-Major, we're leaving." Peterson turned back to Rainey. "Good luck with it, Ed. You're going to need it."

***

From his position in the storm drain underneath the building, Carlos could hear the entire conversation clearer this time than he had a few minutes earlier. Above his head, a grate gave access. Taking a deep breath, he gripped it by the steel and prepared to heave it upwards.

***

With both men facing away from the grate, neither saw or were prepared for what happened next. With a groan, the steel entryway opened into the EOD building, thumping off the concrete with a clank that caused all three men to jump. As they stood up and spun around, Carlos hoisted himself into the room and pounced to his feet. All three looked at each other for a moment, wondering what the hell was happening.

***

Son of a bitch!

Carlos didn't allow time for the shock of the moment to sink in – either for them or himself. As soon as his feet touched the concrete, he bounded forward, towards the man in the white suit. The man stared back at him, his face a mixture of horror and recognition.

In an instant, Carlos was beside him. Thrusting out a hand, he grabbed him by the collar of his exorbitant suit and yanked him towards him. In tandem, his forearm looped over the man's head and came crushing against his trachea. The man spluttered. Jerked. Pulled. Like a rat trying to squirm away from a cat, he fought to find a way out of Carlos' vice-like grip. But as the oxygen to his brain diminished, so too did his capacity for struggle.

Of the two remaining men, only one of them reacted in a meaningful way. The black one removed a standard-issue nine-millimetre automatic from his holster, levelling it at Carlos' chest. Carlos studied the eyes – they never lied. The man had fired before. He'd also killed. That steely look of determination and pride came only from having served your country. He would shoot. Carlos knew he didn't have the luxury of time.

As the man in the white suit faded, Carlos eased his grip slightly. He needed him debilitated but not unconscious. He wanted him to hear every word.

"I don't know who you are, but I assume you're a soldier," the black man began. "I need you to calm down and let Secretary of Defence Rainey go."

Carlos threw him a look. "Secretary of Defence? Strange, that. He introduced himself yesterday as 'Brigadier-General Edward Triton'," Carlos hissed. Rainey tried to speak but it came out as a muffled rasp.

"Okay, I don't know what he's done or what he's told you, but I can assure you this is not the way to deal with this," the black man warned. "Let him go and we can make sure he's dealt with properly – together."

"I heard him"—Carlos pointed at the other man—"call you Sergeant-Major. What's your name?"

"Wesley Anderson."

"Well, with all due respect, Wesley, you have *no* idea what I've been through in the last twenty-four hours. I've been pulled from combat, flown halfway across the world, and thrown into a prison cell. My second-in-command, Julio Gyle, is being tortured as we speak."

Another muffled cry from Rainey. Carlos reacted by squeezing him tighter.

"What!" This time it was the other man. "Listen, soldier, I'm the Chairman of the Joint Chiefs, Charles Peterson. If soldiers are being mistreated in this facility, I need to know."

"Well, Mr Chairman, Mr Secretary here is going to take us to my friend...or I'm going to snap his scrawny neck like a fuckin' twig!"

CHAPTER FIFTY-EIGHT
OUT OF THE WALLS

CASPIAN AIR FLIGHT 434
16: 45 GMT-4

Ivanovich watched with rapt attention as the man in seat 47B – the same one York had spotted earlier – fidgeted with his belt, looked across his shoulder, and glanced to his watch with a nervous and frightened repetition. Across his forehead, beads of sweat dotted his brow and dripped into his thick beard. Something had him spooked, and Ivanovich had an idea what.

Five minutes earlier, after shoving a toilet brush halfway down his throat, York had convinced the one remaining terrorist to make a phone call. With the added incentive of losing his testicles, the resilient yet horrified Muslim had allowed the fear of being tortured to rule his emotions. He'd called the sleeper agent and told him the plan was still in place and to meet him in the bathroom for a status report in thirty minutes.

Since then, five had passed, and this man was the only person on the entire plane who looked as though they were planning to get up. But Ivanovich had to be careful. Bad travellers often fidgeted and perspired like this. He couldn't make his move until certain of the man's identity.

"I got nothin' in first-class, Sergei. Levsky hasn't moved

either," York informed him through the earpiece.

Ivanovich acknowledged the transmission and let his mind wander to Levsky as he waited for his "terrorist" to make a move. The man would have to go through the first-class cabin to get to the toilet. In doing so, Levsky would have ample opportunity to spot Ivanovich. And, whilst having to add one more body to the rising count didn't bother him, the problem was the lack of space to hide them. He didn't know what he would do to the sleeper agent when he got him alone in the toilet, but he didn't think it would be anything less than violent. People were going to notice the sleeper's absence. And if they didn't, the sight of an ostensible flight marshal pulling the dead or unconscious body of a man up the aisle to join an increasing number of missing passengers would cause most people to either panic or start asking questions about Ivanovich's legitimacy.

But what other choice did he have? Either he took care of the sleeper, or the plane exploded on approach to New York. Both of those were undesirable outcomes, but only one assured he stayed alive long enough to complete his mission. And in the game of terrorism, you often had to do things you didn't like.

"We got a problem, Sergei," York whispered.

Ivanovich sighed, wondering what could be wrong *this* time. "Come on, York. Start telling me good news."

"Wish I could...wish I could. We got a fat lady in the toilet, and she ain't doing no singin'. Looks like she's gonna be in there for quite some time, too."

"Fuck!" The passengers around Ivanovich looked up, startled by his outburst. But the man in seat 47B never moved. "On my way," he whispered, shaking his head.

The journey past Levsky went without a hitch this time, but Ivanovich wondered if his luck was running out. One of these trips Levsky would look up and catch a glimpse of a face he'd thought he'd buried. Ivanovich needed to steal a hat, or tie his hair back...or do something to ensure he only bore a passing resemblance to the infamous Sergei "The Butcher" Ivanovich.

He found York standing outside the toilet, keeping an eye on both the door and the area around it.

"So what do you wanna do now?" York asked with a hint of desperation in his voice.

"*Me?* This was your idea, York! You figure it out!"

"Well, I can't exactly knock on the door and say: 'Gee, missus, we really need the bog because, well, see, there's a terrorist on-board we're trying to trap'!"

"Use your imagination. Tell her the toilet's blocked and we need to fix it or the smell's going to drive all the passengers out of the first-class section."

"Goddamnit, she's already driving the passengers out of the first-class section! I can smell it from here."

"Just come up with something! I don't care what. I'm going back to check on our friend, before he decides to blow us up for the hell of it."

The irony of the situation seemed to be growing by the second. Soon, they'd be rescuing baby seals or doing some other heroic action. Ivanovich laughed at the thought, as the people around him looked at him he was some kind of freak.

Let them wallow in their own self-satisfaction, Sergei. Soon, they'll all be eradicated by an event that would make nine-eleven look like a car bomb.

The thought caused him to smile. Yes, soon America would be involved in a war like no other. Nothing would prepare her for the carnage and mayhem that would engulf her shores in the coming months and years. And he hoped to be a part of it. Today's mission was the beginning. He knew what he had to do. It didn't mean he had to like it, but there were certain sacrifices required for the greater good.

And as Ivanovich looked at Levsky on the way back to the economy section, he realised he'd been presented with a priceless opportunity.

CHAPTER FIFTY-NINE
DISCHARGE

HARVEY POINT
15:50 LOCAL TIME

Charles Peterson had never seen Ed Rainey look so scared in all his life. The usual bravado that Rainey exuded was all but gone, replaced by palpable fear. Peterson didn't blame him. In Carlos' hands, Rainey looked like a small child.

With the absence of all the soldiers, there was no one left to protect Rainey. Peterson sensed he knew that and was trying to stall until they came back.

"Where is he?" Carlos demanded for the fourth time in the last two minutes. Again, Rainey refused to answer. "Goddamnit, my military career is screwed as of this moment, and right now I hate you more than any person on the planet. Do you really wanna test me, you slimy son of a bitch?"

Through restricted vocal cords, Rainey answered, "I don't know what you're talking about."

Carlos wondered if he should just snap the bastard's neck and be done with it. The more he thought about it, the more it appealed to him. He couldn't salvage his career now. Not after this fiasco. Gyle was still in trouble, and the never-leave-behind-a-man motto ingrained into Carlos throughout his military career now erupted in rage. To hell with them all. They wanted to play a game? Well, now they were going to find out that playing games came with a price.

Carlos increased the pressure on Rainey's throat, completely cutting off the oxygen to his brain. Rainey thrashed wildly, his arms and legs flailing.

"Try not to struggle. It'll be over quicker. Unless you wanna tell me where Gyle is right now and we can walk there in a more peaceable way."

Rainey's struggles lessened by the second, while Peterson and Anderson looked on in shock, wondering how to handle a man who'd clearly snapped. Even Anderson's gun, seconds earlier pointed at Carlos, now lowered as the futility of the situation dawned on him. Carlos was being smart. He'd dragged Rainey's body off the floor to his height, giving a shooter nothing to aim at. It also used Rainey's weight against him; a hangman's noose.

"One last chance!" Carlos growled.

"That's enough!" a voice called from behind. Carlos edged around slightly, enough to keep his eyes on everyone. *Son of a bitch!* The diminutive leader from earlier – the one who'd socked Carlos in the ribs – was standing behind him, in his hand a nine-millimetre Beretta.

Carlos weighed up his options. Neither man would dare shoot, not with the Secretary of Defence's life at risk. That gave him time. Letting Rainey back down to the floor, he eased his grip around SecDef's throat. Rainey spluttered, jerked, and tried to break free, but Carlos held firm.

"Well done, son," Rainey croaked.

Carlos frowned. "What are you talking about?"

"You can put your guns down now, gentlemen," Rainey ordered, casting sharp glances at Anderson and the newest arrival. "Mr Carlos here has passed."

Suddenly it dawned on Carlos. "Passed? This was a goddamn *test!*" After the last exhalation of air, Carlos' entire body tensed. As anger surged through his veins, his grip around Rainey's throat increased. Rainey's eyes bulged in his head, his veins popped out into his skull, and his mouth made the sound of a man who knew his life was about to end. Carlos, his teeth gritted, yelled, "You son of a – "

Fully intent on snapping the neck like a twig, Carlos became acutely aware of a stabbing pain just below his right hip. His eyes, glazed over now by something he couldn't understand, dropped to his front thigh.

Blood.

It dripped from the gaping wound in the fabric of his fatigues. Carlos could see the innards of his leg – could almost see daylight through the aperture. He stumbled backwards, letting go of Rainey in the process, and turned to face the leader. His gun was still up, the smoke from the barrel leaving no doubt. Carlos looked at him in a far-off way. And then, with a sigh of what could only be considered as relief, dropped to the ground. The floor felt cold, but his entire body burned. The strange sensation kept him alert for about twenty more seconds.

Then the world went black.

PART III

CARTE BLANCHE

16:00 – 21:00

CHAPTER SIXTY
LAST RESORT

```
NEARBY WILLOW GROVE
INTERSTATE-276 WEST
PENNSYLVANIA
16:01 EST
```

Vladimir Pushkin cursed as an eighteen-wheeler pulled into the left lane, cutting him off and causing him to lose sight of Troy Davies' taxi. In the right lane, a large truck carrying a load of stones spewed black smoke as it struggled to negotiate the hill. Pushkin, trapped between the two behemoths, had no choice but to flash his lights, honk his horn, and hope the eighteen-wheeler found the power to overtake.

To his chagrin, it had taken the better part of an hour to find Davies and his taxi. This had nothing to do with the startlingly pinpoint accuracy of the GPS, but more to do with New York and its surrounding cities containing somewhere in the region of a hundred thousand taxis, most yellow. Finding it had been a stroke of luck...and now it seemed he was destined to lose it again.

"*Idi na khui!* Goddamnit, move that piece of shit!" he yelled, honking his horn numerous times. Still the truck inched forward, travelling under fifty miles per hour. Losing his patience, Pushkin pumped the clutch (he'd chosen a manual transmission because of familiarity) and shifted into fourth with a jerk. Yanking the wheel left, he mounted the grass verge. The tires spun for a moment, then found traction. He slapped on the windscreen wipers and shifted into third. The extra infusion of power sent the SUV forward with a lurch, and he floored the accelerator. The SUV shot past the eighteen-wheeler, whose driver honked his horn in return, and Pushkin pulled back into the lane in front of him.

He was tempted to remove his Makarov from his waistband and pump two rounds into the fat American's head, but that would only draw even more attention. Instead, he forced himself to breathe, to relax.

Ahead, he could still see Davies' taxi, about a quarter of a mile up the road. Neither the driver nor his passenger seemed to have noticed the incident behind.

He gunned the SUV. As the gap closed, he wondered how to handle the next part. If he ran Davies' taxi off the road, causing an accident, there was still a chance the man would live. If he pulled up next to him and fired a half-dozen rounds into the back seat, that chance was less likely but still possible. No, he needed to be positive, and the only way to do that was to make the taxi stop, approach it, and kill both occupants. Only then could he be sure.

When the gap closed to twenty yards, Pushkin made his decision. Grabbing his seatbelt and strapping himself in, he powered forward until the nose of his SUV came level with the rear of the taxi.

***

When the SUV came abreast of him, Davies noticed it was black. That got his attention fast. Most people shunned dark-coloured vehicles in favour of flashy, more sporty models. When he looked up, his breath left him with a jolt. The man seated behind the wheel had all the distinctive characteristics of a Russian. Having spent the last two years of his life in the country, Davies had learned how to distinguish the locals.

Glancing back to see nothing behind, Davies roared, "Hit the brakes! Now!"

The taxi driver gave a start, looked in the mirror, and said, "What the hell are you on about?"

Davies leapt forward and screamed, "Hit the goddamn brakes! *Now!*"

"Listen, jerkoff, I'm not going to – "

Davies turned to see the SUV smash into the rear of the taxi. The screech of metal-on-metal filled the air. Then, with a groan of rubber on asphalt, the taxi's rear-end slid to the left.

***

Pushkin followed the taxi into the spin, keeping the nose of his SUV tight against it. When the taxi driver pumped his brakes, Pushkin hit his in tandem. Downshifting, he yanked the wheel hard to the right and aimed for the centre. He downshifted once more and jammed his foot on the accelerator. The SUV broadsided the vehicle with a thump, lifting the right side completely off the ground. The taxi flipped over several times, narrowly missing some cars, clipping a few others, before coming to rest on a grass verge across the road.

Pushkin ignored the constant tooting of horns and skidded his vehicle to a stop ten yards farther down the interstate. Grabbing his Makarov, he opened the door and stepped out onto the grass.

He saw the driver first. His head, a crimson mass, was slumped on the steering wheel. He realised the horn wasn't coming from the other road-users but from the taxi. Ignoring the dead driver, he continued towards the rear, gun up.

***

One minute Davies had been telling the taxi driver to stop, and the next he was lying face-down in the back, showered with glass, and wondering why his entire body felt crushed. He tried to say something, but only blood aspirated from his mouth. Then, instinctively, his hand reached for the pocket of his coat, where his pistol had last been.

Scratching. Ripping. Tearing.

He couldn't find it. Panic gripped him. He tried to move but his body wouldn't respond.

Then he saw motion above. Someone was standing at the front of the taxi, his – or her – shadow blocking out most of the light.

Davies tried to pull himself forward, towards the left-hand passenger door. Excruciating pain shot through his arms and legs. It was like nothing he'd ever experienced before. His entire body screamed at him to let go. To succumb to the overwhelming desire to fall asleep. And as much as he wanted to survive – as much as he *had* to survive and warn his bosses about what was coming – the only thing he could think of was how tired he felt and how much he wanted it to be over.

Do your duty! Get up and finish the job!

Davies knew there was no other option. Plan A had failed, through his own fault; but he'd prepared a backup plan in case it ever came to this.

***

Vladimir Pushkin had never felt pity for any of the people he'd murdered, but as he looked at Davies crawling along the back of the taxi, he felt a twang of something. Then, as quickly, the feeling dissipated and Pushkin raised his gun.

Davies never saw it coming. Two blasts echoed through the interior of the cab, and Davies' arm slumped to the ground. Satisfied he was dead, Pushkin moved to turn away. He saw it then. On the floor beside Davies' hand was a small device. He bent into the cab and took a closer look. With a start, he realised what the device was: a PDA. On its screen were two words that sent a shiver of dread through Pushkin's body.

MESSAGE SENT.

CHAPTER SIXTY-ONE
REALISATIONS

```
ATARIC
16:05 EST
```

Seated behind his desk in Reid's office, his fingers flying over his keyboard, Hunt was desperately trying to find a site that corroborated Daedalus' claims about "Station Blue" being a top-secret facility buried underneath New York City. Unsurprisingly, he'd found nothing. Not even a snippet of a similar story. As far as the world was concerned, such a facility didn't exist – at least not in New York.

That didn't bother him. While other people would have needed proof to substantiate such claims, Hunt knew in his heart ATARIC was a company shrouded in secrecy. The elevator notwithstanding, there were also several other things – like the power consumption and the information being sent to Jamie Signfeld's email address – that were bothering him. Plus, the "gas-main repairs" outside the office were a convenient cover to allow secretive work to take place.

But he needed proof before he could take it to Reid. Otherwise, he'd just dismiss it as the paranoid ravings of a man who craved alcohol. It didn't matter how sober Hunt was, if he didn't have proof, Reid would laugh him out of the building.

The picture wasn't enough. Sure, it showed Reid leaving ATARIC, it showed the ostensible repairs happening outside it and, along with the Internet report, it *might* be enough to convince someone of strange goings-on, but without proof it was all conjecture.

Hunt thumped the table with his right hand and slid the chair out from underneath it. With a sigh, he stood and walked out of the room, to the confusion of Reid and Collins. He took the stairs two at a time and continued to the toilet.

How had his life become this? Everything had been perfect a few years ago. Great job – despite a horrid boss – a lovely wife, great house, a baby boy; and now...what? Looking in the mirror, Hunt asked himself how he'd let it get this bad. Where had it all gone wrong?

For so long he'd overcome the tribulations to the point where life had been...promising. Now, like someone whipping a carpet from under him, everything in his life had come crashing down.

Nothing had come easy for him. He'd had to work for everything. But at least back then he had people to confide in; people who would support and believe in him. Now, the only person he could rely on was himself. He was familiar with the feeling; it came from having two parents who worked insane hours and left their son with a sadistic minder. If Reid wouldn't believe him, he'd just have to find a way to make him – or do what he'd always done: deal with it on his own.

Before he knew what he was doing, he'd taken his phone from his pocket and had dialled Karen's office number. A secretary answered after a single ring, and he deliberated whether he wanted to involve Karen in his life again. As much as he loved her, he didn't want to give her false hope. If there was a chance they could reconsolidate their marriage, he wanted it to be for the right reasons.

"Hello? Is anyone there?" the secretary demanded.

"Yes, hello? Is Karen Hunt there?"

"She's in her office. May I ask who's calling?"

"It's her husband."

"Mr Hunt, I'll forward the call."

"Thank you."

A few minutes passed – this time to the sounds of *Eye of the*

Tiger – and then Karen's voice came over the handset. "Peter, are you okay?" The concern in her voice imbued Hunt with hope. She still cared, which meant there was still a chance of saving the marriage.

"I just had a nasty fall, but I'm fine," Hunt lied.

"What happened? I mean, you said I called you. Peter, I wouldn't lie to you about anything. I wanted to call you, but I never did," Karen replied, her voice becoming guarded.

He frowned. "What do you mean 'you wanted to call me'?"

Karen hesitated. "Something happened in the office yesterday, Peter. I'm trying to deal with it myself, but I'm afraid you're going to find out."

Hunt, his voice now more serious and direct, said: "What happened, Karen?"

"There was an incident yesterday involving one of the male employees."

It sounded like she was having a hard time recounting what had happened. Hunt figured it was either because she was embarrassed by it, or afraid of what he might do when he found out. Either way, she was right. He had already planned what he was going to do. Now it was just a matter of finding out what had happened and how serious it was.

"What happened, Karen?"

Karen sighed. "I don't think I should tell you over the phone. Listen, Jack told me you have no way home tonight. How about I come over and give you a ride? We can talk about it then."

He knew what she was doing. By waiting past her law firm's closing hours, Karen made sure he couldn't drive to the office to find the person responsible. At least this way it gave her a little time to placate him.

"Okay, that sounds good. But I'll likely be working late. It'll probably be after seven before I'm finished."

"That's okay. I have a few things to clear up here before I finish. I'll see you at seven?"

"Okay. And Karen?"

"Yeah?"

"Whatever this is...whatever happened...I know you think I'll do something stupid, but I'm not that guy anymore. I'm giving up the drink, Karen. And this thing with ATARIC...who knows? Maybe I'll get my old job back."

"Peter – "

"Don't, Karen. I'm going to make this work. I promise you. Whatever happens, I'm going to have you and Jack back in my life. I'm not giving up on you. Please don't give up on me. I'll see you later."

Hunt hung up before Karen could offer a rejoinder. As much as he wanted to take Reid's keys, get in his car, and drive to the Leo and Walken building to sort out what had happened between Karen and the male employee, he knew doing that would effectively end his marriage. He had to show Karen he'd changed. He had to make her understand the Peter Hunt she'd known over the past year was gone. If he could earn her trust back, maybe he could earn his life back also.

As he opened the door of the toilet, he jerked back when Harold Johnson's furrowed face came within inches of his own.

"Hello, Peter. I heard you had a little accident earlier. The kind of accident that might lead to certain individuals believing you'd been drinking on the job. Now, I don't think you're dumb enough to do something like that, but the bosses want reassurance.

"I didn't drink on your stupid time. All right, Johnson?" Hunt asked, brushing him aside.

Johnson held his ground. "Afraid it's not that simple, Peter. Fielding wants you in his office – right now. If I were you, I'd pray he doesn't smell drink on your breath."

"Don't worry, Johnson. If you think this little stunt is gonna rid you of me, you got another thing coming. I know how to handle James Fielding.

"Sure you do. Just try not to mix up your words, Hunt. Wouldn't want him thinking you're drunk."

And just like that, something went *click* in Hunt's mind. *Just try not to mix up your words, Hunt.*

James Fielding.

Jamie Signfeld.

CHAPTER SIXTY-TWO
SECONDARY

```
APARTMENT COMPLEX
ST. PETERSBURG
RUSSIA
00: 10 MSK
```

Scott Harden thrust out a hand and fumbled for the nightlight on his desk. The constant hum of traffic outside had kept him awake for most of the night. That, and the dread of receiving a message he didn't want or need. And as the PDA in the pocket of his khaki trousers bleeped, his heart sank.

Turning the light on as slowly as possible, he reached into his pocket and removed the device. A message on the screen informed him he had new mail. The sender was "T. Davies". It read:

If you receive this message, Scott, the scenario we talked about during our conversation in Russia twenty-four hours ago has come to be. That means I'm either dead or dying. It also means you are now the last person in the world who knows what I knew.

I didn't know who to trust in any of the American agencies, but you have contacts from your days in the Marines. You need to get in touch with your commanding officer and tell him you wish to speak with the President. He will tell you he'll forward the message to the White House switchboard and that's all he can do. You tell him to tell the White House it involves Station Blue. You'll have a direct line to the President before your CO hangs up the phone.

You need to tell Walsh everything I told you – EVERYTHING. You need to make him understand it's happening NOW. That before the end of this day, Station Blue WILL be attacked. I should have gone straight to him in the beginning, but I thought I could handle it myself. You're the last hope, Scott. I hate to put this all on your shoulders, but there's no one else.

I just hope my death will in some way prevent what will surely be thousands more deaths if the terrorists succeed. Don't let that happen, Scott. Don't let my death be in vain.
Troy.

Wiping away a tear, Harden removed his phone from the desk in the drawer, scrolled through the numbers, and picked "CO" from the list. The phone rang a couple of times and then a husky voice croaked a hello.

"Sarge? It's Scott Harden." Harden paused a moment to let the name sink in. "Desert Storm in ninety-two? Took a bullet in the leg outside Kandahar?"

"Yeah, I remember. Damn, you got injured pretty bad that time. Thought you were gonna bleed to death on us. You still on active duty, Gunny?"

"No, sir. Retired in ninety-nine. Just before Desert Storm Two started. In fact, I've been living in Russia for a few years now. Got a job guarding high-level diplomats over here. Dangerous, but the pay's good."

"That's good to hear, son. So, what can I do for you?"

"Well, you know about the Marine 'get-out-of-jail-free' cards?" Harden meant the one-time-only favour former Marines called in from time to time. Usually it involved getting some act of wrong-doing expunged from official record. Depending on how well liked or how decorated a Marine was, the card extended to making even high-level crimes like robbery or statutory rape disappear. Though its existence was treated as an urban legend, many Marines had used it to start new lives or wipe the slate clean. Now, Harden was going to use his for one massive favour.

The man on the other end laughed. "Come on, Scott. You know as well as I do that whole thing is a myth. Besides, you're living in Russia. Even if it were true, there's nothing we could do for you there." There was a pause, and then he continued, "What have you done anyway?"

"That's just it, Sarge. I haven't done anything. It's kind of like an NYPD captain calling all cars. I need one huge favour from you guys."

"Okay, well you tell me what it is and I'll see what I can do."

Harden paused for effect, then said, "I need to speak with the President ASAP."

The man laughed again. "Why don't I organise a video conference with the Queen of England while I'm at it? You do realise for a soldier to speak with the President in any way requires him to be vetted at the Yankee White clearance level?"

The sergeant was referring to the Single Scope Background Investigation undertaken by the Department of Defence on all people working with the President. He also knew this didn't extend to people talking with the President, but there were certain protocols that needed to be followed, and he was trying his best to dissuade Harden from this decision.

"Listen, Sarge, I know it's a hell of a lot to ask. I wouldn't even think of calling if it weren't red-level. I need to speak with President Walsh post-haste. Just give him a message from me. Tell him it involves something called 'Station Blue', and it's a matter of life and death. He'll know what that means."

"Give me your number there and I'll see what I can do. I'm not promising anything, Scott, but damned if you haven't piqued my curiosity."

Harden gave him the number and said, "Thanks, Wes. You're a legend."

On the other end, Wesley Anderson hung up, his face contorted in a frown. Just what was "Station Blue" and why did an ex-Marine living in Russia suddenly have a desperate need to speak with the US President about it? Just when it seemed all the pieces were finally coming into place, a new one had just abruptly landed on their laps.

For a moment, Anderson forgot about Jack Carlos being shot, and wondered how many more pieces remained.

CHAPTER SIXTY-THREE
PRIMACY

26 FEDERAL PLAZA
16: 15 EST

Back behind his desk, one hand on a mug of coffee and the other cradled around his phone, William Forrester "listened" as Greg Hatchett relayed the results of Hollingsworth's evaluation, his mind anywhere but the conversation. The OPR man had so far recommended an indefinite suspension. Other than that, Forrester hadn't a clue. Hatchett had a fondness for verbiage.

"...which is why I think a suspension is of paramount importance in Hollingsworth's case. I believe he still hasn't fully convalesced after the incident in Baltimore. His mental state is fragile. I still haven't ascertained what happened at the airport today, but I'm of the belief it has rekindled dormant memories and feelings. Keeping him in the Bureau at this point in time could be detrimental. I recommend suspension and mandatory counselling sessions until such times as his mental state is akin to what's required of an FBI agent. There will be a further investigation pertaining to both shootings at the airport this morning, and we'll require an interview with you, William."

"Whatever's necessary to get to the bottom of this. Thank you for coming down, and I'll see to it your recommendations are put in place."

"I would like to conduct that interview now, William," Hatchett replied, his tone becoming sterner.

Forrester had a feeling this was coming. When an OPR representative got their claws in, they were almost impossible to break free of. And as much as he wanted to co-operate and get it over with, he didn't have the time right now. Currently, four crime-scene investigators were probing through Davies' home in Seagate, while Bastich and the others were narrowing down leads on where Davies might be right now. He wanted to be ready to bolt the second they had a location.

"I'm afraid that's impossible, Greg. I have paperwork to finish up for Director Baker before I leave tonight. It's my ass if it's not on his desk tomorrow morning. Right now I can't spare any time."

"It'll only take an hour, maximum."

He laughed, more so to break up the tension than anything else. "I only have an hour. Gotta get home to the kids. My wife's working a double shift tonight at the hospital. I'm sorry, Greg. It's just going to have to wait."

"I can be here tomorrow morning at seven."

Forrester shook his head. The OPR had a habit of making gofers of people, even high-ranking officials like Forrester. They liked to throw their weight around as though they could order the deputy director of the FBI to do anything they pleased. He would have none of it.

"I'll be here tomorrow morning at eight a.m., sharp. Not a moment before, Greg. You're welcome to come at seven, but I won't be here," Forrester finished, hanging up before Hatchett could make a rejoinder. Dialling the number of his deputy, he instructed him to issue Hollingsworth his suspension, confiscate his badge and firearm, and see him out of the building. He could have done it himself, but Hollingsworth would have plagued him with questions and complaints. This way, it would be done quickly and quietly, with minimum fuss.

Something still nagged at him, though. In all the madness, he hadn't time to cogitate on what had happened at LaGuardia this morning. He hadn't lied when he said he had paperwork to finish. Along with the reports he was supposed to have done this morning, he now had to write one on what had happened today. Being the deputy director didn't exempt him from that.

But there was something else. Something he couldn't quite put his finger on. Wracking his brain, Forrester again didn't hear Mike Delaney come in. This time, though, the agent's face was contorted in a frown, his eyes narrowed.

"We've located Davies," he announced."

Forrester bolted from his seat. "Why the long face? Let's go get the SOB!"

"Red!" Delaney called, stopping Forrester in his tracks. "He's dead. An NYPD officer found him in a taxi five minutes ago. Shot twice, in the back of the head. The cab driver was dead too. No bullet wounds on him. ME's on-site right now."

"Jesus! Have we any idea of motive...or what happened?"

Delaney shook his head. Not to say no, but because what he was about to say was profound. "The murders at Seagate this afternoon?"

Forrester frowned. "What about them?"

"I'd bet my pension the person who killed those four people is the same one who put two bullets in the back of Troy Davies' head."

"What makes you say that, Mike?"

"Lots of things. The grouping of the bullets in Davies' head – too similar. It just screams of someone well-versed in firearms. And the bullets found at Seagate came from a nine-millimetre Makarov. The ME's determined the ones that killed Davies are the same. Probably from the same gun."

Just like Hunt a few minutes earlier, something went *click* in Forrester's head now. His face furrowed in a frown, he watched as this morning's altercation in the airport flashed before his eyes. He heard Hollingsworth, his tone clearly agitated.

The guy drew down on me with a Browning, Red! If I hadn't got my Type Two on, I'd be dead right now.

The conversation was about Davies shooting Hollingsworth. Forrester had remembered the anger in his voice

Now, wide-eyed, he seized Delaney by the shoulder. "The preliminary forensics report from LaGuardia!

"What about it, Red?"

"The PAPD officer who was shot – did they find what bullet killed him?"

"Yeah, a forty-five. Why?"

He said it was a Browning Davies used. But the PAPD kid – he was shot with a forty-five, not a nine-millimetre! And Hollingsworth carries a Glock 21 – calibre...oh, fuck me

"Jesus Christ, Delaney. Ring down to the lobby! Tell them to stop Hollingsworth right now!"

"What? Why!"

"Because he shot dead a PAPD officer, and I want to know why!" Forrester snarled.

CHAPTER SIXTY-FOUR
MEDEVAC

HARVEY POINT
16:25 LOCAL TIME

A pool of crimson slicked the floor.

A pint. Maybe two.

Enough.

About ten yards away, Jack Carlos lay on a gurney, his lifeless eyes staring up at the ceiling. On his face, a mask pumped him full of a mixture of oxygen and morphine. The combination left him a little blanched and intoxicated.

But alive.

The bullet, a through-and-through, had missed the main arteries and veins in his leg. The blood-loss came from the wound itself. The nine-millimetre round – quite a ghastly, powerful thing – had exploded a half-inch exit hole around his thigh. After they'd spent five minutes looking for a clamp and stitches in the shambolic hut that served as a "first aid" station, Carlos passed out a second time. Another five minutes were spent debriding the wound, before someone found a personnel file with Carlos' blood type. One transfusion and shoddy stitching later, he was loaded on a gurney while a chopper was called to transport him to the nearest medical facility.

Except it hadn't arrived yet. And now half a dozen men were running in different directions, none with the slightest clue what was happening. All the while, Carlos remarked how lightheaded he felt and how much he wanted to sleep

When Dominguez walked past him for the third time, his arm subconsciously jerked up and grabbed the man by the forearm. He turned to Carlos, expecting to see a look of anger, but all he could see was concern.

"Gyle...where is he? He needs a medevac too," Carlos said, sounding like a cheap imitation of Darth Vader.

Dominguez gripped Carlos' shoulders, looked him in the eye, and said, "Your buddy is fine. He's in the next room."

Carlos shook his head. "No! He was injured...needs help!"

"Sergeant-Major, he's fine. Nobody was torturing him. It was all a charade."

He shook his head more forcefully this time, gripping Dominguez tighter. "I know my soldiers, man! I know their voices...their screams. I *heard* him screaming. Where...is he!"

"I swear to you – Master-Sergeant Gyle is in the next room, being debriefed by Sergeant-Major Anderson as we speak. There was never any torture."

Despite the protestations of Dominguez, Carlos sat up in the gurney, using the Latino's arm for leverage. "Then explain this to me!" he hissed, pointing to a huge gash and beginnings of a bruise on his naked upper body.

"I'm sorry about that, I truly am, but I give you my word, as a fellow Marine and soldier, your friend is fine." *Doesn't he remember it was me who gave him those bruises?* In his disorientation, it seemed Carlos had forgotten. Dominguez sensed an opportunity.

"I want to see him -"

"You've lost a good bit of blood and have been sleep-deprived for over twenty-four hours. We need to get you to a medical facility ASAP," he replied, gesturing for Carlos to lay back on the gurney.

But he shook his head. "I'm not going anywhere until I see, for myself, Julio is fine."

"I'm afraid I can't permit that. You need medical attention."

"Either you bring him to me, or I get off this gurney – shot, and dripping blood – and find him my damn self!"

"As you wish, Sergeant-Major." Dominguez looked to one of the base soldiers and nodded. The young man walked towards the nearest doors, his every movement tracked by Carlos' glazed eyes. So riveted – so anxious – he was that he never noticed Dominguez until it was too late.

The diminutive Marine slipped in behind him and injected a hypodermic syringe into Carlos' jugular vein.

As his senses became disorientated, the world black, and his body relented to the sleep it had craved for the past twenty-odd hours, Carlos noticed one last thing. As the soldier opened the door, another one wheeled out a second gurney. This one, though, was quite different.

On the slab was a zipped-up body bag.

CHAPTER SIXTY-FIVE
KARMA

CASPIAN AIR FLIGHT 434
16: 30 EST

They were already fifteen minutes over the time limit and no one had made a move for the toilet. At least not since the fat woman had left it twenty minutes earlier. Maybe it was something to do with the god-awful stench, but as Ivanovich sat in his seat, waiting for movement of any kind, he realised their window of opportunity was closing by the second. In forty-five minutes, according to the pilot, they would be entering US airspace. Fifteen after that, this bird would be landing...one way or another.

Maybe the sleeper agent had grown a brain. After all, it had been well over an hour since any of his buddies had been seen. Even though the pilots had done a terrific job of convincing everyone the terrorists were still on-board, holed up in the cockpit, the entire scenario would raise suspicions in even the most trusting man. It wasn't the modus operandi of a hijacker. You never let your guard down around potential threats, even if they were a bunch of terrified passengers. If that was true, it meant the remaining terrorist was waiting it out until the plane entered United States airspace. That didn't bode well for *anyone.*

Ivanovich glanced over to York, standing at the entrance to the first-class cabins, who shook his head. People were too terrified to even think about going to the toilet, which theoretically should have made their jobs easier. The problem was, *nobody* was going.

"What you want to do now, Sergei?" York asked. "You ask me, I think that fat lady *did* do some singing in the john, man, 'cause our asses seem screwed six ways to Sunday right about now."

"We still have about thirty minutes, York."

"Yeah, and then what? This guy doesn't move out his seat, we start randomly blowing the crap outta ethnic minorities for the hell of it? I say he's about the only one right now who looks any way likely of being this sleeper agent. Way I figure it, we need to drag his ass to the toilet; do a little strip-search."

"Yes, let's make all the passengers as xenophobic as hell about every foreigner on-board. That ought do us favours no end."

"Lot better than standing here with our thumbs up our asses. At least that way we deal with potential threats."

"Jesus, you really are a psycho. I'm not going to commit Hitler-esque mass murder because someone's a Muslim. We wait and we watch."

"Wonderful. I'll order us some popcorn, shall I?"

"Granted, it's a shit plan, but it's also a shit scenario. We take what we can get."

Ivanovich keyed off and watched as York hurried out of the cabin, shaking his head as he went. He knew the feeling. Being former military had imbued York with zero patience, instincts that were, more often than not, dependable, and a deep-seated feeling of being unable to be the helpless onlooker. It was almost impossible for him to remain patient in a situation like this. But cooler heads needed to prevail. Ivanovich had also spent time in military circles, not to mention law enforcement ones, but he'd come to realise successful terrorists were those who kept their nerve when things got out of control. Which was why he didn't blink when the pert young stewardess – the one he'd told earlier about the possibility of another terrorist on-board – came to him with a sharp-dressed man in tow. It was only when she scurried off that Ivanovich realised something was amiss.

Ivanovich appraised the man in front of him: A little over six foot; solidly built; a square jaw with a day's growth of beard on it; and the confident swagger of...*Jesus, this guy's a cop!*

"Something I can do for you, Mr...?" Ivanovich asked. With a quick dart, he scanned the floor to see if his man had made a move yet.

Nothing.

"Williamson. Daryl Williamson. Your name?" The blue eyes were interrogative. They bore through Ivanovich, yet sparkled like those of a youthful rookie on his first day on the force.

"Tom Flynn," Ivanovich replied in an American accent.

"So, Mr Flynn, you're a TSA-registered flight marshal, yes?"

Ivanovich nodded. "Sure am."

"That's mighty strange. You see, there's very seldom more than one flight marshal on a plane. I know for a fact Richard Denton was the one assigned to this one. You know how I know this?"

Ivanovich shook his head, alarm bells pounding, and reached for the gun tucked in the waistband of his trousers.

"Because I'm the TSA-registered senior flight marshal sent to assess him. And I don't know you, Mr Flynn. So..." Before Ivanovich could react, Williamson's hand jerked to his side. In a flash, a weapon appeared, its barrel pointed directly at Ivanovich's face. "...just who the hell are you?"

CHAPTER SIXTY-SIX
CONTROL

ATARIC
16: 35 EST

As Hunt waited outside Fielding's office for the chairman to show up, chastened by the fact he hadn't seen what was right in front of him, he wondered how many more things were that obvious. The fact that the e-mail address was an anagram of Fielding's name didn't surprise him, though he should have seen it earlier. Uneducated computer users often picked passwords that were, if not obvious, easily guessable. And although Fielding was nothing if not prudent, word around the office – even when Hunt was last here – was that cancer had ravaged his once healthy body. Pain had a way of making people careless.

Hunt had known for quite some time that ATARIC ticked all the wrong boxes. There was something out of kilter about this place – it was steeped in secrecy. The more he thought about that, the crazier it seemed. A place like this being a front for a top secret weapons development facility? There was paranoia...and then there was being delusional.

What annoyed him further was that Johnson had told him to come to Fielding's office immediately. It had been almost half an hour and still no sign of the SOB. Fielding didn't half-mind going berserk at people who didn't come at his beck and call, yet he expected Hunt to wait like a dog outside its master's door?

Screw this.

He turned and headed for the stairs. Halfway there, the sound of expensive loafers echoed off steel. He froze, then turned back to the office. When James Fielding appeared over the cusp, Hunt was standing at his door, leaning against the steel enclosure.

He noticed first that Fielding was out of breath. That would have been normal for a man of his age. The blood on the cuffs of his shirt, however, would not.

"Peter...sorry to keep you waiting," he wheezed. "Come inside."

Fielding's office was not what you'd expect for a man of his standing. It was bereft of any extravagant items (like Reid's fridge and Johnson's widescreen TV) and had the vacant feel of a room soon to be unoccupied. A desk, two chairs, a table and computer was all that remained. No filing cabinet, no secretary with her own separate desk, just a barren room that depressed Hunt even more. Though he'd faced his share of tribulations, he did not envy Fielding's current lifestyle. The old man, stubborn to the end, had refused chemotherapy. His toothpick-like body looked like it wasn't going to last the conversation. In stark contrast, Hunt felt bad about the extra thirty pounds around his gut.

To add to the already-clandestine feel, Fielding shuffled over to the blinds and pulled them all closed. Maybe it was an attempt to make him feel uneasy, but it took a huge amount to impress or intimidate Hunt. Certainly a stick like James Fielding held no worries for him.

"How long have we known each other, Peter?" Fielding asked, taking his seat and gesturing for Hunt take the other one. His voice was hoarse and weak, and Hunt had to listen with rapt attention to understand him.

"I'm not sure. A good few years, I suppose. Why?"

"I'm not going to lie to you. I had high hopes for you. I planned to make you chief of staff before you started snooping into things that weren't your concern." Hunt rose his hand to interject, but Fielding cut him off sternly. "Don't interrupt!" He coughed for a few seconds, removed a couple of Kleenexes, and continued, "Yes, chief of staff. And a fine one you'd have made. It's just a shame your nose got the better of you.

"When the problem of installing Jack Reid's operating system initially presented itself, yours was the first name that came to my mind, Peter. You're the smartest computer programmer I've ever met. You breached our firewalls in ten minutes, for God's sake! It's no secret everyone here considered you COS. Even though Johnson held that honour, they knew you were ten times his better. You could have had it all, but curiosity killed any chance of that.

"I didn't know what to expect by bringing you back here today. I'll be the first to admit I didn't even expect you to take the job. Johnson warned both myself and Dave Haskens you would be more trouble than you were worth, but I saw no one else who could handle this with the speed and efficiency you could. So far you've met my demands and then some. Dave informs me we should be well-on schedule for Wednesday.

"However, it has come to my attention your actions today have not been as noble as I have alluded to. You see, earlier our systems were infected by a rather nasty virus. Thankfully it's all been cleared up, but I have been given reason to believe you are in some way responsible for it. As of yet I haven't corroborated these claims. No, I would rather hear from you personally, Peter. I ask you this as your friend and not your boss: Did you have any part in infecting our computers with that virus?"

Hunt didn't wait for any length of time to pass before giving his blunt reply: "No."

"It's just...it's got all the hallmarks of your brilliance, Peter; albeit slightly rushed brilliance. And since Mike's basically been watching you like a hawk today, I'd say that's a good reason why it was rushed." Fielding waved his hand dismissively and continued, "I can understand why you'd do it. You saw an opportunity to get even with us and you took it – conjecturally, that is."

Hunt leaned forward in his chair. "How can I make this any clearer for you? I had nothing to do with that virus."

"I hope for your sake that's true, because I'm going to make you an offer."

"Yeah? What's that?"

"In light of what you've done today, and what you'll – I hope – have done by Wednesday, I'm going to offer you your old job back; with a little extra perk. I'm going to make you assistant chief of staff."

Dumbstruck, Hunt mouthed, "What?"

"I'm going to give you another chance. You'll need to get yourself sobered up, though."

Hunt frowned.

"Yes, I know about the alcoholism, Peter. I've been keeping tabs on you since we let you go."

"Why are you doing this now? Today – was it a test?"

"In a way. I don't need to test your capabilities as a computer programmer. They're second to none. But I needed to see if you could survive in this environment after everything that's happened to you. I'm willing to take a chance on you."

"Why?"

"Maybe it's because I'm an old man about to die and sentimentality has clouded my judgement. Maybe it's because I consider you a protégé. Or maybe it's because you're the best damned computer programmer in this city, if not the country. You have your issues, but what genius doesn't? I would rather have you here, with all your baggage, than let you go to some other rival computer firm and outfox us there."

"What about Mike?"

"What about him? Mike's a sycophant. He'll do what he's told. What he won't do is what you'll do."

Hunt tried to make his next words sound like he wasn't fishing for a compliment. "And what would that be?"

"He won't run the floor; make decisions without the backing of me or Dave; take his own initiative and kill potential problems before they can manifest; and, most importantly, he doesn't have the slightest clue about computers."

"You knew that when you hired him?" Hunt asked and Fielding nodded. "So why the hell *did* you hire him?"

"Make no mistake, Peter; Mike Johnson is a tyrant to those who report to him. In the harsh light of day, the man's statistics are unassailable. He *makes* people work. He gets one-hundred-and-ten per cent out of everyone in this building. But he's only good at motivation. He can only do what someone tells him to. You, on the other hand, like Jack Reid, will take matters into your own hands. You know the minutiae of computers. And you will, without asking for permission, make decisions that will keep this company one step ahead of its competitors. I know this for a fact because I've seen it in the past."

"Forgive me if I seem a little sceptical," Hunt replied, "but you knew all this the last time as well and you still fired me. You sided with Johnson. What's changed?"

"It's no secret a man analyses and reanalyses his life when he knows it's about to end. We all make mistakes. I've come to realise I handled the situation with you unprofessionally. But I'm willing to forget the past. If you get sobered up – and I'm talking full-blown rehab here – then the job is yours, including a twenty per cent pay-rise."

"How do I know this isn't a scam?"

"One thing I always liked about you was you were invariably very prudent." Fielding paused and opened his desk. He removed a manila folder and set it on the table. "That's a new contract. In it, it states you are to be given a pay-rise, the position of assistant chief of staff, and a ten-year contract which cannot be waivered. You sign that, Peter, and you've got job-security for the next decade.

"Now, I know you all too well. You won't be assistant chief of staff for long. Jack will probably – and this is between me and you – be taking Mike's job as managing director before I leave here in three weeks' time. Your future is here, Peter. It's always been here. We've made mistakes in the past, but this time I promise you it'll be different. Sign that contract and you'll be back here in six weeks' time, fully sober, ready to kick-start your life again."

Hunt removed the file from the envelope and spent five minutes reading through it, committing all the important details to memory. Nothing seemed incongruent; no loopholes that might be exploited at a later date. The document seemed legitimate. Had they still been together, he would have taken it home and let Karen read it. They weren't, but maybe having his old job back would convince her things had changed. This moment of human weakness allowed him to sign it without thinking. By doing so, he was wholly unprepared for Fielding's next words.

"Now that we've got that out of the way, let me make one thing clear: When we find the employee responsible for today's virus, he or she will be arrested for destruction of property, disruption of business, and, by God, any other crime our lawyers can think of. And since you've signed that contract, Peter, you fall under the category of 'employee'. Good day."

And with that, Fielding gestured for Hunt to leave.

CHAPTER SIXTY-SEVEN
INCOGNITOS

CASPIAN AIR FLIGHT 434
16: 45 EST

Ivanovich knew flight marshals were armed. The aftermath of 9/11 put paid to concerns for gun-safety on-board airplanes, and demonstrated the need for armed marshals on every flight. As a precaution, the marshals were given firearms loaded with frangible ammo. They wouldn't penetrate the sheet-metal of the cabin but, if fired at the right area, would neutralise a terrorist.

Ivanovich's eyes, locked on Williamson's, never faltered. He held the man's gaze with the confident authority the KGB and Spetsnaz had browbeaten into him.

He ignored the gun. By itself, it was just a lump of steel. The person holding it made it a deadly weapon.

Nothing. Just the expressionless mien exclusive to hardened law enforcers. That meant he would fire if necessary, but even with the low-velocity rounds that were standard-issue for flight marshals, Williamson would want to avoid a gunfight in a pressurised cabin. And even if he did fire, Ivanovich was wearing a ballistic vest – a leftover habit from his KGB days. Undetectable by modern-day X-ray machines, it wouldn't stop anything over a .22, but provided Williamson didn't opt for a headshot, the combination of the low-velocity rounds and the vest would ensure a non-lethal impact.

"How about you start by telling me your real name?" Williamson said.

"You're taking a huge chance here. Those terrorists are still holed up in the cockpit," Ivanovich replied, continuing to use the American accent.

"You see, I don't think they are; much the same way I don't think you're really American."

"You think you're the only law enforcement officer on this plane?"

"Are you saying you're an agent and not a TSA marshal?" Williamson demanded.

"What I'm saying is you know a hell of a lot less than you think you do."

"Why don't you enlighten me, then?" Williamson asked, with a wave of his gun.

Ivanovich, still using the accent, decided to try to reason with him. "Let's start by you lowering that gun. We got a powder-keg of emotion in here, and any little thing could set this plane off." He realised the irony of that statement, but he couldn't tell Williamson about his fears of a sleeper agent. Not yet.

The flight marshal gave him a dubious look in reply, but slowly lowered his weapon. "Make a move and I'll put you in the ground, powder-keg or no powder-keg," he warned. "Who are you?"

"My name is Dmitriev Fyodorov," Ivanovich replied, deciding to remove one incognito and assume another. "I'm an FSK – formerly KGB – agent."

Williamson frowned, his gun-hand jerking slightly. "So why pose as a TSA flight marshal and use a weak-ass American accent?"

"Look around you. Right now this plane is one large smorgasbord of nationalities and races. Russian people don't exactly engender trust in others. Americans, on the other hand..."

"So what was your plan? Break into the cockpit and subdue the terrorists yourself?" Williamson snorted.

Ivanovich had little choice. Until he got Williamson off his back, he couldn't do anything to find the sleeper agent. He had to tell him the full story.

However, unbeknownst to him, the transmit button on his two-way radio was still on. York had heard the entire conversation, and had made his way back to Ivanovich's cabin to see for himself what was happening.

The squelch of Morse code in his ear caught Ivanovich by surprise. Looking down, he saw his transmit button was on. Clicking it off, he heard, "Nod if you can hear this."

Ivanovich bobbed his head once.

"Good. Turn the volume down so he can't hear me."

Ivanovich, shielding his hand from view, adjusted the knob to its lowest setting.

"I'm across the cabin from you. I'm going to try and sneak in behind him."

Ivanovich gave the slightest shake of his head.

"No dice, Sergei. This guy is not a flight marshal. Repeat, *not* a flight marshal. Look at him. He's about forty, looks well-experienced, yet he holds his gun with a isosceles stance? Not on your life. What were we taught in our military careers? The Weaver stance. Ain't no way this guy's a veteran law enforcement agent using anything other than that. Whoever he is, he is *not* who he says he is."

Ivanovich felt his blood turn to ice, his own words ringing in his ears: *Russian people don't exactly engender trust in others. Americans, on the other hand....*

They'd been too busy looking for a Muslim that they hadn't considered the other possibility.

The sleeper agent wasn't Muslim at all.

He was American.

CHAPTER SIXTY-EIGHT
TERRA INCOGNITA

UNKNOWN LOCATION
UNKNOWN TIME

He awoke slowly.

Light shone from above. Disorientating. Garish.

A high-powered halogen bulb.

He blinked once. Twice. A third time.

Then his hand rose to his skull, to stop the pounding that threatened to turn his brain to mush.

Jack Carlos' first coherent thought was how much he wanted to go back to sleep. How much he wanted to be rid of the pain. How much he *needed* to understand what the hell was going on. But fate would not allow him any of those luxuries. It had, instead, condemned him to...where the hell *was* he?

Using his hands for leverage, he pushed himself to a sitting position. The absence of bright light required his eyes to readjust again. Other than the halogen, complete darkness shrouded the room.

He looked down and saw what he was lying on – the gurney from earlier. Swinging his feet onto the floor, he took a moment to brace himself before putting weight on his legs and standing.

They didn't hold.

The second his weight came crushing down on them, they turned to jelly. His hands shot out to grip the gurney, and as he collapsed to the ground, it toppled over and fell on top of his ribs, forcing the air out of his lungs along with an exasperated curse.

What's going on?

Anger coursing, adrenaline surging, he fired the gurney off him and then regretted it.

What the hell did they drug me with?

Ignoring the pain, he rolled to his belly and pushed himself to his knees.

Too quick.

A wave of nausea, coupled with vertigo, washed through him. He turned to one side and heaved, tears clouding his eyes with the pain of his empty stomach trying to rid itself of bile. When was the last time he had eaten? Sometime into the fifteen-mile run in Afghanistan yesterday?

Carlos heaved for a few more minutes, then rolled onto his back again and breathed deeply to try to alleviate the sensations.

Another upheaval began in his stomach, travelled as far as his throat, before he stifled it. The taste of it caused him to shudder uncontrollably.

Turn onto your side before you choke on your own puke, Jack, for Godsakes!

He rolled again to his stomach, this time pushing slowly to his knees. Taking a minute to steady himself, he planted his stronger leg on the floor and pushed himself to a standing position. Again, his knees wobbled, but this time he was ready. Just as the numbness threatened to collapse him in a heap again, he fell forward, spreading his hands out. They hit something solid, a wall, and Carlos held himself aloft until the feeling returned to his legs.

Diazepam. Son of a bitch!

Carlos had, eight years earlier, been involved in a takedown of a narcotics ring in South America. A young sergeant at the time, he'd seen first-hand what drugs could do to a person. How they dulled your senses to the point of uselessness; how they suffused your body with a feel-good high that sometimes lasted only mere minutes; and how the comedown was *always* depressing. Not to mention how the body craved the same high again but could never manage it. It was said that an addict spent his/her life trying to recreate the high from that first trip, oftentimes failing miserably.

Diazepam. A muscle relaxant. He had heard of snipers using it in moderation to help steady the nerves in high-octane war-zones. Marketed under its trade name "Valium", it was also used by police negotiators as a means of drugging terrorists in hostage situations.

Why would that SOB drug me?

And then it hit him. The zipped-up body bag. The shooting in the leg. Ever since Adi Ghar and the flash-priority orders to go home, everything seemed like some kind of surreal dream. The secrecy, the isolated locale, the two "soldiers" he and Gyle had tied up; the only thing that made sense about the whole scenario was the ending, when Anderson and the Chairman of the Joint Chiefs had stumbled upon something not meant to be and had done their utmost to rectify it.

Had either of them been involved in the drugging?

Who *had* drugged him? The spider-webbed memories were a foggy haze. He shook his head; cleared his eyes. The memories were there, on the periphery, yet they taunted him like a child hiding behind a parent and sticking a tongue out at a sibling. He could not clear the mist between him and the answer.

The truth.

And the truth shall set you free.

Freedom.

The word triggered a flash. Back to the cell, earlier today, just before he'd broken out. Why was his mind showing him this? What significance did it have, other than the occurrence of the word "freedom"?

C'mon, Jack, what the hell are you thinking?

Bits and pieces. Flashes of past events. The cave...the dynamite...Baxter.

Baxter!

The captain who'd started this fiasco. Carlos hadn't for a second believed him. Who made rank as captain and then took a job driving soldiers around? No, he was much too young to be entrusted with the information he'd been given. As of right now, he was the one who didn't fit in, more so than anyone else.

With his balance regained, he moved away from his leverage and studied the room. Aside from the gurney and halogen light, only one other item occupied it – a wash-handbasin. He moved along the marble floor and stopped beside it. The sensation of water on his sleep-deprived body was heavenly. He splashed himself several times until all the sweat, dirt, and – possibly – tears washed from his face, leaving only the beard which hadn't been shaved for days. Then, he rinsed the god-awful taste from his mouth.

Okay, so these guys don't mind breaking the rules. They're resourceful, efficient, intelligent. They've removed us from all civilisation, to a remote location, in a CIA facility. But this whole thing has stunk since the beginning. Why the hell did they –

Movement.

In his peripheral vision he saw a shadow dart across the entrance to the room. He spun around, hand shooting down on instinct for his gun.

Shit.

He moved toward the gurney. Crouching. Ignoring the slight report of his rubber soles on the marble floor.

One on knee, he reached up and fumbled for the switch. After a few frustrating seconds, he found it.

The room descended into darkness. He blinked again to readjust his vision.

No movement. Nothing in the corridor except more shadows and an absence of light. What the hell was this place? A building of some kind, but how had he ended up here having spent the last eight hours in a jungle? Who'd left him here and, more importantly, why?

He moved left of the gurney, keeping low on the tips of his toes, ready to pounce if necessary. The morphine was starting to wear off, but he steeled himself to ignore the increasing pain. He moved along the marble floor, each step more careful than the last. When he came to the door, he stopped, dropped to his behind, and lay against the wall. As slowly as possible, he poked his head out until he could see both directions. The right-hand corridor led to a double door. A green light above it cast a pale glow onto a wooden floor.

Brilliant. All I need.

The left side led to a branching corridor. Carlos couldn't see any signs of life in either direction, but he could see oblique objects hanging from different walls – pictures, awards, achievements. He couldn't read them in the dim light, but this place had to be a business of some kind. Maybe the intruder worked here.

I wish I had a gun.

Maybe this was another test. The day had turned to night, and it was no secret anti-terrorist units revelled in nocturnal environments. Carlos had spent the majority of his career under the cover of darkness. Force Recon Marines conducted more nocturnal operations – not to mention training exercises – than any other US military group. If they wanted to test him, someone had done a hell of a bad job tracing his history. This was Jack Carlos' speciality.

Okay, what'd they teach you in Advanced Marine Training, boy? Assess the area. Evaluate the threat-level. Determine quantity and quality. Okay, okay. I was standing...away from the door. He – or she – darted past my right. So, they're now on my left. Only one I know of. Minimum threat. The area's dark.

Wishing for Julio's Swiss Army knife, he patted down his pockets for any items he might use as a weapon. They'd stripped Gyle of everything except his underwear, yet they'd allowed Carlos to continue wearing his military fatigues. In the knee of his Khaki trousers, hidden in a space for a kneepad, he found his secret weapon he'd forgotten about. A Microtech HALO retractable knife. The matte-black finish would make it impossible to see even in the brightest light.

Removing it, he made sure the blade snapped out without any obstruction, then pocketed it in his easy-access pouch on the rear of his trousers.

The corridor was still empty when he stepped into it a few seconds later. His rubber-soled boots made a different report on this surface; a slight squeak like the one he'd heard during his first Knicks game at Madison Square Garden. God, how long ago had that been? Carlos had been sixteen or seventeen at the time, and his father had thought the NBA to be a ticket to the big time. Never mind that he was at best a second-string player. Never mind that no scout had seen him play more than five minutes in any one game. He'd thrown Carlos out of the house when, two weeks later, he told him he wasn't continuing with his studies and basketball. The next day, Carlos joined the Marines.

And the military had shaped him into the man he was meant to be. A leader. A warrior. One who had nothing to fear from a scampering security guard.

Carlos advanced forward, towards the branching corridor. His shadow danced along the wall beside him. Other than his muted approach, nothing stirred in the gloomy surrounds of the hallway. He thought back to the cavernous cave in Adi Ghar, where all this had started; at least he'd had a gun then.

The tiny shafts of what daylight remained percolated through the blinds on the right-hand windows, only to be swallowed by deep shadows of impenetrable darkness. Carlos found himself wishing for his NVGs. He felt another tickle run down his spine.

For a moment, he thought he saw furtive movement coming from the branching corridors, but he realised, with a sigh of relief, that it was his shadow moving from one wall to the other. Still, he retrieved the knife from his pouch and readied himself.

Slipping in beside the left-hand wall, he slid along it until he was in line with the corridor. Then, making sure no other part of his body was visible, he moved his head out far enough to see down the left side. The corridor stretched for about twenty yards, whereupon it stopped at a set of double doors flanked on both sides by blinded windows. A boardroom, perhaps. An ordinary bulb illuminated a small patch on the floor beneath. He noticed a change again; this time to a plush carpet.

What the hell is this place?

No sign of life.

Carlos moved to the right-hand side and performed the same manoeuvre. This length of corridor spanned only a few metres, to a left-hand turn which coalesced into further darkness. Who knew what lay beyond that? Numerous guards? Barren emptiness? Carlos didn't know, but felt compelled to go that way instead of left.

He stepped out into the corridor without thinking. Without fully checking the rest of it. And then he realised he'd erred. Badly. Fatally.

From the shadows of a recessed cubbyhole emerged the figure which had darted past the door...how long ago now? Carlos couldn't know. Didn't know.

The only thing he knew was the man held an Uzi in his outstretched hand.

CHAPTER SIXTY-NINE
BETWEEN THE EYES

CASPIAN AIR FLIGHT 434
16: 58 EST

For a moment, Ivanovich couldn't do anything but breathe as his mind raced through the possibilities. The chances of an Al Qaeda splinter cell entrusting an American with the job of sleeper agent was slim, but Ivanovich had seen stranger things. Many of them on this very plane.

"Okay, I'm going to ask you one more time, then I'm going to get testy. What were you doing posing as a TSA flight marshal?" demanded Williamson.

Ivanovich inched left, towards an empty first-class seat. The movement, as he'd intended it to, momentarily distracted Williamson. The ostensible TSA marshal moved to cut off Ivanovich's path and, in doing so, opened his body to an attack.

Ivanovich moved before Williamson could. If this guy was a flight marshal, he would be well-trained in close quarters combat. He needed to catch him by surprise, before he had a chance to fight back.

He brought his knee up into the man's crotch with every ounce of strength he could muster. The force lifted Williamson off the ground a few inches, as his breath left his body with an explosive exhalation. As Williamson fell to the ground, Ivanovich grasped the weapon and wrested it from his hands with a violent jerk. Williamson tried to scream as he hit the cabin floor with a thump, but the attack had robbed him of his voice. He could only lie there as Ivanovich twirled the pistol and brought it crashing down across his temple.

"It's okay, everyone," Ivanovich announced, in his American accent, before anyone could scream or draw attention to the first-class cabin. "I'm a federal agent. This man is working with the terrorists. I need everyone to remain calm. If anyone makes a racket, they will find out what's happened and they will kill all of us. Myself and my colleague"—Ivanovich gestured to York—"are going to try to retake the cockpit. But for us to do that, we need all of you to remain calm and silent."

That seemed to placate them.

Ivanovich rifled through Williamson's pockets, finding a wallet, loose change, and an extra clip for the weapon: a Glock 22, equipped with a silencer. The bullets were not low-velocity, nor were they frangible. Instead, they were hollow points.

Who the hell are you, really?

Inside the wallet, he found pictures of Williamson and a black middle-aged woman – presumably his wife. No ID, no credentials, and not the remotest suggestion he was who he claimed to be. Yet he'd carried – or smuggled – a weapon on-board, and had been surreptitious enough to spy on Ivanovich's earlier conversation with the flight attendant.

York had circled around the cabin and now slotted in beside Ivanovich. "Nice speech. Bought us a little time, but the plane still lands in thirty. This our guy?"

Ivanovich shrugged. "Can't tell. No ID and no TSA – or *any* – credentials. No device for detonating, either."

"If he's not our guy and he's not a flight marshal, who the hell is he?" York asked, then shook his head. "Look, we're outta airspace, Sergei. Maybe we were wrong about the whole sleeper thing."

"I don't think so. Here, take this." Ivanovich handed him the Glock. "I'll be back in a second."

Ivanovich stood, walked to the middle-class cabin, where

he found the attendant from earlier – Holly – serving drinks to someone who looked like they'd seen their fair share of alcohol already today. When she saw him, she gave a slight start, turned, and walked briskly down the aisle. He stepped up his pace and caught her by the arm before she stepped through the curtain into the economy-class section.

"Let go of me!" She tried to sound angry but fear belied her attempt.

"I don't know what that man told you, Holly, but whatever it was, it isn't true."

"Please, just let go of me," she whimpered.

"What did he tell you, Holly?"

"He said you were a terrorist...the one you told me you were trying to find."

Why the hell would he do that?

"Look, if I really *was* that terrorist, do you think I would tell you about the sleeper agent and the suspected bomb?" Ivanovich replied, making sure he whispered the last word.

Holly brushed away a lock of blonde hair. She stood with her hands on her hips in a show of resolution, then said, "Listen, whatever your name is, I don't know what's happening on this plane, and I don't want to know."

"Listen, Holly, I'm trying to make it so we all get on the ground in one piece. Now, for all I know that guy could be the sleeper agent I'm looking for. How did he make contact with you?"

"He asked me who were the men walking around the plane, and I told him you were a flight marshal. Then he told me to take him to you."

"You didn't tell him about the bomb?"

"No. He got all wide-eyed when I said you were a flight marshal. Didn't say anything else."

"Okay, this is really important, Holly. I need you to take me to his seat. Will you do that for me?"

"Fine, but that's all – "

Holly's words were cut off by the arrival of a man behind Ivanovich. Without wasting a second, she dashed into the economy section, leaving Ivanovich bewildered...until he turned around. And was duly hit by a savage punch to the face, felling him.

Above him stood Aleksandr Levsky, his face contorted with contempt. In English, but with a thick Russian accent, he said, "I thought I buried you in Saint Petersburg twelve years ago, Sergei Ivanovich. But it seems I was mistaken."

Levsky drew back his boot and levelled a kick at Ivanovich's skull.

CHAPTER SEVENTY
EXECUTIVE DECISION

PEOC BUNKER
THE WHITE HOUSE
17: 00 EST

The last few hours had been frustrating. The information, which had come courtesy of the British government, had been corroborated and verified, but it was only in the last fifteen minutes that the plane's identity had been fully ascertained. Now, the President and his cohorts had received word *Caspian Air* flight 434 was the only airplane within an hour of American soil which hadn't made contact when prompted by fighter jets.

"Sir," urged Richard Duke, "we need to make a decision now. The plane is almost at the fail-safe point." Gone was the briar pipe and the laid-back poise replaced by the concerned look of someone who feared for the safety of his country.

"I'm well aware of the plane's location, Rick. And I'm acutely aware of the decisions I have to make. You reminding me of them is not going to change anything, nor is it going to slow that plane down. So, please, spare me the harangue."

"I'm not haranguing you, Mr President. I'm informing you of the facts. That's my job. I am the National Security Adviser, sir, but while I do work for you, it is also my job to secure and protect this country. Which means I have to tell you the things you least want to hear. Right now, there is a four-hundred-ton plane in the hands of an unknown faction of terrorists, inbound for New York City. There is a distinct possibility this plane will be used as a weapon against our country, sir – *again*. We have less than ten minutes to make a decision, or face the possibility of a recurrence of nine-eleven, Mr President."

"We've had this speech already, Richard," interjected Matthew Clark. "We don't know what their plans are, and we haven't heard a thing from them since this alleged 'hijacking' took place. No demands, no gloating about gaining control of the plane, nothing. We don't even know if they're even *in* control. The pilot squawked seventy-six-hundred – you said that yourself."

"Which is *not* standard protocol, Matt. And if you knew anything about these kinds of situations, you'd know that. So, please, let the adults do the talking," Duke rebuked.

"That's enough, Rick," the President ordered. "I'm not going to make a decision until I have irrefutable evidence this plane is going to attack our country. Until you can prove that to me, you're wasting your time with lectures and hectoring."

Duke leaned forward, trying to hide the sneer of disgust. "You have the evidence. You have more than enough to make this decision. Flight four-three-four is the only one within a hundred-mile radius of American soil that hasn't made contact when prompted. It is also the only one that has squawked seventy-five-hundred in the last six months. So forgive me, sir, if I do not share your optimism on this matter...but the simple fact is that plane is on course for this country, under control of terrorists. We made the mistake of letting nine-eleven happen. I will not be involved with another catastrophe of its magnitude again, Mr President."

"What exactly are you saying, Rick?" the President inquired.

"If you don't make a decision in five minutes, sir, I am tendering my resignation. You can conduct the cleanup and explain to the American people how we knew about flight four-three-four for hours before the attack and did nothing about it."

"Assuming there'll be an attack," Clark observed.

"I wonder how smug you'll be, Matt, when thousands of lives have been wiped out and the American citizens are screaming for the people in government – the very people they put there to prevent another nine-eleven – for answers."

"What happens if we shoot it down and later discover the squawk was accidental and the secondary one – the seventy-six-hundred squawk – was an attempt to rectify a mistake?" Clark returned.

"If you can give me a plausible explanation for why that pilot squawked twice and in-between ceased radio contact with air-traffic control, I'll stand down right now. But until that moment...until you give me a valid explanation for what's happening on that plane other than hijacking, I am going to assume it is on course for American soil for one reason only. Occam's razor, gentlemen. The simplest explanation is usually the correct one."

"That may be, Rick, but the simplest explanation doesn't have to account for the minutiae of the situation," Walsh stated. "We're dealing with a double-edged sword here, and no matter what choice we make this evening the outcome will be catastrophic for this administration."

"To do nothing, sir, would be an act of gross negligence, never mind a dereliction of duty," Duke replied matter-of-factly.

"Doing *something* would also be state-sponsored murder," Walsh replied, not missing a beat. "So either way, we're screwed. But don't worry, Rick. I'll make my decision in – "

The door to the PEOC bunker opened and a breathless woman staggered into the room with a phone in her hand.

"Mary, what the hell!" the President demanded as his secretary handed him the phone.

"I'm sorry, Mr President. The Chairman of the Joint Chiefs told me it was a matter of national security."

"It's okay, Mary. Thank you. You can leave now."

"Yes, sir," the terrified woman replied and quickly stepped outside.

"Chad, what is the meaning of this? I'm about to make one of the most important decisions of my life. Whatever it is, it can wait."

"Mr President, you may have to make another one. I know about Station Blue, sir. Everything."

The President exhaled, gripping the phone tighter. "I don't know what nonsense you're talking now, *Charles*, so why don't you enlighten me about this 'Station Blue'?"

"I have no desire to play a charade with you today of all days, Mr President. Your inside man – the one they call 'Davies' – is dead. Killed today by the same people who are going to attack Station Blue, sir. *Tonight.*"

"Listen, Chad, this vendetta against me...it's getting kind of old. Whatever you think you know, you don't. I suggest you drop it or you'll be dropping your resignation off at my office first thing tomorrow morning. Are we clear?"

"You'll have it...in the morning. But you know what else you'll have, James?"

Walsh blinked. In three years of being Chairman of the Joint Chiefs, Peterson had never called the President by his first name. Trying not to seem disconcerted, Walsh quickly replied, "What's that?"

"The deaths of all the workers – the ones who know nothing of Station Blue – at ATARIC. How many are there? A hundred? Two? I've corroborated this intel at the highest levels. Call Jon Baker at the FBI. Ask him if Troy Davies is dead. When he tells you he is, call my advisor, Wesley Anderson, and ask him about the message he received from an ex-Marine called Scott Harden. You've been keeping secrets your entire term, James. How ironic one of those is about to proverbially bite you in the ass.

"I called you with this information hoping you would see past your clandestine ways to acknowledge what I was saying and help those people. But I've realised a long time ago, *Mr President*, that you care little of the menial people that put you in that seat. Station Blue – ATARIC, call it what you will – is going to be attacked tonight. I just hope you have the fortitude to make the right decision. I would hate to think you would let those people die to save your own skin. Good evening to you, sir."

Peterson hung up before the President could make a rejoinder.

Walsh moved to stand but the shock of the moment brought him to his seat again. How had Peterson found out, and was Troy Davies really dead?

"Sir, where are you going?" Duke asked.

"I need a little time to think, Rick."

"I hate to be brusque, Mr President, but we need a decision now. We're running out of time, sir."

"Order the F-Eighteens to make it land. Whatever it takes.

Morse code, post-it notes, I don't care! If four-three-four does not comply, they are ordered to shoot it down."

"Mr President, you can't be serious – " began Clark.

"I am serious, Matthew. I will not have another nine-eleven on my watch."

"Mr President, four-three-four will be over the general populous in approximately twenty-five minutes," Duke revealed. "If we can't get it to acknowledge our order to land, we'll have to shoot it down."

"Do what you have to do. I need to make a phone call." The President stood again, this time keeping his balance.

"Sir, there's a phone here," Clark said.

"The conversation is private, Matthew."

"Sir, don't you think it'd be best you were here in case you need to rescind the strike order?"

Walsh looked up, all the emotion draining from his face, and said, "If we can't make it land in the next half-hour, there'll be no rescinding anything. For *anyone*."

CHAPTER SEVENTY-ONE
SHADOWS

UNKNOWN LOCATION
UNKNOWN TIME

The darkness worked in his favour.

The interloper hadn't made his move yet. For the last ninety seconds, it was like they had been suspended in reality. Carlos could have easily slammed the Uzi into the man's throat, crushing the windpipe and drowning him in his own blood. He could also have grabbed the machine pistol, turned it in the blink of an eye, and unleashed a barrage of bullets into the man's sternum. Or, he could have wrenched the guy's neck, instantly killing him. Right now, he was in the mood to do all three. But each of them allowed for the possibility of spasmodic reactions, and they were bad news. He'd lost three men in past war-zones to enemies who'd been hit with a clean headshot but still their fingers locked on the triggers of their rifles. He wanted to avoid the clean sweep.

He kept to the shadows. Until he knew who he was dealing with – this could have been one of the soldiers from the jungle earlier – he had to assume they had the same training as he did and that their eyes worked as well in the dark as they did in light.

Okay, wait until the gun lowers. Then, knock it out of his hand –

"You Carlos?" the man in the shadows asked, his voice timid and wrought with fear.

Carlos blinked. Who was this guy, and how did he know his name?

"Who the hell are you?" he replied, his eyes never leaving the gun.

"Somebody who thinks they've made a huge mistake. Here", he said, handing over the Uzi, to Carlos' bewilderment. "Take it."

Without a pause, he snatched the machine pistol from the man's trembling hands, spinning it to face him immediately thereafter. "What the hell's going on here? Who are you and what are you doing in this building with an Uzi?"

The guy stepped out of the shadows. Carlos tensed when his hands moved toward his face, but relaxed when the man started biting his nails. Whoever he was, he certainly wasn't a soldier. On his left shoulder, Carlos noticed a tattoo. He couldn't make out all of it because of the sleeves of the man's shirt, but he saw what looked like two elongated fangs. It reminded him of something from his past, but he couldn't remember what.

"Man, I knew I should have told that SOB to keep walking. What the hell was I thinking?"

Carlos studied him. He was of Oriental descent, but his accent indicated he'd been born in the States. Dressed in black trousers and a blue top with epaulettes on the shoulders, he assumed him to be a security guard. A baton dangled from the rear of his trousers and a walkie-talkie hung on his belt. Somehow Carlos couldn't imagine a company issuing their security guards with high-end weaponry like an Uzi. Someone else had given him the gun.

"What's your name?" he asked, lowering the weapon and coaxing the terrified young man out of the shadows.

He bit his nails again. "Jin. Look, man, I'm sorry about pointing that gun at you, but I didn't know who the hell you were or what you were doing here. Some guy downstairs tells me there's a man on the fourth floor, in the washroom, lying on a gurney. I thought he was joking, but then he handed me the Uzi and told me to take it to you."

Carlos' eyes narrowed. "What did he look like?"

"I don't know, man. It was dark. Looked like a soldier, maybe. A major or something. He spoke with authority – scared the shit out of me. He told me it was a matter of national security and that I'd be arrested if I didn't comply."

"Why didn't you just hand me the gun, then? Why did you hide?"

Jin shook his head in disbelief. "When's the last time you handed over a weapon to a man who looks like he doesn't need one to kill someone? I was scared, okay? I don't even know why I agreed to that man's demands, but I was afraid he might find some kind of loophole to deport me...even though I was born in this damn country."

Carlos assumed the man in question was Rainey. Or that SOB who'd socked him in the ribs in the jungle earlier in the day. Either way, this seemed more and more like another test.

"You work here, right?" he asked and Jin nodded. "What is this place, and why is it abandoned right now?"

"It's a government building. That's all I know. Don't ask me what branch 'cause they didn't tell me and I didn't ask."

"Are you the only security guard here this evening?"

"There's three more. On the three floors below this one."

"So, if your route is the top floor, what were you doing downstairs?"

"I went out for a smoke. A few months ago the owner found out one of the security guards was smoking in the building. He fired him the next day. So now we do all our smoking outside. It's a denial of human rights, if you ask me."

"And this guy just approached you – "

Before Carlos could finish, the window beside him shattered inward with a burst of serrated glass that showered both men. Jin screamed and reflexively put his hands to his head to protect himself, not realising what had happened. Carlos did, however. He had enough experience to grab the man and drag him to the ground. His momentum carried him into the windowsill, his ribs cracking off the unforgiving oak. The same ribs the diminutive punk had socked earlier. The same ribs he'd clattered off the rocks in Adi Ghar. His breath left him with a jolt followed by a scream. The latter wasn't his, however. Jin shrieked again as the window above their heads sundered in another shower of glass.

With a terrified whip of his head, Jin scanned the hall in an effort to determine what had happened. Then, he staggered to his feet, only to be hauled down by Carlos.

"Stay down! On the ground, below the windows! You trying to get yourself killed?"

"The hell is going on!"

"This guy outside – did you see anyone else with him? Anyone in the buildings around this one?" Carlos whispered, easing to his belly and crawling to the other side of the petrified Asian-American.

"Anyone *else*? What the hell are you asking me?" replied a stupefied Jin.

"Just answer the question!"

"No, I didn't see anyone else! All right? What was I supposed to see – a damn sniper?"

Carlos' silence answered the question.

"You're kidding me, right? You're telling me I'm being shot at by a sniper? What the hell have I gotten into here?"

A sniper using subsonic rounds and a suppressor, judging from the lack of a weapon report. Only two groups in the world used that combination – terrorists and the military. *What sort of test calls for the use of live ammunition?* Even his initiation into Force Recon hadn't been that severe, and he only knew of one group who performed live-fire training exercises with any regularity: Delta Force. Did that mean he was dealing with a terrorist?

His eyes dropped, for the first time, to the Uzi in his bloodied hands. Not an Uzi. In fact, a MAC-10. An American-made machine pistol analogous to the Israeli Uzi but less accurate and less reliable.

Not terrorists, then. The MAC-10 was a military-issued weapon last used in the Vietnam war. Its unreliability led to it being discontinued, and finding one nowadays was nigh on impossible. Unless you were military. Whoever had given it to Jin knew it was useless against a foe more than fifty metres downwind. The sniper would be at least a hundred metres away, probably on the same level or slightly higher. It would be like firing on an elephant with a pea shooter.

"Which way to the elevator?"

Jin remained silent, staring at the opposite wall, his hands joined as though in prayer.

Carlos shook him with his free hand. "Where is the elevator, goddamnit!"

Jin, shaken from his stupor, pointed left and said, "Down this hall, through those double doors, and to the right."

"Okay. I need you to listen carefully," he began, adopting his military inflection. "We're gonna crawl down this hall, through those doors, and we're gonna get on that elevator. Then you're going to get your ass as far away from this building as possible. Go through the back door – the opposite side to where the shots are coming from."

"Wait a minute – how do you know where the shots are coming from? How do you know there aren't two snipers out there? We could be walking into a trap!"

"The sniper's leeward to our location. He's using the wind for distance-shooting and higher trajectory. He's about seventy-five to a hundred-and-fifty metres away from us. And he's using subsonic rounds with a suppressor. That's why we're not hearing anything."

"That tells me where he is and what's he doing, but not *how many* of them there are. I think we should stay here and wait it out."

"I'm not debating this with you. They know we're in this building. The only chance we have is to get out of here now, before they start coming in to look for us."

"Who are *they*? And why are they doing this to us? And why the hell don't you use that gun and get us the hell outta here!"

"Because using this gun would be pointless. And whoever gave it to you knew that. Listen, the only chance you have of making it out of this building is if you stick with me. Now, I'm going to start crawling along this floor. You can join me...or you can stay here and take your chances. Either way, I'm going."

"No, you know what – I'm getting up off this floor right the hell now and walking out of here. And neither you nor that son of a bitch out there are going to stop me."

Before Jin could make a move, Carlos levelled the MAC-1o at his chest, evoking a high-pitched scream of terror.

"Let me tell you something about me, Mr Jin: I haven't bathed, slept, or eaten for thirty-six hours. In the last twenty-four I've been through more time-zones than a Rolex. I've been shot at, beaten, and had to listen to my best friend get tortured, all before getting shot in the leg, drugged, and seemingly left to die in this dump. I'm itching to go on a killing spree." With a raise of his eyebrows, Carlos cocked the gun. "So maybe you *should* be a little more scared of me than you are right now."

"Okay, man. Whatever you want – whatever you want! Just point that thing away from me. Please!" Jin screamed, with a capitulatory wave of his hands.

"On your stomach. Now! Keep your head down, eyes forward, and don't stop. When we get out into the foyer, stay low. I'll call the elevator. Move!"

CHAPTER SEVENTY-TWO
POWER PLAY

```
ATARIC
17: 10 EST
```

The day had been weird, to say the least. And it was about to get weirder.

Jake Collins had called time, taking his men with him. He promised to be back early tomorrow morning, with more men if necessary. So far, they'd installed the new operating system on a hundred-or-so computers and were on-course to have the job completed in the allotted timeframe.

Harold Johnson had long since retired for the evening, but not before giving them another ultimatum. They could either stay late and get as much done as possible, or work like Trojans tomorrow. Reid had decided to stay, and Hunt couldn't leave until Karen came to pick him up at seven.

The rest of the workers had either left or were in the process of leaving. Soon, the building would be like a ghost town, with only a half-dozen baton-toting guards for company.

They were alone in Reid's office. Hunt hadn't said or done anything since Fielding's ultimatum...except to tell Reid, who'd checked and rechecked to ensure no accusations could be levelled against either of them. The silence was indicative of their current mood, and neither seemed bothered to try to strike up any kind of conversation. When Hunt's cell phone rang, he thought it a blessing in disguise. Until a few moments in.

"Hello – Peter? Peter Hunt?" asked a deep-throated man.

"Yes. Who is this?" Hunt replied, shielding the receiver from Reid.

"Mr Hunt, we spoke about six months ago. I'm Fred Nance from Ambit Energy. You hired me to look into the power consumption for a building on East Thirty-Eighth Street?"

Hunt shook his head. "I think there's been some kind of mistake, Fred. I did originally hire you, but I cancelled your services, with full pay, about six weeks ago."

"I'm aware of that, Mr Hunt, but I'm not calling on behalf of the company. Sir, you were right when you said the kind of power consumption used by that building exceeded anything an ordinary business would consume. That's not why I'm calling."

Hunt, now fully engaged in the conversation, softly replied, "And why *are* you calling?"

"I'm not even supposed to be telling you this. I could lose my job, but my gut feeling is something fishy is going on. Mr Hunt, that building is scheduled for power-down at seven...*tonight*...and I can find no documentation to verify the shutdown is legitimate."

Hunt found this odd. He'd hired Nance to probe into ATARIC's power consumption, and the thirty-year veteran had done more than that. He'd uncovered several startling facts. Firstly, the building never powered down. Despite Fielding's vehement warnings to shut down all computers before leaving at night, ATARIC still somehow managed to use more power during that time than it did throughout the day. And no reason – whether a backup system for files, a backup generator, or anything like that – could explain what would use that power. Unless, as Hunt had suspected all along, something else was using the power...another building like this one, only on basement level three.

"Okay, so what does that mean?" Hunt urged, sensing a lull in the conversation.

"What it means is simple: Someone other than the owner of the building has scheduled a power-down for tonight. And the only way I can think of to do that while avoiding the documentation is to bribe an official."

"You're saying someone bribed the electric board?" he whispered, trying to keep Reid from hearing, but he had seemingly taken an interest.

"No, I'm saying someone bribed an *official* of the electric board. And whoever it was, they went to great lengths to ensure no one ever found out about it. Peter, we're not dealing with some prank or a power play by another company here. I hate to even think it, but this kind of thing ominously resembles terrorism. That building...its power consumption is on a par with Langley's. There's something going on there besides software manufacturing. And it's being targeted by someone because they know what."

"I understand that, and I've made allusions to it in the past, but I don't understand how you've made a connection"—Hunt glanced to Reid—"to terrorism."

"Because someone at the Office of City Engineers downloaded the schematics for that building...three days ago. And I've got a feeling that person was bribed by the same person who bribed the electric board official."

CHAPTER SEVENTY-THREE
DUPLICITY

CASPIAN AIR FLIGHT 434
17: 13 EST

Ivanovich – sitting in a spare seat in the first-class cabin, his hands secured by a set of flex-cuffs taken from the unconscious flight marshal's pocket – scanned the floor for York, but the American was nowhere to be seen. With time running out and the pilots preparing for final approach, this was the last thing Ivanovich needed.

Above him, Levsky pranced around like a cougar after ensnaring its victim, in his hands a gun that looked remarkably like the one Ivanovich had handed to York. With a quick twirl, he jammed it against Ivanovich's temple.

He never flinched. Instead, a slight smile spread over his face.

"How did you manage to survive Saint Petersburg, Sergei?" Levsky asked calmly.

"Your gofers didn't check me for a vest, Levsky."

"Yes, a little oversight on my behalf." Levsky cocked the hammer against Ivanovich's skull. "I won't make that mistake again."

"Doesn't matter. Either you kill me now, or we die in

fifteen minutes when the plane touches down."

Levsky nodded. "Yes, the 'sleeper agent'. I've spoken with the lovely Holly. I know all about your charade, Sergei. I just can't figure out why you, of all people, care."

Ivanovich laughed. "Our Middle-Eastern friends don't know the meaning of the word 'terrorist'. I've got more important things to do with my life than to be an ornament on the hood of some obese American's car."

Levsky stepped back, his face etched with a sneer of contempt. Ivanovich, puzzled, watched as the former KGB director's snarl morphed into a cold smile. With his free hand, Levsky smoothed his pressed suit and took a seat beside his arch-nemesis, crossing his legs and tucking the pistol into Ivanovich's ribs.

"What like – killing more families?"

Ivanovich felt the gun press deeper into his abdomen.

"You know, my wife – Helena – was a lovely girl. So full of life and energy...before you robbed her of it."

Ivanovich could see the slightest hint of pain in the old man's cold, blue eyes. Nothing more. Hardened by years of being a victim and viewer of senseless violence, Levsky had shed all the tears he would ever shed long before today.

Ivanovich, on the other hand, had last shed a tear as a teenager. He would not beg for his life, nor would he give Levsky the satisfaction of an apology.

"Williamson – he was yours, right?" Ivanovich asked, aiming to discover the real identity of the TSA flight marshal.

"Of course," Levsky replied with a smile.

"You can kill me right now if you want, Levsky, but it won't matter. You'll be dead in ten minutes."

"Perhaps. Just so you know, though; I've informed the pilot that the terrorist situation on-board has been dealt with. He told me he already knew that, but you told him to keep the rest of the passengers believing it hadn't. Why would you do something like that?"

"Because keeping everyone out of the loop was the only way I could make the sleeper agent relax. If he knew the terrorists were dead, he might have panicked and blew the plane up before we even got to American soil. I needed time to find him. Believe what you want, Levsky, but I'll bet my life there's a sleeper agent on this plane."

Levsky exhaled. "There is no sleeper agent, is there, Sergei?"

"What are you talking about! Why would I make it up?" He turned in the seat, feeling the gun press tighter as Levsky compensated for the movement. "Seat 47B in the economy-class section. The man occupying it is our most prominent suspect. You have to get to him before the plane starts its final approach!"

Levsky frowned. "*Our?* Who else have you on this plane, Ivanovich?"

Ivanovich hesitated, a momentary flicker of fear passing over his features "My English is not so good, Levsky. I haven't used it in a while."

Levsky shook his head, kneading the gun deeper into Ivanovich's side. "No, no, Sergei. Your English is perfect." A snarl morphed onto Levsky's face, and his voice dropped to a mellifluous whisper. "Who else do you have on this plane?"

"It doesn't matter who I do or don't have on the plane, Levsky," Ivanovich retaliated. "You have to get to seat 47B and find out what that man is doing. You are running out of time!"

"Have you forgotten your KGB training? You have no proof, Ivanovich."

Ivanovich snarled. "I haven't forgotten anything. It may be racial profiling, but the man in that seat fits the mould of a terrorist almost a hundred per cent. Right now, he is the only suspect we have." Ivanovich sighed. "Levsky, for Godsakes, forget about me. You've got me. You won. But it isn't going to matter if we all die in the next ten minutes."

Levsky looked like he was considering it, but after a moment of deliberation he shook his head. "It's bullshit, Sergei."

"I know a goddamn terrorist when I see one, Levsky! That man is the sleeper agent."

"He isn't, Sergei."

"How can you possibly know that?"

Levsky turned to face him, the cold smile back on his face. But it was the eyes that chilled Ivanovich to the bone.

Oh, no! Wrong again.

"How do I know, Sergei?" Levsky asked in an eerily calm

tone. "Simple..." he began, his face morphing into a snarl again. "Because that would be me."

***

The thought had never crossed Ivanovich's mind. That Levsky could be the sleeper agent was unthinkable. But at the same time, it made perfect sense. Levsky may have lost a family to a soldier-cum-terrorist, but he'd lost his mind to the hunt. Along the way he'd had others do the distasteful deeds. When he'd finally come face-to-face with Ivanovich, Levsky had looked him in the eyes and pulled the trigger. Rather than being a release, Ivanovich's "death" had changed the old man. The taking of someone's life was a feeling of power like no other. It appeared Levsky had become addicted.

"Who else have you got on this plane, Ivanovich!" Levsky lashed out with a punch that seemed weaker than the last half-dozen he'd thrown.

Ivanovich grinned maniacally, blood dripping down his shirt. "Looks like I was wrong about you, Aleksandr. Tell me, when did you affiliate yourself with Islamic fundamentalists? Somehow I just didn't picture you as a self-sacrificing man."

Levsky laughed. "Do you really think I give a damn about them?"

"Then why do this?"

"Enough questions! Where is he?"

"I don't have anyone on-board. You're wasting your time."

Ivanovich had to force himself to keep looking down. Any movement of his eyes would be taken by Levsky as a sign. *Where the hell are you, York?*

At that same moment, York's voice came over clear in Ivanovich's ear. "We've got a huge problem, Sergei."

To paraphrase you from earlier, York: 'No shit, Sherlock. Where've you been all day?'

York continued, "Two F-Eighteen Hornets just flanked us, and they sure as hell don't look like they're here to escort us."

No, they're here to shoot us down. Somebody on the ground found out, and looks like Mr President is trying to avoid another nine-eleven.

Ivanovich could do nothing in his current position. Without York's intervention, he was dead. Ironically, even with York's intervention he would probably die anyway. Somehow, he needed to get a signal to him.

"What happened you, Levsky?" he asked, hoping York was still listening.

"Reality." Levsky encompassed the entire economy section with a wave of his hand. "All these people are sheep. They go about their lives one monotonous day to the next. Americans, Russians, Spaniards; nationality is irrelevant."

"And you want to blow them up for *that*?"

"What I want and what I will get are two different things, Sergei Ivanovich. I expected more from you; a terrorist, no less. What was it that lured you to the *dark* side? All those years fighting terrorists with the KGB. You were one of our prized assets. A man so ruthless he scared even himself."

"You're flattering me, but still failing to tell me why we're sitting on a plane twenty years later, both of us now terrorists."

Levsky sneered. *"Terrorist?* Don't insult me by grouping me with your terrorists!"

"You're about to kill four hundred people. I wouldn't call you a hero."

"I am a *martyr,* Sergei."

Is this the same man who murdered half of Russia searching for me? What the hell have they done to you, Levsky? Ivanovich knew of civilians being reprogrammed to adhere to the beliefs of Islam and other fanaticisms, but this was Aleksandr Levsky, the most ruthless and despotic director in the history of the KGB. A battle-hardened warrior with a mind as sharp as anyone Ivanovich had ever known. You didn't reprogram people like that – not unless they were scarred to begin with. Losing Helena had broken Levsky's spirit, making him an easy target for anyone to exploit. Still, that didn't explain how or why he'd sided himself with Islamic fundamentalists.

"Martyr? What noble cause are you supposed to be fighting for, Levsky?" *Come on, York. Where the hell are you?*

"Nobility is a mark of weakness, my dear Sergei."

The voice was coarse, Ivanovich noted. Levsky sounded as old as he looked. A tired man, a tired mind, and perhaps a tired command of right and wrong. But still dangerous – especially with...*wait a minute! Where the hell's your cane, Levsky?* Ivanovich scanned the floor around the old man.

No cane.

He came here without it? Why? What would make him leave his deadliest weapon behind?

Something didn't fit. Levsky would never leave it behind – unless it was lost or removed from his possession. He could walk perfectly without it – in fact, Ivanovich knew he'd no need for it at all – but the poisonous darts it shot were an insurance policy to tip the odds in his favour. He'd be feeling bare without it right now.

For the first time, he noticed Levsky's Armani suit was spoiled with blood. The exertion of punching Ivanovich had also popped open a few buttons, revealing a hairless chest which made even Ivanovich cringe. In a moment of chilling clarity, he knew what had happened to the once-proud KGB director. The lack of hair was not because of senescence or any other natural cause. The skin beneath was pervaded with asymmetrical scars and hyper-pigmented lesions, some reddish-purple, others black. The hairs had been singed off.

Reprogramming...via electric-shock torture.

Just enough to bring him around to their way of thinking, but evidently not enough to wipe all his memories.

Levsky had become a sleeper agent in every sense of the word.

CHAPTER SEVENTY-FOUR
COVER AND CONCEALMENT

UNKNOWN GOVERNMENT BUILDING
UNKNOWN TIME

From the recesses of the shadows, Carlos reached out and eased open the double door. On his stomach, tight against the left-hand wall, he knew he was in a position where the sniper couldn't see him. So when a pane of glass above him shattered, and a chunk of wood exploded where his hand had been seconds earlier, he jerked back, eyes and veins bulging in a gesture of wild shock.

The wind whistled through the aperture, biting into his cheeks, hardening the blood from a dozen tiny lacerations.

Beside him, Jin stifled a scream. Carlos didn't hear. Heart pounding, mind racing, he tried to figure out how the sniper knew their location. Even a high vantage point wouldn't allow him to see everything. It was possible he'd seen the door being opened and fired a warning shot, but he didn't think it likely. With an absence of light in the corridor, it would be impossible to see in from two metres away. Either the sniper was firing blind, or using some kind of night-vision scope.

But I kept tight to the wall, and the only thing visible for any length of time was my hand. It's like he...knows where we are!

Cameras!

Carlos scanned the wall and ceilings for any, finding only a bare coat of white paint. He turned to Jin, realising for the first time the security guard was on the verge of hyperventilating. He gave him a shake and clicked his fingers beside Jin's head a few times.

"Are there any cameras in this building?" he demanded.

Jin nodded, shaking out of his attack. "Every floor."

"Why can't I see them?"

He explained the cameras were fibre-optic and recessed into the walls to appear the same colour as the paint. Carlos wondered what kind of government organisation had the wherewithal to install such high-tech equipment. The only ones he could think of were those outside the purview of Congress – officially denied buildings with a seemingly endless bankroll.

Well, Harvey Point is a CIA training facility. It would make sense this building is CIA-owned too.

"Is there a surveillance room on this floor?"

"No, it's on two."

"Okay, change of plan. We need to get to the second floor. Are there cameras in the elevators?"

Jin shook his head. "No. The only place there aren't. Listen, I don't feel comfortable– "

Carlos shot him a look. "They know *exactly* where we are. The only hope we have is getting to that surveillance room and killing the feed to the cameras. Have you got a flashlight?"

Jin retrieved a small Mag-Lite from his pocket and handed it over. Carlos switched it on and played the beam through the open door. It looked like a small foyer. In the middle of the room a set of wooden stairs descended into darkness. Flanked to the left and right of those were numerous cubicles that abutted each other so closely he wondered how anyone could work at them. In the background, the beam reflected off several panes of vertical glass that extended from the marble floor to the ceiling, ten feet above.

Brilliant. They could see us from California.

"Which way to the elevators?" Carlos asked pointedly.

"I told you – to the right," Jin replied.

The closed right-hand door hindered Carlos' view. He could make out the green glow of an illuminated display, but didn't trust the reflection off a cubicle as a precise milestone. Strangely, the rest of the room was pitch-black.

"Why are the lights off?"

Jin shrugged. "They were on when I came through here fifteen minutes ago."

Carlos clicked off the torch and turned to Jin. "Here's the plan. I'm going to use the flashlight to draw his fire. When I signal you, move for the elevator. Get to it as quickly as you can, but stay low! When the doors open, shout to me and I'll come running. By the time he repositions himself for a shot at the foyer, the doors will be closed. Do you understand?"

Jin nodded.

Carlos grasped him by the collar. "Do you understand? Yes or no?"

"Yes," Jin replied, vigorously nodding his head.

"Okay, wait for my signal."

The plan was a stopgap. It would buy him no more than thirty seconds. If the sniper *was* tuned in to the building's security cameras, he would soon discover the flashlight was a decoy. Carlos needed to get Jin to the foyer before that happened.

Turning the flashlight on, he raised it to the opening, feeling the piercing cold wind bite into his bare skin. His heart leapt as the polished handle slipped through his sweat-slicked fingers and threatened to tumble into the yawning chasm outside. Grasping it tighter, and making sure his hand didn't protrude above the edge of the opening, he turned his gaze to Jin and counted him down.

One...

Two...

Go!

The security guard tried to leap to his feet, foolishly, and panicked when Carlos bellowed at him to stay low. His feet went from under him, and he crashed to the ground with a groan of embarrassment rather than pain. Carlos, his heart in his throat, ordered him to stay down and crawl as fast as he could through the double doors ten feet away.

He felt something sting him. Looking up, he saw the flashlight still there, but blood flowed freely from the back of his hand where an inch-long piece of serrated glass teetered at the edge of his skin. He raised his eyes farther and saw where it had come from. The wind had been howling so loud he hadn't heard the window above him implode, sending fragments of glass tumbling down. Like a rain of fire from above, the window two levels up imploded next. Grimacing, he tightened his grip on the Mag-Lite and urged Jin to move faster.

He can't see your hand to shoot it. He's just playing with you, he consoled himself.

He watched Jin push through the double doors as another shower of glass assaulted his fingertips. If Carlos' willpower alone could have propelled Jin, both would have been standing in the elevator right now.

Jin angled right, still on his stomach, legs and arms pumping in tandem. Smeared across the carpet, Carlos could see a trail of blood mixed with shards of glass.

The elevator pinged. Without waiting for Jin's beckoning, Carlos pulled his hand back inside and bolted to his feet. Ignoring his own advice to stay down, he lowered his shoulder and charged through the double doors. He tumbled into the room, tucked his head hard against his chest, and rolled along the marble floor.

To his right, Jin hollered at him to get into the elevator. His pleas were drowned out by another explosion of glass and a deafening whoosh of air as one of the vertical panes disintegrated.

How the hell!

Outside, the newly shattered window was a void of darkness. No pale glow of lights from offices on floors above or below. No buildings nearby. Just black emptiness that seemed to stretch for miles. He could not see any sign of a sniper. But as another pane nearby shattered, he knew there was more than one. The sniper who'd been firing at him could not have repositioned himself so quickly.

Running on empty, his mind and body screaming for its first break in thirty-odd hours, he found from somewhere the energy to dive through the doors of the elevator. From behind, chunks of marble spat out of holes created by a succession of bullets.

"Close them. Now!" Carlos roared.

Jin stabbed at the button as another hail of bullets chewed ground at their feet, rising up the back of the elevator and destroying a mirror. More glass showered the prone Carlos, but he hadn't the energy to raise his hands to protect himself. The closed doors were assaulted by another burst of fire, and then the elevator descended.

"I thought you said he couldn't reposition so fast!" Jin raged, helping Carlos to his feet.

"I know what I said! Just get me to that surveillance room."

"There's more than one of them, isn't there?" Jin looked him in the eyes. "I knew it! I told you. We should have stayed!"

"I don't have time to debate this, Jin. Just get me to that room!"

The elevator opened on the second floor. Carlos couldn't believe his eyes. A corridor, illuminated by the tenuous light of a far-off bulb, stretched beyond the capacity of his eyes. Flanked on each side of it were steel-framed doors complemented by a dull carpeted floor. Shining his flashlight, Carlos illuminated the path ahead, revealing unadorned, stucco-finished walls. In the distance, a lone window overlooked more darkness.

At least he won't have as many opportunities to shoot at us now.

"Which way?"

Jin pointed down the hall, and Carlos looked to the heavens. "It's the last one on the right. You'll know it when we get there. It's the only one with a wooden door."

Brilliant. It's also the only one you can see from the window.

Retrieving the MAC-10, Carlos crisscrossed his hands so he could use it and the flashlight together. He stepped out of the elevator. To his left, another hallway coalesced into darkness. He played the beam down it, limning the way ahead. A few more rooms with windows – offices. The corridor ended abruptly at a water fountain.

"Those are the offices of some of the middle men and women," Jin explained. "The rest, with the exception of the surveillance room, are storage."

Carlos nodded, turning his beam down the long corridor again. He could see particles of dust rising with every movement. "Shouldn't this floor be cleaner than this?"

Jin shook his head. "Afraid not. Like I said, this is mostly used for storage. The surveillance gear is here because it was an eyesore."

"Wait a minute." Carlos frowned. "Didn't you just say those

were offices?"

"Middle men. Hardly the sort to complain about their working environment."

"Is there anyone working late?"

"Usually. Most check out around four-thirty, but there's always stragglers. I haven't come on any, though."

"What time is it now?" For Carlos, the concept of time had been lost hours ago. He only knew it was evening.

"Five-fifteen."

"How far to the surveillance room?"

"About two hundred yards."

"Okay, get behind me. You can stay on your feet this time, but if I shout, get down and stay down."

Carlos moved slowly down the hall, his every breath hanging in the cold air. As he passed each door, he fanned the beam along them, checking if all were closed. From behind, Jin's shallow breaths blew warm on the back of his neck, assuaging the sensation in Carlos' spine.

Their shadows danced along the walls as they approached the solitary, flickering light. *It's like the set of some low-budget Hollywood flick.*

Despite years of training, the hairs on the back of his neck rose with each step. To make things worse, Jin's Mag-Lite dimmed as they moved beyond the reach of the lone bulb. Carlos thought of asking him for another, or a spare battery, but he wanted to maintain silence.

The window ahead edged closer, but he could see nothing but darkness outside. He quickened his pace, afraid the light would die before he reached his destination.

To his surprise, the door lay open. He turned into the surveillance room and dropped to a crouch, his eyes oscillating with the movement of the flashlight. A row of switched-off monitors dominated a large table to the left. Beside them, five swivel chairs were scattered across the interior, lying upside down. In the middle sat another table, with stacks of newspapers, a kettle, and a calendar adorned with half-naked women.

When Carlos' fading beam illuminated the right-hand side, however, his breath caught in his throat.

On another table was a zipped-up body bag.

CHAPTER SEVENTY-FIVE
PREPARATIONS

THE WHITE HOUSE
17: 17 EST

President Walsh ducked into the Oval Office and closed the door. Shaking his Secret Service detail had taken a calculated act of deception. The First Lady's hysterical scream would only keep them distracted for a few minutes until they couldn't find the mouse. He hoped he only needed that length of time.

U.S. presidents are not permitted to carry a cell phone, for security reasons, but most do. Walsh had one in his desk, which he retrieved. Moving back over to the door to watch for his guards, he dialled a number from memory.

"Hello?" a familiar voice answered.

"Are you free to talk?" the President inquired.

"Of course."

"What's the status over there?"

The voices in the corridor grew louder. Someone was approaching the door. Walsh switched the phone to his other ear and passed by his desk. He slipped into his private bedroom and locked the door behind him. Darting across the lush carpet, he turned the key in the other door leading back into the corridor.

"We're nearly finished," the man replied. "I anticipate your team will be ready well before the two-week timeframe your *other* advisors have estimated. They would be ready within twenty-four hours, but I'd rather make sure two of them have the right mindset to be leaders. It's a work-in-progress, but I foresee no difficulties."

"Do you know who's made the cut?" the President demanded. He could hear the door to the Oval Office opening and the heavy footfalls of Secret Service agents pounding towards his location. He hoped they would check the door to his private kitchen first.

"In a manner of speaking."

"Then I need you to call it off, Ed," the President whispered.

"What do you mean, 'call it off'?" Edward Rainey demanded.

"Finish it!" Walsh hissed. "You know who's who. Call off the tests and assemble your chosen teams at the main entrance of Harvey Point. A plane will be there in thirty-five minutes. The Attorney General will be on-board with non-disclosure forms for all the men to sign. Make sure they know they are not signing a US document. Explain to them they fall under no jurisdiction at present, but all of that will be sorted out soon."

"Why? We haven't even set up the governing body for STRIKE Force yet. Getting these men here was difficult enough, James. Now you want me to make them sign non-disclosure forms? What's going on? What are they agreeing never to disclose?"

A knock on the door caused Walsh to jump. "Mr President, are you in there, sir?" demanded Walsh's detail chief, Carl Lewin.

The President couldn't stay silent. If they didn't find him in a few minutes, they'd start a room-by-room search. If caught with the phone, though, it would be confiscated and Walsh would lose the ability to make off-the-record calls to Rainey.

Walsh covered the mouthpiece and spoke up, "I'm here, Carl. One moment, please." He walked away from the door, turning his attention back to the phone. In a low tone, with one eye on the door, he began, "Listen, Ed, I don't have a lot of time. This might be the last call I make to you today. I just corroborated intel that suggests terrorists are going to attack Station Blue tonight at seven. I talked with a man named Scott Harden who received a message from Troy Davies warning him to alert us to this attack. He told me Pavel Kirov has assembled a team to breach the facility."

"That's impossible. Station Blue is impenetrable. You know that, James."

"We have to consider the possibility they know as much as we – "

The booming voice of Lewin cut the President short. "Sir, is there someone else in there with you! Who are you talking with?"

"No one, Carl. It's just the TV."

"Sir, I really must insist you open the door. I don't feel comfortable with this current situation, Mr President."

"Please just give me one minute, Carl. Can't the President of the United States have peace to go to the toilet?"

"Of course, Mr President."

Walsh moved into the en-suite. "Ed, I'm running out of time. We have to believe they know as much as we do. We have to act now."

"What are you suggesting?"

"I can't reach Jon Baker or Roger Clemence. William Forrester tells me they're in Station Blue right now. They can't be contacted until they reach the surface of ATARIC. And there's no one left in ATARIC who's cleared into Station Blue."

"You're not saying what I think you're saying."

"I need you to mobilise STRIKE Force within the hour. Have them sign non-disclosure forms and bring them up to speed on ATARIC."

"You can't be serious! We don't even know if this attack is going to happen. It could be a hoax, and you want to tell a team of varying nationalities one of our biggest secrets!"

"We have no choice. I don't want to mobilise any other team because it will take too long. Yours are all there, gathered and ready. They're our only hope."

"Mr President, I strongly advise against this course of action. We have no idea if these men will even agree to join STRIKE Force, much less sign a non-disclosure form to safeguard one of this country's biggest secrets. This is a legal nightmare, sir. A disaster waiting to happen."

"The nightmare is already happening, Ed. We have got to respond now, or we'll wake up tomorrow to headlines we've been dreading for years. We cannot allow Station Blue to become public knowledge."

"At the risk of it becoming foreign knowledge, sir?"

"If that situation occurs, we'll deal with it quickly and quietly. We can contain a military and political spread. We *cannot* contain a public one. These terrorists need to be stopped before they can create an event that will facilitate that."

"Sir, the *Posse Comitatus Act* prevents us from using the military for law enforcement. I strongly urge you to think this through. Take some time – "

"This is not law enforcement, and we haven't got any time! Our window of opportunity is vanishing. I need those men on-site *before* the terrorists arrive. I can't debate the legality or morality of this situation right now. The more time we waste, the more likely it is we'll be too late."

Levin's voice boomed again, this time more forcefully. "Sir, may I ask to whom you're speaking?"

Walsh sighed. "Carl, I'm in the bathroom."

"Mr President, I'm after sending one of my agents to the surveillance room. He tells me the cameras show you in the Oval Office, a few minutes ago, retrieving a cell phone from your desk. Sir, we've had this discussion before. It is too big a security risk for you to have a cellular phone. I'm coming into the room, Mr President. If you are at the door, sir, please step aside now."

"Edward, do this! Do it now! That is a direct order from your Commander-in-Chief," the President yelled as the door to the bedroom exploded inward and an irate Carl Lewin stormed over to Walsh, grabbed the phone from his hand, and ground it under his foot.

"Sir, I've been your bodyguard for twenty years," Lewin began. "How many times have I told you cellular phones are like a neon-lit sign that tells every terrorist in the world your exact position?"

"I know, Carl. I know." A weary-looking President walked past Lewin and slumped onto his bed.

"I'm sorry, Mr President. It has to be this way, sir. And much as I would like to let you rest, I'm getting requests all over for you. You're needed in the bunker."

The President nodded.

Of course he was. What else was new?

CHAPTER SEVENTY-SIX
ABOULIA

UNKNOWN GOVERNMENT BUILDING
17:20 EST

He couldn't breathe. Nor move. All he could do was stand in the middle of the surveillance room, eyes fixed on the body bag. Off to the side, Jin threw him urgent looks which Carlos neither saw nor would've cared about if he had. Fear paralysed him, and for the first time in his military career Jack Carlos did not know what to do next.

His mind screamed continuous "oh Gods" as he tried to keep the image of a dead Julio Gyle from taunting him in vivid high-definition.

Jesus Christ, what do I do if it is him?

If the body was in fact Gyle, it made everything Carlos had been told from the beginning an elaborate lie. That changed the entire complexion of the day. But why, and for what purpose? If the military weren't responsible, just what the hell was going on?

From somewhere in the deep recesses of his mind the word "sniper" materialised. And from somewhere else equally as deep, Carlos summoned the courage to move, knowing that if he didn't, he might well end up in another body bag himself.

The journey lasted an interminable amount of time. No matter how much Carlos willed himself to go faster, the distance to the bag seemed to stay the same. And then, to his surprise, he was standing beside it.

It felt as though he was two people at the same time. One part of him stared at his trembling hand, while the other urged him to get it over and done with. And yet another part of him vacillated between action and inaction, keeping him suspended in a state of aboulia.

Heart pounding in his ears, Carlos fought through the crippling fear and extended his arm to the body bag. He grasped the partially open zip and pulled it to him with what seemed adequate force. It refused to budge. Carlos yanked it, panic beginning to settle. Still it wouldn't budge. He tried to zip it up, reposition the jaws, and hope it would realign itself and open.

It still wouldn't move.

Goddamnit!

Carlos yanked forward and backwards. Again and again. The tears started dripping down his face, mistakenly thought by Carlos to be sweat. The more it refused to give, the more they poured. Until the flap of the zip broke off in his hands. He fell backwards onto the ground, landing hard on one of the upturned chairs. The guttural roar which followed was like nothing he had ever heard. It sounded like the cry of a defeated, broken man.

At that moment, Jin thought of saying something but kept silent.

Carlos struggled to his feet. Looking towards the sky for some kind of inspiration (even though he didn't believe in a deity) he was consigned to defeat when nothing came. Then, he felt the handle of his knife, and the hope which had vanished reappeared. Starting below the zip, and careful not to drive the blade too deep, he sliced a line down the body bag. The HALO retractable knife swished along the non-porous vinyl with rhythmic undertones. When he reached the end, Carlos returned to the middle and separated the two pieces.

The midsection appeared first. No Kevlar vest, but Carlos remembered Gyle had been stripped of all his clothing back in the jungle. This could still be him.

Legs next. No military fatigues, but that didn't mean

anything either. The body was outfitted in tan trousers and a plain tee-shirt, which were generic and could be bought in any decent shop. Carlos knew he was temporising. It was why he hadn't cut above the zip. He did not want to see the head, because seeing it would bring closure. Right now, uncertainty was the only thing keeping him sane. Opening this Pandora's box would bring no favourable outcome for anyone.

But he had no choice.

Gulping, he moved to the top of the table. Of all the missions, all the conflicts with foreign *and* domestic enemies, Carlos did not truly know the meaning of fear until that moment where he cut away the zip and exposed the head.

As he stared at it, transfixed by the moment, he realised one thing. Something which electrified his body with utter terror.

It was staring back.

CHAPTER SEVENTY-SEVEN
AMENDS

LEO & WALKEN LAW FIRM
17: 22 EST

Karen Hunt had spent the last two hours finalising a report on her latest case. The documentation had required her full attention and she hadn't noticed the time edge past five – the end of the working day. Those who worked later were entitled to overtime, though had she realised, she would have left immediately.

She looked down from her first-floor office and saw that everyone had left. The lights and computers were turned off, leaving the floor shrouded in darkness, except for the light coming from her office and the one beside it.

Johnson Walken's.

Karen gulped. Turning her attention back to the computer, she saved her document and logged out of the system. She then removed her memory stick from the USB port and slipped it into her purse. Satisfied, she rolled her swivel chair back, swung around, and stood up...right into the arms of Walken.

Karen let out a scream that echoed through her office, stifled quickly by the beefy hand of Walken. Her eyes went wide and her head started shaking vigorously at the thought of enduring another episode, but Walken's eyes didn't hold the same conviction or anger they had some forty hours ago. They look tired – glazed over by something Karen couldn't imagine possible: tears. Was Johnson Walken feeling remorse for his actions?

"I'm going to take my hand away, Karen. Please don't scream; I'm not going to hurt you." The words were spoken softly, with a lack of enthusiasm Karen had only encountered in people who were resigned to defeat. She had heard it once in Peter's voice – when she'd taken his son and left him.

When he removed his hand, she calmly asked, "What do you want, Mr Walken?"

Karen jumped to the side as he came towards her, but he walked past and slumped into her chair, sighing. "I want you to know I'm sorry. Truly, I am. I know that doesn't excuse what I did. It was a moment of weakness, Karen, and I promise you that it will never happen again."

Karen bit her lip, then studied him for a second. Earlier, his Armani suit had been impeccable. Now, it was rumpled, his blazer and tie absent, and several buttons of his shirt missing. His beard looked scraggy, as though he'd been rubbing it continuously for hours. The Bluetooth headset which never left his head was also gone. He had obviously removed the distraction of phone calls to allow time to think, and it appeared he'd been doing a lot of that.

"I'm sorry I scared you. But I knew no matter what way I tried to approach you, I'd frighten you. I didn't mean to do it in here, but when I saw you getting ready to leave..." he trailed off, turning away.

"Why didn't you just ring the phone? You didn't have to make it seem like you were trying to rape me again," Karen said sharply and then felt a twinge of sorrow as he turned back, his face contorted in a mien of emotional pain.

When he spoke, it was in a heartbroken way that made Karen, as much as she despised him for what he'd done, feel pity. "I need you to understand that I'm a happily married man, with two daughters I love and adore." Walken removed his wallet and showed her a picture of his girls, aged eleven and nine. The tears began to stream down his face but he didn't wipe them away. "Sarah and Madison." Choking back more tears, he showed her another picture, this time of his wife, and continued, "And my wife, Kimberly, who I love very much."

Karen felt herself welling up from the emotion of the situation, but steeled herself and remained poker-faced, hands on her hips to show she would not be bowed by his adept acting skills. "You should have thought about them when you were trying to rip my skirt off."

Walken sniffed back the tears, wiped his eyes, and said, "I'm sorry, but you have to trust me when I say I've never been unfaithful to my wife...until forty-eight hours ago. That's what I'm trying to say. What I did was wrong – I know that – and I'm sorry I tried to bribe you into silence. But there have been no other incidents with any women in this office. What happened with you was a huge, unforgivable mistake, but you have my word it has *never* happened before, and I don't know why it happened now."

"Mr Walken, I don't know what you expect me to say to this." Karen shrugged her shoulders.

"I'm asking you as a desperate, emotionally fraught man: Please don't go on record with this. I will resign if that's what you want, but allow me the dignity of walking out of here with some kind of reputation. I know I don't deserve it, but I'm begging you," he pleaded, those blue eyes which had scared her immensely forty-eight hours ago now imploring. Harmless. Devoid of rage. The lifeless eyes of a man who'd realised karma was catching up to him.

"As much as I'm sympathetic, I've already made my decision. In the morning, I'm taking this directly to Walt Leo."

Walken considered this for a moment. As Karen watched, she saw a momentary flicker of anger flash behind his eyes. Then, with a quickness that startled her, he rose from the chair and walked to the door. As he opened it, he turned back and said, in a deep, haunting whisper lacking any emotional baggage, "You know me well enough to know that if you do there'll be repercussions, Karen. What I offered you just now was a one-time deal. When I walk out this door, it's gone and the gloves are coming off." He paused to let Karen ponder that.

She stared at him blankly.

"Have it your way," he said, closing the door behind him.

CHAPTER SEVENTY-EIGHT
SEEDS OF DOUBT

```
ATARIC
17:24 EST
```

Since hearing the word "terrorist", Hunt had done two things: First, he'd hacked into the phone company and replayed Nance's conversation for Reid. His college extracurricular activities – phishing scams – proved invaluable in finding the right server, file, and timestamp – all of which had taken fifteen minutes. When Reid heard the conversation, he'd done as Hunt expected – shrugged it off as insanity and insisted they get back to work.

So he had done the only thing he could. He showed Reid Daedalus' article about "Station Blue" and told him to read it. After he'd finished, Hunt clicked on a link and enlarged the picture of Reid leaving from ATARIC alongside countless trucks and other equipment of the ostensible "gas-main" repairers.

"What's all this?" Reid had demanded, turning from his chair to fire an angry look at Hunt. "And what has it got to do with Nance's call?"

Hunt had sighed, cursing his former best friend's inability to read the situation. "For the last couple of years I've been telling you there was something off about ATARIC. All the secrecy, the buttons in the elevator that require key-cards to operate – everything about this building screams 'front'. From the outside, it looks like a normal computer firm. In here, it's something different. You know it, Jack, and you're lying to yourself if you deny it. All the times Fielding and Haskens disappear for hours on end. Where do you think they go?"

Reid had thrown him an askance glare. "Your paranoia has exceeded even my expectations, Peter. You're trying to tell me ATARIC and the 'Station Blue' this Daedalus guy keeps talking about are the same thing?" Reid laughed. "It's funny, in all the times I've worked here I've never seen any evidence to suggest there's a secret underground building below this one." Reid pointed back to the document. "What you've read there is the work of a man seeking attention, Peter. A man who wants hits on his website. You've been duped into believing his crap, the same way he believes the government has been duping the rest of us."

"Will you please stop bandying around this crap that ATARIC is more than a computer firm, Peter? There's no conspiracy. They fired you because you were a liability. And frankly, you still are."

The conversation had ended there. No witty retorts from Hunt, just a nod of acceptance and the realisation that everything he said would be misconstrued as the ramblings of an alcoholic. That he'd been sober for almost twenty-four hours mattered little. There and then, he understood that he was on his own.

He picked up the phone, dialled the direct line his wife had given him after their last conversation. It rang for several minutes before Karen answered. "Hello?"

Hunt could hear the distraction in her voice. Along with something else he couldn't determine. "Karen, it's me."

"Oh...hi, Peter. I was just getting ready to come to you. I'll be there in about thirty minutes."

He remembered Nance's words and found himself in a quandary. All the proof pointed to something happening tonight. It wasn't his concern, though. He could tell Karen to come pick him up and leave them to sort their own secretive mess out. Or he could stay and try to warn them.

"Peter, are you there?"

"I'm still here, Karen."

"Are you okay? You sound distracted."

I'm not the only one.

If this was the paranoiac ramblings of a conspiracy nutcase, what Hunt was thinking of doing would be for nothing. Telling Karen to not come would be the end of any reconciliation between them. But if terrorists were truly on their way, walking away now would haunt him for the rest of his life. Whatever relationship he might salvage with Karen would be tainted by the knowledge he'd let terrorists gain an advantage in their war against his country, not to mention the deaths of anyone in the secret complex.

"Listen, Karen, about that. Looks like me and Jack are going to have to burn the midnight oils tonight, babe. How about I come over to your mother's when I'm finished up here? We can talk about that 'incident' then."

Karen's voice now became less distracted and more angry. "Are you blowing me off, Peter?"

"What! How can you think that? Karen, there is nothing else in this world I'd rather be doing than being with you and my son right now. But I made Jack a promise and I'm trying not to renege on my promises, babe."

"Don't call me that, Peter. Not now. An hour ago you said you'd be finished at seven. What's changed since then?"

"There's a lot more work involved than I originally thought. I'm just trying to keep ahead so that I have a better chance of getting my old job back," Hunt lied.

Karen's voice dropped to a cold whisper. "If I find out you've lied to me, Peter, to go on some drinking session...or whatever...we're finished. Completely. I'll hand-deliver the divorce papers to you myself!"

The line went dead.

Hunt replaced the receiver and then gave a start as Reid grabbed him from behind and spun him around. With a clenched jaw, he asked, "Why the hell are you lying to Karen?"

"It's none of your business, Jack," he replied, grabbing a heft of Reid's blazer and pushing him away.

Reid came back at him, poised for battle. "You're a lying son of a bitch, you know that?" Without warning, Reid jabbed with his left. The attack caught Hunt off-guard, and as he tried to compensate his footing to counter Reid, he twisted his ankle and went down – just as the jab connected with his jaw.

Reid continued, "You're going to ring your wife back and tell her to come pick you up as originally planned. Then, you're going to sort out your marriage, your life, and your job. In that order. Or I'm going to tell Karen you lied to her, and she's going to divorce you and take your kid."

As Hunt lay there, he couldn't help but smile. Everyone else always had the answers. They made it sound like a walk in the park. A walk through hell would have been a better analogy, though.

He rose, wiped away the blood with the back of his hand. Still smiling, he reached around to the back of his trousers.

The second thing Hunt had done after hearing the word "terrorist" was retrieve his pistol from his workbag.

CHAPTER SEVENTY-NINE
RENAISSANCE

UNKNOWN GOVERNMENT BUILDING
17:30 EST

Carlos had seen corpses of all descriptions: charred, mangled, dismembered, disfigured. But nothing could have prepared him for the sight he beheld after opening the body bag. It was always said a man should never look into the eyes of someone he kills. It was also understood you closed the eyelids, wherever possible, of a soldier killed in action.

Someone had failed to show this body that mark of respect.

As disconcerting as those lifeless, staring eyes were, they were not the reason why he felt unwell.

The body did not belong to Julio Gyle, to his relief, but neither was it a soldier. He had been around them long enough to notice the tell-tale signs. This man's hair was longer than military regulation, and he lacked the scars and wounds indicative of combat experience. Yet Carlos knew he'd been involved in many battles. A tattoo on his left shoulder depicted a wolf baring yellowed teeth, its paws grasping a rifle. He had seen it before. It was a tattoo of Shadow Wolf, a private military company whom the US government outsourced various missions to for insane prices. This man was a mercenary. Not as well-trained as any aspect of the United States military, these men were freelancers who ironically earned more than a soldier could ever dream of.

But Shadow Wolf was based in the Midwest, a far cry from Carlos' current position. Who'd killed this man, and why had they dumped him in this building? What did Shadow Wolf have to do with today's tests? The more this day unravelled, the less sense it made.

"What's wrong?" Jin spoke up for the first time in almost fifteen minutes.

Carlos forced a weak smile. "Nothing."

"'Nothing'? There's a dead body on my snack table. That's the very opposite of nothing. Who the hell is that guy?"

That's what I'd like to know. "Someone in the wrong place at the wrong time."

Jin smirked. "I know the feeling." He paced over to the console and turned on each monitor. The black-and-white images showed various parts of the building, including outside the main doors, what looked like an underground garage, and a looped feed of the numerous corridors on each floor. On the third switch, Jin noticed something. Moving closer, he used his sleeve to wipe away dust. He blinked twice to make sure what he was seeing was real, but there could be no mistake. In one of the corridors, a man was walking towards the camera, the rifle in his hand swinging from side to side as he cleared the pathway.

"Jack! Look at this." Jin turned and tapped an engaged Carlos on the shoulder. "We got company!"

Carlos turned, looked to where Jin was pointing, then asked, "Where is that?"

Jin stared at him but remained silent.

Carlos seized him by the shoulders. "Where the hell *is* that?"

Swallowing a gulp, he replied, "This floor."

Carlos gripped him harder. "*Where* on this floor?"

"He's beside the fountain."

Carlos moved briskly towards the monitors and turned them off. Wheeling around, his eyes roved across the room, landing on the table and the body bag. Pointing beneath them, he said, "Underneath there." When Jin's eyes went wide and his head shook, Carlos added a sharp, "Now! You wanna make it through this night, you better start doing *exactly* what I say."

As Jin scurried underneath the table, Carlos removed the clip from his MAC-10 as he moved towards the entrance. The thirty-round magazine was missing about half a dozen bullets. Shoving it back in, he positioned himself against the frame of the door. He thought about opening it outward to use as cover, but remembered it was wooden.

Wonderful.

Edging outward, he saw the lone bulb was still flickering, casting intermittent shards of light across one spot on the dilapidated carpet. Beyond that, he could see very little. If the man was already in the corridor, and if he knew how to use the shadows to his advantage, Carlos wouldn't see him until he reached the bulb. So, he waited patiently, eyes never remaining on one spot for longer than a few seconds. When staring in the dark, two things tend to happen: objects disappear, or ones that aren't there suddenly appear.

If he was a mercenary, he was a good one, Carlos decided a few minutes later. Most ordinary people didn't know how to mask their approach. Had Carlos not seen him on the camera, he would never have known of his presence.

He edged out once more. Flickers of light spat into shadows of darkness, but revealed nothing remotely resembling a human. Had Jin made a mistake on his location? Was the mercenary even on this floor at all?

When the butt of a rifle hit him square in the jaw, Carlos staggered back in shock more than anything else. To his right, a figure emerged from the shadows, gun pointed directly at Carlos' head.

"Move back into the room. Now!"

The voice was uncharacteristically gruff, but he recognised it immediately. At that same moment, he realised how the man had slipped by him. The light had been flickering on and off in five-second bursts. The man had bided his time and passed by in darkness, slowly following the contours of the wall until he reached the surveillance room and got a look inside. What he couldn't have known was that he was going to assault his commanding officer.

The man was Julio Gyle.

"Julio, it's Carlos!" he warned before Gyle could do something he'd later regret.

"Jesus...Bear! Are you okay?" he asked, offering a hand to pull Carlos back to his feet. The two embraced, forgoing the tears they strangely felt like shedding. Carlos noticed he was dressed in his military fatigues again, but couldn't see anything else in the dim.

"Jesus, am I glad to see you, Julio! I've been going out of my mind here. What the hell happened you? How did you end up here?"

"I guess I could ask you the same question. Those bastards told me you were dying," Gyle revealed.

"*What?* They told me the same thing about you. But I wasn't even being tortured."

Gyle gave a weak laugh. "Neither was I. Those *pendejos* hit me once and then left me alone for God knows how long. But all I could hear was your screams. Bastards came in and out every thirty minutes, telling me you were getting worse all the time."

"Jesus!" Carlos laughed. "They tape-recorded our screams and kept looping them over! Son of a bitch. So how'd you get here?"

"That's the thing; I don't remember. They drugged me. Next thing I know, I'm waking up in this shithole."

"You come here to get a look at the surveillance feed too? How'd you bypass the sniper?"

Gyle gave him an incredulous look. "Sniper? I didn't see any *sniper*. You're the first person I've run into. What's going on, Bear?"

Carlos turned around and saw Jin was still underneath the table. He signalled him that it was okay, and the security guard slowly withdrew from his hiding place.

"This is Jin, Julio. Long story," he continued, noticing Gyle's frown. "Let's just say we've had a bit more eventful evening than yours so far."

"If you can call being shot at by multiple snipers 'eventful'," Jin replied.

"Multiple snipers? Okay, what the hell's going on here, Sergeant-Major?"

Carlos filled him in on everything he could think of, including the body and the connection to Shadow Wolf. When he'd finished, Gyle blew out a soft whistle.

"You thinking these snipers are Shadow Wolf?" he asked as

Carlos restored power to the monitors.

"I'm thinking we should have walked when Baxter dropped us off this morning." Carlos turned to the security monitors. From what he could see, there were no other people in the building...yet. Without turning, he asked, "Jin, is there any way the snipers outside could jack..."

The dual realisation hit him like a runaway train. Shadow Wolf, like most PMCs, had varying degrees of subsidiaries. The main mercenaries were known as the "Wolves". The next tier down from those was the "Jackals". Each group had a distinguishing, unmistakeable tattoo on their left shoulder corresponding to their group name. One of those groups was called the "Sabretooths", and their tattoo was a depiction of the extinct sabre tooth tiger complete with elongated fangs – the same fangs he had seen protruding from under the sleeve of Jin's shirt when he'd first confronted the "terrified" security guard.

The second realisation, which left no doubt in his mind, was Jin's words to him five minutes before: *Jack! Look at this.*

Carlos hadn't told Jin his first name.

CHAPTER EIGHTY
LAST GASP

CASPIAN AIR FLIGHT 434
17:35 EST

Things were beginning to slip from Ivanovich's iron grip. Ever since terrorists had taken control of the plane, the likelihood of the day ending well had diminished with every passing hour. It was hard to believe he'd dismissed the journey to America as a simple task, and yet it had turned into the hardest. In the next few minutes, fighter planes were going to blow him apart – if Levsky didn't get there first. As he sat, flex-cuffed in the chair, he felt helpless. The reality was that nothing he could say to Levsky would make the old man change his mind. Ivanovich, for the first time in his life, resigned himself to defeat, sat back in his chair, and closed his eyes.

After a while, his sense of hearing became hyper-acute. He heard the whistle of something soaring through the air. Heard it impact something with a soft thump. Then heard a groan of pain. When he opened his eyes, Levsky fell into his lap, body shaking convulsively, froth gathering at the corners of his mouth. He looked at Ivanovich, his normally cold eyes now searching for an explanation on his face. Then, they morphed again. Unlike before, though. This time they were large and liquid with incipient tears. Ivanovich had seen the look before, each time on the face of a dying man. The gaze of someone seeking absolution, but knowing it could not be granted.

With one final, convulsive shudder, Levsky breathed his last. Ivanovich let him slide to the floor beneath. Then, he saw York standing ten yards away, twirling Levsky's cane in his hand.

"Took you long enough," Ivanovich said, gesturing for York to remove the flex-cuffs.

"You're welcome, Sergei." York shook his head and set about the task of extricating Ivanovich.

"Levsky was the sleeper."

York abruptly stopped, looked to see if Ivanovich was serious, and shook his head even more. "Didn't see that coming."

When the cuffs were removed, Ivanovich flicked his wrists a couple of times to get the blood flowing again, then asked, "What about the F-Eighteens?"

"They're still abreast of us – two of 'em."

Ivanovich lifted Levsky's body onto the seat; wiped away the froth from his mouth. At a casual glance, Levsky would appear to be sleeping. The last thing Ivanovich needed was to incite panic. No one had noticed Levsky's death, but they'd only remain ignorant for so long. Hopefully long enough for Ivanovich to get the hell off Death Flight 434.

"What about our marshal friend?"

"Still unconscious. I gave him a scenic view beside our Islamic friend."

Ivanovich had forgotten about the one remaining terrorist locked up in the captain's toilet. "Good. Go get the rest of the radio equipment from the overhead compartments. Then, meet me in the cockpit."

"I know what you're thinking, Sergei, but it ain't gonna work. We're talking run-of-the-mill radios here. We'll never reach those fighter planes. They're on a completely different frequency."

Ivanovich started towards the cockpit. "I know that. But we're still over water, and the Navy use the same frequency as conventional radios. Start scanning all them, between a hundred-and-fifty to two hundred megahertz. Maybe we'll get lucky."

"We got *zero* time, Sergei."

Ivanovich turned and regarded him with gimlet eyes. "Then why are you still here? Do as I ask, York. Get the radio equipment, scan the frequencies, then come to me in the cockpit when you've got something. Think you can handle that?"

York flushed. "What's with the 'tude, Ivanovich?"

Ivanovich came beside him and leaned in. "I need you to be productive, York, instead of being a pessimistic son of a bitch. That's why the attitude."

"Fine. I'll go get the radio stuff."

"Thank you."

On the way to the cockpit, a small balding man stopped Ivanovich and asked him what was going on. He ignored him, pointing to the cockpit door, but the man would not be undone.

"My wife and I are getting very worried about these terrorists." He glanced around nervously, then added, "And to tell you the truth, if you guys don't storm that cockpit pretty soon, there's about a dozen volunteers ready to do it for you."

Ivanovich had assumed so many incognitos today he had a hard time placing who this man thought he was. Then, he remembered he'd identified himself as a federal agent.

Adopting his American accent again, he said, "That would be a mistake." With the sleeper agent dead, Ivanovich decided it was time to inform the passengers. Raising his voice: "Ladies and gentlemen, may I have your attention." He waited until everyone looked up. "My name is Richard Hawkins and I'm an agent with the Federal Bureau of Investigation."

Several hushed conversations were exchanged, then one young man spoke up, "Hey, shouldn't you be keeping your voice down? The terrorists might hear you."

"Folks, the terrorists were neutralised during the first assault on the cockpit. They've been out of the equation for hours."

The balding man clenched his jaw. "*What?* So why the hell did you have us believe they were up there?" This question created a cacophony of similar ones from all the other first-class occupants.

Ivanovich raised his hand. "Listen, I need you to calm down while I explain." When Ivanovich paused, most assumed it was to allow the passengers to settle down. In reality, his mind probed for a decent cover story. "I'm the FBI's Russian liaison.

Earlier this morning, before this flight departed, the US government received intelligence that suggested this plane would be hijacked. Forty-five minutes later, after sifting through Middle-Eastern chatter, they discovered the terrorists had a backup plan – a sleeper agent on-board. Since the plane was already in flight, they couldn't ground it. So myself and my partner took it upon ourselves to orchestrate a takedown. We later learned of this new intel. We had to make the sleeper agent believe the plane was still under terrorist control, otherwise he may have blown it up."

There was a sharp intake of breath from all.

"Relax. The sleeper agent has been neutralised."

A large black man bolted out of his chair, his face irate, and levelled an admonishing finger at Ivanovich. "Man, that's just like the po-lice. Keepin' every goddamn person in the dark."

"Sir, please return to your seat. We've managed to avoid violent outbursts amidst a terrorist hijacking. It would be kind of stupid, don't you think, to have one when the situation has been resolved. Now, if you'll excuse me, I have to speak with the pilot."

"You feds all the same. Keep everyone in the dark 'til you need them, then expect us to help you. I ain't doing you no favours, pig."

Masquerading as a federal agent was no fun. In his terrorist persona, Ivanovich would have pulled a gun and kneecapped this SOB. Instead, he said, "I'm going to the cockpit. If you're still standing when I come back, I'll arrest you."

Ivanovich ignored the man's predictable riposte and hurried to the cockpit. He found the decimated door closed and opened it without announcing his arrival. The first officer wheeled and regarded him with a cold stare before turning back to the console.

"I'm sorry about earlier," Ivanovich began, flipping down a spare seat behind him. "I made you guys tell the passengers we were still in danger to lure out a sleeper agent. He's been dealt with. How far are we from the airport?"

The first officer turned again. "Listen, buddy, we don't know who the hell you are, but right now we have more important things to worry about it," he replied, pointing out the window at the F-18s.

"That's why I need to know how far we are from the airport."

"Well, considering everything that's happened, we're remarkably only ten minutes behind schedule. In five minutes we'll be preparing for final approach."

"Have you tried communicating with the fighter pilots?"

"The radio is *broken*."

"I've got someone working on it anyway."

This statement got the undivided attention of the captain. "Why are you so eager to contact those fighter planes?"

"Captain," Ivanovich began in a didactic tone, "do you really think they're here to escort us in?"

"Of course not. They know the plane's been hijacked. They're here to make sure we don't pose a threat to the United States."

"No, Captain. They're here to blow us out of the sky...unless we can convince them this plane is no longer under control of terrorists. In five minutes' time, we're going to be over land. So that gives us about four minutes tops before they open fire. So if you're a religious man, now might be a good time to pray. If not, I suggest you convert."

CHAPTER EIGHTY-ONE
HAIL MARY

PEOC BUNKER
17: 37 EST

The bunker was quieter than the President could ever remember. On a large suspended screen behind Walsh, a map of the United States glimmered, the red contour of a plane pulsating as it inched closer to a broken yellow line signifying the fail-safe zone. In less than five minutes, the plane would reach land and shooting it down would cost the lives of an indeterminable number of people on the ground.

The President kneaded his brow with his fingers to alleviate a pounding headache, then looked up at the conglomerate of men in front of him. They awaited his command, prepared and ready to execute their duties after the plane splashed into the ocean.

"Sir." Duke broke the silence. "The F-Eighteens are in place, ready to fire on your order."

The President nodded. "Have they been able to make contact?"

Duke, sombre, shook his head. "No, sir. They've been scanning every frequency. No response."

The President folded his hands across his chest and took a deep, composing breath. "Give me an optimum time-frame here.

How long are we talking about?"

"Three-and-a-half minutes, maybe four. Any longer and we risk civilian casualties if we shoot it down."

"Get me General Flynn on the horn." Flynn was the Air Force chief of staff.

"Yes, Mr President." Duke busied himself with dialling the number.

"And someone call Secretary Moore at DHS. I want Coast Guard cutters in the vicinity of the crash site immediately after the plane impacts. We can't take a chance that nobody will survive."

"Yes, sir," Clark replied, then paused. "Mr President, if I may?"

"What is it, Matthew?" The President was not in the mood for histrionics.

"That phone call you – "

Walsh cut him off with a stern glare and a raised hand. "Matthew, within the next five minutes, in all likelihood, we are going to have a catastrophic situation to deal with. Right now is not the time to be prying into my private dealings. Contact Secretary Moore and work with her to co-ordinate search-and-rescue teams."

Clark nodded and picked up a phone.

"Sir," Duke announced, "I have General Flynn on line three."

The President picked up the red, secure telephone in one hand, while he massaged his stubble with the other. A glance to his watch – two minutes fifty seconds. Such a short time to make the biggest decision of his life.

Walsh turned to the map. The plane continued its inexorable journey towards land. He glanced down to the floor, then to his aides. To rest a decision of such magnitude on one man's shoulders was insane, but the people had chosen him to make impossible choices. In his ear, he heard Flynn call, but Walsh didn't answer. He needed more time. But time was the commodity he least had.

God forgive me.

Walsh inhaled, let it out. "General Flynn, this is the President." He paused for what seemed like forever. "I authorise you to shoot down *Caspian Air* flight four-three-four. Repeat, you are authorised to shoot down *Caspian Air* four-three-four. Do you acknowledge?"

"I copy, Mr President. *Caspian Air* four-three-four. Repeat, four-three-four."

Walsh hung up, his head buried in his chest. When he looked up, his face was ashen. "May God have mercy on their souls...and ours."

For the second time in thirty minutes, the door to the PEOC bunker crashed open and the President's secretary stumbled breathlessly into the room. By right, it was the Chief of Staff's job to come to the President with any important telephone calls or urgent messages, but Clark was otherwise committed and Mary Clancy had shown enterprise and taken it upon herself to relay them.

"Mary, unless the person on the end of that phone has some kind of *deus ex machina*, I'm really not in the mood."

Mary hurried to Walsh. "Mr President, this is a flash-priority call from Captain Mike Malone, USS *Enterprise*."

"*What!*" The President grabbed the phone before she could explain any further. "This is the President. What is this about, Captain Malone?"

"Mr President, you'll forgive me if I forgo protocol. I've just received and corroborated a message from a *Caspian Air* flight four-three-four. Sir, it is my understanding we don't have a great deal of time here, so I'm going to cut to the chase. The plane is no longer under control of terrorists, Mr President. They have been neutralised and the aircraft is back under control of the pilots."

Walsh sat up in his seat, all the colour returning to his face. "Richard! Get me General Flynn back on the phone right now!" the President ordered. Duke cast him a confused look and went to say something. "Now, Rick. *Now!*"

Five seconds later he had Flynn on line four. The President stabbed the loudspeaker button. "General, call off the attack!"

"Mr President, I don't understand – "

"Wayne, that is a direct order. Bring those birds home *now!*"

Deafening silence from the other end. Walsh felt his stomach roll up into a ball of ice. "What's going on, Wayne?"

Silence.

"Wayne, answer me!"

Was it too late? Had they already shot it down? The President worried a nail; massaged his stubble.

"Mr President, our fighters were go-mission," Flynn began,

his voice taut; urgent. "They've ceased communication until the mission is resolved. We're trying to raise them on the emergency frequency right now."

Oh...my...God.

The President cupped his face, rested his elbows on the table. Though not a religious man, the gesture was symbolic of prayer.

"Mr President, we're saturating all radio channels right now. Standby."

Walsh rose from his chair, paced around the room, his hands steeped and pressed against his lips. Over the loudspeaker, he could hear Flynn barking orders. The President looked to the ceiling and fought the urge to bite his nails again.

"Standby...standby..."

The map now showed the airplane's nose touching the fail-safe line. Walsh allowed himself the fleeting thought the fighters hadn't prepped quick enough and now couldn't fire. But they were professionally trained to be ready for this scenario.

"General Flynn," a tenuous voice said over the loudspeaker. "We got Eagle One on the spark."

The President hurried back to his seat.

"Eagle One, this is CSAF. Those orders are red-lighted. Repeat, you are no-go for launch, no-go for launch! Acknowledge. Over," barked Flynn.

The subsequent thirty seconds of silence were the longest of James Walsh's life. As he waited, he heard every laboured breath, spit swallowed, and beat of his heart. Every tick of his timepiece pounded in his skull.

"Mr President, General Flynn. Sir, the fighters have been successfully called off. The plane is still airborne. Awaiting further instructions."

At that moment, Walsh's face went pale as the adrenaline ebbed from his body. The emotions of the last twelve hours finally caught up to him, and he crumpled onto the desk with an explosive, sobbed exhalation of pure exhaustion.

CHAPTER EIGHTY-TWO
CHOICES

ATARIC
17:39 EST

Hunt had never brandished a weapon at someone before.

He sucked in a deep breath – it was all he could do to keep his hands from shaking – and ordered Reid to take a seat. His former close friend looked at him as though he were an alien. Eyes darting from the gun to Hunt's face, Reid said, "What are you going to do – shoot me, Peter?"

He thrust the gun forward menacingly. "Just take a goddamn seat, Jack!"

Reid shook his head in disbelief, sighed, and slipped into his chair. "What the hell happened you, Hunt?"

The ghost of a smile crossed his face, but he ignored the question. Keeping his gun trained on Reid, he moved over to the office blinds and peered through an opening. A guard was roaming around the cubicles, doubtless checking to see if all computers were off. Hunt knew if he saw Reid's office lit up, he would check it. Drawing all the blinds shut, he moved over and turned down the dimmer lights as far as he dared.

"I didn't want it to happen this way, Jack, but you gave me no choice."

Reid gave him a derisive snort, then said, "You know, in the last couple of hours I saw my old friend come back to life. Hell, you were in your element today – apart from that one incident. But I gotta say, of all the things I expected you to do, this"—Reid gestured to the gun—"was not one of them."

Hunt moved back to the window and separated two blinds. "Yeah? Well sometimes you gotta do stuff you don't like. The world throws you a curveball, and sometimes you haven't got time to stop and ponder. Sometimes you don't even have time to act – you're just *re*acting."

Reid lifted his left hand and gesticulated as he said the next sentence. "And you think that makes what you're doing right now okay? You need help, Peter." As he listened to Reid's calmly spoken words, the gesticulation worked as planned. His attention was drawn to Reid's moving hand, while Reid gently lifted his receiver and set it on the table with the other hand. Speaking up to cover the noise, he pressed button #1: "Why don't you just put the gun down and let's take a walk? Get some fresh air. If you do that, I promise I won't tell Karen about *any* of this."

Hunt noticed the guard was hurrying towards the entrance of the building. Moving closer to the periphery of the office, he drew the blinds open and raked the floor below with his gaze. The guard was joined by a second, who pointed frantically to the security office by the front door. He watched as they piled into the small room. The newcomer lifted a phone and they huddled together. Frowning, Hunt turned back to Reid, gun still trained on him, and checked his hands. Both were on his thighs.

"Peter, did you hear me? Please...just put the gun down and we can sort this all out."

An expression of realisation flitted across Hunt's face. He moved back to the window, unsurprised to see both guards back on the floor, pointing at Reid's office, moving with purpose towards it.

"Peter, they're coming, aren't they?"

"Nice play, Jack." He moved over and set the receiver back in its cradle. Then, he moved into a kneeling position behind Reid's seat as the clangour of boots on metal began.

"What are you doing, Peter? It's over. Put the gun down and maybe you won't walk out of here in cuffs."

Hunt ignored him again. The noise grew louder as the first guard reached the door. It opened inward, and he heard a rustle as the man fumbled for his flashlight. The powerful beam glared into the left-hand corner, accompanied by a call for anyone inside to speak. Hunt jammed the Browning into the nape of Reid's neck as the guard raked the light around the rest of the interior. When it landed on Reid and the gun, a sharp intake of breath followed.

Hunt looped his free hand over Reid's neck and lodged his forearm against Reid's throat. "Up!" he bellowed. Reid slowly lifted himself from the chair, in tandem with Hunt. When both were standing, Hunt said to the guard, "Turn the flashlight off and step into the room. Tell the other guard to join you. *Slowly!* Hands on your head where I can see them."

When both were inside, he continued, "Now, close the door behind you and slowly – *very* slowly – reach up and turn the dimmer switch up halfway. I see any unnecessary movement, Reid gets a bullet in the head."

The guard did as instructed.

"Good. You back there," Hunt said to the rear guard. "Take your flashlight, Motorola, and baton – toss them to me."

The guard removed and rolled each item individually along the floor. Hunt, gun still trained on Reid's head, carefully stooped down and picked up the radio, then put it in his pocket. He kicked the other items under Reid's table.

"Okay," he said to the nearest guard. "Now you. Everything except your radio. Roll them to me now. Slowly!"

The front guard had already dropped his flashlight. He added his baton, kicked both to Hunt's feet, who lifted his leg and let them roll into place beside the others.

Hunt switched his aim to the first guard. "Take your Motorola, and radio in a code nine to the perimeter guards." ATARIC's "code nine" was guard-speak for "false alarm". Only the security guards and the brass were supposed to know it, but during one of Hunt's forays into the system, he'd discovered the list and committed it to memory.

The guard looked dubious. Hunt moved in closer and brought the gun against his head. "Now! And in case you're thinking of warning them, be aware I know *all* your codes. You say anything I think is suspect, I will shoot you. Understand?"

He nodded, clicking the transmit button. "Edwards, this is Shaw. We're code nine on that previous report. Everything's quiet in here."

"Damn. I was looking forward to coming in. Freezing my ass off out here."

"Sorry, can't help you on that."

"Sure you can't. All right, Shaw. Copy on the code niner. Over and out."

Hunt shuffled towards the door, keeping the gun tight against Reid's temple. When he was beside the second guard, he instructed him to come closer. Before he could step forward, though, Hunt mashed the butt into his temple. With a grunt, the heavyset man collapsed to the floor.

He turned to the other one. "Now you're going to radio James Fielding and Dave Haskens. Tell them there's an emergency on the floor and their presence is required A-S-A-P."

Shaw shook his head, looked uncertainly towards Reid, then eyed Hunt. "I don't have the ability to contact Mr Fielding *or* Mr Haskens."

He let the gun trace a line from Shaw's head to his crotch. "Unless you wanna spend the rest of your life as a woman, I suggest you rethink that answer."

Shaw's Adam's apple bobbed. He looked again to Reid, who offered nothing but equal fear. "Even if I did have their number, or tried them on the radio, it wouldn't matter. They can't answer."

"And why's that?" Hunt was not in the mood for temporising.

Shaw motioned to speak, hesitated, and closed his mouth again.

Moving closer, Hunt switched his aim to the unconscious guard. "Either you tell me right now, or he gets a bullet in the head."

"Come on, Peter," Reid interjected. "We know you're not going to do that."

"Shut up, Jack!" He jammed his forearm tighter against Reid's throat. Reid struggled, sounds of constricted choking whistling out of his mouth. "Let's get one thing clear here, Shaw," Hunt began, his face morphing into an angry snarl. "Right now, I'm someone you really don't want to fuck with. I'm not going to give you some lame Hollywood countdown here. What I will give you, though, is the time it takes Reid's face to turn blue from asphyxiation."

With his gun-hand, he reached forward and, using his other forearm for leverage, yanked back on Reid's throat. Even as he was doing this, he kept the gun pointed forward and, if Shaw attempted to move, could still fire. Reid thrashed wildly, the choking sounds now elevating to desperate gulps for air. Hunt held strong, arching his back for even more leverage.

Shaw looked like a deer caught in headlights, vacillating.

"Come on, Shaw!" he snarled. "What's it gonna be? D'you know that if you cut off oxygen to the brain for over a minute, there's a ninety per cent chance of brain damage? You want that on your conscience?"

Reid, his face turning a deep shade of purple, croaked, "Do it!"

"All right, all right! I'll do it."

Hunt released the pressure, and Reid sucked in great mouthfuls of air.

"I only have a number to be used in serious emergency situations. When I ring it, Mr Fielding will take it to mean something is horribly wrong in here. You have to understand once I do that I *cannot* guarantee your safety."

"I don't care. Do it!"

Shaw replaced the Motorola in his shirt pocket. From a pouch on the knee of his trousers, he removed an ordinary-looking cell phone and extended a not-so-ordinary-looking elongated antenna from its top. Without inputting a number, he pressed the dial button. Hunt could hear the odd reply as crisp as though he were listening himself: "The number you have dialled is not recognised". Shaw let it repeat four times, then pressed a button. A dial tone followed, then three rings, before a female voice broke the connection and asked for a security number.

"Four-four-one-two," Shaw enumerated.

This time eight rings followed, before the unmistakeable weakened voice of James Fielding answered. "Who is this?"

"Mr Fielding, it's Craig Shaw. Sir, we have a serious situation on the floor that requires your immediate attention."

"I'm in the middle of a crucial meeting, Mr Shaw, and I do

not like my time monopolised with trivial matters. I shall be there in five minutes, but if the problem is not on the scale of World War Three, you shan't."

"Yes, sir. I understand."

When the lift doors opened five minutes later, all three were waiting beside it, Hunt still locked together with Reid. He turned his gun on a startled James Fielding and ordered him out of the lift.

To Hunt's infinite surprise, from behind Fielding two men stepped from the shadows, brandishing their own pistols which they now trained on Hunt's frame. He felt Reid go limp with relief.

"Put the gun down now!" the first one, a balding, middle-aged man, ordered. For all his bravado, he didn't frighten Hunt. The second man, however, did. His face, chiselled and hardened not by age but by the things he'd seen and done, was expressionless, but his eyes told Hunt more than anything else ever could. Even if he hadn't known the intimacies of the man's life, he still would have known enough to take the director of the FBI, Jonathan Baker, deadly serious.

Hunt, knowing there was little other option, released Reid and surrendered the gun to a man he knew was the director of the NSA, who proceeded to handcuff him.

"What did you think you were going to accomplish, Peter?" Fielding asked, padding up beside him. "I told you there'd be consequences if I found out you were complicit in the computer problems today. These latest actions reinforce my belief you are a guilty man. A desperate man."

"You warned Shaw if this emergency wasn't serious you'd fire him. Well, if you don't listen to what I have to same, James, what will happen tonight may very well be the beginning of World War Three," Hunt said with what even he had to admit was excessive dramatics.

CHAPTER EIGHTY-THREE
PROPINQUITY

UNKNOWN GOVERNMENT BUILDING
17: 45 EST

In the centre of the surveillance room, seated in one of the swivel chairs, Jin struggled against the duct tape holding him firm. Above him, Carlos and Gyle circled like vultures inspecting their prey. Despite their intimidating presence, Jin looked serene.

"What's Shadow Wolf doing here?" demanded Carlos. He'd lost track of how many times he asked that question, or a similar version of it, in the last ten minutes. But, like every time before, Jin stared into the distance and ignored it.

Carlos' face darkened. It was bad enough that his own government had betrayed him. Now, members of his country were attacking their own troops? It pissed him off. Without thinking, he stormed over to the chair, threw it backwards amidst Jin's yelp, and followed it to the ground. There, he jammed his forearm into Jin's throat so hard he thought he'd crushed the man's windpipe.

"How many of you are there, and how did you know we'd be in this building!"

Jin, his eyes bulging pits of fear, croaked, "Secretary of

Defence!"

Carlos pulled away and muttered SecDef's name as though the very mention of it would condemn them to even more misery. He reached over his shoulder and removed the MAC-10 from his back holster. Ignoring the look of horror on Jin's face, he turned back and set the muzzle against the operative's nose. "How many?" he asked pointedly.

"Three. Me and two snipers." Jin was brave, but lying to a man who could, with the very weapon in his hand, pick off targets at a hundred yards was suicidal.

"Why are you in here?"

The question confused Jin.

Carlos' voice grew impatient. "Why are they out there and you in here?"

"Oh." Jin nodded. "SecDef wanted someone on the inside to assess your performance in a combat situation."

Son of a bitch! "This is another goddamn test? So why the hell are they using live-fire?"

"You *know* the answer to that, Sergeant."

Enemy combatants didn't use blanks or rubber bullets in conflict. The newly assembled "best anti-terror squadron in the world" needed its members to be unflappable, and even the most supreme military drills could not compare to live-fire training.

Gyle, who'd moved into a crouched position in the corridor, spoke up, "Bear, we got a serious problem here."

Carlos shook out of his trance, moved over to his sergeant. "What is it?" Even as he finished the sentence, he knew. The sound, though tenuous now, was growing rapidly. Outside, he could see a tiny speck in the distance – the beam from a spotlight mounted on a helicopter. "Dammit! How long?"

"About three minutes." Gyle turned to Carlos. "And this ain't no ordinary chopper, *amigo*. We wouldn'tt hear it if it was – not yet. This one's double-rotored – transport chopper."

"What! What kind of transport chopper?"

Gyle shook his head. "Can't tell. What I can tell you is that it's *big*. Probably talking 'bout a twenty-seater."

My God, thought Carlos. *Twenty Shadow Wolf mercenaries. You gotta be fuckin' kidding me.* "Has it got ordnance?"

Gyle turned but didn't answer.

"Julio! It is armed?"

Gyle cocked his head, his face deadpan. "If it is, we're screwed."

Carlos turned back, shaking his head. Steeping his fingers, he stared into the distance, ruminating. Twenty mercenaries against two soldiers – even highly trained Force Recon Marines – amounted to an insuperable scenario. No matter how well-planned their attacks were, the numbers would overwhelm them eventually. This had all the hallmarks of a final test, and someone was determined to make sure it separated the men from boys.

"Bear, whaddaya wanna do? Inbound in about ninety," Gyle said.

Carlos grabbed Jin's chair and hauled it back to its wheels. Placing the muzzle against his crotch this time, he asked, "Where are the snipers located?"

"What? No." Jin shook his head. "I don't know. I was in here when they took their positions."

Carlos jerked left, pulled the trigger, sending a slug directly at Jin's thigh from less than a foot away. Jin screamed as the bullet impacted, expanded, and exploded out the underside of his leg.

"Jesus Christ, Bear!" Gyle breathed, barely believing what he was seeing.

"Julio, go check on the chopper," Carlos ordered.

Gyle looked doubtful. "Sergeant-Major?"

"Now, Julio!"

As Gyle exited, Carlos clamped his massive hand around the wound. Jin's whimpering escalated into a piercing scream that almost drowned out the approaching helicopter. "I avoided the major arteries. Tell me where the snipers are positioned and the pain stops. Don't, and I'll put another bullet in your femoral artery and leave you here to bleed to death."

"You – you're...crazy!"

Carlos increased his grip, his eyes narrow and burning with hatred. "What I am is tired of playing this bullshit game. You're gonna tell me what I want to know, or I'm gonna drag your ass outta this seat and throw you out that fuckin' window."

Jin, his face scrunched in a tight rictus, mouthed through

tears, "I don't...know."

With his free hand, Carlos removed his HALO knife and sliced through the duct tape. Ignoring Jin's terrified whimpers of protest, he seized him by the shirt and hauled him to his feet. Jin's right leg buckled as Carlos forced him forward, and he collapsed, his scream inaudible over the thunderous thrum of the landing helicopter. He roughly jerked him back to his feet and dragged him into the corridor. Removing the MAC-10, and ignoring the look of perplexity on Gyle's face, he fired a three-round-burst at the nearest window. The glass shattered into minute pieces, blown away by the side wind of the helicopter.

"Bear, what the hell are you doing?" Gyle demanded as he watched his commander drag a kicking and screaming Jin to the window.

Carlos ignored him. For a fleeting moment, the nexus of the helicopter's searchlight washed over him, bathing the corridor in garish light. Then, as the chopper swivelled right, the only remaining light emanated from the moribund bulb. Carlos, dazed, shook his head and blinked a few times. The momentary distraction allowed Jin to struggle free of the vice-like grip. He tried to scamper down the hall, but his leg gave way to the sickening sound of broken bone. Jin hit the floor hard, the anguish-filled scream horrifying enough to make the hairs on Carlos' neck stand.

Showing no remorse, he advanced on Jin again. "Where are the snipers? Tell me or a broken leg will be the least of your worries," he demanded, pointing to the window. When he didn't answer, Carlos lifted his boot and threatened to bring it down.

"All right! I'll tell you!" Spittle flitted from his mouth. "The first one's in the crow's nest of a crane five hundred yards south-east of the main doors. The other one...I honestly don't know where he is. He's roaming."

"And the chopper?"

"I don't know anything about it! Our parameters specified only a handful of us were to be involved. We decided on three. One to infiltrate...two for cover fire."

"What's the endgame?"

"We were told to put you through the paces. Live-fire combat in a controlled environment. I'm wearing a tracking device – that's how the snipers know where we are."

"We're talking high-quality marksmen here, aren't we? Those aren't the Boy Scouts out there."

"Both have won the NRA's World Series of Shooting. Our mission wasn't to kill you. It was to test you."

Carlos scowled. "So how we doin' so far, Jin?"

"Pretty good, by my reckoning. But none of that matters now," he said in a way that suggested Carlos should know why.

"What are you talking about?"

Jin gave a short laugh-cum-grimace. "Come on, Sergeant...you really think that chopper is Shadow Wolf's? Even I know better. That's a military bird. Whoever set up this little soiree...they're ending it. You can bet the farm the snipers are being debriefed as we speak. In the next sixty seconds...I'm gonna get the signal for abort."

Carlos shook his head, turned to Gyle. "Julio, what's the status on that bird?"

Gyle moved away from the window and came beside his commander. Whispering into Carlos' ear: "Bear, I think he's right. And it ain't a chopper."

Carlos frowned. "What are you talking about?"

"V-Twenty-Two Osprey, *Papi.* It landed and two men sped in different directions. One went to the crane; couldn't see where the other went."

"Julio, it could be another part of the test. Make us think it's over and then lure us out into the courtyard." Carlos turned and looked at Jin, turned back, and whispered, "He could be setting us up."

"Could be, but I don't think so." Gyle's eyes narrowed, his voice lowering even more. "Bear, when those two guys jumped out of the Osprey, about ten seconds later another man stepped out. I only saw his face in the spotlight for about two seconds, but I'll never forget that *pendejo*. It was the brigadier general who ordered us home from Adi Ghar yesterday."

Gyle was taken aback by the reaction that elicited from Carlos. For the past few minutes, his face had been beset with a mixture of anger, confusion, and rage. Now Gyle observed something much more horrifying.

Death.

The unflinching, ineffable countenance of Death itself.

***

The white suit was as garish as the light from the V-22 Osprey, but Edward Rainey was nothing if not obsessive about appearance. With the swagger of an overbearingly confident man, he sauntered to the main doors of the North Carolina regional headquarters of the CIA and used his personal key card to open them. Though the CIA was a civilian organisation and did not fall under the purview of the DoD, presidential orders are something even Central Intelligence can't ignore. This facility, by Rainey's request, had been vacated twenty-four hours earlier. Rainey had planned to involve the chosen leaders in one final test (it was he who'd ordered the brutish Latino to drug Carlos) but the President had cut that short.

Now, it was Rainey's duty to placate two soldiers who wanted him hung, drawn, and quartered. Not to mention convincing them to sign non-disclosure papers and board a plane to participate in a mission neither of them could ever talk about again.

As he stepped through the doors, he didn't realise Carlos and Gyle had already witnessed his entrance via the CCTV monitors in the surveillance room.

***

Carlos, his leg still smarting from the bullet wound, moved down the second-floor corridor as fast as his body allowed. Beside him, a fully-fit-but-tired Gyle matched his commander's pace.

"Bear, think about this for a minute! You're gonna walk away from Jin – a man you shot two minutes ago? How's *that* going to look on the service record, *amigo?*"

Carlos stopped suddenly, turned to face Gyle. Grasping him by the shoulders, he said, "Julio, after this is over there *is* no more service for me. What I've done today – I'll be lucky if I don't get court-martialled. You go back there and stay with Jin until the cavalry arrives."

Gyle shook his head. "No way, *muchacho*. We serve together, we die together. *Semper Fi.*"

"That man we've just seen – "

"I know who the *puto* is, Jack." It was the first time Gyle had called Carlos by his forename in a combat environment. But it got his attention.

"What do you mean?"

"I figured out who Triton really was a coupla hours after they split us up. I knew the SOB looked familiar, but in Adi Ghar I was too tired to make the connection. It only took a while to realise I'd seen the *pendejo* on television. Triton is SecDef."

"Which is exactly why you need to stay with Jin. I'm the commander here. I take the fall for anything my team does. I've already accepted my military career is over as of now. Fuck it, I was getting fed up with bureaucracy anyway. But you're almost ten years my junior, Julio. This doesn't have to be the end of both our careers."

Gyle held Carlos' gaze with steely eyes. Without blinking, he said, "I meant what I said before. Nothing you say will make me change my mind."

"Julio – "

If possible, Gyle's eyes became even more intense and unblinking, cutting off Carlos' train of thought. "Bear, we started this together...damned if we aren't finishing it that way."

"Listen, Julio, we've been like brothers for years. What I'm going to do to Rainey when I get my hands – "

Gyle grabbed him by the shoulders, eyes now morphing from determination to rage. "No, Sergeant-Major: When *we* get our hands on Rainey. That *cabron* is going to pay. *Celer, Silens, Mortalis.*"

Carlos nodded. "*Celer, Silens, Mortalis,*" he echoed.

Both of them bumped fists, walking down the corridor side by side at a military canter. Jin screamed for help, but neither listened. The soldiers' creed of *Licentia haud vir secundum*, "*Leave no man behind*", vanished from their personas, replaced by their unit's own creed.

Swift, silent, deadly.

CHAPTER EIGHTY-FOUR
PROBLEMS AND SOLUTIONS

```
HALLIDAY & PITT LAW FIRM
MANHATTAN
17:55 EST
```

Karen entered the building of the Halliday and Pitt law firm. She knew quite a few of the lawyers who worked there but only because she'd come up against them in court. At the reception desk she inquired if they had anyone who specialised in cases of sexual harassment.

"Yes," replied the receptionist, "we have three lawyers who deal in cases of harassment – of any nature. Would you prefer a male or a female to represent you?"

Karen thought for a moment, then answered, "Female, please."

"All right, Miss...?"

"Mrs Hunt. Karen Hunt," she replied. "Would it be possible to talk with someone right now?"

"I'll see what I can do. Please take a seat."

The receptionist went off to her left through glass doors, knocked on the first door, and entered after a moment.

Karen didn't know if she was doing the right thing. She had intended to discuss it with Peter, but since he was now working late, she had decided to proceed.

The receptionist came back through the glass doors.

"You're in luck, Mrs Hunt. Marjorie can see you right now. Come with me."

On the second floor directly opposite them, two men came out of a room.

"I'll see you at the weekend, Mark. We'll have a round of golf," Johnson Walken said, shaking hands with Mark Pitt. He looked down to the floor in time to see Karen rise and follow the receptionist through the glass doors and into the first room.

"Who works out of that first office, Mark? It wouldn't be Des Green, by any chance?" Walken inquired casually.

"No," Pitt answered. "That office belongs to Marjorie Wallace. Why do you ask?"

"Oh, no reason, no reason. I'll see you soon. Thanks for all your help." With that, Walken walked to the escalator and left the building.

So, he thought, Karen *was* taking things further.

CHAPTER EIGHTY-FIVE
TRANSFER OF POWER

ATARIC
18: 05 EST

Hunt struggled against the handcuffs cutting off circulation to his hands, as Jon Baker struggled to move him towards the exit. "You're making a huge mistake! This building is going to be attacked within the hour. Jack, tell them about the Web site we found! Show them the document and pictures. You have to listen to me, goddamnit!"

Reid exhaled. "The lunatic ramblings of a paranoid, delusional conspiracy theorist? My God, Peter, will you listen to yourself? I thought you were prepared to face the real world again, but it seems you're more insane sober than you are inebriated."

Fielding said, in a strong voice that belied his weakness, "Jon, please get him the hell out of my sight before I do something my frail body will live to regret."

Baker roughly forced Hunt forward, only to be met by stiff resistance. Reid, knowing he was as strong as Hunt, took over. He grabbed Hunt around the waist and half-lifted half-pushed him to the exit.

"*Insane*, Jack? Why don't you take a long look around you?

And then ask Fielding why the directors of the FBI and NSA are in this building."

Though Reid had recognised them, it was only now the incongruity of their presence dawned on him. "Mr Fielding, why *are* they here?"

Fielding looked more disappointed than upset. "Not you too, Jack? You may not be aware, but I once served this country, and I still have many prominent friends on the Hill. Directors Baker and Clemence are here to say their goodbyes – before I..." Fielding paused and dabbed his eyes with a handkerchief.

"Oh, bullshit!" Hunt raged. "That's a convenient cover story. But why did you come *up* in the lift? Huh? Answer me that!"

"We didn't," Fielding responded. "We came *down* from the directors' office on the fifth floor."

"I watched the goddamn numbers myself! You came from the basement!"

"You were mistaken, Peter." Fielding shook his head and signalled Baker. "Jon, please, take him out of the building and arrest him."

Reid had already taken Hunt as far as the front door, but now he stopped. Not to hand him over to Baker. Instead, he turned to face Fielding. "He's right. You came from the basement. I saw it myself. Why are you lying, sir?"

"Goddamnit, Reid! Hunt is no longer an employee of ATARIC. He's about to be arrested for your attempted murder. Unless you want to join him, shut up!" Fielding raged.

It was the presence of the FBI and NSA directors which did it. Reid no more believed Hunt's story than he believed in a deity. But the appearance of two top DoD officials added credence to his ramblings, and Fielding's deceitful anger tipped the scales. Hunt was no longer crying wolf. Now, he had a firm believer on his side.

Reid tried to cut Baker off before he could manoeuvre Hunt outside, but he didn't get there in time. As soon as Baker opened the door, Reid knew something was off. He couldn't see a security guard anywhere.

ATARIC's entrance was never unmanned.

Hunt sensed it too. Digging his heels into the ground, he brought Baker's forward momentum to a crumpling halt. The FBI director grunted and growled as he tried in vain to move

Hunt's behemoth body.

"Mr Reid, gimme a goddamn hand – "

Reid moved fast. With his left hand, he grabbed a heft of Baker's coat and dragged the director off Hunt. His right shot down into Baker's holster and removed the Glock from it. As Baker stumbled into his arms, he simultaneously locked his left hand around Baker's throat, and settled the barrel against his head with his right.

"Jesus Christ, Jack! What are you doing?" Fielding spluttered. Beside him, Clemence snapped out his gun and trained it on Reid.

With his right foot, Reid kicked shut the door and locked it. "Okay, everyone remain calm. I can explain."

"Please humour us, Jack," Fielding spat.

"I've worked in this building for over ten years. I've given long nights of service, James," Reid said, eyes daring Fielding to respond to the use of his first name. "I've never seen the front door unguarded. Have you?"

"Of course not! I explicitly forbade it."

"There's no one there now. So I'm thinking maybe Peter has a point. Because if I was going to attack this building, taking out the guards would be my first move."

As he said that, the lights above him flickered for a few seconds, then powered down.

"And that would be my second," Reid said to pitch blackness.

CHAPTER EIGHTY-SIX
TRANSPORT

ON-BOARD A V-22 OSPREY
18: 10 EST

Jack Carlos buckled up as the Osprey rose into the sky, the double rotors on its wings moving from vertical to horizontal once it reached optimum height. A thin keening knifed into the interior as the plane shuddered in the crosswinds.

Carlos appeared calm, but beneath the unshaken exterior his temper was surging. Beside him, Gyle's eyes burned with hatred as they roved around the interior. In every seat except four, soldiers of varying nationalities talked in hushed tones. All spoke English. Finally, Gyle's eyes landed on Edward Rainey and the man with whom he was speaking.

Attorney General Walter Norman.

Fifteen minutes earlier, Carlos and Gyle had been on the hunt, determined to locate Rainey and get revenge for what he'd done to them. Instead, they'd run into Norman on the first floor. He'd spoken with them for five minutes, explaining the situation, the extenuating circumstances, and the authority vested in him by the President to offer them anything they wanted in reparation. However, if they agreed to overlook their treatment over the last forty hours, both would be given the esteemed position of team leaders of STRIKE Force's two squads. Since neither had any inkling what it was nor any inclination to join it, they declined and demanded to be transported to 1st Force Recon headquarters at Camp Pendleton, California.

Norman then played his trump card. He told them that, along with the position of commander, both would be bumped up four and five pay-grades respectively to the rank of "major". No written exams would need to be taken. In addition, the remaining members of their Force Recon squadron would also advance one pay-grade, with one member of their choosing becoming team commander. Their company commander, Major Miller, would tomorrow learn of a transfer order from the President stating both Carlos and Gyle would be joining DEVGRU, while also being warned any resistance would be met with a downgrade to O-1. Thus, they would simply cease to exist...to everyone except a select few.

And that was before Norman told them about "Station Blue". Before divulging any information about the top-secret facility, Norman had asked for two things. First, he needed their signatures on the non-disclosure form, along with their word that neither would pursue Edward Rainey or any others responsible for their incarceration. And second, he needed them to agree to join STRIKE Force and partake in a black operation that would remain secret indefinitely. For that, they would receive an immediate upgrade to O-4, have the last thirty hours of their lives expunged from record (including Carlos' attack on Rainey and the shooting of Jin), as well as acquiring level-one SCI military clearance (top-secret) as a perquisite of becoming STRIKE Force's leaders. To settle their doubts, Norman showed them a signed presidential writ corroborating his promises. They would be free to continue their duty as Marines, in the capacity of STRIKE Force leaders, without the fear of a court martial. Refuse, and their military careers would doubtless be over and they'd be remanded in a stockade indefinitely.

Carlos hated his country for having the audacity to treat its soldiers like that. But, after mulling it over with Gyle, both acquiesced. Though they felt like they'd sold their souls, the alternative was an impossible choice to make, no matter how vehemently either disliked their country at that moment. To be remanded in a stockade meant only one thing: disavowed, locked up, and the key thrown away.

"Station Blue" hadn't shocked him. In fact, Carlos had heard various rumours over the years about similar underground bases. He'd been in Cheyenne on a few occasions, in official and non-official capacities. Terrorists knowing of "Station Blue's" presence, though, scared him immensely. Fighting a war against terrorists using US weapons was a terrifying premise. And for all he knew, chemical and biological weaponry might be housed there also. A born and bred American, Carlos couldn't allow terrorists to gain an inexorable advantage in the War on Terror. 9/11 had been a catastrophe, but it would pale in comparison to the resultant death toll if terrorists managed to procure weaponised nerve agents or other WMDs.

As titular team leaders, Carlos and Gyle received the schematics of ATARIC and its underground structure, "Station Blue". As the Osprey headed for New York City, ETA just over an hour, they began conversing on optimal routes of entry, staging points, perimeter boundaries, and anything else which would give them an advantage over the terrorists.

Their planning, however, did not account for the terrorists already being on-site.

CHAPTER EIGHTY-SEVEN
ZUGZWANG

OUTSIDE ATARIC
18: 20 EST

Getting off the plane had been the hardest part. Immediately after landing, several fire trucks, police cars, and bomb squad vans surrounded and pinned in the 747 to prevent it from taking off. From the vans emerged dozens of ESU members, clad in full body armour and armed with MP5 sub-machineguns. They took up positions around the perimeter of the plane, training red dots on all possible exit points. Chatter from various channels suggested the plane had been retaken by the crew, but the ground-men took no chances. They opened the exit, inflated the slide, and one by one ushered every passenger into the arms of bulky men who took them to a staging area where identifications were made.

Ivanovich and his team stayed until the last of the passengers exited. Knowing they would be compromised if the authorities detained them, they removed a floor hatch and quietly slipped into the avionics room. From there, they located the landing gear. From above and below, they heard the shouts of various men as the last of the passengers came out. Once the pilots were accounted for, heavy footfalls pounded above

Ivanovich's head as the officers cleared the remainder of the plane. Urgent cries then echoed as dead and unconscious bodies were discovered throughout. Several minutes later, they declared the plane "secure" and left.

Through an aperture in the landing gear, Ivanovich and his team exited. Red-and-blue lights swamped the nearby area, and farther down the runway massive spotlights had been erected over a staging area. To the rear, the runway's landing lights glared for approximately a mile.

Ivanovich led his team left, away from most light sources. Moving from shadow to shadow, they covered a half-mile before coming to an eight-foot chain-link fence. Each man boosted the other over, the last jumping to catch Ivanovich's hand and then pulling himself over as well.

More spotlights, this time illuminating a short-term parking lot. Ducking and weaving to avoid the concentric circles of light, they moved across the car park until they came to a van outside the reach of the spotlights. York hotwired it and drove to the main gates. Here, a security guard let them pass after Ivanovich showed him TSA credentials. Twenty minutes later, they were parking five blocks from ATARIC.

Although Kirov had assured him the building's power would be terminated at seven, he didn't like to rely on someone else to do a job he could do himself. He found the service box and shut down the breakers serving ATARIC. As he did, his men quietly removed the perimeter security guards before any alerted the interior ones. With everything set, they donned night-vision headgear and moved into position beside the front doors. Here, Ivanovich learned of his first serious problem.

The doors were locked. His team couldn't find keys on any of the security guards they'd eliminated. Along with the supplies they'd smuggled on-board the plane, Ivanovich had stopped at one of Kirov's safe houses close to ATARIC (whose occupants' job had been to collect intelligence) and retrieved more, including plastic explosives. Removing the door wouldn't be a problem, but entering the building this way put Ivanovich at an immediate tactical disadvantage. For the mission to be successful, stealth was paramount. Doing it any other way would bring swarms of police before the mission even commenced.

Ivanovich gritted his teeth in frustration and slipped in beside York. "Is it possible to pick this lock?"

York, wearing body armour, night-vision gear, and holding an AK-47, said, "With time. But we ain't got time, Sergei. The second they find a flashlight in there, someone's calling the pigs."

"If we go in any other way, the police will be on top of us in no time. We have to do this quietly. Get started on the door. I'll go set up perimeters so we'll know when someone's coming."

"Okay, Sergei. But this ain't gonna be a Hollywood lock-picking. It's gonna take a little time. If we break a window, by the time the cops get here we'll have the area secured and be downstairs – they'll just think it was some punk kids."

"I want to keep a stealth approach until there's no other choice. I'll be on our pre-arranged private channel if you need me. Keep the other one open for communication with the team. I need to make a phone call. I think there's someone who might be able to help. You let me know the second you breach those doors so I can call him off if need be."

"*If*, Sergei. I'll let you know if I breach the doors. Don't count on it, though."

"Fifteen minutes, York. If you haven't it done then, you aren't going to."

CHAPTER EIGHTY-EIGHT
CATCH-22

ATARIC
18:30 EST

The light from a solitary torch limned the figures of Reid and Baker, both still locked together. Roger Clemence used the light from Fielding's torch to draw a bead on Reid. He'd have preferred Hunt, but the crafty bastard had obscured himself behind a computer.

"Jack, just put the gun down and let Director Baker go," Fielding said softly. The light bobbed as the weight became too much for his weak limbs to hold steady.

"We're wasting time here, James. You know this isn't just some power outage. Right now, you've got a bunch of terrorists surrounding this building. The doors are locked, but that won't stop them. They're coming in. We need to be somewhere else when that happens," Reid responded. He dragged Baker a few feet to the left. He'd done this several times. Each time, Fielding had to readjust, re-aim, and steady the Mag-Lite. Every such movement for a man in his condition was energy-sapping.

"I told you already, Jack. *There is no underground base!* This is a computer firm, and when this is over, you and Hunt are going to prison for a long time."

Reid shuffled to the right. "You may be on death's bed, Mr Fielding, and willing to die now to keep this place secret. But you've got security guards, two employees, and two high-ranking officials of the DoD here. Are you prepared to sacrifice their lives?"

"These nonsense ramblings about terrorists are at best paranoia, Jack. If you lay down the gun now, I give you my word you will not be prosecuted for any of this. Please do not let Peter Hunt drag you into his world of delusion."

"I've known Peter a lot longer than you have. He's crazy, weird, troublesome, hag-ridden, and I'd say right now just about at the end of his tether. But one thing he incontrovertibly is *not*, sir, is a liar."

"If that's what you think..." Fielding trailed off.

The merest flicker of a frown flashed over Reid's face. Something wasn't right. When Clemence asked him, seconds later, to put the gun down, he felt his stomach roll up into a ball of ice. Both men were standing shoulder-to-shoulder, Fielding doing his best to keep the light trained on Reid and Baker. Neither of them knew were Hunt was, nor seemed to care. They were striving to keep conversation, but for what reason Reid couldn't imagine. No matter how distracted Reid became, Clemence would never chance shooting him with Baker nearby.

He advanced a few feet right, as fast as he dared, until he bumped into a desk. Keeping a tight grip on Baker, he used his right hand to open the top drawer. Setting the gun inside, he tossed aside several items, none of them heavy enough to be what we wanted. He retrieved the gun and did the same for three other drawers. In the last one, he finally found what he needed.

"Mr Baker, I'm going to hand you a flashlight. I want you to point it exactly where I tell you." He placed the Mag-Lite into Baker's right hand and pointed left, into the darkness. Baker hesitated at first, until pressure was applied to his throat. He fanned the fulgent beam outward, irradiating desks, computers, and an upstairs office. The light suffused the shadows and illumined specks of dust. He instructed Baker to slowly pan to the left, towards Hunt. As the beam moved over each workstation, Reid could see no one. Just before it got to Hunt, though, it paused momentarily on a wall. There, he saw the moving silhouette of someone sneaking through the darkness from desk to desk. Baker jerked left, hoping Reid hadn't seen.

But he already knew what was happening. He'd forgotten about the remaining security guard, who was probing the darkness to find Hunt. He also knew that, since he was the only one who knew his position, he couldn't warn Hunt without compromising him.

If Reid did warn Hunt about the guard, he would have to take evasive action. Doing so would alert Clemence to his position and he would kill him. If Reid didn't warn Hunt, the security guard would eventually find and kill him. And if he let Baker go and tried to save Hunt, Clemence would kill him instead and then kill Hunt.

Catch-22.

CHAPTER EIGHTY-NINE
FINAL PREPARATIONS

OUTSIDE ATARIC
18: 40 EST

ATARIC's front doors were anything but easy to pick. The lock design was tubular, which ruled out conventional lock-picking techniques. Without a lock-picking gun, it could take York up to an hour.

With a grimace, York flicked his radio to the dedicated channel. "Sergei, it could take me hours to pick this sum'bitch. You should call your backup."

"Already done, York. He'll be there in five minutes. When the door is open, call me."

"Copy that."

York didn't like being out in the open like this. His team were well-trained in the art of stealth and knew how to conceal themselves, but the longer it took them to get inside, the more chance they'd be spotted by a passing motorist or pedestrian. And the entire team, save for York, were Russian. So many foreigners outside a well-respected establishment like ATARIC would raise suspicion.

It didn't help that ATARIC was exposed. It may have been good place to house a top-secret weapons development base, but its location provided little cover, the only hiding spots behind elm trees dotted around 38th Street. York, though, had been in the service before converting to terrorism, and knew the best way to remain inconspicuous was to blend with the crowd. His men perambulated the streets, talking on their phones, jogging in circular routes, and doing the prosaic things that nocturnal human beings did while York remained focused on the comings and goings of pedestrians from the cover of darkness.

He hoped Ivanovich's backup was forthcoming.

***

The *El Rio Grande* restaurant opposite ATARIC steadily gained more customers as the night grew old and the city's denizens stopped in after a hard day's work. In the vestibule, shielded from view, stood the deputy director of the FBI, William Forrester. His business, however, was not food. His gaze was focused on ATARIC; he watched proceedings through the bevelled door, his veteran eyes leery of the sudden influx of people around the computer firm.

His stunning revelation about Dan Hollingsworth's illicit actions had come too late. By the time the order to arrest him had gone through the pipeline, Hollingsworth had disappeared. An APB had been dispatched to all law enforcement agencies within the state and to the US Border Patrol. He was confident Hollingsworth would be found.

With Davies dead, he thought it best to personally deliver the news to Baker. When he'd arrived at ATARIC, though, he spotted suspicious activity outside. Parking his car in the restaurant's lot, he slipped inside to survey the scene.

Their movements suggested terrorism. Forrester had seen enough to know how their kind operated. Not as methodical and meticulous as trained soldiers, but comparable nevertheless. He flipped open his cell phone, dialled Baker's number. The last three times it had gone to voicemail. This time was no different.

Where the hell are you, Jon?

When a car turned off 3rd Avenue onto East 38th Street, swamping ATARIC with full-beam headlights, the light penetrated the shadows of darkness obscuring a man from Forrester's vantage. He immediately sensed the man hadn't been hiding in the dark for nothing. He remained stationary, allowing the beams to pass over him, thinking nobody had noticed.

Forrester was already on the move. His gut told him something untoward was happening. He wrenched his cell phone out again; hit the redial button.

Still no answer.

Goddamnit, Jon!

He brushed past flocks of ingoing customers, exited through the main doors, and stepped into the cool breeze. Replacing the cell phone, his hand went to the other side and gently removed his service pistol. Keeping it low and out of sight, he started to cross the street but stopped abruptly when he saw a man round the corner of 38th Street and disappear into the shadows.

Forrester moved back to the footpath. He waited sixty seconds, but the man never emerged. He jammed the pistol back into its holster and moved along the footpath to an amber crossing on 3rd Avenue. He jogged across and angled left. Crouching, he moved in behind a parked bus. Pedestrians regarded him with confused and amused smiles, but he ignored them. He shuffled left, stepped off the footpath, and slid along the side of the bus until he came to the front of it. Crouching again at the wheel, and ignoring splashes of water from vehicles whizzing past him, he tilted his neck until he could see past the nose of the bus.

For a moment, he thought he'd gone too far. But when another vehicle rounded 3rd Avenue, he saw two men at the front door. One was shielding the other, but from Forrester's vantage he could see a strange device in the other one's hand.

He darted to his feet, grabbed his gun again. Rounding the bus, he hit the footpath at a sprint, gun extended. "Move!" he bellowed at the people nearest him, confident the hum of the traffic beside ATARIC would drown his cries and those of the people he'd just terrified.

When he closed the distance to fifty yards, another vehicle turned off 3rd Avenue. Forrester stopped dead in his tracks as the man working on the door turned a fraction, the light enveloping his face. Forrester knew him...knew him well, as it turned out.

Dan Hollingsworth.

CHAPTER NINETY
CORROBORATION

ATARIC
18:57 EST

Reid and Hunt were handcuffed, seated in chairs, and being watched raptly by two security guards – the second had just woken up, and continuously caressed the back of his head, where Hunt had slugged him earlier.

The only way Reid could save his and Hunt's life had been to surrender.

Baker, Fielding, and Clemence were huddled together, discussing what to do, when Baker's phone rang for a third time. This time, however, he was free to answer it.

"Hello?"

"Goddamnit, Jon! Where the hell have you been?" Baker could barely hear Forrester over the hum of traffic. "Red? I'm at Station Blue. Why?"

"I've been trying to get you for hours. Troy Davies is dead. And right now there are a group of men trying to get into ATARIC. Two of them are working on the front door as we speak. Jon, Dan Hollingsworth is working with them."

Baker closed his eyes, shook his head, inhaling and exhaling loudly. "I have two people here who seem to think terrorists have planned an attack on Station Blue tonight."

Forrester laughed at the irony. "I'd say it's a pretty safe bet they're right. That's why Davies ran from us at the airport this morning. He knew Hollingsworth was trying to kill him. Davies didn't know who to trust. He was trying to tell us about the attack but we weren't listening.

"Jon, I don't know how many are out here," Forrester continued. "I counted five, but these bastards look good. There could be upwards of a dozen. Hollingsworth's working on the door right now. I can't get any closer without risking my position."

Baker signalled for the security guards to lift Hunt and Reid to their feet. "Red, do me a favour. Get a couple of agents to the FEMA building at Hunters Point. If these guys know about ATARIC and Station Blue, there's a fair chance Hunters Point has been compromised. They'll never breach the biometrics, but their presence there will verify this threat."

The reply was laced with anger. "Why waste time? I'm standing here looking at them, Jon. That's all the verification you need. If you're in the upstairs facility right now, get the hell out of there. I'll try to stall them, but there're too many to engage alone. I'll call in backup as soon as I hang up."

Baker shielded the phone and pointed at Reid and Hunt. "Get the cuffs off them," he said, tossing the keys to the security guards. He turned to Fielding, who was about to protest but was silenced by a stern glare. "James, get everyone into the elevator now. We're going to Station Blue. Move!" He placed the phone back against his ear. "Red, we're moving – " A double bleep indicated Baker had another caller waiting. "One minute, Red. I've got another call. Stay on the line." Baker pressed number two and said, "Hello?"

"Jon, it's President Walsh. I've been trying to reach you for hours."

"Sorry, Mr President, I've been in Station Blue. I've only gotten topside in the last half hour," he replied, moving towards the elevator with the guide of the security guards' lights.

"That's what this is about, Jon. I've been presented with compelling evidence to suggest Station Blue will be attacked by terrorists this evening."

"Yes, sir, I've just received similar intelligence. We're taking pre-emptive measures right now."

The President continued in a sterner tone. "Jon, I don't need to remind you what will happen if terrorists gain access to Station Blue and acquire top-secret weapons and technology."

"No, Mr President, you do not." Baker stepped into the elevator, followed by the security guards and their freed prisoners. He gestured for Fielding to proceed, and ignored Clemence's angered looks.

"I've issued an edict to involve STRIKE Force in this. They're about twenty minutes out. They've been briefed on everything. They'll secure ATARIC, but I need you to stay and secure Station Blue and its weapons in the event they're unsuccessful."

"I thought STRIKE Force was only latent. You're saying it's operational?" asked Baker as the elevator began descending.

"As of now, yes."

"Understood, Mr President. We're on the way to Station Blue now. We will defend the facility until STRIKE Force neutralises the terrorists. In the event they don't, sir, I will initiate the plan we talked about before. Terrorists will never get their hands on our weapons, sir. You have my word."

"Thank you, Jon, and Godspeed."

Baker pressed one. "Red, you still there?"

"I'm here."

"That was the President. He's corroborated the attack, but he's going to send STRIKE Force to deal with it. We're going to lose comms in sixty seconds. I need you to stay outside and liaise with the STRIKE Force commander. Give him full co-operation. He's been fully briefed on Station Blue."

"Understand, Jon. Watch your back."

"You too. I'll talk to you soon."

As the elevator descended to basement level three, ATARIC's front door opened and Amos York stepped into the building, radio in hand.

CHAPTER NINETY-ONE
PLACEMENT

STRIKE FORCE STAGING AREA
ONE BLOCK FROM ATARIC
19: 27 EST

Leaving behind a warren of streets, Major Jack Carlos pulled his van over at the corner of East 39th Street and stepped into the cool breeze. He'd selected the location because of its proximity to ATARIC and the presence of Eastgate Tower Hotel directly across the street from it. Its lobby would serve as STRIKE Force's staging area.

The Osprey had landed at JFK fifteen minutes earlier, the Attorney General and Secretary of Defence absconding from the area as soon as they could find a vehicle. Carlos had requisitioned a van from the airport parking lot and used its GPS to find ATARIC.

He walked to the sliding door of the van and spoke up: "Okay, you all know why you're here. What we've been through in the last days and weeks has been unorthodox and, in some cases, inhumane; but you've all signed non-disclosure papers. You've all made the decision to join this team. Myself and Master – " Carlos caught himself. "Myself and Major Gyle are the provisional commanders of this unit. We'll do all the talking, but just in case any of you find yourselves in a situation, we are a military task force reporting directly to the President and *no one* else.

"I want a soft perimeter set up around ATARIC; Snipers in Eastgate and the Rio Grande. The rest I want split up between interior and exterior duties. Decide among yourselves who will be on entry, but do it quickly. I want the exterior group monitoring all law enforcement channels. Your job is containment. Do *not* let anyone into the building. Spread out throughout the area so no one can see you, but restrain any civilians who could compromise our presence. I'm going to get us a staging area right now. Stay out of sight until I do."

Gyle exited the van and began walking with his commander to Eastgate. "I could get used to 'Major Julio Gyle'. It has a nice ring to it." He laughed. "So what's the plan, *Papi?*"

"Recon. We wait for these guys to get here, then we take 'em down."

Carlos sensed someone was following them. Angling right, away from Eastgate, he took Gyle by the arm and led him across the street to an intersection. Gyle, knowing his commander had a reason for doing so, kept quiet. When Carlos rounded North-East 39th Street, he pushed Gyle into the vestibule of a bar and slipped into position beside him. When the man walked past the door, he reached out and yanked him inside.

"Who the hell are you?" he asked, spinning him about-face.

"Deputy Director William Forrester, FBI," Forrester replied. He then inquired if it was okay to reach into his pocket. When he did, he removed his badge.

Carlos studied it briefly. "Majors Carlos and Gyle, sir, United States military," he said, handing back the credentials. "My apologies, but may I ask what you're doing here?"

"You can drop the charade, Major. I know about STRIKE Force."

"Then you know we're here to prevent terrorists from gaining access to Station Blue?"

Forrester shook his head, sighed. "The situation has become more complicated than that, Major Carlos. The terrorists are already here and have occupied the building. As far as I'm aware, they cannot bypass the biometrics to gain access to Station Blue, but my confidence in that is evaporating by the minute."

They traded looks. Their approach had been designed on the assumption they'd arrive before the terrorists. If they were already here, his team were severely compromised.

"Sir," Carlos began, "our protocols were tailored for an on-site recon and takedown. We aren't tactically ready for a full-scale assault."

Forrester shook his head again. "I don't understand, Major. The protocols for those two entities are remarkably similar. What's the problem?"

Carlos gestured towards the street, and they began walking back to the hotel. "Mr Forrester, there's a big difference between a clandestine operation and a full-scale assault. Our men are prepped with the knowledge these terrorists are forthcoming, sir. Their being on-site changes the complexion of the situation."

"How, Major?" Forrester replied sharply, angry that Carlos hadn't elucidated himself.

"We were at a tactical advantage when we thought they weren't here. I was going to place my snipers in the Eastgate Hotel and the El Rio Grande restaurant. We were going to recon the area, learn their positions, and take them down accordingly. Sir, without that intel, I don't know where these terrorists are. Going blind into a battle-zone severely diminishes our chances of success."

They stepped into the lobby of the hotel and walked to the main desk. Here, Forrester produced his credentials and asked to speak with the manager. The receptionist informed them she'd be downstairs imminently. While they waited, Forrester queried Carlos about the chances of a successful mission without positional advantage.

"Sir, it's like a chess game. You strategically position your pieces to offer an auspicious advantage. Imagine you couldn't see the other player's pieces. Your chances would drop drastically."

"Okay, but can it be done?"

Carlos nodded. "Of course. We did it in Afghanistan. It was a tactical nightmare, but we did it. But Afghanistan was expansive territory. Finding terrorists in a concrete jungle at night time, sir, is a much more complex task."

"Major, we cannot let terrorists get their hands on American top-secret weaponry. Right now, Director Baker is in Station Blue. I need to know you're capable of averting this crisis." Forrester stared at him with a blank expression.

"I haven't had time to evaluate this team, sir. We've been thrown into this situation without any familiarity with each other. That's an oversight on DoD's behalf. But I will say this: These men are reputed to be the very best. Myself and Major Gyle are former Force Recon. So believe me when I say if there's a way to do this, we'll find it."

A middle-aged women – dressed in a blouse, jacket, and medium-length skirt, her hair neatly arranged in a chignon – emerged from an elevator. Forrester asked if they could speak with her privately. Inside her office, Carlos explained he needed the lobby cleared of all patrons immediately so his FBI task force could use it for their base of operations. The woman's attractive features hardened as he told her a redacted story about a known terrorist expected in the vicinity shortly. Her blue eyes narrowed as she regarded his every word with an unflinching gaze, looking for any indication his story was fabricated. What she saw instead was the mien of someone trained to dissimulate all emotion.

Hands on hips: "What am I supposed to tell my patrons? This is the lobby's busiest time. They're going to demand an explanation."

If he'd been off-duty, Carlos would have flirted with her. She was his kind of woman: strong, fiery, and independent. "Miss...?"

"Pierce," she replied, hands still firmly rooted on her hips, eyes unwavering.

"Miss Pierce, I give you my word that when my operation is complete we will egress the building immediately and your hotel will be compensated for any losses. Right now, I need you to make up an excuse. I don't care what, but *don't* mention terrorism. I need the lobby cleared as fast as possible, and all its entries and exits locked down once everyone has left. Can you do that?"

"I suppose I could do it in thirty minutes."

Her indignation and unwillingness to acquiesce annoyed Carlos. "Ma'am, we don't *have* thirty minutes. I will give you five, and then my men will escort any stragglers to a detention point. I don't want to do that. I would prefer to keep our presence here off the radar. But if you give me no other choice, I'll have to."

"This is highly unorthodox. Don't you need a warrant for something like this?"

"Miss Pierce, the situation demands a blunt approach. This is a time-sensitive mission. If there was any other way, we'd do it. There isn't. Please start escorting your patrons out of the lobby. I want everyone – employees included – out of here now."

Pierce looked to Forrester, let her gaze wander back to Carlos and Gyle, and then locked her eyes on all three but remained silent.

"Please, madam," Forrester pleaded. "Do as we ask."

"Fine, but I *will* pursue compensation."

Pierce stormed out of her office, wondering how she could explain the need for an exodus from the lobby without raising a panic. Her relationship with her patrons had been amicable for years. Lying to them now, if discovered, would damage trust between them. If that happened, she'd make damned sure the FBI was held accountable.

Sons of bitches.

In the office, Forrester asked Carlos how long it would take to prioritise his men and have them mission-ready.

"After the lobby's clear, about ten minutes."

"In twenty minutes, we're going into ATARIC, mission-ready or not, gentlemen," Forrester replied.

CHAPTER NINETY-TWO
OVERSIGHT

OUTSIDE ATARIC
19: 35 EST

Standing on the corner of 3rd Avenue, Vladimir Pushkin appraised the vista in front of him. He'd never served in any military service, but had years of experience as an ersatz private military commando, though he'd never allow himself to be called such a thing. His first instinctive reaction told him Ivanovich's team were already inside ATARIC. Their weapons, appearances, and demeanours all screamed either "terrorist" or "Russian".

His second instinctive reaction told him someone else was present. Not cops. Not even New York's famed Emergency Service Unit.

He jogged across the street to look for a vantage point. Checking for any spectators, he tossed his workbag onto the roof of a bus and clambered up after it. Crawling to the front offered him a vantage of both the El Rio Grande and Eastgate Tower Hotel. But his eyes locked on the van parked equidistant to both. It appeared empty, but he waited sixty seconds; a lone man stepped out, dressed in full tactical gear, minus a helmet, and walked a circuitous route to the Eastgate.

Pushkin grimaced. The mannerisms of this man told him everything he needed to know. He was military. Their presence changed the entire scenario. Ivanovich's group of poseurs would be annihilated by this superior phalanx of soldiers. No way to contact Ivanovich (even if he had, Pushkin doubted if he wanted to) meant Ivanovich would be walking into an ambush the moment he exited "Station Blue". In a way, it solved his problem of determining how to kill Ivanovich. But if Ivanovich died and HRT reacquired the technology and weaponry he'd stolen, today's work would be for nothing. He couldn't afford to let that happen, but he could do little against these protean super-soldiers. Even a one-by-one elimination was impossible. HRT worked in dual groups, no man ever left alone by his partner for more than thirty seconds.

He could pick them off from his current vantage, using the gear in his workbag, but none of it was silenced and at this hour the muzzle flashes would give his position away immediately. Besides, he had no idea of their numbers. Alternatively, he could wait for Ivanovich to exit ATARIC, and then create a distraction to aid him. He'd tail Ivanovich to his safe-house, kill him, and requisition the material.

One thing he knew for certain: he couldn't do nothing. He'd come too far, invested too much, and sacrificed his anonymity to ensure this mission succeeded.

Failure was not even a consideration.

CHAPTER NINETY-THREE
LEVEL THREE

```
LEVEL THREE STATION BLUE
19: 42 EST
```

Of all the things Peter Hunt expected to be on level three, what he saw now was not among them. A mammoth laboratory – easily twice the size of ATARIC's main floor – comprised much of the three-storey atrium. Hunt and the others were standing on a raised balcony – some eighty feet above a garish white floor – which ran the width of the entire laboratory, all four corners equipped with an exterior elevator. Baker guided them to the nearest one.

"What the hell is this place?" Reid demanded, looking over the edge as they neared the glistening floor.

Ignoring the vehement headshake from Fielding, Baker begin to narrate the purpose of "Station Blue". He explained that, in the aftermath of 9/11, the President initiated two top-secret schemes to maximise the security and efficiency of the United States. The first one, codenamed "Station Blue", began as an intelligence-gathering facility analogous to the NSA. (As he said that, Hunt suddenly figured out the purpose of the "Jamie Signfeld" account). During the next twelve months, it became a victim of its own success. The intelligence gathered equalled the

NSA's, presenting the opportunity for an expansion. With weapons-development facilities existing in numerous locations throughout the country, the President was at first sceptical about upgrading "Station Blue". But his advisors convinced him that ATARIC provided an ideal front, whose location would both be undetectable and impenetrable. Within days, "Station Blue" became a development and intelligence community, free from Congressional oversight, its existence a highly guarded and esoteric secret; one which had now fallen into the hands of terrorists.

It took a moment for Reid to compose himself. Then he asked, "You said *two* top-secret schemes. What was the other one?"

"Jon, they aren't cleared for any of this," Clemence fumed as the elevator touched down.

Baker regarded him with gimlet eyes. "They risked their lives to warn us about this attack, Roger. The least we can do is fill in the blanks."

"They aren't a part of this!" Fielding interjected. "They're menial workers at best. This is my livelihood...my legacy!" the old man croaked.

Baker stepped onto the white floor, turned back to Fielding. "Well I'm making them a part of it, James! Because we have a situation here in which their being kept in the dark benefits no one. So if you want to order them back upstairs to face certain death, do it. But if there's a conscience left in that decaying body of yours, shut the hell up and let's figure a way out of this goddamn mess before we're *all* dead!"

Fielding retreated as though he'd been slapped. He gave Baker an appraising look, as if seeing him for the first time. Then his eyes dropped to the floor and he mumbled "Fine."

"As I was saying..."

Hunt blocked out Baker's narration, staring instead at the complex which seemed endless. The white floor was littered with desks; computers; wreathing cords duct-taped to the floor, leading to machines marked by variegating colours; countless antechambers locked down by reinforced doors with bullet-resistant glass, leading into bigger labs which Hunt couldn't see clearly; and to top it all off, several images of cell phones with diagonal lines stroked through them. At the end, a set of stairs led up three levels. These stairs, though, were separate from the raised balcony and led to an area only accessible by climbing them. Hunt keyed back into the conversation to hear Baker explain that level two housed a conference room for meetings with department heads, a lunch room, and an amenities room. Level three contained the bio-hazard labs.

"Wait a goddamn minute! You're talking about chemical and biological weaponry?" Hunt asked.

"Mr Hunt, I understand your concern, but those labs are hermetically sealed. Every substance is documented and handled by professionally trained scientists. The chambers are bulletproof, not to mention being equipped with cutting-edge detection systems: infrared sensors, motion sensors, temperature-alteration sensors, x-ray scanners, as well as a purification and filtration system designed to decontaminate air in the event of a leakage. They are safe, Mr Hunt, and rigorously checked to remain so. Right now, they're locked down, and only James can open them. The terrorists will not gain access, I promise you."

"But it's biological and chemical warfare!" Hunt protested. "We were supposed to have discontinued chemical and biological testing and stockpiling."

"You see, this is why you people don't need to know anything about this!" Fielding grumped.

"James!" Baker warned.

"They're civilians, Jon! They don't understand what it is to be a patriot." Fielding locked his gaze on Hunt. "This country needs a place like this; needs people like myself and Dave Haskens – people willing to do what's necessary to protect the future of America!"

"You wanna know what it is to be a patriot, James?" Hunt began in a low, seething tone. "It's about dedicating your life to something you thought was real, only to find you've been lied to for years, and then having the self-control to remain calm and not report the place to the Chemical Weapons Convention!"

Fielding gave him an incredulous look, but before he could speak, Hunt continued, "We're wasting time with territorial pissings. You don't want this place discovered, and we don't wanna die. So let's come to some kind of compromise. We'll do whatever we can to fend off these terrorists. Myself and Jack are

– were, rather – experienced hunters. So if there are any conventional weapons in this place, start doling them out."

"And what do you want in return, Hunt?" Fielding glared.

Hunt took Reid to one side and conversed with him. Several salvos were exchanged, before Hunt turned back to Fielding and said, "We're just as much patriots as you are. We'll keep this place secret, help you with the terrorists, but in return we want to be a part of it."

Fielding gave another vehement headshake. "Not going to happen, Hunt. I've put my life into this building, both upstairs and down. If one person learns about this place who shouldn't know anything about it, I may lose the entire thing."

"You're about to lose your life, James. Either here tonight, if you don't do as we ask, or in another month when your body gives in. Me and Jack put ATARIC on the map. Without us, you wouldn't be where you are today. You said it yourself: you had high hopes for me. Well I'm giving you the chance to rekindle them."

"James." Baker got Fielding's attention. "You may own ATARIC, but Station Blue belongs to the government. You report to the President, and as his chosen representative for this facility, I'm ordering you to stand down and accept this offer."

"Jon – "

Baker rose a hand. "I will get them to sign non-disclosure papers when this is over. I give you my word." Fielding's expression remained blank. "For Godsakes, James! We're running out of time." He switched his gaze to Hunt and Reid. "Your offer is accepted, gentlemen. Weapons are in the last two labs on this floor."

Above their heads, the whirr of an elevator sounded. Hunt noticed it wasn't any of the four exterior ones. The sound was too tenuous for that. The elevator they'd travelled to this facility in was now going back up.

"Should it be doing that?" Baker's wide-eyed stare answered his question. "What does that mean?" Hunt continued, a little more agitated.

Fielding spoke up. "It's okay. It just means someone called the elevator. Without a key-card they can't get down here."

"What if they have a key-card?"

Fielding shook his head. "The only people who have key-cards are Dave Haskens and us," he replied, pointing to Baker and Clemence.

"Where is Haskens now?"

"Dave left when the meeting ended. He's at home," Fielding replied.

Hunt shook his head and frowned. "Let me understand this. We stopped on level two, entered a highly secure hatch, and climbed down stairs to this facility. You're telling me Dave left here how long ago?"

"About an hour, I suppose. What's your point, Hunt?" Fielding asked.

"I've been watching those elevators all day. Haskens did not exit through ATARIC this evening. So how did he get out?"

Fielding looked to Baker, who reluctantly nodded his head. "Dave lives close to Hunters Point – "

"He used the secret tunnel," Hunt revealed, nodding.

"How'd you know that?" It was Baker's turn to be angry.

"For an intelligence-gathering facility, this place sucks. The article I intended to show you by a man called 'Daedalus' hints at this location. In fact, I'd say he's got it spot on."

"He mentions the secret tunnel?" Baker was sceptical.

"Right down to the ostensible ownership by FEMA. The article is the reason why I found out about the terrorist plot."

The elevator didn't reach level three. Hunt noticed that beside the ladder they'd descended, there was an electronic readout displaying its current floor. Presently, it read: ONE. He moved to the end of the hall and climbed the stairs to get a better view. Perplexed by his actions, the rest followed. "Apparently this place isn't as well-kept a secret as you guys thought," he continued, eyes rooted to the display. "If some low-level computer hacker can find it, a well-funded terrorist group can do the same with a kid's detective set."

Hunt watched the display for several minutes. When it didn't move, he gave a sigh of relief and started back down the stairs. As he looked back up to reassure himself, he felt his blood turn to ice.

The display now read: B1

Grabbing Fielding, he pointed to it and said, "What does that do for your key-card theory!"

CHAPTER NINETY-FOUR
INCURSION

ATARIC
19:49 EST

Carlos flicked down his goggles and stepped through the main doors. Gyle covered him from behind, angling right as he entered. He moved in a crouch, rifle oscillating. In infrared, the room appeared as a variation of colours ranging from red to blue, denoting the hottest and coldest points. The computers were yellow, the radiators red. Gyle scanned his entire quadrant, searching for the silhouette and heat source of a human.

Eight more soldiers entered, moving in cover formation, their footsteps skilfully cautious. Two of them took the stairs to Fielding's office, two more, Reid's. The remainder began checking the five floors above.

Carlos stood in the middle of the main hall, flanked on both sides by desks. The vista triggered flashbacks to the CIA building a few hours earlier. This time, though, he was prepared. Rifle in hand, he moved alongside each desk, rolling chairs back, checking foot-space underneath. He didn't for a second think a terrorist would be hiding there, but he couldn't afford to take the chance. When he finished the main hall, he checked the men's and women's toilets. He kicked open every stall, his rifle dropping into position each time as the wooden doors clanged against tile. Within sixty seconds, the toilets were cleared.

Carlos came back to find his men returning from their quadrants. All of them, Gyle included, reported "clear". Carlos grabbed Gyle and led him to the main doors, where he signalled Forrester to join them from across the street. "There're no terrorists in here," he began. "So either there were never any to begin with..."

"I saw them, Major!" Forrester replied sharply.

"...or they're already downstairs."

Forrester's face waned. "That's impossible. You need a key-card to access the elevator. Only five people possess them. Four of them are downstairs. The President is the last one."

"There are ways around key-cards, sir," Gyle said.

Forrester took a step back, shaken. "We talked about putting in a retinal scanner, but employees use that elevator every day. It would have only raised suspicion."

"There are also ways around elevators," Carlos mused. He turned back, to where the rest of his team had assembled in a huddle, and said, "Guys, get that elevator door open now."

While they set about that task, Forrester asked, "What are you thinking, Major?"

"Open the hatch in the roof and use the governor cable to descend to the bottom."

Forrester looked at him as though he were crazy. "That's suicide! And besides, the elevator only takes you to level two. To get to level three, you have to go through a hatch that's protected by retinal and fingerprint scanning. Even if the terrorists can falsify a key-card, they can't fool biometrics."

Struck by an unnerving thought, Carlos turned on his heel and forged ahead to the elevator. He brushed aside two of his men as Gyle guided Forrester through the darkened room. Carlos used every inch of his six-foot-four frame to reach up to the roof of the elevator. It made a dull sound when he rapped on it. "Plastic," he mumbled. Turning to one of his men, he said, "Make a four-foot-wide hole in this roof, soldier. We're going down the governor cable."

"Major, you plan on telling me how you think you're going to do that? That cable will rip your men to pieces."

Using the beam of a flashlight so Forrester could see, he

tugged on a line lapped around a cylindrical object on the bottom of his vest, on the end of which was a hook. "Rappelling line, sir."

"Fine, Major, but that doesn't explain how you think you're going to get past the biometrics."

"Sir, the terrorists didn't need to use the governor cable. It stands to reason they also have a countermeasure for the biometrics."

Forrester looked him dead in the eye. "What are you saying, soldier?"

Marines were never called soldiers, but Carlos was no longer a Marine. He let the disrespect slide. "They didn't come here without knowledge of this place. If they're on level two right now, you can bet the farm they know about the hatch."

Forrester gritted his teeth. He was beginning to dislike Carlos' omissions and cryptic nature. "You didn't answer my question, son. What countermeasures?"

"None that are savoury, Mr Forrester..."

***

Dan Hollingsworth exited the elevator last. Around his shoulder, a black workbag hung. The weight and contents of it sagged his shoulders. He continued to the hatch – a large cast-iron door six feet high by two feet wide, on the corner of which were two electronic devices – where Ivanovich and the rest of his team were waiting. Barely able to control the incipient tears, Hollingsworth lifted the strap over his head and set the bag on the floor beside Ivanovich. He stepped back from it as though the contents were toxic. He covered his face and eyes with his hands, feeling the hardened cast of erstwhile tears, the chafing prickle of stubble, and the whittled form of his nails.

Ivanovich ignored him and removed the first item from the bag. He placed the small object on the fingerprint scanner. After several seconds, the machine beeped and a message appeared: FINGERPRINT RECOGNISED. PLEASE PROCEED TO THE RETINAL SCANNER. Replacing it in the bag, he removed the second – a human head, from which dripped blood. He grasped it with his entire hand and placed it against the retinal scanner. A similar message appeared, and the hatch emitted a hissing sound and cracked open.

"Nice work, Dan." Ivanovich handed him a cell phone. "A man will ring you in ten minutes with the location of your wife and child."

As Ivanovich and his men descended the ladder, leaving the bag and its contents to one side, Hollingsworth clutched the phone, fighting back tears, and hit the call switch for the elevator.

***

Carlos had just hoisted himself to a standing position on the roof when the elevator doors closed, entrapping Gyle, Forrester, and two other STRIKE Force members inside. Before any of them had a chance to hit a button, the elevator dropped precipitously. The suddenness caught Carlos by surprise. His feet went from under him, and he hit the roof with all his weight, punching through the plastic as though it were a sheet of paper. The rappelling line whirred as it unwound, then inexplicably jammed. Carlos slammed to a halt, suspended above the floor in a supine position, like a bungee jump gone horribly wrong. Before anyone could reach up, the hook above snapped off and Carlos fell the remaining five feet to floor.

"God-*damn!*" Carlos exhaled, helped to his feet by Gyle. "Why are these sons of bitches coming back up so early?"

As the elevator doors opened, Forrester's eyes grew wide, his face twisting into a sneer of contempt. He moved before anyone else could, grabbed a perplexed Hollingsworth, and slammed him into the wall so hard he thought he'd broken his back. A painful expulsion of air escaped from Hollingsworth's mouth as Forrester rested his pistol against his head.

"I think you've got some explaining to do, Dan! Starting with why the hell you're working with..." He trailed off as he noticed a crimson liquid pooling out from underneath a bag behind Hollingsworth's feet. Carlos had already noticed, and got there before Forrester. He lifted the item by its hair, which was tainted with a smear of blood. More blood dripped from what remained of a severed neck. When Carlos turned it to face Forrester, the deputy director's shoulders slumped.

"You know him?" Carlos asked, still holding the ghastly

head.

"I tried to get him to come," Hollingsworth sobbed. "I told him these bastards had my wife, but he wouldn't listen."

Forrester slammed him into the wall again. "What are you talking about, Dan! Who has Julie?"

"They kidnapped her and Ben yesterday." He broke down in a paroxysm of tears. "They said they'd kill them if I didn't do exactly what they told me."

Forrester closed his eyes, sighed. "That's why you shot the PAPD kid. The terrorists wanted you to kill Davies, didn't they?"

Hollingsworth nodded.

"But the kid got to you before you could reach Davies. And then you did what any desperate father would have. You killed him to get to Davies, but he was already gone. But why did you come back? Why didn't you chase after him?"

Hollingsworth composed himself. "Because, after I failed, they told me I'd be given another chance to get my family back. They said to continue as if nothing had happened and wait for a phone call. I got that call earlier tonight. They gave me an address and told me to take the man who lived there to this location. But he wouldn't come," he continued, tears beginning again. "I told him everything! He said he wouldn't negotiate with terrorists. I knew what they needed him for. So I..." Forrester let him go and Hollingsworth dropped to his knees. "I did it for my family!" His entire body shook with sobs. In a heartbroken, childlike voice: "I did it for my family."

Carlos, not wishing to be insensitive but aware time was not on their side, pointed to the head in his hand. "Can someone please tell me who this is?"

Forrester sighed. "That would be someone I thought was downstairs with the others. It's Dave Haskens."

CHAPTER NINETY-FIVE
THE GREATER GOOD

```
LEVEL THREE
19: 53 EST
```

Once they heard the hatch opening, everyone – Fielding included – knew this was no longer a game of cry wolf. Their worst nightmare had come to pass, made brutally clear by the clangour of boots on metal rungs. Fielding knew what he had to do.

"Upstairs. Now!" he bellowed. "Everyone to the third floor. Follow the gangway around to the biological pods."

Baker turned, knowing Fielding's plan but also aware it had one major flaw. "James – "

"Jon!" Fielding shook his head. He continued in a sombre tone. "It has to be done."

"What's going on?" Hunt asked.

Fielding grabbed Hunt and gave him a small push. "Not now, Peter. Up the stairs!"

As the reverberating clangour grew closer, the conglomerate sped up the staircase. Fielding's weakened body should have slowed him down, but the adrenaline coursing through him allowed him, remarkably, to keep pace with the younger group. At each landing, Fielding grabbed the newel post and swung himself around, taking the stairs two at a time, but not three like he had in his military days. The thought sent him back to the jungles of Vietnam, and for the first time since being diagnosed with cancer, Fielding cracked a genuine smile. He was doing the right thing; what needed to be done.

Up ahead, Clemence rounded the gangway at pace, following it left, then right, until he reached the bio-hazard labs. He paused at the door and waited for a breathless Fielding to arrive. Beneath them, the sound of voices echoed off the walls. Orders both in Russian and English were barked. Fielding wasted no time. Ripping out his key-card, he swiped it through a reader on the door, then entered a code into a numeric keypad beside it. A loud hissing sounded, then the door rose and locked into position above.

"Get in!" Fielding ordered. He could make out the shapes of people below, and he knew he needed everyone inside now. "Come on, come on!" he said, ushering Reid and the two security guards in. Hunt, unsurprisingly, came last. He turned to Fielding but before he could say anything, Fielding cut him off. "Peter, get in. We don't have time."

"If you opened the door with your key-card, they can open it with theirs. If we go in here, we're trapped."

"No. Only my key-card opens and closes this door. Haskens, much to his displeasure, has no access to this room. Get in now, Peter!"

Hunt nodded, but when he stepped through the door he realised Fielding wasn't following. Turning, he saw him outside. Hunt asked, "What are you doing, James?"

For a fleeting moment, Fielding was reminded of why he admired Hunt so much. No one in the company, save for people of equal standing, had the hardihood to call him by his first name. But Hunt had always done so when angry, mad, or attempting to acquire Fielding's attention. The rest of the time, he deferred to "sir". Now Fielding was glad he'd had the chance to reinstate Hunt and make things right. It made what he was about to do somewhat easier.

His face, though sombre, also bore a look of acceptance. "I'm sorry about tricking you earlier, Peter, but I also meant what I said in the office. You are the best computer programmer in this country. And I have every confidence you and Jack will keep this place running when I'm gone." Behind him, the rataplan of numerous boots ascending stairs grew closer. "It's time. Everyone step back from the door."

Hunt watched as Fielding moved to the card reader again and removed his key-card from his pocket. "Why aren't you coming in here?" he asked, but he already knew the answer.

"I'm afraid the labs can only be hermetically sealed from the outside. It's a safety feature to ensure that, in the event of leakage, someone caught inside can't open the door and contaminate the rest of the lab."

The sound grew stronger. Closer. Accompanied by sharp orders.

"Once the door's sealed, use the computer with the red screensaver to operate the fans. This building, as I'm sure you're aware, is powered by a generator in the event of a blackout. It will keep the fans circulating for over three days. Help, as Jon will tell you, is already on the way. The terrorists won't get into this room. All you have to do is wait it out."

"Wait!" Hunt cried as Fielding motioned to swipe his card. "If you stay out there, they'll kill you and take your card."

"They won't," Fielding said, swishing the card through the reader. The door fell twice as fast as it had ascended. Then, like the hiss from the air brakes of a truck, it sealed...just as the first of the terrorists rounded the gangway. Fielding, with his back to them, grimaced as he gripped the card in his thumb and forefinger and exerted pressure. His feeble, bony fingers couldn't bend the material. Panicking, Fielding crouched over and put every last ounce of energy into it. A loud snap filled the air, but any hope of it coming from the card dissipated when Fielding's piercing scream trilled loud enough to be heard through the bulletproof glass. Clutching a broken, bloodied finger, he lunged to the banister and flung the card through an opening in the Perspex. It fell three storeys to the ground below, nestling alongside a snarled cord.

Fielding watched as the leader peered over the Perspex sheeting. He muttered something in Russian to one of his comrades, who broke away from the group and retraced his path downstairs.

"James Fielding, I presume," Ivanovich said.

Fielding was surprised at the fluency of his English. "What

do you want?"

"What I want is of no concern to you."

In the lab, Hunt looked on in horror as the long-haired man raised a pistol. Though the gun wasn't silenced, the bulletproof glass reduced the sound to a muffled bang. The image, though, would endure in his head for years to come. Fielding did not flinch, nor beg. He stood ramrod straight, despite the pains which ravaged his body, just as he had in his time with the military. The bullet snapped his head back with enough force to break his weakened neck, the blood cascading like a waterfall as the defunct body crashed through the Perspex and tumbled over the banister. It fell the remaining distance to the ground below, impacting with a horrendous thud and the crack of more bones.

Ivanovich regarded a horrified Hunt with gimlet eyes. The intense stare caused him to break eye contact, and sent a shiver down his spine. When he looked back, Ivanovich mouthed two words that made his skin crawl.

"You're next".

CHAPTER NINETY-SIX
CELER, SILENS, MORTALIS

LEVEL THREE
20:01 EST

Forrester had decided to accompany Hollingsworth to his wife's location, so Carlos exited the hatch last. When he reached the ground, he saw his team were disposed around the first floor, mostly to check the labs, but Carlos also knew they were committing hiding places to memory. Even though the lights were operating, his men moved much the same way they had upstairs, albeit without goggles.

Upstairs, he could see the silhouettes of several people on a gangway. Unlike the one he'd been standing on ninety seconds earlier, this one was about fifty feet above the main floor. He looked up to see if the eighty-foot-high gangway gave access to the lower one he occupied. It didn't appear so, and he began wondering how he was supposed to get to the terrorists. He got his answer fifteen seconds later.

Having moved into the middle of the atrium to catch up to his team, he was caught in the open when a unitary terrorist emerged from a staircase. He froze, hoping stillness would help, but wearing an all-black outfit in a predominately white environment did him no favours. When the terrorist's head rose, he noticed the incongruity at once. First, his rifle came up. Then, he went to roar.

Carlos, forgetting he held a silenced rifle, wrenched his HALO knife from a pouch and snapped the blade out with a flick of his wrist. With another one, he sent it whistling across the ten-metre void. Just as the terrorist started to turn to alert his comrades, it struck him to the right of the larynx, burying itself to the hilt. The young man tried to cry out, but the knife lacerated his jugular vein. A sea of red exploded from the wound, accompanied by a sickly gurgling. He collapsed, clutching at his throat, as the life ebbed from his body.

Carlos covered the distance and, grabbing the back of the man's head away from the protruding blade, yanked the knife free, wiping the blood on the sleeve of the dead man's jacket. Re-sheathing it, he grabbed the body around the legs and dragged it around the corner, out of sight. Gyle appeared beside him and congratulated him on a perfect throw, but Carlos pointed to the stairs.

He took point, leading his three-man team to the foot of the stairs. The remainder were still upstairs, but Forrester had assured Carlos he'd send them down. He and his men needed to remain unseen until then.

"What do you wanna do, *Papi?*" Gyle asked, as Carlos raised a hand.

"There's about at least half a dozen upstairs. Plus, Directors Baker and Clemence are in the facility somewhere. We need to do this quickly and quietly, Julio. I'm going to lure a few of them downstairs. You guys pick them off." He turned to face the other two members, Larry Lansdale and John Mason.

"You guys up for this?" Carlos didn't need to ask the question, but he wanted to ensure they weren't distrait. Both gave different variations of an answer which left no doubt. "All right. I know enough Russian to get a few of them downstairs. If you haven't already, affix silencers now. Let's do this."

Carlos climbed to the first landing. In a loud, deep voice, he shouted, *"Vy mOzhite mne pamOch?"* Meaning: "Can you help me?" He said it again to make sure, and then waited. Within seconds, footsteps pounded above his head. Two sets, he judged, moving back downstairs to join his team.

"Get ready."

Carlos and Gyle took position behind one of the labs, while Lansdale and Mason mirrored them on the opposite side. Carlos raised two fingers and they nodded.

The first one descended into view seconds later. Carlos watched him from the corner of his eye. Waiting. The terrorist bore the unmistakeable features of a Russian. Fair skin, emaciated face, but strong, determined eyes. Carlos still waited. He couldn't afford to wait much longer, or the man would discover his dead comrade.

C'mon, where the hell are you?

The second one should have been right on the first's heels. That he wasn't suggested either Carlos had mistaken the pounding from above, or they were being cautious. Either way, he could only let the first advance another five yards.

The second appeared just as the first crossed the threshold. Carlos nodded to Lansdale, who swung out in tandem half a second later. Even as he was spinning, Carlos' rifle began its upward trajectory. When he planted his feet firmly, the MP5-SD locked into position tight against his shoulder, the sights coming to rest on the second Russian's head.

A single round loosed. It hit just forward of the ear, fragmenting when it struck bone. Carlos would forever remember it as a horrible but deadly shot. It ripped the face explosively from the skull. Forehead, nose, and mouth coalesced into a red mist, the blood venting from a dozen lacerations. Like a puppet whose strings had been severed, the second Russian pirouetted to the ground.

Lansdale's shot was much better, but his advantage was proximity. Nevertheless, the round hit the first terrorist above the bridge of the nose. Lansdale's rounds, Carlos now learned, were hollow points. On impact, it expanded to twice its size. A cloud of pink-red spewed from an inch-wide exit hole, and the Russian ceased all functionality.

Carlos turned to find five more men joining him from the elevator, among them Nathan Murphy and Kürt Fromm. The German hurried to Carlos and gave him a situation report.

"Count four more upstairs, *Chef*. They're guarding a room with six people inside. It appears they can't get in."

Murphy, standing beside the body of James Fielding, whispered, "Major, think you better come take a look at this."

Carlos didn't know how he'd missed it. When he came over, Murphy handed him a bloodied key-card. "Found it about ten yards away. Looks like someone was trying to break it. Probably this guy," Murphy finished, pointing at Fielding. "I'm thinking it opens the pods upstairs. I'm also thinking those pods contain hazardous materials."

"What makes you say that, Sergeant?" Carlos looked him in eye.

"If the windows weren't bulletproof glass, they'd have shot their way in by now. The door looks to be sealed airtight. Only one kind of room needs *that* much security."

Carlos nodded, musing. "So this key-card is the only thing standing between those terrorists and a stockpile of biological weaponry? Okay, if that's true, they're going to send more of their men down here to find out what's keeping the others. We stay our ground and pick them off as they come."

Fromm raised his hand and said, "I think I have another way..."

HAPTER NINETY-SEVEN
STRATAGEM

```
LEVEL THREE
20: 10 EST
```

Sergei Ivanovich had not heard as much as a whisper from any of the three men he'd sent to retrieve the key-card. In between, he'd tried Haskens' on the door, but a buzzer had sounded. He figured Fielding's desperation to destroy the card meant his was the only one which opened the bio-hazard labs.

Pavel Kirov's mission had been to rid "Station Blue" of all its technology. His *original* mission. The emergence of a spy within the ranks had changed that. Now, it had become a quick in-and-out mission to retrieve as much technology and weaponry as possible. There had been no mention of how much that equalled suicide.

Ivanovich had worked for Kirov for almost two decades, but of late he'd begun making several high-profile mistakes. Lapses of concentration and judgement, forgetfulness, and an argumentative relationship with Kirov had pushed Ivanovich down the pecking order. This mission had seemed to be his salvation, but the impetuosity with which it had been planned and initiated bothered Ivanovich from the beginning. Yes, their security had been compromised by Troy Davies (dead, unbeknownst to Ivanovich) and, yes, it had required a quick response to ensure all their planning didn't peter out into nothing. But the most efficient way of dealing with it would have been to neutralise Davies. Then, they could have orchestrated a better plan for breaking into "Station Blue". As it was, this was a fool's errand with only one possible outcome: Ivanovich's death. The one thing Kirov had forgotten, it seemed, was that Sergei Bogdan Ivanovich was no fool.

Despite York's protests to leave at least one member outside as a lookout, Ivanovich had taken the entire team into ATARIC – eight, including himself. It wasn't that he thought he needed the help. He'd always been a keen observer. He knew, the same way Pushkin had, that American soldiers were present outside. He also knew someone on the team, or perhaps a freelancer hired by Kirov, was going to kill him before the night ended. So he'd devised his own escape plan.

Knowing his life might be at risk during the operation, Ivanovich had done research on every aspect of ATARIC, including "Station Blue". On the first floor of level three, an elevator led to an underground parking garage. A tunnel continued from the garage, went underneath East River, and emerged from a FEMA building in Hunters Point. He had learned that accessing this tunnel from Hunters Point was almost impossible. Retinal scans, fingerprint scans, voice recognition pattern checks, and special holographic devices were needed before access could even be dreamed of. The President and those privy to "Station Blue" knew it would be suicide to attack the structure that way, so they'd concentrated the bulk of their security measures at ATARIC and a frontal assault. In doing so, they'd decided that the route back through the tunnel needed to be bereft of biometrics. The idea was that, in the event of a break-in, people in level three could lock down those labs which were bulletproof, and jettison the material from the remaining rooms into vehicles in the parking lot. To escape the tunnel quickly, the blast door at the end was opened by a button inside. Which meant Ivanovich needed only Dave Haskens' key-card to open the elevator, and his path from there to freedom was a 2.7-mile tunnel.

Which was why, when the room descended into darkness twenty seconds later – as he knew it would – Ivanovich snapped a small object onto the banister of the gangway and tossed something else over the top. Before the assault team could flick down their NVGs, he leapt over the opening.

***

Robert Archer (often said to have an apt surname) had been a sniper with the FBI's Hostage Rescue Team before being transferred to STRIKE Force. A patriot whose loyalties lay only with America, Archer had considered the redeployment a gross misuse of power. HRT consisted of only fifty-odd members, and he'd undergone sedulous training to make the cut sixteen months ago – only for it to be taken from him fourteen days earlier, for what, at first, seemed an unimpressive training camp for soldiers who differed in everything from training regimes to skin colour. But, as Archer soon learned, the team being assembled made HRT look like the Boy Scouts.

Perched atop the eighty-foot gangway, eyes peering through a ten-power Unerthl heat-vision 'scope, Archer was the last of Carlos' eight-man insertion team. As it turned out, he was also the key one.

Kürt Fromm's simple, but deadly, plan *did* involve killing the power. Carlos had found a way to cut the feed to the generator for sixty seconds. After that, the system would reboot and lock out any further attempts. Fromm's plan, though, also involved Archer taking down the remaining terrorists with his rifle.

As the room blackened, he worked the first round into his sniper rifle. Subconsciously counting down time, he lined the cross hairs on the bridge of the first terrorist's nose and squeezed the trigger. The silenced round bared out of the gun, covering the distance in under half a second. It struck the target's philtrum on a downward trajectory, blowing a hole out the back of his neck, taking the medulla oblongata with it in a shower of blood. The "Death Shot".

Before the man began to fall, Archer chambered another round.

Forty-five.

CHAPTER NINETY-EIGHT
TUNNEL VISION

LEVEL THREE
20:20 EST

Ivanovich landed on the floor, hearing the unmistakeable sound of someone's head being blown apart. He hated to leave York – someone whom he'd worked with for years – behind to meet certain death, but survival instinct kicked in. Ivanovich was not prepared to die for nothing.

He discarded the rappelling line, tracing the contours of the walls and wreathing cables back to the elevator. He'd memorised the path earlier, but following it in darkness proved to be harder than anticipated. He didn't know how long the lights would remain off, but he needed to be at the elevator before they came back on.

How he wished for a pair of night-vision goggles. Another oversight in a mission full of them. But he couldn't do anything about that now.

He tripped on a cable. Stumbled. Once. Twice. Then hit the ground with a thud as loud as the sound of another head being blown to pieces. *Goddamn cables!*

Ivanovich didn't stay down for long. Unaware of the cuts across his hands, he pushed himself back to his feet. But the fall had disorientated him. Not knowing which direction he now faced, he was forced to guess the way to the elevator. Blindly reaching out for a landmark that might guide him, his hands landed on something solid. He scratched it. Clawed it. Panic gripped him. What was it?

The corner of the lab nearest the elevator!

On wobbly knees, he staggered in the general direction of the elevator, hands sliding along the wall until they reached inky blackness as the lab disappeared. He almost stumbled again. Caught himself as his body threatened to upend into the abyss. He angled right, probing now with feet instead of hands.

Another sound from above. He ignored it. It seemed the cables ended in tandem with the labs. But Ivanovich's sensory-deprived body worked against him. Without anything to hold on to, his entire world spinning vertiginously, he fell to the ground again. He gagged as dizziness engulfed him. Overcome by the efforts of the last twelve hours, Ivanovich's lassitude caused his entire body to shake convulsively.

He fought on, dragging himself across the floor with his hands, what remained of his adrenaline not allowing him to realise his path to the elevator might as well have been made by Hansel and Gretel.

Driven by an ineffable desire to survive, Ivanovich pulled himself by one hand until he could go no farther. When he reached up, he felt what could only be the console of the elevator. Infused with an extra burst of adrenaline, Ivanovich wrested Haskens' key-card from his pocket and thrust it upward. Waiting. Another second. Now!

As the power returned to the box, and the room was irradiated with fulgent light, Ivanovich stretched every inch of his six-foot frame to reach the card reader. With all the energy he could muster, he swiped it through, stabbing at the OPEN DOOR button thereafter. As the doors opened and the sharp orders of the assault team echoed through level three, Ivanovich collapsed into the elevator, barely able to reach up and hit the button for the doors to close.

***

The combination of the silenced rifle and darkness bewildered the four remaining terrorists. After the second had fallen, the remaining two ducked below the Perspex, figuring something to be wrong. The action proved futile, Archer's rounds penetrating it as though it were sheet-wood. When he felled the third, the final one sought cover on the ground. Archer, perched thirty feet higher, picked him off with what others might have considered murderous ease. Nevertheless, when the lights returned, all four terrorists were dead, and the rest of the team began clearing the area, starting with the release of the men inside the bio-hazard labs.

***

When the elevator doors opened in the parking lot, Ivanovich summoned the energy to stand. He couldn't understand why he suddenly felt enervated. His entire system felt like it was shutting down. It took every ounce of energy to cross the garage to a unitary van parked next to the tunnel. He found the door open, the keys in the ignition. The owner had felt confident to leave it like that. Ivanovich silently thanked him.

He collapsed into the seat, beads of sweat popping out on his forehead and arms. He took a deep breath – all he could do to stop his body from shaking.

With a flick of his wrist, he started the van, put it into drive, and gunned it.

***

The sibilant sound of the hermetically sealed doors opening made Hunt sigh in relief. For one minute the fans in the bio labs had shut down. Though they'd circulated enough air to allow the occupants to breathe for at least thirty minutes, the intervening sixty seconds were the most terrifying of his life. The thought of being slowly asphyxiated was even scarier than looking into the eyes of the man who'd said "you're next".

As he exited the claustrophobic environment, he saw four dead bodies on the gangway. All of them were in a supine position, most of their faces unrecognisable. He started to search for one with long hair. Ignoring the protests of several men in full body armour, he knelt beside the deceased terrorists, ignoring the urge to gag.

He felt his body go cold. None of the terrorists had long hair. Turning to the nearest soldier, he said, "He's not here! The leader is missing!"

Reports boomed from downstairs: "Major, we got a trail here! Looks like there's a bogey still alive. He's taken this elevator."

Carlos, standing on the gangway beside Hunt, eyed the four men beside him. "Secure this facility now. Then, escort these gentlemen topside." Turning to the remaining four, who were downstairs – Gyle among them – he said, "Secure the elevator. No one gets in or out." Though they were confused, they moved to the elevator and disabled its console.

Jonathan Baker smoothed his ruffled suit and stepped out of the bio-hazard labs. "Major, let myself and Director Clemence accompany you. We've seen this SOB. We'll make the ID." He didn't notice Clemence's smirk of disapproval.

Carlos, too tired to stand to attention in the presence of a superior, said, "Director Baker, there'll be no following."

Baker levelled him a confused frown. "Quit prevaricating, Major. What are you talking about?"

"Sir, I did my homework on this place. There's a contingency plan to deal with scenarios like this one."

The frown morphed into an angry glare. "That is *not* applicable now, Major! The terrorists have been neutralised. The leader is the only one who remains. I am ordering you to follow him now!"

"Sir, this base is compromised. Tonight's attack was unsuccessful, but now that Station Blue is terrorist knowledge there will be more attacks. Several of them. The contingency plan is the *only* thing applicable right now. I studied the schematics. There will be no collateral damage. Its design specifically prevents that outcome. You need to arm it *now*."

Hunt interjected: "Can someone please explain to me what's going on and what this 'contingency plan' is?"

In a loud military inflection: "Everyone listen up. You need to start making your way down to the ground floor, over to one of the four elevators, and up to the larger gangway. Then you need to start climbing the hatch to basement level two. Director Clemence first. He has the key-card to operate the elevator. Go!

Now!"

Baker grabbed Carlos by his vest. "This is madness!"

"You need to take me to it *now*, sir. How long will it take after you activate it?"

"Ten minutes."

"We need to get everyone out of here before then."

Hunt, passing by on one side, paused when he heard the word "activate". "What are you activating?"

Baker shook his head as though Hunt's words had torn him from a reverie. "Mr Hunt, you need to follow Director Clemence to the elevators. Now."

"I'm not going anywhere. This sudden rush to get out of this facility – why? What is this 'contingency plan' you people keep mentioning?"

Baker sighed. "It's a bomb, Mr Hunt. We're going to blow the facility up. Do you really want to be around when that happens?"

Trying to ignore the fear threatening to cripple him, he replied, "What about the leader?"

"This side has been sealed, and there's no way out from the opposite end. The bomb will destroy this facility, ATARIC, and the entire tunnel from here to Hunters Point. Now please, Mr Hunt, make your way to the elevators."

CHAPTER NINETY-NINE
ENDGAME

LEVEL THREE
20:30 EST

The van sped through the tunnel at close to fifty miles per hour, its lights bathing the cylindrical enclosure as far as the eye could see. Ivanovich wiped away another bead of sweat from his forehead. He blinked a few times to rid his eyes of it; squinting as it began to irritate them. Despite the sub-zero temperatures inside the van, his face was flushed, breathing laboured, and his entire body on the verge of complete mental and physical exhaustion. He'd consoled himself the symptoms could be explained simply by jetlag. And he'd been convinced of that until pain had erupted from his stomach up to his sternum.

He grimaced again as another sharp pain stabbed him, then burned a path to his chest like a fuse had been lit. It became harder to think. Harder to see. Harder even to breathe.

Mind racing through all of things he'd done over the past twelve hours, he began to wonder if someone had injected him with something. The more he tried to remember, the more a haze settled over his mind, his thoughts becoming oneiric flashes embellished by the surreal surrounds of the tunnel.

The stabbing pain travelled from his chest to his eyes. Burning. Like someone was torching the retinas. Ivanovich slammed the brakes to keep from crashing, his hands immediately shooting to his eyes when the van stopped. He knew the exit couldn't be much farther, but the only thing he wanted to do was douse his eyes with water.

The searing pain advanced to his ears next. The sharp, piercing trill that accompanied it was like no sound he had ever heard and no pain he'd ever experienced. Torn between saving his eyes or his ears, he vacillated. By the time the sound reached unfathomable decibels, his ears were already bleeding, his hands doing little to staunch it. It did not trickle as much as it flowed.

Trying to plug the dyke with everything from his fingers to his hands, he felt another trickle come from his nose. It gave way to an avalanche. What followed was an incongruous bleeping that came from inside his body. Stunned, he patted the area of his chest making the noise, then realised it was in fact his phone.

He had just enough time to read the Russian text message before the crippling pain grew so intense the veins on his forehead literally exploded, and he keeled over on the seat, the backlit display keeping the message illuminated for thirty seconds:

My dearest Sergei: I expect that right now you are experiencing the most gut-wrenching pain imaginable. Do not fight it. It will be over soon. You have served me well through the years, but your usefulness has ended. Your death will prove that Tartarus is a very potent killer. And when I unleash it against the Americans, it will be a day to savour!

Would that you were there with me on that victorious day, but I cannot tolerate any more mistakes. You may remember the comment you made about the wine in the Meridien hotel several hours ago. Tartarus can be dispersed rather easily through the water supply and can withstand temperatures exceeding 150 degrees centigrade. It takes upwards of twelve hours, though, for symptoms to start showing. I had hoped you would have acquired the weapons before you succumbed to its ravages. But once symptoms start, death follows in minutes, sometimes seconds. I will spare you the horrific details, as you are probably well aware of what this animal can do.

You have become a martyr for my cause, Sergei Bogdan Ivanovich, and I salute you.
— *Pavel Kirov.*

***

Inside a small four-by-four floor hatch, equidistant from the last laboratory and the parking lot elevator, the contingency plan for "Station Blue" lay dormant. Until now, only two people had known of its existence, and only one had the key. A set of stairs led down into what Carlos now compared to the Abyss. They seemed to descend forever. Guided only by the guttering flame of Baker's lighter, the journey down was reminiscent of a catacomb in a Hollywood blockbuster.

Once Baker found the light switch, though, what greeted them would never have graced the silver screen. Carlos had never seen anything like it. On first glance, it looked like a miniaturised version of the atomic bomb. It was roughly cylindrical in shape, measuring approximately ten feet high by three wide. The entire exterior was pockmarked by tiny indentations no larger than the dimple on a golf ball. Stencilled on the bottom right-hand corner were the letters CP-101. To the left of them, a panel rose the entire height of the bomb. In the middle of it, a key stood vertically. Around the opposite side, another one mirrored it.

"What's CP-one-oh-one mean?" Carlos asked.

"Contingency Plan one-oh-one," Baker replied. "Now move over to that other key. We haven't got a lot of time here."

"Still, one-oh-one?" Carlos pressed as he moved to the back of the bomb.

"Orwell's *Nineteen Eighty-Four*," Baker explained. "Room one-oh-one is the worst nightmare imaginable. Poetic, isn't it?" Baker said with a grunt.

When Carlos had positioned himself, Baker said, "On the count of three, turn the key ninety degrees clockwise. One, two, three!"

They cranked the keys in unison. CP-101 emitted a loud

sound which reminded Carlos of the buzzer in Madison Square Garden. When he returned to the panel, a backlit display began counting down from 10:00:00.

"That's it! It's set. Let's get the hell out of here!" Baker ordered.

***

For a reason he couldn't fathom, Hunt stayed behind until everyone else had climbed the stairs to basement level two. It wasn't until he saw Major Carlos and Director Baker exit the floor hatch that he began ascending the ladder. The level-two hatch had been left open by its last users, so Clemence hadn't needed Baker's presence to disengage the biometrics. When Hunt exited it, he found seven of Carlos' eight-man insertion team, two security guards, Clemence and Reid standing in a huddle beside the open doors of the elevator.

"Jesus Christ!" he exploded. "Why are you all standing here? There's fourteen of us! We won't all make it on one trip." He seized Clemence by the collar. "Take seven of them upstairs now and come back down with that key-card."

Clemence pushed him away and smoothed his expensive suit. "Careful there, bubba. You're not talking to one of your employees now."

Hunt moved in until his face came inches from Clemence's. In a low, menacing whisper: "I don't care who you are. If you don't get your ass into that elevator in the next ten seconds, I'm going to throw you back downstairs, lock that hatch, and leave you here to die. You understand me?"

Gyle, who'd been watching the conflict with something of an amused smile, stepped in before Clemence could reply and said, "He's right, Director. We need to get bodies topside now. Sir, take the security guards, these two employees, and three of my men with you now. Get them outside the building, and then come straight back here."

Clemence looked like he was going to protest and exercise his chain of command, but Gyle cut him off again. "Sir, we don't have time for ranks or egos. We got less than ten minutes to get everyone – including the rest of my team topside – as far away from this building as possible. Quit being a *pendejo* and get into that elevator."

Clemence wanted to ask what a "pendejo" was but thought better of it. He ushered in the two security guards, Reid and Hunt, and three men selected by Gyle. The doors closed as Carlos emerged through the hatch, turned back, and pulled Baker through.

"Sitrep!" he called as he secured the hatch.

"Elevator's on its way up. Just five of our team and Director Baker left. Director Clemence will get them squared away topside, and take her back down for us."

Carlos nodded as he stood up. Gyle notwithstanding, the remaining members of the insertion team were Lansdale, Fromm, and Mason. That they hadn't lost any men struck Carlos as something of a miracle.

***

When Clemence stepped into the main hall of ATARIC, he expected the lights to be on. Instead, a pitch-black room greeted him. In the shadows, he tugged at his jacket, trying to remember which pocket held his phone. Any source of light was better than nothing. He had just found it when three STRIKE Force members brushed past him and swept into the room, knocking it out of his hand. It hit the carpet, then an exasperated Clemence trod on it as he tried to locate it.

"What the hell – "

The nearest one turned back, and though Clemence couldn't see his eyes because of the goggles, the eerie green lights were enough to silence him. Angry at the lack of respect for a senior official, Clemence dropped to his knees with a grumble and started searching for the phone. It took him thirty seconds to find it. When he rose to his feet, he realised everyone had cleared the elevator, the doors still open.

"Fine," he mumbled. "Find the way yourselves."

The elevator worked on the power of the level-three generator, and the light from the console was enough to partially reveal Clemence.

He reached out to close the doors, but suddenly realised profuse beads of sweat were dripping down his forehead. Pulling his hand away from the buttons, he tapped his palm against his forehead, then held it to the light. He jerked back, realising the beads pooling from his forehead weren't sweat.

They were blood.

Instinctively, he looked up to the ceiling.

He saw the hole Carlos had made in the roof, but to the right and left of the opening were two unmistakeable opaque shadows.

"Jesus Christ! Guys, it's a – "

Clemence felt something wiry tighten against his throat. Before he had a chance to figure out what, his body was lifted off the ground, the wiry material now acting as a noose. Gasping for air, he kicked wildly as his hands clawed at the material around his neck – what he now realised was a garrotte. He tried to scream but his vocal cords were crushed by his own weight. His face blue from asphyxiation, he gave one last effort, but it only served to rob him of his remaining breath.

When Clemence was dead, Vladimir Pushkin heaved him alongside the bodies of William Forrester and Dan Hollingsworth.

CHAPTER ONE HUNDRED
ROOM 101

ATARIC/LEVEL THREE
20:51 EST

Vladimir Pushkin had stepped through the doors of ATARIC just as Forrester and Hollingsworth exited the elevator. He watched them hand an item to a group of five soldiers. Not expecting any terrorists to be upstairs, the two men walked casually to the door, allowing Pushkin to pick them off with ease. When he'd entered the elevator, he discovered the hole in its roof. With no way to get down to level three, and no desire to die going down the governor cable, he decided to bide his time.

He counted three soldiers exit the lift, along with two civilians, two security guards, and someone who was the director of the NSA, according to the wallet Pushkin now leafed through with the aid of a flashlight. But he counted five soldiers originally, which meant there were still more downstairs.

In the NSA director's pocket, he found a key-card with L3 written on both sides. This, he now realised, allowed the elevator to access level three.

***

"Jesus, it's about time, Roger!" Baker sighed as he heard the lift begin to descend. The stopwatch on his phone continued downwards from 07:05. Seven minutes to evacuate the building. Clemence was cutting it very close.

When the elevator pinged, the doors opened only a matter of inches, hit something, and then closed again. Baker motioned to move, but Carlos cut him off with a raised hand. Deadly serious, he reached down to his holster and removed his pistol. Gyle didn't need a signal to know to go to the opposite side. When Carlos gestured to Lansdale to press the button, both his and Gyle's pistols were fully extended. The SAS man waited for the door to hit the object again, then placed his size fifteens into the gap. Using all his power, he pushed the door open until the item it had snagged on snapped under the pressure and the door receded into the groove.

"Christ!" Baker screamed, trying to push through but held back by Fromm.

In the light of level two, blood glistened off three recumbent bodies on the floor of the elevator. The hand of the one nearest the door lay on the ground in an unnatural shape. Carlos figured it had been positioned in the groove of the door to stop it from opening. He had no trouble identifying the cause of the deaths or the identity of all three.

"Jesus, Red," Baker sobbed, finally making his way through the barricade. "Oh, God, Roger!" The man who had been like a brother for a quarter-of-a-century, and the man who been something of a mentor since Baker's ascension to director of the Bureau, now lay dead in front of Baker's disbelieving eyes. Beside them was Dan Hollingsworth.

Carlos signalled Gyle. "Julio, secure it. Check the roof." While Gyle busied himself with the task, Carlos led Baker away from the ghastly scene. He looked at his watch: 05:59. "Director Baker, we have to assume there're terrorists here that we've missed. We need to disengage the bomb until we deal with them, sir."

But Baker, it seemed, did not hear the statement. He stared into the distance, eyes devoid of sadness, rage, or any other emotion. Catatonia. Carlos shook his head and stifled a curse.

"Julio, status report!"

"Elevator's clear, Bear," Gyle replied, dropping back into

Lansdale's arms. He moved over beside Carlos and said, "*Muchacho,* we didn't miss anything on the way down here. There were *zero* terrorists topside when we came through. I get the feeling whoever killed these three was on recon duty outside. Probably got a FUBAR."

Carlos agreed with a nod. "Baker's indisposed for the moment. We need to flush out those last tangos." He paused to look at his watch. "And we need to do it less than five minutes, Julio. Let's start thinking."

"Major, I think I have an idea," Fromm announced.

Carlos gestured to the rest of them. "Fall in, soldiers. We ain't got time for being shy." Even though they'd only worked together for an hour, there was already an esprit de corps between them.

When Fromm told him his plan, Carlos' eyes lit up and the ghost of a smile crossed his face.

***

Pushkin had watched the exodus via ATARIC's front door while he waited for the elevator to return. He'd let them go because engaging in a fire fight with highly trained soldiers was suicide. Besides, the only thing he was interested in right now was making sure the remaining soldiers downstairs came up. Among them would be Jonathan Baker, and, with coercion, he would take Pushkin back into "Station Blue".

The elevator had been gone three minutes, and he was beginning to think the soldiers below were plotting something when a distant whir sounded. Stepping back into the shadows, he extended his pistol and waited.

He would take the first one with a well-placed shot to the head. While they were determining his location, Pushkin would move left, avoiding any shots fired where the muzzle had flashed. Then he would fire again, move again, and repeat the process until he'd killed everyone, save Baker. He'd catch them off-guard, before they had a chance to –

The elevator doors opened with a ping. But he did a double-take when he saw the inside. The bodies he'd sent down were undisturbed, the rest of the elevator empty. He crept forward, stepped into the elevator, and craned his neck. When he saw the shadow of something that could only be human, he snapped his gun up and pulled the trigger. The fusillade was deafening inside the cramped space.

But when the sound ended, he didn't hear the groan of an injured man. Didn't feel the blood of a wounded one either.

As his eyes and head dropped back to the bodies, a horrified Pushkin realised his mistake.

***

Carlos, dressed in the deceased Roger Clemence's clothes, darted from the floor with the speed of a leopard. Pushkin swung the gun left, bringing the barrel in line with his head, but Carlos used his long arms to maximum effect. He brought the callused edge of his hand down hard on Pushkin's forearm. The pain of the blow took Pushkin by surprise, but his vice-like grip ensured the gun stayed firm in his hand.

He reared back, trying to distance himself enough to get off a shot. But Carlos was already on the move. As Pushkin brought the gun up, Carlos feinted right, momentarily causing Pushkin to defend that side, and then came at the gun with his left hand. Using his palm, he slapped it, getting all his weight behind the move. The gun flew from Pushkin's hand, hit the side wall, and fell to the ground.

Pushkin decided not to dive for it. He stayed on his feet; advanced on Carlos with the stance of a southpaw. His first jab caught Carlos on the jaw, but his reach meant it did little damage.

Carlos spotted the opening. When Pushkin's punch landed, he batted away the Russian's hand and stepped forward. Preparing to lash out with a flurry of punches, he was surprised when Pushkin hit him with a sweeping kick, taking his legs from under him. The Marine crashed back-first onto the unforgiving steel floor, a grunt of pain exploding from his lips.

Rather than go for the gun, Pushkin drew back his leg and aimed a kick at the gap between Carlos' shoulder and mandible. Carlos turned just before the kick hit him in the carotid artery, but Pushkin's foot connected solidly with his clavicle. A wave of pain crashed through his body, up his neck and down his right-hand side. He was sure his collarbone was broken, but before he could check, Pushkin landed a savage blow to the side of his head. He gasped again, blood spitting from his mouth as teeth chattered against each other.

An ordinary person might have been knocked out, but Marines weren't ordinary. When Pushkin stepped over him with gun in hand, Carlos thrust out both of his and grabbed the Russian around the ankles; yanking them towards him. Pushkin hit the floor with a hard thud which dislodged the gun.

As Pushkin tried to scramble backwards to retrieve it, Carlos let go of one ankle and gripped the other one with both hands. With the strength of a bear, he twisted it anti-clockwise, trying to break it. Pushkin kicked out of the hold, his boot cracking against Carlos' chest, sending him backwards yet again.

When Carlos landed in a supine position, Pushkin clawed at the ground to retrieve the gun. Finding it, he thrust it over his head and back down to where he expected Carlos to be.

With all the energy left in his exhausted body, Carlos tossed his legs into the air and flipped himself to his feet. As Pushkin tried to compensate, Carlos closed the gap and kicked the gun out of his hand with enough force to snap the Russian's wrist. Too adrenalized to feel pain, his only acknowledgement was the baring of his teeth in anger. The gun propelled through the air and landed in the shadows.

As Carlos advanced on the prostrate Russian, Pushkin landed a blow to his right kneecap, the crippling pain taking away Carlos' ability to apply weight. Hobbling, he watched as Pushkin returned to his feet to finish the job. In agony, he shambled left, right hand reaching down to his pocket, eyes watching the Russian's every move.

When Pushkin threw a wild left hook, Carlos ducked under it, snapped open his HALO knife, and rose upward, driving the blade deep into the Russian's throat. Pushkin gasped. Gurgled. The sucking noise of his tracheated throat was music to Carlos' ears. With the knife protruding into the mouth, he jerked it upwards further, ripping through sinew and viscera until it struck the chin. Using what remained of his energy, he twisted it sideways and yanked it right. The tined blade cleaved Pushkin's carotid artery and perforated the soft spot under his jaw. It emerged from the neck in an eruption of blood, both men dropping to the ground for entirely different reasons.

Trying to fill his lungs with air, Carlos crawled to the console and stabbed the button. The doors closed and the elevator descended to level two as he checked his stopwatch: 02:47. Trying to ignore the pains that throbbed through his entire body, he pushed himself backwards until he could lie against the wall, ignoring the bodies beside him.

When the elevator doors opened and the rest of his team began to voice their concerns, Carlos mumbled, "No time! Inside...let's go...two minutes."

When everyone had boarded – including the still-catatonic Baker – Gyle slapped the ground floor button and moved over beside Carlos. He noticed the bloodied body of the Russian and immediately knew a fight of insane proportions had just occurred. *Damn, you're definitely one hell of an oso, Jack!* His commander looked like he'd been in a fifteen-round fight with Muhammad Ali, but the guy on the ground was missing a huge chunk of his face. Gyle had agreed to pose as Forrester, giving Carlos backup if needed, but for whatever reason Carlos had declined.

When the doors opened, there were two minutes left on the stopwatch. With the aid of Lansdale, Gyle helped Carlos to his feet and threw him over his shoulder in a Fireman's Carry. Lansdale then did the same with Baker, and they moved through the main hall of ATARIC, Mason's flashlight providing guidance.

When they emerged through ATARIC's front door, they found Nathan Murphy standing alone, obviously waiting for them. Gyle asked him for a situation report and he explained he'd sequestered everyone – including passers-by and the exterior STRIKE Force members – into the Eastgate Tower Hotel, much to the annoyance of one Erin Pierce.

Exhausted at the effort of carrying over twenty stone, Gyle handed Carlos over to Murphy, who literally ran across the street with him, leaving Gyle to shake his head in amused incredulity. The rest of the team sprinted after him, including Lansdale, who made Baker look like a sack of potatoes. Gyle was amazed to discover he couldn't keep pace with the Briton.

Inside the Eastgate, Gyle found everyone – everyone still *alive* – from ATARIC standing in the middle of the lobby, away from all windows and other sources of potential damage. When Pierce recognised him, she walked towards him with a purpose, brushing through the throng as though it wasn't even there.

"What is going on! Why are all these people in my lobby?" she demanded, hands poised on her hips again.

With a tired smile, Gyle laconically replied, "You're about to find out."

***

At one minute to nine p.m., Eastern Standard Time, the device known as CP-101 exploded deep in the recesses of "Station Blue's" level three. It rose in a ball of flame, razing laboratories, immolating the bodies of those left behind, melting computers, weapons, and technology. It incinerated level three in a matter of seconds, continued upwards to level two, the ground floor, and much of the first and second floors of ATARIC. At the topmost point of its explosion, it sundered the windows outward, the flames escaping into the night air, only to be sucked back to the point of origin. The subsequent vacuum took with it dozens of windows, chairs, computers, desks, and razed several offices.

When the thunderous roar ceased, those nearby were too shocked to move, let alone notice several soldiers decamping from the area. By the time anyone had thought to ask what had happened, the news stations were already being fed a cover story.

The two people left behind were Reid and Hunt, who embraced in a way only men who had faced what they had, could.

Neither of them, though, could have possibly known what they'd just initiated.

***

About ninety seconds after the explosion, the phone in

President Walsh's bedroom rang. On the other end, Edward Rainey informed him STRIKE Force had neutralised the terrorists but at the cost of "Station Blue", which now lay in ruins beneath the ramshackle remains of ATARIC.

The President decided it was an acceptable loss. He told Rainey to find a location to house the remainder of the ATARIC employees until the building could be restored. He had no need to ask if a cover story had been created. As he hung up, he rolled back into his wife's embrace, glad this nightmare day had finally come to an end.

He could not have known it was, in fact, only the beginning.

EPILOGUE
THE INEXORABILITY OF FATE

MIDTOWN MANHATTAN
NEW YORK CITY
TUESDAY, JANUARY 7TH, 2003

Enjoying the feeling of warmth on his skin, Hunt walked –
bounced – along the sun-soaked street as the early-morning
commuters made their way to work. The weather was
surprisingly warm for the time of year, but it was not the reason
why his skin felt warm. He turned and looked into the beautiful
eyes of his wife for the first time since he could remember. He
kissed her moistened lips and squeezed her hand. Karen returned
his look, her eyes filled with love, and kissed him soundly. For
once, he felt at ease; felt his life had found meaning again.

"What you did for them – what you did for *me* – I'll never
forget it. You should be given a medal. This city – this country,
even – owes you a debt of gratitude, Peter." Eyes welling up, she
continued, "I'm *so* proud of you. Even though Jack didn't believe
– even though you could have easily walked away and given up –
you still fought on because that's the man you are – the man I fell
in love with."

With Jon Baker's imprimatur, Hunt and Reid were allowed to
tell their wives what had happened in ATARIC, though a

truncated version. Omitting the part about "Station Blue", they'd told them terrorists had attacked ATARIC for reasons unknown, and they'd helped the police fight them off. Baker had promised compensation and commendations for their help, though Hunt believed he'd never hear another word about it. Either way, being named on the news as someone who'd risked his life to save other employees from certain death at the hands of a terrorist bomb made Karen realise Peter was not the selfish man she'd thought him to be.

"I'm glad you took my phone call after learning I'd lied to you about having to work late." He gave an embarrassed laugh.

"When I learned you were trying to protect me, it changed everything. What you did was for my own good, and it made me realise there was still hope for you and me."

He breathed a sigh of relief. He'd been waiting to hear those words for what seemed a lifetime. "I love you so much, Karen."

Karen turned; smiled. "I lo – "

Hunt, standing abreast of her, turned – smiling – to see why she'd paused. This split-second reaction saved his life. When the bullet struck her just below the ear, he was turned far enough so that, when it exited, it missed him by a quarter-inch. Blood and cartilage exploded from the wound as Karen's face disintegrated into mush. He tried to reach out, tried to staunch the bleeding, not realising the greatest surgeon in the world couldn't have saved her. Karen fell to the ground and, without as much as another sound, breathed her last.

"*Karen!*" He fell to his knees, sobs wracking his body. "*No!*" The word came out in one long scream. "*God, please, no!*" He cradled her destroyed face in his trembling hands. "Karen, talk to me. Please don't die on me. Oh, God, please. *Somebody help me!*" He looked up to the street. "*Please, somebody help me!*"

As the first of New York's citizens arrived with extracted cell phones, Hunt screamed so loudly the ambulance men ten blocks away could hear him.

***

On the roof of a nearby building, a man disassembled his sniper rifle and returned it to a black case. From a gusseted pouch he removed his own cell phone. Dialling a number from memory, he got through to a pleasant woman who forwarded him to his employer.

"It's been taken care of," he said with no emotion. "The proof should be on your phone now."

"I have it. Excellent work. The rest of your payment will be in your account within the hour. It's been a pleasure doing business with you."

"And you."

"I don't think I need to tell you it would be wise for you to leave the country for a while."

"When I've confirmed the money is in my account, I'll be on the first plane out of here."

"Thank you, and Godspeed."

"Thank *you*, Mr Walken," the man said as he hung up.

THE END.

AUTHOR'S ADDENDUM

To the reader:

Whoever said all things must come to an end obviously never encountered authors and sequels! With one ending comes numerous ideas for the next chapter in the beginning of a series.

I hope you've had as much fun reading this as I had writing it. As a reader-turned-writer, I think I know what people want from a novel – because I know what I want from one. I live by the credo that every chapter must end with a bang, and every novel likewise. Needless to say, I hope you understand why it had to end the way it did. It may seem cruel, and I despaired over writing it, but it was a necessary evil, the reason for which will hopefully become apparent in the future.

For now, I thank you and bid you adieu. It's been quite a journey, I hope you'll agree.

Daniel McKeown, October 22, 2011.

About the author

Daniel McKeown has been writing for over a decade. To date he has penned over half a dozen novels and several short stories. An avid reader of thrillers, his own work reflects his desire to read something which never ceases to surprise, thrill, and ultimately hook the audience.

McKeown has seized on the economic lull, using his free time to return to university to study for a degree in English and History. The one-day-a-week course allows him time to pursue his passion; writing a series of thrillers about two ordinary men who are forced into the world of terrorism.

When he isn't hard at work behind the screen of a laptop, or studying for an upcoming exam, he can found doing one of two things: reading a novel, or working out in his home gym, where many of his best ideas have come to him.

McKeown lives in the countryside of South Armagh, Ireland, where he is currently at work on the aforementioned thriller series.

CPSIA information can be obtained at www.ICGtesting.com
Printed in the USA
LVOW10s0435251114

415497LV00001B/1/P